W9-BEH-910

By Allison Pataki

The Traitor's Wife

The Accidental Empress

Sisi

Where the Light Falls (with Owen Pataki)

Beauty in the Broken Places

Nelly Takes New York (with Marya Myers)

The Queen's Fortune

Poppy Takes Paris (with Marya Myers)

The Magnificent Lives of Marjorie Post

The Magnificent Lives *of* Marjorie Post

The Magnificent Lives *of* Marjorie Post

A Novel

ALLISON PATAKI

Ballantine Books
New York

The Magnificent Lives of Marjorie Post is a work of fiction. All incidents and dialogue, and all characters with the exception of some well-known historical figures, are products of the author's imagination and are not to be construed as real. Where real-life historical persons appear, the situations, incidents, and dialogues concerning those persons are entirely fictional and are not intended to depict actual events or to change the entirely fictional nature of the work. In all other respects, any resemblance to persons living or dead is entirely coincidental.

Published in the United States by Ballantine Books, an imprint of Random House, a division of Penguin Random House LLC, New York.

BALLANTINE and the HOUSE colophon are registered trademarks of Penguin Random House LLC.

LIBRARY OF CONGRESS CATALOGING-IN-PUBLICATION DATA

Names: Pataki, Allison, author.
Title: The magnificent lives of Marjorie Post : a novel / Allison Pataki.
Description: New York : Ballantine Books, 2022.
Identifiers: LCCN 2021000317 (print) | LCCN 2021000318 (ebook) |
ISBN 9780593355688 (hardcover ; acid-free paper) |
ISBN 9780593355695 (ebook)
Classification: LCC PS3616.A8664 I22 2022 (print) |
LCC PS3616.A8664 (ebook) | DDC 813/.6—dc23
LC record available at https://lccn.loc.gov/2021000317
LC ebook record available at https://lccn.loc.gov/2021000318

Printed in the United States of America on acid-free paper

randomhousebooks.com

2nd Printing

First Edition

Book design by Virginia Norey

Title page art from an original photograph by
FreeImages.com/Vichien Boonyong

For Marya, friend and first reader

I am not the richest woman in the world. There are others better off than I am. The only difference is that I do more with mine. I put it to work.

–MARJORIE MERRIWEATHER POST

Beauty is truth, truth beauty,
That is all ye know on earth, and all ye need to know.

–JOHN KEATS

The Magnificent Lives *of* Marjorie Post

Prologue

Mar-a-Lago, Palm Beach, Florida
1968

"MRS. POST, THE PRESIDENT AND FIRST LADY ARE HERE TO SEE you."

"Thank you, Frank. You can show them in." I smooth the ripples of my slate-blue skirt and rise, my spine going straight, my heart speeding to a gallop. From across the room, I catch my reflection in the mirror—the thick glint of diamonds at my neck, my ears, my wrists. Eyes a vibrant blue, bright and alert, even if surrounded by an etching of fine lines wrought by my many full years. Long silver waves of hair, pulled back, tidy and upswept. Oh, and this room. This grand room, its sprawling confines pierced by windows that open out over lush lawns and sapphire sea. Yes, it's fine indeed; I've done some job on this place. I clear my throat, allowing just the subtlest of nods. I was right to request that the meeting take place here, rather than at the White House.

The click of footsteps on the stone floor, and I know that the president approaches. I wonder if he suspects anything; if he knows about the offer I am going to make him. *Mrs. Post, the president and first lady are here to see you.* It could have been any number of presidents being announced by my staffer. These commanders in chief keep changing every four to eight years, but I remain at my post to greet and host them all. I blink, and I'm a girl of fourteen, dressed in bright blue, bandying with Alice Roosevelt at a White House ball. And then there I am, in command of a castle floating between cloud and sea, a space grander than anything my friends the Vanderbilts or Windsors have ever enjoyed. I am Lady Bountiful, ladling soup to women with as much hunger in their eyes as in their sunken frames. The prism of memory shifts yet again, and there I am, crouching low, surrounded by the murdered Tsar's treasures in a dark Moscow warehouse. Next I'm racing through torpedo-laced waters, the Nazis nipping at my wake, the RAF bombers overhead ripping the sky with angry thunder. Then I am in my library, the perfume of summer blooms intoxicating as I greet a tall, timid, big-eyed brunette, doing my best to put the young Mrs. Jackie Kennedy at ease.

But all of that is in the past. I blink again, coming back to the present, as this new president and first lady cross the threshold of my living room and stride toward me. Lady Bird Johnson is rose-cheeked and smiling as she extends her arms for a hug. "Oh, Mrs. Post, how wonderful to be here. Every time I step into one of your homes, it's like I've stepped into some beautiful Neverland."

I smile, returning the first lady's greeting. I may live like an empress, but I've never asked an emperor to pick up the bill. And since I've never had a crown for which to answer, I suppose you might say I'm that much better off. I turn next to her husband, eager to make my offer that could change the lives of these presidents. I've changed so many lives already. And I've changed your life, too. I know that as a certainty. How can that be, you may ask, when you do not even know my name? Who *am* I?

Well, the answer is, and has always been, that I am Mrs. Marjorie Merriweather Post.

Part One

Chapter 1

Battle Creek, Michigan
Winter 1891

I WAS RAISED IN RELIGION, BUT IT WAS NOT GOD WHO LOOMED largest over my girlhood and its earliest memories. That was Charles William Post, Charlie, or simply C.W. to those who knew him best. To me, he was only ever Papa.

He cut no particularly imposing figure, what with his narrow frame, standing at just over six feet tall, and his fine, blue-eyed smile. But the man molded my world, and then he went on and changed everybody else's as well.

You might say the same about my education, too, for although I went to school for all of my girlhood, it was on Papa's lap that I did the learning that would shape me. How Papa could spin a story, building worlds in my young mind until I came to believe that just about anything was possible. Because to Papa, anything was. There were the tales of the tall Springfield lawyer whom Papa admired, a family friend by the name of Mr. Abe Lincoln, who taught himself to read as a boy in a drafty log hut with nothing more than a tattered Bible and yet somehow found himself in charge of the White House. Of course Papa—and then I—knew all the presidents, but I loved the stories about Mr. Lincoln the best; Papa had made this singular man a friend while they lived in Springfield, after they'd both sprung up from nothing but their own grit and the fertile frontier soil.

Oh, but there were other good stories, too. Papa's words had me forging across the Great Divide on the back of a mule, just as he'd done as a young man with his brother, my Uncle Cal, the pair of them sifting for gold amid the red mud and the pines. He had me battling Chicago's Great

Fire or else waiting out a night of dust storms in Oklahoma, shivering beneath a heap of scratchy wagon canvas as the coyote yips mixed with the wind skittering against a flimsy tin roof. He talked of pianos that didn't need human fingers to play and buggies that didn't need horses to pull them.

It always seemed to me that by the time I arrived in the world, Papa had tried his hand at pretty much everything: he'd been an inventor in California, a salesman in Illinois, a farmer in Nebraska, a rancher in the wild Oklahoma Territory. Success had come in fickle fits and bursts, with plenty of failure mixed in, but he'd managed to wed the sweetheart of his youth in the midst of it all. My mother, Ella Letitia Merriweather, a pale beauty with gray eyes and a reserved demeanor, came from a far more affluent family but the same Springfield roots.

The borders of my young mind and memory can barely contain Papa: fine-featured, with an easy charm and smarts to best anyone else in the room, a sharp humor and a kind voice—but then sick. Suddenly and frightfully sick.

It was this sickness that fueled our journey that winter, a journey that would end in a way that none of us, not even Papa, the incorrigible dreamer, could have possibly conceived.

Battle Creek welcomed us with a wall of cold air, the sort of air that stuns, needling your cheeks and causing the breath to stick in your nostrils on the way in. Beside me, Papa leaned on Mother to limp off the Michigan Central line train car and onto the frigid platform. After weeks of travel, we had arrived, and for that I was grateful, but I feared that our stop might be Papa's final destination.

"Your father is near the end of mortals," Mother had whispered to me on our long journey up from Texas, both her words and the skin around her lips pulling tight with worry. Our train car had rocked back and forth in a doleful rhythm as swaths of ice-slicked farmland rolled past our frosted window. Papa groaned where he lay in the berth, the extra blankets doing little to warm his thin, trembling frame. I didn't know if perhaps he'd heard Mother's words and was trying to respond or if he was simply giving voice to the pain that gripped his failing body. I also did not understand why Mother couldn't put a tender hand on him or lean close to offer some soothing words of comfort, anything to lend him just a tiny bit of warmth. But then I'd rarely seen her do such a thing.

And to be fair to Mother, it wasn't she to whom Papa called out when he had the strength for words. "Budgie," he'd whisper, his breath a sliver of pearly mist in the cold compartment, his voice so faint that I almost couldn't hear my nickname over the rolling thrum of the train's forward motion.

"Yes, Papa, I'm here," I'd say, taking his wilted hands in mine and lowering myself down to pass the hours by his side. Singing the chaste Christian hymns he'd sung over my bedside. Thinking with an ache, but knowing better than to say aloud: *Papa, please don't leave me. What would I do without you?*

Papa's symptoms were a list of words that meant little to me at my young age. Migraines, melancholy, dyspepsia, insomnia, anxiety—all in all, a nervous disturbance of both the body and the mind. Papa wasn't the only man to suffer such symptoms, but it seemed to me that nobody could have possibly had them worse.

When at last the train lurched to its stop and we stepped out onto the platform, a weak winter sun was lowering itself over the bustling Battle Creek station. Grateful to be free of the train's close-packed air and the scent of the many bodies riding within, I gulped in several large, cold breaths and immediately detected the belches of train soot mixed with the aroma of the countless cows that filled the flat surrounding countryside. There was another tinny smell, one that I'd soon come to know well enough: the promise of snow.

Porters jostled around the crowded depot, seeing to trunks and boxes and weary travelers. Passengers shuffled about, looking for loved ones and luggage. I stood there shivering, glancing up at each parent in turn and wondering who was in charge: Mother? Or Papa, even though his body was so visibly useless? A porter in a smart cap and dark wool coat approached us, pushing a chair and looking to Papa with eyebrows raised. "A wheelchair, sir?"

"Indeed." Papa, leaning on Mother's arm, nodded his feeble acceptance and collapsed into the chair's caned seat with a relieved sigh.

"To the San?" the porter asked, looking from Papa to Mother.

We, like nearly everyone else on that darkening platform, had come for one reason: to seek the treatment of the famed Dr. John Kellogg. A physician by trade, the brilliant Battle Creek healer attracted the sick from the East Coast to the West—old money and new—and even from across the oceans. Slumped in his chair, Papa let loose a low, faint groan.

"No, to this address," Mother answered. Even though Dr. Kellogg and his wife had adopted dozens of children over the years, they did not look kindly on little ones roaming the campus, disrupting the hundreds of feeble patients and busy medical staffers, so Mother had arranged for us to take furnished lodgings in a house just several streets from the San campus.

"It is the home of a widow, a Mrs. Elizabeth Gregory." Mother handed the porter a paper with our destination scrawled in her stiff cursive, and she watched, rigid as the frozen lampposts, as the young man oversaw the unloading of our few trunks and boxes. While Papa's body had gone slack with sickness, as though his bones could no longer hold him entirely together, Mother's figure seemed to coil ever tighter under the strain of our situation. I don't remember any hair color of hers other than white.

"I understand that the address is near the Sanitarium campus of Dr. Kellogg?" Mother asked the porter, who nodded and assumed control of navigating Papa's wheelchair through the crowded depot.

"Oh, yes, ma'am. Everything in Battle Creek is near the San." Mother nodded her terse approval, taking my hand in her too-tight grip as we followed the young man and made our way down the platform toward the noisy street.

Papa groaned as the porter did his best to gently lift him from the chair into a waiting wagon, where Mother and I also took seats. "You take care now, sir," said the kind young man. "Dr. Kellogg will have you fixed up in no time. We see miracles every day—folks limping off the train for treatment who end up skipping their way out of town." Papa did his best to answer the attendant with a dim smile and a nod. Mother simply folded her gloved hands in her lap, eyes fixed on some indeterminate point across the flat, frost-covered farmland. I sat up a bit straighter as Papa turned his gaze toward me and offered me a wink. We'd heard that Dr. Kellogg's ways were unorthodox and his treatments expensive, but all our hopes hinged on the man. Papa was near the end of mortals, to hear Mother tell it, and we had come here at the end of our hopes and our pennies; if anyone could heal Papa after years of these baffling ailments, we hoped it would be Dr. Kellogg.

Mrs. Gregory answered the door at number 61 South Division Street just a beat after Mother's quick series of knocks, giving me the impression that she'd been standing right on the other side, awaiting our arrival. "Ah, the Posts have come," she announced at the threshold of her home, her loud voice sounding deep and authoritative from out of her broad, ample chest. "Heard the train when it rolled into the station. Welcome, welcome. Come in. You must be frozen through. Come all the way from Texas, haven't you?"

I didn't need to be invited twice; I quickly stepped inside, grateful for the blast of warm, bright air that filled Mrs. Gregory's modest entryway. The house smelled like steamed apples and cinnamon, and I felt my entire frame soften. Mother followed behind me, and Mrs. Gregory helped Papa to enter. "Come now, in you go. I think you'll find our Battle Creek winters a touch harsher than anything you get down there." Mrs. Gregory's features were large, her cheeks ruddy, and I immediately saw her resemblance in the small group of clean, sturdily built children who gathered in front of the house's stairwell. I smiled toward them. "Well, don't just stand there staring like I never taught you a single manner," Mrs. Gregory said, chiding the youngsters with a stern tone that was tempered by her smile. "The Posts have traveled far enough, and they are frozen and tired. And probably hungry. Help them with this luggage." Our hostess's commanding words sent her offspring into a flurry of dutiful motion, and they descended on us, taking our coats and hats, our trunks and the leather valise Mother clutched.

"Course they'll be bunking together," Mrs. Gregory said, gesturing toward her children, "given our Gregory homestead is a modest house. But you'll have plenty of room." She guided us up a steep, narrow stairwell to the second floor. I noted how Papa clutched the banister, white-handed and hunched, as he labored up the stairs, with Mother and me moving slowly behind him. "Nothing fancy like in those spa towns of Newport or Saratoga Springs, but I keep it clean. And there's always plenty to eat. This'll be for Mr. Post." Mrs. Gregory led Papa into the first bedroom at the top of the stairs, modestly sized and simply furnished with a single bed, a wooden dresser appointed with a pitcher and washbowl, a plain chair, and a rug woven in dark blue and maroon.

"Mrs. Post, I'll put you and the little one in here, right adjacent." With that, Mrs. Gregory leaned forward and looked squarely into my eyes. "And what might your name be?" she asked, her deep voice softening just slightly. Before I could answer, she cocked her head sideways as she remarked, "Well, don't you have just about the prettiest eyes I've ever seen? A shade of blue you can see right through. You look like your daddy." Mrs. Gregory took a pinch of my left cheek in two of her strong, callused fingers. "There's no denying that one came from your stock, Mr. Post."

Papa laughed feebly. "This is Marjorie," Mother interjected. "And this will do just fine." And then, a beat later, Mother nodded once, adding: "Thank you, Mrs. Gregory."

"Happy to have you," Mrs. Gregory replied, standing back to full height, her head almost bumping into the pitched ceiling. Patting down the front of her starched apron, she said, "Now, you get settled in. Wash up if you like. Supper'll be on in an hour, and I sure hope you're hungry."

Papa grimaced and Mother's scowl seemed to indicate that she had little appetite, but I felt my stomach rumble just then in appreciation.

THE SKY HAD promised fresh snowfall, and snow it did. I awoke the next morning and pressed my nose to the cold pane of our bedroom window, looking out at a street brushed in white. My breath turned to mist on the pane as I took in my first view of this foreign winter scene. "Cold," said Mother, sighing beside me as she rose slowly from the bed, her thin white braid slipping down her back. Of course to her, since she had grown up in

Illinois, this glimpse of a frozen landscape was nothing new, and she looked unimpressed—and tired, weary before the day had even happened to her. I saw her breath as she spoke, her voice quiet and reedy as she said, "Now it's finally time to see what this Dr. Kellogg can do."

The aromas of coffee and frying meat—bacon, I hoped—wafted up to our bedroom as we washed and dressed. I was hungry, and excited for another one of Mrs. Gregory's meals. "Breakfast," Mother said. "And then it's off to meet him."

Him meant Dr. Kellogg; that I knew well enough. We had come all that way, on a long winter's journey that could have sapped the last of Papa's reserves, Mother carrying all of our remaining money on her person, and now we had no choice but to submit fully to the hopes we had placed in Dr. Kellogg and his celebrated San.

That morning, the day of Papa's first appointment, Mother and I bundled ourselves under knit scarves and hats, mittens over our gloves and extra socks on our feet, then we piled wool blankets high on Papa and made ready to push him the short distance to the campus in the wheeled wooden chair that Mrs. Gregory offered us.

Our hostess saw us to the door, pressing a small parcel of golden biscuits, still warm and dripping with melting butter, into Mother's hands. "Dr. Kellogg is a Seventh-day Adventist, so you best not let him see these sinful little buns," she said as she winked at Mother, her tone indicating that she herself was not of Dr. Kellogg's faith. "The doctor runs that facility with an iron will . . . controls just about everything from what folks wear to what they eat and drink." Mrs. Gregory adjusted my scarf so it came right up to my nose. "And I'd suggest you refrain from wearing a corset the next time you're heading to the campus, Mrs. Post. The good doc does not approve of the things."

Mother inhaled a sharp gasp of scandalized breath. "But . . . would that not be . . . immodest? I would hardly wish for Dr. Kellogg to think that we Posts are—"

Mrs. Gregory chuckled as she interjected: "My dear Mrs. Post, unless you are a slide of harmful bacteria, the good Dr. Kellogg likely won't look at the shape of you for more than a passing minute. You must remember—

the man has been married for decades and has very proudly shared with the world that he and his wife have never . . . well . . . consummated their union."

Mother took my gloved hand in hers and shifted on her feet. "Indeed . . ." was all she offered in reply.

Mrs. Gregory looked down at me, her round eyes narrowing. "You certain you don't want to leave the little one here with me? I don't see how that hospital is any place for a youngster."

Papa winced slightly and I stepped closer to his wheelchair. "I will stay with Papa," I said, my tone resolute.

"Then that's settled." Mrs. Gregory gave me a nod, the hint of a smile upturning her lips. "And I'm certain he will be happy to have you."

A thin coating of snow had fallen overnight, and sporadic patches of frozen water dotted our path along the busy streets. "It's ice," Mother said, noting my intrigued stares. "Don't step on it or you'll fall. Now, keep up."

The street was noisy with the sounds of horse carts and foot traffic, and the wind blew so cold that it stung the inside of my nose and caused my eyes to water. Within minutes I was thinking that perhaps I regretted my decision to quit the warm, cozy confines of Mrs. Gregory's home. "Hurry along, Marjorie," Mother said, pulling my hand to keep me going at her quick pace as she wheeled Papa's chair across Washington Avenue. His eyes were shut; I only knew he was breathing because I saw the weak streams of vapor that slipped out of his nose every few seconds.

Finally, we reached the campus and approached the main building by way of a neat path that cut through a patchwork of frigid but tidy lawns. The grass was ice-wrapped and crunchy beneath my feet. The San grounds were huge, clearly the prosperous headquarters of a thriving empire, what with the sprawling network of tall brick buildings, each lined with rows of gleaming windows. The central hospital building stood back a ways from the street. At the building's tallest point, an American flag flapped in a bitter wind that promised more snowfall.

Mother marched like a soldier, pushing Papa's wheelchair briskly through the final steps and toward the large front doors. As we entered the lobby, a blast of warm air greeted us, along with a clean, lemon-tinged scent. Potted plants filled the bright space, and the ceiling soared overhead to a height unlike anything I'd ever seen. The space was vast, but for me the best things about it were the warmth and the lack of wind, entirely unlike the gray streets along which we'd trudged to get there. I wiped my seeping eyes.

"Stop your fidgeting," Mother scolded, her voice a tight whisper as she looked around the busy lobby.

We could not have been standing there more than a minute, studying our surroundings, before a slender, smiling nurse approached us, her apron and skirt starched white and stiff. "Welcome to the Battle Creek Sanitarium," she offered in greeting, her expectant smile inviting us to offer her information about ourselves and our reasons for being there.

"Yes, thank you," Mother said, removing her gloves. "My name is Mrs. Charles W. Post, and this is my husband, Mr. Charles W. Post. He is here for treatment with Dr. Kellogg."

"Yes, of course." The nurse nodded, clearly having been aware before Mother's words that Papa was to be the patient. She scribbled something in a booklet with a pencil.

"Will we be seeing the doctor this morning?" Mother asked. Her eyes leaked moisture onto her red cheeks, and I thought it was nice to see a bit of color on Mother's face, even if that color did come from a harsh winter wind.

"Dr. Kellogg?" the nurse asked, looking up from her papers.

"Yes," Mother said.

"Ma'am, Dr. Kellogg has thousands of patients." The nurse glanced around the crowded, sprawling lobby, as if to indicate—in case Mother had not yet noticed—just how far the doctor's domain stretched. "But yes, Dr. Kellogg does see each patient personally. Though I cannot say precisely when he will see Mr. Post."

"Well, I hope it will be soon," said Mother, her gaze sliding toward Papa's slumped figure. He had not spoken much that day, other than some faint and indecipherable mewling. Even at my young age, I knew what Mother was refraining from saying: by the look of it, we didn't have much time.

The nurse stood slightly taller, fixing a cool, courteous smile to her features as she said: "You have come to the right place, Mrs. Post. Now, we will take Mr. Post with us for some preliminary examinations and questioning, and you may come back this evening to fetch him."

At this, my father slumped even deeper into his chair, as if yielding the final reserves of authority over his body to this new figure and to this bright, clean place. My mother, gripping the back of his chair, eventually stepped to the side, leaving the handlebars for the nurse to grab. But I edged closer to Papa, my body unwilling to cede its place beside him. The nurse looked down at me, her smile flickering for just a moment with a peevish blink, but then her features softened. Her chin tilted downward as her eyes met mine, and she said, "Not to worry, my dear. We shall take fine care of your father."

You had better. My young mind reeled, even if the words remained unspoken. *Because he is the only one I've got.*

Chapter 2

AFTER THAT, OUR DAYS FELL INTO A RHYTHM, RISING AND SETting around Papa's sessions at the San and the needs of his failing body. Mother and I would wake to the smell of Mrs. Gregory's cooking—lured out of our warm beds by the scent of sausage or bacon and fresh-baked biscuits. In the pale morning light, we would wash and dress, our bodies shivering as we slipped from our nightclothes into stockings and sweaters. We'd descend the creaky stairs and eat the hearty breakfast that Mrs. Gregory laid out for us, appreciative of the hissing cookstove that dispersed its warmth throughout the space. Then we'd climb back upstairs and prepare Papa for the day. We'd wheel him to the campus, usually over ice or snow, and deliver him for his full schedule of treatments—sessions in the indoor swimming pools, private appointments with doctors and nurses and massage therapists, lectures, and group meals of Dr. Kellogg's personally prescribed vegetarian dishes in the massive dining room.

Back at the house, I'd sit with Mother while she sewed or read, occasionally finding some entertainment as Mrs. Gregory's kittens chased one another or a spool of yarn. But really, I passed the hours eagerly awaiting Papa's return at the end of the day.

Papa took no meals at home with us. The San provided for each patient a diet built on vegetables pulled straight from the earth and bland bran products made according to Dr. Kellogg's own handwritten recipes. Salt was forbidden, as were caffeine and sugar. No coffee, tobacco, tea, or wine. Fresh air, regardless of the weather, was prescribed each day, as well as indoor exercises and water treatments in the many pools.

Our Battle Creek days stretched to weeks and then months, and I remember the giddy excitement I felt in the early spring when I was finally going to have the chance to meet the mysterious Dr. Kellogg, a man whom I knew Papa to see regularly for his treatments but who had thus far, to me, remained cloistered behind the inner walls of his labyrinthine hospital. "He has summoned us for a private meeting in his study," Mother announced at the table that morning. "He wishes to speak about Mr. Post's . . . progress."

Mrs. Gregory, who sat opposite Mother, was stitching the waistline of a pair of Papa's trousers. The woman frowned into her lap as she said, "Might I suggest, Mrs. Post, that you ask the good doctor when Mr. Post might be allowed to eat some real food? I'm taking these pants in yet again, but the weight keeps coming off him, and pretty soon, there won't be anything to keep 'em up."

Mother shifted in her chair. "I'm certain we will hear about dietary matters . . . among other things."

Mrs. Gregory rose and placed her mug in the large washbasin, allowing Mother to sit and finish her own drink. "I say the man needs to eat more than that rabbit food they offer them up at the San. But I'm no doctor."

I accompanied Mother and Papa as we made our way to the San. The air had lost the knife-edge of cold, and the smell of manure hung thicker in the breeze. I now needed only one layer of stockings when we took our walks. As we entered the lobby of the San, a dark-haired nurse checked us in and then whisked us down a hallway through which we'd not previously been invited. Attendants and patients filed past, the bright corridor filled with a well-ordered air of purposefulness. Eventually, we came to a closed set of double doors, and the nurse paused, knocking gently. Another attendant, this one male, answered from within. I followed behind Mother as she pushed Papa into a quiet, clean antechamber. I could see an office through another doorway, and just a moment later I heard the softly spoken words: "Come in." The attendants nodded toward us, and we walked slowly toward that beckoning voice.

In that first glimpse of the doctor, I was struck by the overall impression of colorlessness—of a pearly-white umbra so pristine as to appear sterile. He was like untouched snow, entirely unlike the farmlands surrounding us that were covered in a brown-gray layer of muddied, late-winter slush. Dr. Kellogg was white from head to toe, from the shock of hair atop his head and his thick, plentiful mustache to his starched white suit and tie and all the way down to his polished shoes. Even his pale eyes appeared somehow devoid of color.

The male attendant and the nurse left us alone, shutting the door quietly on their exit, and Dr. Kellogg stood from behind his gleaming, massive mahogany desk. He looked first toward Mother, then to Papa, who slumped under a wool blanket in his wheelchair. "Ah, Mr. Post," the doctor greeted my father by name as we stood at the threshold of his study, the space large and sparkling clean, the walls neatly decorated with several framed portraits—serious-looking men whose names I did not know at my young age. Orderly bookshelves were arranged with weighty leather tomes that showed not a single speck of dust. "Please, sit." Dr. Kellogg raised a hand and then retook his place behind his large desk as Mother took a seat opposite him. I shuffled closer to her and sat in her lap. Papa's wheelchair was beside us.

"The Post family." Dr. Kellogg tented his fingers close to his goateed chin, and I noticed the immaculate crescents of his ten tight-clipped fingernails. He went on: "Charles William Post. Chief medical complaints: nervous disorder, melancholy, digestive trouble, lassitude."

Mother nodded as the doctor ticked through a list of ailments with which she was all too familiar. It was said that Dr. Kellogg knew the details of every patient who stepped onto his campus; one did not become the most famous doctor in the world without a blade-sharp mind and a knack for retaining particulars.

Dr. Kellogg fixed his light, bespectacled gaze on Mother as he continued: "Mrs. Post, your first name is Ella, is it not?"

Mother leaned back in her chair, the faintest hint of color tinting her otherwise pallid cheeks. "Why, yes. Ella Merriweather Post."

Dr. Kellogg nodded. "A fine name. My wife's, as well."

Mother smiled, a fleeting, sheepish expression entirely unusual on her ordinarily taut features.

Then the doctor turned his piercing, pale eyes on me. "And you, young lady, are named . . . ?"

I tilted toward Papa in his wheelchair. "This is Marjorie," Mother said. "It's an honor for both of us to make your acquaintance, Dr. Kellogg."

Both? I thought. *Aren't we three in number?* Or perhaps she had already stopped counting Papa.

"And . . . the girl . . . she can stay for this?" Dr. Kellogg arched a tidy white eyebrow.

"Oh yes," said Mother, her lips tight once more. "She's seen everything. She and her father are very close."

Dr. Kellogg cleared his throat before he continued. "You do know, Mrs. Post, that I am not only a doctor, but an inventor as well?"

Mother nodded. "Yes, sir."

Dr. Kellogg weighed his next words in silence a moment, pressing his narrow fingers flat on top of the polished surface of his dark wooden desk, so that the crescents of his nails drained of color. "I believe that this nation is making itself sick with the poison we put into our bodies. I don't allow my patients to eat the stuff." A dismissive wave of his hand. "To try to treat our sick without addressing the horrid eating habits that caused the illness in the first place would be akin to trying to clean a house by simply emptying the slop jars. We must treat not only the results of illness, but the underlying causes that bring on the original complaints."

Mother blinked rapidly, the lean of her body toward the doctor affirming her absolute attention. Dr. Kellogg went on: "I have been trying my new foods on Mr. Post. I have invented a new spread made of puréed nuts, which I have taken to calling peanut butter. Another new thing I've invented is a concoction made of oats, wheat, and corn, which some of my patients here call cereal." He shrugged, an expression of indulgence. "Mr. Post came to me as someone who has spent a lifetime indulging in animal flesh, sugar, caffeine—poisons, all. No wonder he was sick." Dr. Kellogg braided his hands in a tight, controlled gesture. "No more. I've eliminated all liquor and coffee, and prescribed my healthful drink I make from ground bran and molasses. I've ordered him to wear looser clothes. To adopt salubrious sleeping habits. I've prescribed daily sessions in the pure outdoor air."

"Yes," Mother said, her voice faint.

"I've done everything I know to do. And yet, with Mr. Post . . ." Dr. Kellogg sighed, pressing his mustached lips together in a momentary frown.

I felt my back go straighter where I sat. Finally the doctor spoke again, but his words were not welcome: "Nothing seems to be working."

I felt the breath leave Mother's chest in a slow, weary exhale. I looked down at my hands in my lap. I knew it to be true, had known it before the renowned Dr. Kellogg had declared his findings: Papa was getting weaker by the day. I couldn't remember the last time we'd had a conversation of any meaningful length. Any attempts by him to speak now were inevitably accompanied by a shuddering wince and quickly abandoned. I missed Papa's words, his smile. His laughter. I missed all of him so badly it made my throat tighten with a dry ache.

"Since Mr. Post's arrival, this affliction of his has appeared to be both bodily and yet, somehow, of an emotional nature as well . . ." The doctor went on, and my young mind wandered as I watched the man gesture with his long-fingered hands; I noted how his skin gleamed, so papery and colorless that a fine webbing of purple veins ran visibly around the base of his palms and along his wrists. I heard snippets of the words he and Mother spoke, phrases like "attenuating further loss" and "options to ease the suffering." More than any of their words, I could understand the meaning in how Mother's entire frame seemed to sag ever further as the conversation continued.

Eventually, the words that seemed to herald the conclusion of our meeting came from the doctor: "I understand that your funds are limited, Mrs. Post. And with the child to provide for, I would regret to leave you with no resources to address . . . well, what comes next."

Mother swallowed, sitting silently for a moment before she answered in a low, toneless voice: "I understand, Doctor. And I appreciate the thought you put toward our future."

Dr. Kellogg nodded once, folding his hands together on top of his dark, shiny desk. "When the time comes, we shall do what we can to help you transition out of treatment and into the next phase, Mrs. Post." A pulling back of his shoulders and a thrust of his goateed chin and, with that, we knew that our time with the busy doctor was concluded. An attendant appeared unbidden at the door, quietly entering the room and standing sentry-like at the threshold.

Mother clutched to my hand as we left the doctor's study. As an attendant pushed Papa ahead of us and down the hallway, Mother paused a moment, and I saw her chest rise with an abrupt intake of breath. And then, breaking down right there in that busy, clean hallway, Mother gasped out the words: "There's nothing more he can do, Marjorie. Nothing more any of us can do. We've tried everything."

I'd never seen Mother cry, and the result now was mute stillness on my part. If Mother was without an idea, if a man such as Dr. Kellogg stood powerless before Papa's illness, then what could I, a scared young girl, possibly do? Before I could offer some words of comfort, Mother pulled herself back to upright, dabbing her nose with the handkerchief from her pocket. Staring down the hallway, where Papa's frame was being wheeled away from us and toward the bright, airy lobby, Mother sighed, saying: "Now we just pray. It's in God's hands."

Chapter 3

Battle Creek, Michigan
Spring 1892

WE WERE SITTING DOWN TO SUPPER A FEW WEEKS LATER WHEN Papa returned from a long day, his face as gray as the low clouds outside that threatened more spring rain. But our hostess's tone was bright, and she nodded as the San attendant wheeled him in. "You are just in time, Mr. Post. Come on in and join us at the table." Mrs. Gregory was not one for luxury—it didn't seem that anyone in Battle Creek was—but true to her word, she always kept her home clean and warm, and her table was always heaped with tasty food. That evening's meal appeared to be a particularly appetizing beef stew.

The bowl at Papa's seat was always returned to the cupboard unused, and yet, meal after meal, our hostess continued to set the place for him. "Evening." Papa limped to the table and dropped himself into the empty chair, staring longingly at the aromatic dishes that Mrs. Gregory had just begun to serve to Mother, her own children, and me.

"You're welcome to partake, Mr. Post," Mrs. Gregory said, as she glanced from Papa back down to the beef stew. "Your pay covers room and board, and I always make plenty, so why don't you just go ahead and eat your supper?"

"No, thank you," Papa said, shaking his head slowly. With great effort, he added: "I mean no offense, but Dr. Kellogg would not approve. He gave us our evening meal."

"And what was that?" Mrs. Gregory inquired, lifting an eyebrow as she ladled a scoop of thick juices and soft carrots onto a slice of fillet and then took her own seat.

"Oh, this evening it was a lukewarm bran drink, along with creamed beets and celery, and a perfectly tasteless broth of peas and puréed nuts." Papa managed a weak grin as Mrs. Gregory spread her napkin over her lap with a sigh.

I did not know what Mother thought of these treatments and meals up at the San, but Mrs. Gregory made her disapproval plain enough. "No wonder you're wasting away." Our hostess frowned, shaking her head as she lifted her spoon. "A body in need of healing is a body in need of good, wholesome food."

When neither Papa nor Mother answered, Mrs. Gregory added: "I don't doubt that the good Dr. Kellogg means well, but I can't abide the way he starves you all and rants against the food that the good Lord put on this earth for us. The food at my table is good, clean food. And I know a thing about healing myself."

The table fell silent at that, and I turned my attention to the bowl of beef stew before me. *Healing.* Mrs. Gregory had told Mother and me that she practiced something she called Christian Science, and in truth, I had noticed that she had her own steady following in the health-conscious town of Battle Creek. Sick individuals often came unannounced to her front door, appearing at random times of the day asking for guidance and prayer. She had a gift, a reputation for offering at-home cures, I heard them say. I saw enough to know that, though not a boastful woman, Mrs. Gregory did not do anything to deny these claims. She, like nearly everyone in the town, was fixated on the idea of health and how best to find and keep it.

Not one for idle gossip or small talk, Mrs. Gregory often filled our mealtimes by reading from a cherished volume she seemed to carry from room to room with her: a thick book called *Science and Health.* And on many a cold evening that past winter, once supper had been cleared and the dishes set to soaking, Mrs. Gregory had gathered us all in her parlor before a hearty fire, and there she read aloud or she prayed, encouraging each of her children to participate. "It's the healing power of the spirit that cures our feeble frames," she'd said on more than one occasion. She spoke long and boldly, warning us that "our ailments come not from the body but from the soul."

Papa did not eat from the bowl of offered beef stew that evening, but from the way his pale features stitched together, I could tell that he was thinking over what our hostess had said. And as the weeks passed and Mother's improbable admiration for Mrs. Gregory seemed to grow, she took an increasing interest in our hostess's ideas of healing and spirituality.

One night, as we sat before the fire, Mother patched up Papa's socks as Mrs. Gregory read aloud from her worn copy of *Science and Health*. When our hostess took a break from the book splayed across her lap to sip her tea, Mother cleared her throat and leaned forward. "I wonder, Mrs. Gregory . . ."

"Yes, dear?"

Mother's tone was tenuous as she asked: "Might I have a turn reading?"

"Course you can," said Mrs. Gregory.

Mother took the heavy book, which looked even thicker in her small hands. Then, with her voice clearer and more confident than I'd heard it in months, she began to read aloud: "God is good. God is Mind, and God is infinite; hence, all is Mind."

Papa looked on, his features furrowing in keen concentration as Mother continued: "Spirit is the real and eternal; matter is the unreal and temporal. Spirit is God, and man is His image. Therefore man is not material; he is spiritual." My mind failed to grasp these long and meandering sentences, laced as they were with words beyond my comprehension, and soon my attention turned toward Mrs. Gregory's cat as it nuzzled my legs. But even as I began to doze off, lulled by the warmth of the hearth and the fullness in my belly, by Mother's cadenced reading, I noticed that my parents remained fixed in their chairs even as the spring twilight turned to dark night, and that all three of us moved to our bedrooms much later than usual that evening.

The next night, Papa returned and sat down as we were eating supper. It had been a pleasantly mild day, with the promise of a gentler season evident in the longer hours of sunlight, the lessening of the bite in the wind. For the first time since we'd arrived in Battle Creek, Papa did not look as if he had to thaw his trembling body before the fire. His cheeks had a faint glow of color, but it did not appear to be simply a chapping from the frigid air.

Dinner that night was a fragrant spread of whole roasted chicken cooked with carrots and potatoes, the steam curling in languid ribbons over the table, filling the small dining room with a medley of delicious smells. Papa stared at our plates heaped with food as the dish before him remained empty.

"I've said it before, and I'll say it again," Mrs. Gregory said, staring squarely into the pale blue of Papa's eyes. "You're welcome to join in our supper. There is nothing here that will harm you—except fear."

Papa raised his hands to decline, as was his custom, but then he paused, the tint in his cheeks brightening the slightest bit. And then, to my surprise, he shrugged. "Perhaps just a small bite."

Mrs. Gregory bit her lower lip, perhaps bridling a grin, and then, ignoring the tepidness of the acceptance, she heaped a plate of chicken with rosemary potatoes and carrots for Papa, spooning the flavorful broth generously over the entire dish. "When you finish that, you can have more. Eat anything you want. It is what you need; you've gone for too long without good food."

Apparently Papa agreed, however silently, because he ate his entire portion. I stared on in wonder, exchanging a wordless glance with Mother. Mrs. Gregory, for her part, did not mask her approval. When the meal was over, she declared: "I'll put the leftovers in the icebox, Mr. Post, and should hunger pangs bother you during the night, you just come help yourself."

I AWOKE THE following morning and found, to my surprise, Papa there to greet me at breakfast—having walked down the stairs on his own—with the first real smile I'd seen on his face in many months. "Papa!" I ran to him, my delight overtaking me as I let out an undignified hoot and squeal for which I was certain Mother would reprimand me, but I didn't care. I squeezed him in a hug, and to my dizzying joy, Papa returned the embrace. I took the place beside him at the table.

Papa helped himself to Mrs. Gregory's offerings that morning: ham and eggs, pancakes, even a slice of toast soaked in her homemade butter.

"Glad to see you've got your appetite back, Mr. Post," said Mrs. Gregory, sitting down at the end of the table with a satisfied expression on her face. "I was starting to take offense that you didn't want any part of my cooking." She winked at me, and I returned her smile, helping myself to another serving of pancakes.

A few days later, Papa stunned us by declaring he felt up for walking to his appointment at the San. Mother and I were free to walk beside him rather than behind his lumbering wheelchair. He waved at the folks on the street, and they stared back in mute wonder, unable to believe that his was the same body they'd seen bundled up and close to death on so many days prior.

Whether he told Dr. Kellogg he was doing it or not, I wasn't sure, but Papa began to join us regularly at Mrs. Gregory's table for supper. After the evening meals, while Mrs. Gregory's two oldest daughters washed the dishes, Papa would participate in the readings and prayers with gusto. "You know something, Mrs. Gregory?" he said one night. "I believe that your care is healing me more than any of those meals or treatments that Dr. Kellogg has prescribed."

"It's your new faith that is healing you, Mr. Post," said Mrs. Gregory, a broad smile brightening her features as she sat in her armchair, her well-worn copy of *Science and Health* making its rounds through the small group gathered in her parlor.

"Five pounds a week, that's how fast I'm gaining flesh!" Papa declared, his tone as light and peppy as his steps.

Late spring saw Papa, somehow, almost entirely revitalized. He began to skip treatments and lectures at the San, opting instead to take me on long walks through the thawed fields surrounding Battle Creek. Each day it seemed he was spending less time at Kellogg's campus and more time around town, chatting with others about his recovery. For a man whom the famed doctor had deemed a hopeless case, whom Mother had declared near the end of life, it was nothing short of wondrous, and Papa would say so to anyone who inquired.

But then, just as we felt it was time to celebrate Papa's extraordinary healing, to heave a long-held sigh of weary but grateful relief, illness returned to the Gregory home. And this time, it wasn't Papa's bed around which death lurked. It was mine.

Chapter 4

AT THE TIME, I THOUGHT IT WAS GOD HOVERING OVER MY BEDside, but I realize now that it was probably Papa. Scarlet fever and then mumps seized my young body, bringing death close and turning my world into a series of foggy mirages. My mind slipped in and out of fitful sleep; my memories of that time are scant, strung together with long periods black and blank. When I did wake enough to see my surroundings, I noted that Mother and Papa prayed over me at all times. They read aloud from the Bible. They read from *Science and Health,* too, as Mrs. Gregory attended with the dedication of an expert nursemaid.

They'd waited twelve years for me. Nine lonely years had passed before they'd even conceived, but that baby, a boy, had left them before he'd had a chance to breathe his first. Three years later I'd arrived, impossibly plump and healthy and somehow all theirs. Papa had fallen ill soon after finally becoming my father, only to make a miracle recovery. But now I was going to be taken from them both.

I don't remember how, but I know that I came through the illnesses after some weeks. "Your faith was so strong, Marjorie. It saved you," Mother told me, stroking my hand with her own in a rare gesture of affection.

Mrs. Gregory boldly stated it, and Mother and Papa wholeheartedly agreed: Trust in the Lord had been my salvation. Faith and hope and love. Those virtues had conquered the illnesses and would do so all the days of my life. That was what Mother and Papa declared to anyone who would listen. Any remaining doubts as to their new friend's religious zeal were washed clean with an expunging force more powerful than baptismal waters: their new faith had saved not only Papa, but their only child as well.

* * *

"First I was saved. Then my Budgie was saved. There has to be some reason for that," Papa declared in the garden behind Mrs. Gregory's home. It was a mild morning filled with sunshine and boisterous birdsong, even the perfume of flowers in the air, all confirmations that the stubborn midwestern winter was finally well and gone. Papa's mood was as bright as the day; it had been so since my recovery. He was simply convinced that we'd both approached death only to have our lives spared in the final moments—and that there was some large and meaningful purpose at the center of it all. "There has to be a reason," he said over and over that spring. And he was determined to find out what that reason might be.

As spring warmed to summer, and both Papa and I reentered the world of the hale and healthy, he began to approach our days with a vigor I'd never before seen in him. One morning, a humid one filled with an irregular breeze and the loamy odor of the surrounding cow pastures, Papa whisked me away from Mrs. Gregory's parlor to take a walk outside. Our outings always resulted in some adventure. Sometimes we'd walk to the banks of the nearby Kalamazoo River and look for the fish jumping. Other times we'd remove our socks and shoes and, if the day was warm enough, dip our toes in Battle Creek or skip flat stones across its surface. Sometimes we'd walk to the depot and watch the trains coming and going, their smartly dressed passengers bound for far-off places like Chicago and Kansas City, San Francisco and New York.

The city of Battle Creek was already awake and bustling with purposefulness that day. The streets teemed with horse-drawn carriages and clattering wooden carts bearing the bounties of fresh produce that came from the many surrounding farms: potatoes, eggs, timber, creamy milk. A gentle breeze rippled through the busy town, carrying on it the scents of railroad smoke, horse droppings, fresh-tilled soil, and hope.

We walked slowly, Papa and I, enjoying each other's company. Enjoying the fact that we could take such a stroll together—something that had not been possible for us on so many of the days before this one. "See that over there, Budgie?" I nodded as we passed the new school, a large brick building where girls were allowed to attend up through high school. "I don't hold with this idea that girls are any less capable than boys when it comes to schooling," Papa declared, looking down at me with a sideways grin. "Why, anyone who would claim such a thing has clearly never met my clever little Budgie here." He gave my hand a squeeze.

I smiled and turned from Papa, looking back at the school and then over the buildings all around it. Everywhere, it seemed, there were new structures rising up like stalks of corn climbing out of the fertile earth: sawmills and factories, new churches, wooden beams promising new houses for young families. A trolley clamored up the wide street, and Papa gripped my hand tighter as we waved at the streetcar, its bell jangling as it passed. I turned to Papa with an excited laugh, and we kept walking.

Some of the homes we passed had windows and doors ajar, and occasionally I could make out the smells of breakfast and cookstoves as we walked. Just then the milk wagon in front of us paused, and the capped milkman hopped down from his perch to fill the empty pails left out on the front steps beside us. "Mornin', Marty," Papa said, greeting the milkman by name.

"Charlie Post, good to see you," the man answered, offering a smile for Papa and then one for me. The milkman continued his morning delivery in front of us, and Papa and I watched as housewives and children opened front doors and greeted Marty before retreating back indoors with their cold, cream-filled pails. A few of them said hello to us as we passed; some knew Papa by name.

Papa squeezed my hand as we paused at the intersection of Van Buren Street and Washington Avenue. "Budgie?"

"Yes, Papa?"

"Did you see how that lady took her milk jug in a hurry and then had to get right back inside?"

I nodded. In truth, I had not noticed, of course; as a young girl, I was much more excited by the noisy streetcars and the horse-drawn carts, but I knew that Papa always had something important to say.

"It's because they've all got to get back to their chores. Always chores. Just like our Mrs. Gregory. She wakes before the sun to get the fire going, to fry up the eggs and bacon, mix up batter, heat the kettle. Then as soon as breakfast is served and cleaned up, it's time to start fixing lunch. And same goes for supper."

I could tell by the way his light blue eyes glistened, fixing on some distant point, that Papa had a mind full of thoughts just then, and so I listened, always happy to be his confidante. He went on, sure as I'd known he would: "I've been thinking . . . wouldn't it be nice to make their lives just a bit easier? So that all of those mothers and wives could be out here enjoying the day as we are?"

I shrugged, nodding. "Sure, Papa. That'd be nice."

Papa seized on a lull in the traffic and guided me across the street, my legs running at double time to keep his pace. "Where are we going?" I asked as we walked.

"Right here"—he gestured—"Osgood Jewelry. See if we can't find something pretty to cheer your mama up."

In contrast with Papa, Mother had been in low spirits lately. Even though we were all healthy once more, there were some days when she hardly left her bed; when she did, she had little appetite for food or company. Maybe she was fed up with taking care of sick people, I figured. I did hear her complain to Papa about the lack of money, that we were now living off the last of the funds that she'd brought to the marriage in her dowry. I thought it a shame that her spirits had started to sink just as Papa had finally come out of his sick spell, but they never did seem to agree on much, and I guessed that included when to feel good and when to stay in bed, feeling rotten.

But given Mother's complaints about money, I did not understand how or why Papa now planned to buy her something from a jewelry store. Apparently he had some funds of which I wasn't aware, because he leaned close and smiled. "Come on, Budgie. Wouldn't you like to look at some shiny baubles?" And I was won over.

"Hey there, Burtie." The bell overhead tinkled as Papa greeted the clerk inside the jewelry store. Papa knew everyone in Battle Creek, it seemed.

"Marjorie, this is Mr. Harold Burt," Papa said. "You'd best be nice to him if you want a good deal on your jewelry when you get a bit older. Burtie, this here is my little Budgie. Marjorie. Ain't she just about the loveliest thing?"

"She sure is, Mr. Post." Mr. Burt wore spectacles and a crisp suit, and he stood behind a display case of women's brooches, where he appeared busy polishing the glass with an off-white rag. As the front door clanged shut behind us and we walked up the store's central aisle, Mr. Burt eyed Papa with the same expression I had come to recognize on so many of our neighbors' faces: a combination of incredulity and wonder. "Sure is good to see you looking so fine, C.W. Why, to see you now, I'd never guess you'd been in such a bad way."

Papa spread his thin arms wide in front of him, a beam lighting his face. "God is good, Burtie. God is good. That's the truth. And now I'm here to show my pretty little thing some of your pretty little things."

"You let me know if you have any questions." And with that, Mr. Burt went back to polishing his glass display case. I could smell the aroma of his cleaning solution—a tangy mixture of vinegar and lemon scents. Papa began to whistle as I looked at the display cases that met my eye level, marveling at the rings and bracelets, a necklace with a large red jewel, cameo pins, and women's combs crusted in shimmering blues and greens.

As Papa's eyes traveled across the crowded space, they fixed on the far corner at the rear of the shop, where piles of clutter were stacked by the back door. He crossed the store toward the heaps. "Hey, Burtie, what do you make of this?" Papa asked.

"That? That's old junk," Mr. Burt answered, barely looking up from his cleaning to glance in Papa's direction. "A rusty corn toaster. I'm fixing to throw all of that out back into my wagon, take it over to the junkyard. Doing a late spring-cleaning even if it's summertime."

"You're planning to throw this one out?" Papa was fixated; I could tell from the way he flipped the machine over and studied its underbelly. "Mind if I take it home? Fiddle with the thing a bit?"

Mr. Burt chuckled, inspecting the glistening surface of his glass display case from all angles. "You'd be doing me a favor, C.W. One less piece to load."

"Change of plans, Budgie," Papa declared, crossing the store toward me with the toaster under one arm and taking my hand in his free one. "The jewelry will have to wait. We're taking this home to your mother."

An old corn toaster? I suspected Mother would prefer the jewelry, even if we couldn't afford it, to a piece of rusted old scrap plucked from Osgood's junkyard pile.

Mother had risen from bed, and she eyed Papa with obvious misgivings when she saw his arms laden with Osgood's toaster. "What are you doing with that . . . thing?" she asked as we approached the front of the Gregory house.

Papa's ebullient mood would not be pierced. "This here, Ella, might just change our future."

Mother scowled. Papa didn't notice, lugging his haul toward the back and setting it down in the garden. Mother and I followed. "What is it?" she asked me.

"A corn toaster from Mr. Osgood," I answered.

"The jeweler?" she asked. I nodded. Mother's face told me that she wanted more information, but I only shrugged, as confused as she was.

"What are you intending to do with a rusty toaster?" Mother asked Papa, her gray eyes narrowing as she pulled her shawl tighter around her shoulders.

Papa rolled up his sleeves, hoisting the machine to examine its underside as if he hadn't been near-crippled just a few weeks earlier. "I figure I can putter with the thing."

"What for?" Mother asked.

"See about making some dry food, like what the poor souls are served up at the San. Only, something with taste."

"Why?" Mother asked.

For the first time since we'd returned home, Papa paused, standing upright and pressing his hands to his hips as he turned toward Mother and explained: "Who knows better than I do the power of the foods we eat? I will create a food that can nourish and heal, just as I have been healed." He looked at me, and I saw that deep flicker in his eye, one that I would come to know well. And then he winked at me. "No more of this poisoning ourselves with our food, Budgie."

"You?" Mother said. "You are going to create a new food?"

If Papa heard the skepticism in Mother's voice, he chose not to acknowledge it but instead to answer, "I've been saved, Ella. Now it's my purpose to offer healthy foods to other folks. A food that's easy to prepare *and* easy to digest. I know I can do it. And I'll do it right here."

"C.W." Mother sighed, as if preparing to patiently reason with a child. "They do that sort of thing at the San, but they have Dr. Kellogg to oversee it all. And teams of doctors and scientists. You really think you can do something like that at home? Alone?"

Papa shrugged, offering me half a grin before he turned back to his rusty toaster. "I'm not alone, Ella. I've got Budgie here."

Chapter 5

Battle Creek, Michigan
Spring 1901

He called it Grape-Nuts. As the new century steamed in with the speed of a freight train, Papa broke wide open a new industry for the American people, and ten years after his arrival in Battle Creek, he had the success and fortune to show for it. It was Papa who had noticed that housewives and mothers did not want to spend hours preparing pancakes and bacon every morning over hot fires, and so he'd given them something we now all knew and ate. We introduced the world to cereal, and with that, the world—starting with breakfast—changed forever.

But Papa didn't stop at breakfast cereal; he also created a substitute for coffee, a healthy, caffeine-free bran drink he'd called Postum. And just like that, Papa had made tasty new breakfast options that were easier *and* healthier—and available to every American household for a fraction of the old effort and prices.

One afternoon, I returned home to a piece of paper with his tidy, familiar handwriting on it: "Dearest Budgie: See me in the office."

I smiled. I lived for notes such as this one, summonses after the school day and the walk back home. Not only because they meant an invitation to join him out in the white barn, but also because these summonses took me away from Leila, my tiresome companion who worked in part as my after-school tutor and in part as Papa's secretary. At twenty-two years old, Leila was closer in age to my fourteen years than she was to Papa's forty-six, but she behaved as if she were a mother figure. With her wide brown eyes and her quick, lively opinions—offered on all matters pertaining to the household, it seemed, whether solicited or not—Leila's presence was entirely opposite to that of my mother. It overtook the house, in the same way the scent of her Pears soap and overly sweet perfume, a mixture of cherries and vanilla, filled each room. And yet, Mother seemed each day to be yielding bits of her status as "lady of the house" to the irksome young woman.

"Oh, Marjorie, my dear." As if on cue, my companion entered the room and saw me. "I didn't hear you come in. Well then, let's get started on your schoolwork, shall we? And then your chores. I don't think the chickens have been checked since this morning when—"

"Can't right now, Leila, sorry. I've got to—"

"Now, Marjorie, don't you argue with me, young lady," Leila interrupted, her tone suddenly imperious, even as her features held tight to her smile.

"Papa's orders," I said, waving his note as my victory flag. "He wants me out at the barn."

Leila's limpid smile slid ever so slightly, but before she could reply, I turned on my heels and skipped out of the room, making my way toward the back door and out into the yard.

I breathed in deep, relishing the mild spring afternoon and its wash of country smells—thawing mud, the fires cooking in Papa's workrooms, the familiar aroma of the dairy farms that surrounded Battle Creek. It felt good to be out of the house, where I no longer had to listen to Leila or worry about my footsteps disturbing Mother. "Marjorie, I am trying to rest," had become her constant refrain. But even more than the escape from schoolwork or Leila or Mother, I loved these notes because they meant I was invited to go see Papa, and that always meant some exciting—and often unforeseen—adventure.

"Papa!" I shouted happily as I skipped into the big white barn, one of my favorite spots on the family farm that Papa and Mother had bought together and the building that Papa had turned into his main factory and warehouse for his popular Grape-Nuts cereal and Postum bran drink. "I got your note—I'm here!" Papa was always happy to see me, and he'd often halt whatever it was that he was doing and run to scoop me up into a full-bodied twirl.

But not that day, it seemed, as I bounded eagerly into the barn. That day, I found my father's lithe, agile frame leaning over a workbench, a newspaper spread open before him and a scowl fixed to his face. "Overnight success?" He barely nodded in my direction, his body remaining hunched over the journal. "They call me an 'overnight success'? There was nothing fast about it! It was work, work, and more work!" Papa slammed a fist down on the paper. I stepped beside him and scanned the offending article, immediately understanding my father's sour mood. The piece was just one of the many that sought to compare Papa to our Battle Creek neighbor and erstwhile friend, Dr. Kellogg, painting Papa less as a worthy and respectable rival and more as an opportunistic interloper who had piggybacked on Dr. Kellogg's success—a narrative that I knew to be patently false. And one that rankled Papa more than anything else he could read.

Years earlier, when Dr. Kellogg had laughed Papa off the premises of the San, refusing to hear him out or consider partnering with him for a mass-market breakfast cereal, denying him any blessing or any of the San's formidable resources, Papa had set up his own shop on our modest parcel of farmland just outside of the Battle Creek downtown. There was nothing interloping about it—Papa had developed his homegrown experiments from scratch. Sure, Dr. Kellogg had come up with a few bland recipes of wheat and bran and dry corn mixes that he'd been foisting on his patients in the San dining hall; but the doctor had never even considered the idea of mass-producing tasty breakfast foods and marketing them to the public. What about the millions of folks who couldn't afford to stay at the San and pay for the dubious privilege of Kellogg's spartan therapies and bland menus? Only Papa had asked that question; only Papa had set to work to find an answer for them.

Besides, anyone who'd ever suffered through a meal at the San knew that Dr. Kellogg's original recipes were so flavorless as to make the idea of mass marketing them seem laughable. Papa had created his recipes not only to be healthy, but also with widespread appeal at the fore. C. W. Post wasn't a carpetbagger at all—nobody had taken on America's outmoded breakfast habits the way he had. Nobody had even thought to do it, nor had anybody had the smarts or the drive or the ingenuity to pull off such a feat.

Now, ten years later, Grape-Nuts was the most popular cereal in the country, and Postum was the unrivaled replacement for coffee. Our days of worrying about money were long behind us. But Papa was still fueled, perhaps even more so than in the past, by a savage drive to succeed. He'd believed that there was a reason his life had been spared, and he believed it more with each passing day. "More, more, more!" was his daily driving hymn—he was always scouring our world for the next thing that someone had labeled "can't be done."

Because Papa had needed space for his experiments, we'd moved out of Mrs. Gregory's home to the farm where we now lived, just east of town on Marshall Street. The property had the old white barn where Papa now worked, and behind that a sprawl of cornfields and apple orchards, with low-lying hills in the near distance that grew thick with berry bushes and white oaks. We had stables and horses, and in the back of the barnyard there was a chicken coop, with egg-laying hens that Papa told me it was my job to name. Having just studied ancient Rome in school, I decided to give them all proper matriarchal names of the empire—Lavinia, Portia, Flavia—and I enjoyed feeding them each morning.

I loved having the space to roam out of doors—when Leila allowed—but my favorite place was the barn, where Papa worked with his staff. There, Papa and his team, which now involved my Uncle Cal, would let me help by putting the hot glue on the labels of the Postum boxes, or counting out the orders as we loaded up crates for delivery. I loved being near Papa as he called his excited commands to his right-hand man, a local guy named Shorty Bristol. I would jump up and down on the massive storage drums filled with the uncooked ingredients. Oftentimes Papa, Uncle Cal, and Shorty would let me rake the oats and bran as they warmed over the roasting trough, or sample a fresh batch of Grape-Nuts to give my approval. The whole place buzzed with an excitement that here, our work had meaning, and I breathed that in, along with the familiar scents of the cooking fires and the cooling cakes of just-roasted bran and wheat berries, the bubbling molasses that steamed in the tall cylinders.

But on that spring day, as Papa crumpled up the newspaper and tossed it into the nearest fire, I could see that he was not interested in my playing around in his barn or sampling the latest batch of cereal. That day it seemed he had quite a few other things on his mind. "Enough of that rotten ink," he declared, rolling up his sleeves as he turned his focus toward me. "Not going to let that poison stick. We Posts never stay down for long. We always get back up to go another round. Now, how are you, Budgie?"

I squared my shoulders as I answered, "I'm good, Papa." With Papa, there were only good days and great days. On bad days, he wanted to know how I aimed to turn things around to finish out with some good.

He nodded, still eyeing me. "Any trouble from those toughies by the lumberyard today?" he asked. Papa's seawater eyes searched my own as he asked it—he'd taught me boxing, sparring with me in our yard. I was to defend myself anytime the local crowd of bullies gave me, or anyone with me, a hard time walking home from school past the lumberyard.

"None," I said, shaking my head decisively. It was true; I hadn't had trouble with them since I'd clocked the leader as he'd tried to taunt me earlier that school year.

"That's a good girl," Papa said, nodding once. "Like I said, we Posts don't fall down just because someone shouts louder or hits first."

Was he still talking about me? I wondered. The Kellogg family had certainly shouted loud and hit first. Dr. Kellogg and his brother saw my father as not only a copycat but also a traitor, and they'd say so to anyone who would listen, even going so far as to falsely claim that Papa had poached their recipes.

But their foul tactics hadn't worked. Papa hadn't backed down, and he hadn't yielded an inch. He was far more agreeable and good on the business side of things than the aloof, rigid Dr. Kellogg, and that was why my daddy now counted among his close friends our new vice president, Teddy Roosevelt, as well as other giants, like Henry Ford—who was always asking Papa to do business with him on his new horse-free buggy—and Mark Twain, Walt Whitman, William Howard Taft, and other leaders of the day. China's formidable empress, Tz'u-hsi, had taken to eating Grape-Nuts each morning and now ordered boxes of the cereal for her entire court. So did Queen Victoria's rakish son, England's new King Edward. Battle Creek was being called Cereal City, and Papa rivaled only the world-famous Dr. Kellogg as its favorite son.

But while Papa's fame was rising in Michigan and beyond, and though he'd made countless wives happy, there was one wife who was *not* happy with C. W. Post. I was now old enough to understand what previously I had only indirectly sensed, to grasp what I was seeing as I watched my parents' marriage fray. Though she'd nursed us both back from illness, Mother had spent the recent years suffering from her own poor health. She complained regularly of crippling migraines and fraught nerves. When her body wasn't suffering, her mood often was, and melancholy had taken up a permanent residence in our home. It came as some relief that she was often gone to Chicago for doctors' appointments and St. Louis for rest cures.

With Mother's regular absences and periods of bed rest, Papa had overseen my upbringing throughout recent years, telling me that he'd raise me up to be "as proficient with dance cards and teacups as with machinery and balance ledgers." And it seemed he had a lesson in mind for me that day. "Budgie, do you remember the Hinman girls?"

"Of course, Papa," I answered. Mr. Hinman had been my dance instructor just a year prior, at a well-regarded studio in downtown Battle Creek. His daughters, Isabelle and Gertrude, had been popular local beauties, admired in town before Mr. Hinman had sent them to some fashionable finishing school out east.

"They attended the Mount Vernon Seminary," Papa said.

"Yes, sir," I said with a nod, still not certain where this lesson might be going.

"Do you know where Washington, D.C., is?" he asked.

"Yes, sir."

He arched an eyebrow, prompting me to go on. And so, shoulders pulled back, I recited all that I could recall from our civic lessons in school: "Washington City is our nation's capital, named for our first president and situated on the Potomac River between the states of Virginia and Maryland. Though the area was once primarily swamp and marsh, it was decided in the compromises between the Framers when drafting our United States Constitution that a new capital of the United States should be designed—"

"Good." Papa nodded, lifting a hand. "That's a good girl."

I beamed; his approval would never stop being my favorite source of warmth.

"Well, Budge, it's a long way away, that's for sure." He paused a moment, pressing his clean, callused hands together. "But that's where you're going to go."

"Washington?" I asked after a moment. It was a distant point on a map, a place I'd studied only as a list of facts but had never seen. "But . . . the high school right here in Battle Creek allows girls," I stammered. Why would I leave home? I didn't want to leave the farm, the barn, the chicken coop, my friends in town, Shorty and Uncle Cal as constant visitors. I didn't want to leave the Post headquarters and warehouses. I didn't want to leave Papa.

He must have sensed these thoughts even though I did not voice them, because he went on with a measured tone: "Now, Budgie, there's a whole world outside of Battle Creek, and I aim for you to take it on."

I felt the fight go out of me as I heard the conviction in his voice. It was decided, whether I wanted it or not. Nobody overpowered Papa once he'd set his mind to something. "But there's more," he said. "And you can quit giving me that frown, because it's not all bad."

"Oh?"

"I'm going with you."

"To . . . to boarding school?" I frowned again, confused. Was such a thing allowed?

"Well, not to Mount Vernon, no. I think I'm beyond the hope of any finishing school, no matter how first-rate it is. But I'll be going with you to the capital."

"You will?"

He nodded. "That's right. The Posts have big things up ahead. And I think our nation's capital is the place to be."

I didn't doubt that what he said was true, simply because I had learned years earlier never to bet against C. W. Post, but that didn't mean I understood what could possibly be coming next.

Chapter 6

Washington, D.C.
January 1902

I WAS THE ENVY OF EVERY GIRL IN MY CLASS AT THE MOUNT Vernon Seminary as I left our school's brownstone, riding by covered coach with my parents until we stopped under the grand portico of the White House. President Theodore Roosevelt had been in office only a few months, taking over after President McKinley's shocking assassination the previous autumn, and he was hosting a New Year's reception to usher in his first full year as commander in chief.

Compared to the raw January nights we had known back in Battle Creek, the night felt balmy here in what had previously been Potomac swampland. As we stepped inside, greeted by liveried attendants in immaculate suits of dark blue and cream, the White House glowed warm and bright. Papa helped me out of my mink stole as a footman stepped forward to receive it. Inside, the mob of close-pressed bodies filled every corner of the large space, women with neatly coiffed hair piled high in the bouffant style, men in tailcoats and gloves, the crowd as decorous and plentiful as the arrangements of pine and holly that gave the grand White House rooms their festive holiday feel. Our new president was famously opposed to the American tradition of chopping down trees at Christmas, being a fierce defender of the woods, but I saw that he'd put the White House staff to work at decking the grand rooms with plenty of other yuletide accoutrements, with fragrant wreaths and berried garlands, red bows and colorful blown-glass ornaments.

"Here we are, Budgie. Ella." Papa directed us forward through the large Blue Room. As we took our place in the massive queue, awaiting our turn to greet the president and first lady and members of the cabinet, I noticed how in spite of the candlelit warmth of the house, the relations between Mother and Papa could not have been frostier. It had been that way for months, ever since our move to Washington. Papa had taken a spacious brownstone on Vermont Avenue and had opened up a Post Cereal office just a short walk's distance. Mother had moved with us but, to my surprise, had taken lodgings of her own, a furnished suite of rooms just a few blocks from my school on leafy M Street. There was now not even the pretense of any marital union between my parents; Mother still spent a lot of her time visiting various spa towns seeking cures for her headaches and nerves, and when she was in town, my visits to her home never included Papa.

As we neared the front of the line to greet the president, affectionately called "Teddy" by the press and the adoring public, my eyes fixed on the tall, striking young woman who stood nearby. Alice Roosevelt was in the midst of some lively conversation, surrounded by a gaggle of admiring young men and eager newspaper reporters. The First Daughter was already famous—infamous—as the president's brash and free-spirited eldest child. Newspapers loved nothing more than to fill their pages with stories of her sharp-tongued quips, her midnight escapades with other Washington socialites and their roguish suitors, and her attendance at parties with her pet snake, named Emily Spinach, slithering freely in her pocket. Reporters—and the public—could not get enough details about how Alice and her siblings kept the White House staff constantly on their toes, rigging silver trays to slide down the wide stairways and bringing horses and other animals into the bedrooms of the storied old home.

But the favorite topic, it seemed, was whether America's First Family would be hosting a wedding in the White House during Teddy's tenure. To see the columns tell it, every ambitious young man in America hoped to marry the beautiful Alice and dance at a wedding reception given by the country's most powerful father. Like all the young girls in America, I had read plenty about Alice, and so now I eagerly took in all the details of her appearance in the flesh, noting the flattering cut of her dress, the stylish waves of her upswept dark hair. Her gown was a bright shade already being called "Alice blue" because of how it complimented her bright eyes, eyes that had made her father cry when he'd first beheld her as a newborn, so the story went, for their resemblance to those of the beautiful mother who had borne the baby and then perished on the birthing bed. Teddy had gone on to remarry and now had five more children, and the papers also liked to report on the tiffs between the First Lady and her spirited stepdaughter.

I noted, as I watched her bob her head in conversation, that although Alice had been gifted with her mother's beauty, she had also inherited her father's force of personality—an irresistible combination it would seem, based on the number of admirers surrounding her. I patted down the skirt of my own dress, feeling dim and ungraceful compared to the bright, beguiling wattage being radiated by the self-confident First Daughter. "You look lovely, Budge." Papa leaned close beside me, speaking as if he'd read my thoughts. "But don't think for a minute that I'm going to allow any of these flip young congressmen to ask you for a dance."

This put a smile on my face, and I felt my nerves slacken the slightest bit. At fourteen, I was still a bit young for gentlemen suitors, even if I did sense a newfound power in my figure and appearance. I had noted recently how the young men who came to my school to court the older girls would stop and take note when they saw me passing, their eyes roving curiously over my new curves. I was already taller than Mother, standing well over five feet. I'd sprouted overnight, it seemed, and Papa liked to note, "You're not dainty like your mother. You're hearty, like your Post kin."

And, in truth, I was relishing my youthful allure and newfound beauty. I did my best to dress like the Gibson Girls, the elegant women drawn by the artist Charles Gibson, whose flawless faces and figures graced every article that wasn't already filled with images of Alice Roosevelt. My closest friend at school, Helen Hibbs, and I would clip images of the Gibson Girls and hang them beside our beds at Mount Vernon. I piled my thick, honey-colored hair high on top of my head, just as they did. I tinted my cheeks with rouge and splashed my neck with rose water. And thanks to Papa's generosity, I was well dressed, too. Before sending me off to Mount

Vernon, he'd outfitted me with an entirely new wardrobe, with dresses custom ordered from New York City and London. With Grape-Nuts and Postum continuing to fly off the grocers' shelves all across America, long gone were the days of the Osgood Jewelry store in Battle Creek—now when Papa gave me jewelry, which was somewhat often, it came from Tiffany in New York or Cartier in Paris.

And that night, I was dressed in my best to meet our young new president. A necklace of large sapphires lined my neck, matching the new sapphire earrings that Papa had just given me for Christmas. My gown, a rich shade of violet, cinched my waist while showcasing my new curves. Elbow-length white gloves and kidskin heels embroidered with silver thread made me feel as if I were playing dress-up. A bit of rouge brightened my cheeks, but so did a natural flush brought on by the warmth and excitement in the room.

Finally it was our turn to pay our respects, and I followed Papa and Mother as I offered a deep curtsy. Up close the president was a broad bear of a man, with a thick mustache and a wide, bespectacled grin. The attendant announced our names, but it did not seem that Mr. Roosevelt needed any prompting. "Ah, there he is! Mr. C. W. Post, the man who turned breakfast into America's favorite meal!" President Roosevelt's thick paw pulled Papa in for a vigorous handshake, accompanied by a jovial slapping of the back. "Did I tell you that I asked our kitchen staff here to stock the cupboards with your newfangled invention . . . cereal? The children love it. Now, if Edith and I could only get them to sit still long enough to eat a meal."

Teddy Roosevelt was thicker than my father by almost double, but he had the same quality—something I'd never before seen so clearly in anyone other than Papa—the impression that the sheer size and force of his spirit overspilled the borders of his physical frame. He, like Papa, was a great man. I could understand how the two had become quick friends in recent years, largely via letters. As Papa leaned closer to the president now to make a point on a new labor bill being debated in the House of Representatives, I heard another voice at my side. "So you must be Marjorie Post?" I turned and looked into the cool blue of Alice Roosevelt's eyes. I felt my back stiffen, and my posture pulled a bit more upright as the First

Daughter gazed at me with interest. Then she cracked half a smile and added, "You've just started at Mount Vernon up the street, isn't that right?"

"It is." I nodded, feeling sheepish that Alice Roosevelt knew this detail about me. She smelled fresh, a swirling blend of jasmine and orange blossom.

"I've got a few friends there," she said, her voice deep and self-assured. "And I know a few of the fellows who call there on weekends, working on getting themselves wives." I nodded again at this; gentlemen callers were a regular part of the rhythm of Mount Vernon for the older girls. Alice sniggered, tossing her head back ever so slightly, setting her dark waves aflutter. She had her father's commanding manner, a posture that told the entire room that she was in charge. She leaned toward me and whispered: "A few of the fellows have been asking about you."

I shifted from one foot to the other, caught unaware by this. Or perhaps more so by the fact that it was Alice Roosevelt who was telling me. "Oh?" was all I offered in quiet reply.

"Course," she said, with a shrug of her pale shoulders. And then Alice slid a hand into the pocket of her gown, and I couldn't help but wonder if her snake was in there, slithering around her fingers. She went on: "You're the girl whose daddy reinvented breakfast, right?"

"My father is C. W. Post." Beside me, Papa was gesturing animatedly at the president as he set forth his own thoughts on labor unions and how he was aiming to keep his workers satisfied through fair wages and quality housing on the Post properties back in Battle Creek.

Alice cocked her head, tilting her narrow face. "Why, you're not only awfully pretty, but you're rich to boot."

I flushed at this, aware even as I did so how girlish I must have looked, but I could not help it; Alice Roosevelt had called me pretty. I could tell as we spoke that I was being watched by countless pairs of curious eyes from around the packed room—my proximity to Alice guaranteed that. She offered half a grin, saying, "Better take care, honey. They're going to want to gobble you up faster than a bowl of Grape-Nuts."

"No one's doing anything of the sort while I'm around," Papa interrupted with a gentle nudge to my shoulder. I cringed, mortified that my father had overheard this exchange. But he was all good-natured joviality as he continued: "Miss Roosevelt, good to see you, my dear. I'd say you've got a few petitioners yourself. Looks like that young Longworth fellow aims to toss his hat into the ring."

Alice bobbed her brunette head with practiced insouciance, but I noticed the sudden tinge of color that rushed to her cheeks. Papa smiled, looking from Alice back toward me. "Now, if I may be so bold, I'd like to impose on Miss Marjorie Merriweather Post for her first dance." He extended a hand toward me, and I accepted with a nod.

"See you around, Marjorie," Alice said, turning with a wink and making her way back into the scrum of reporters and eager young men, leaving a scent of orange blossoms in her wake.

"Where's Mother?" I asked, as Papa guided me into the East Room, where the dancing was taking place. "Would you like to dance the first with her?"

"Your mother's head is troubling her," Papa said, his voice momentarily toneless. I followed his stare and noticed that Mother, her face bone-white and unsmiling, had taken a seat in a far corner of the room.

"What do you think, Budgie?" My father pulled my attention back to our dancing. "Nice party, isn't it?"

"Very," I said.

He swung me around as if we were back in Mr. Hinman's Dance Studio, but Papa's long coat and tails were far too splendid for any Battle Creek gathering. "It's a new century," he said, his voice rippling with a lively ebullience, "and the East Coast is where the power is."

I looked up into the bright, light eyes of my father—the eyes he had bequeathed to me. He was the man who had remade America's eating habits according to his ideas and his will. Our family would want for nothing; his bankroll far surpassed anything we would ever need. But it seemed that Papa was setting his sights on an ever-larger landscape, because he was never satisfied unless he was working zealously toward his next conquest. Seeing him there that night, I realized that he wanted national influence. With thousands of employees working for him, Papa wanted to weigh in as a leader on labor and business policies. And why shouldn't he? Not only did the Post Cereal workers love and admire my papa, but he was friendly with scores of senators and congressmen and reporters and even the president as well, all of whom sought his opinions on how to help the workingman.

"Washington City is important. But so is New York," he declared now, as we continued to glide together across the dance floor. I looked up at him, surprised by this turn in the conversation. He went on: "What do you say to this, Budgie? Let's build a home together near New York City."

I stared at him in confused silence; I had always thought we'd return home—to Battle Creek—after I finished school at Mount Vernon. "What about the farm?" I asked.

Papa's gaze was animated as he explained: "There's a fine community outside of New York called Greenwich. The Rockefellers have settled there, and the Setons, the Carnegies. A lot of the wealth and power is consolidating right there. The way I see it, why can't we Posts make a home there as well?"

I still had several years left of school, and this seemed far away to me, even if exciting, as Papa's adventures tended to be. "I . . . I guess that sounds nice. But what about Battle Creek?"

"We'll always keep our place in Battle Creek. That's where it all started, and that's where the Post Company headquarters will stay. But as I've said: there's a big world out there. And I don't need that Kellogg breathing down my neck, stealing my victories and claiming my credit." Daddy shook his head once. "Wait until you see what I have in store, Budgie. I've bought us a fine piece of property, covered in big old trees, with a creek and plenty of land for horses and pastures. We'll build a great house there. We can plan it and furnish it together—however you want it. We'll make it as big as we can, so you'll have room to grow. Start a family of your own someday. But not anytime soon, you hear?"

"Really?" I blinked, my mind spinning faster than our feet were dancing.

"Come over tomorrow and I'll show you the designs. All right?"

"All right," I said with a nod, my thoughts awhirl with the lively string music all around us. It wasn't until after I had agreed that I realized Papa had not once mentioned Mother's place in our new home.

⁂

PAPA HAD FINALLY given in to his friend Henry Ford and purchased one of those new driving inventions, an automobile, and so he arranged to send his chauffeur to pick me up at school and bring me the short distance to his brownstone on Vermont Avenue the next day, but the morning came so clear and unseasonably warm that by lunchtime I decided I'd like to walk.

I arrived to a quiet house. The servants were probably eating their midday meal, and Papa, not expecting me for another half hour, was likely out lunching with some influential senator or curious newspaperman. President Roosevelt had only just begun his first term, but Papa's name was already being offered as the candidate to succeed him in the Oval Office. I couldn't help but laugh at all of the attention, even as Papa good-naturedly dismissed such talk. He was eager to serve his workers and continue to invent foods and drinks that made Americans healthy and happy—he'd never once courted attention in the political arena. Still, it was fun to hear my daddy spoken of with the admiration I knew he deserved.

The house was dim and cool as I entered, the fires in the large fireplaces having sputtered to ash. I walked from the front foyer through the dark-paneled dining room and into the drawing room, where I saw papers strewn all over the velvet davenport sofa and oriental carpets. Papa was always writing down new ideas, penning editorials, concocting potential new recipes or inventions. But as I looked at these papers, I saw with irritation that they weren't in Papa's handwriting. "Leila," I grumbled, recognizing her spidery script. In fact, the remnants of her Pears soap and cloying cherry perfume lingered in the room, even now. The woman had come to Washington with her servile smiles and overeager laughter to carry on her work as Papa's secretary. And while I was grateful that I no longer had to see much of her now that I was living at the boarding school, I knew that she still spent plenty of time in Papa's presence. Couldn't she have cleaned up her mess rather than leaving this sprawl of papers all over his drawing room? Papa extolled nothing more than tidiness; he would not be happy to return to this. As I bent over to pick up the papers, I saw it, right at the top of one of them:

PETITION FOR DISSOLUTION OF MARRIAGE

The blood chilled in my veins. I blinked, staring in stunned silence at the words. The document was a long one, and I read on:

Claimant on the Suit: Charles William Post

There at the end was his familiar signature. Papa had signed the papers, and beside that there was another space, still blank. For Mother's name.

Dissolution of marriage. Divorce. I'd heard the word before, though never spoken aloud by anyone close to me. Papa was going to sue Mother for a divorce? Would she agree? Perhaps she already had? No one had said a word to me. I could barely breathe, and my hand instinctively braced against the punishing boning of my stays, where my breath struggled in and out.

Divorce. Such a thing was unthinkable. The end of their marriage. The end of our family.

True, I had never known my parents to act lovingly toward each other. I'd never seen a gentle embrace pass between them, could not remember having heard one of them speak a tender word to the other. And yet, the idea of a divorce was incredible. Papa and Mother were staunch adherents of the Christian faith. How could he consider such a thing? I lowered myself to the sofa with a ragged exhale as the document slipped from my fingers, floating to the carpet.

My thoughts were a knot, tangled and thorny with urgent questions that I myself had no hope of answering: Did Mother know? Was she expecting this? Did that explain her surly mood, her strained face? Or was it the other way around—that her ailments and her unceasing melancholy had been enough to finally push Papa toward the final break, to seek his own happiness alone?

Not alone. As my mind reeled, the sound of my corseted breath coming and going in constricted rasps, I heard another noise. I followed the sound, my eyes sliding toward the far side of the drawing room and the thick door into the next room: Papa's study. I had assumed that I was alone in the house, that Papa was dining out, but from the sound of the voices on the far side of the heavy wooden door, it seemed that I had been mistaken. A voice, Papa's, mixed with another. Then a warble of laughter, a woman's. And then the smell of Pears soap and too-sweet perfume clung thicker to my nostrils. I heard the second voice again, its sugary, servile tone mixing with a coo of girlish laughter.

Leila.

Leila was in Papa's study, behind a closed door, laughing, while in the next room the wreckage of my parents' marriage papered the floor. More laughter, then Papa's voice, low and throaty, beseeching even, a timbre I'd never heard from him. A long moment of silence—that silence perhaps louder to me than the laughter of the previous moment—then more talking. Leila's chirpy laugh and then casual talk, a quick, easy exchange that spoke of a well-worn intimacy.

I had to go. Immediately. I straightened, my mind a whorl of anger and anguish. I'd walked there from school; I could walk back. I'd send a note with some excuse, tell Papa I had a headache. But just as I crossed the room to leave, the study door began to groan open. I hurried the last few steps to the near doorway, but my eyes flickered backward and fixed on the threshold as I saw them: Papa in just a shirtwaist with no jacket or cravat, his top buttons undone and revealing the scarlet flush of his neck. Leila, her hair loose and untidy, her entire face flushed, a relaxed, triumphant smile on her lips. She turned to face him, and as his hands gripped her by the waist, the two of them paused a moment on the threshold, their bodies flush against each other, Leila fiddling with his unbuttoned collar.

My stomach clenched, and I worried that I would be sick right there in the doorway of the drawing room.

They weren't expecting me just yet, I wasn't due for another half hour, and I did not alert them to my presence on the opposite side of the room. How could I? I slid slowly backward, away from them and out to the foyer. I'd slip out the front and run, far away. And as I moved to do so, I heard the words. Leila's words: "Now, now, Charlie Post, look at the mess you've made. And I thought you were such a fastidious man."

"Well, I am sorry, my dear. I don't know what came over me." The sound of Papa pulling her to him once more, her fresh, compliant giggles. Leila, stepping on the divorce papers to get closer to Papa, a man who was still married. The pair of them, caressing like that, making a jest of the divorce documents that would destroy my family and shatter my mother's fragile heart.

Never could I have conceived of such a thing. Of Papa being capable of such a vile act. Perhaps I'd never really known him at all. I, who'd fancied myself growing from girlhood into womanhood. Who had reveled in my new dresses from New York City, in my cheeky small talk with Alice Roosevelt and my Gibson Girl hairstyle. I'd danced at the ball, had relished the admiring looks of those blue-blooded young men all around me. I'd thought my father had such exciting plans for us, moving toward New York City and beginning a new chapter for our Post family. But the reality was that I was nothing more than a fool.

Chapter 7

Greenwich, Connecticut
Summer 1903

THE CHAUFFEUR OPENED THE DOOR OF OUR AUTOMOBILE, AND I accepted Papa's outstretched arm. As we made our way up the pebbled front path, I examined the façade of the Old Elm Country Club. Soft light trickled through the windows of an old, dignified building painted a crisp white and trimmed with tidy wintergreen shutters. A border of tasteful ivy and low-clipped shrubs added the right amount of natural adornment. Nothing about the clubhouse appeared gilded or flashy, and it was precisely in that fact that one caught the overwhelming whiffs of power and wealth—old, pedigreed privilege, the sort that opted for understated restraint as opposed to flair and sparkle.

"I know I've always told you, Budgie, that 'beauty is as beauty does,' but I'll indulge in a rare moment of vanity now to tell you just how beautiful you look tonight." Papa gave my arm a squeeze, smiling down at me, and I found myself smiling back.

I'd been so cold and aloof with him lately, really ever since I'd stumbled upon the divorce papers and his closeted interlude with Leila. My parents had finalized their divorce, and both had conducted their own separate and awkward conversations with me, explaining their plans. Mother now split her time between Washington and St. Louis, where she took her regular cures. Papa spent time in both Battle Creek and Washington, where I was still enrolled in boarding school. And he had followed through on his plan to build a sprawling new estate up here in Greenwich. He was rarely alone in his travels; though he'd never spoken to me of any formal attachment to Leila other than her ongoing role as "secretary," he had allowed that woman to assume an ever-larger hold on his life and role in our family, so that by this time she was practically a constant fixture.

But not tonight. Not on this lovely summer evening, and for that, I breathed just a bit easier. I was sixteen years old, it was my summer break from Mount Vernon, and I was going to a party—and I would enjoy myself, I decided. I wore a light gown of pale rose satin, my new Cartier diamonds from Papa glistening around my neck (I wasn't blind; I'd seen the way Leila had scowled when he'd presented the necklace to me upon the completion of my spring term at Mount Vernon). The night was a balmy one with a faint saltwater breeze, and my dark blond hair was swept back in a Gibson style that showcased my jeweled throat and freshly made-up face.

As we entered the club, walking past a plentiful spread of oysters and smoked salmon, caviar and a tiered display of small canapés, Papa held tight to my arm. A gloved footman approached bearing a silver tray laden with flutes of chilled champagne. "No, thank you," Papa answered for the both of us. Ever since his healing at the hands of the Christian Scientist Mrs. Gregory, Papa swore off all alcohol, and so I followed suit.

A quintet of strings played gentle notes on the far side of the room as the well-dressed guests mingled, sipping their drinks and nibbling on thin-sliced steak and deviled eggs. Beautiful young ladies meted out soft, controlled laughter as men in tailcoats requested places on their dance cards.

"Not too much like a Saturday night gathering in Battle Creek, is it?" Papa said, echoing my exact thoughts.

I spoke in just above a whisper as I leaned close and said, "It feels as though everyone is staring at us, Papa."

I felt him squeeze my arm a bit tighter, and then he tossed his shoulders back and looked out over the room as he answered: "It's because you're so lovely, Budgie." I knew that was not the case—he knew it, too—but I appreciated his efforts to put me at ease. No, people were staring at us because they had no idea who we were—or what we were doing there.

In all likelihood, Papa had more money in the bank than most of the well-tailored people in that rarefied room—and therefore I did as well—but they had something that we did not: they were of this habitat. This was not Battle Creek, some former pioneer outpost where everyone had arrived within the past few decades—a generation or two earlier at most. This was the East Coast. Here, in this leafy and moneyed town just outside of New York City, the sense of belonging had been bred into the local populace not only for their entire lifetimes but for generations prior. We had stepped into a country club, but it felt like a club in all ways—and we were most certainly its newest members.

Why did Papa feel the need to infiltrate this blue-blooded terrain? I wondered. But this was not the time to ask him, not while scores of eyes held us in their discreet but definite stares. I looked back toward the spread of canapés and decided perhaps I'd make myself a plate, but then a voice caught me unaware. "I was hoping you'd be here tonight." A young man, tall, appearing slightly older than me, had approached without my noticing. I turned, distracted, toward his voice, startled to be addressed in that room. But then I noticed that he was speaking not to me but to Papa.

"Oh?" Papa, serving himself a small bite of smoked salmon, turned toward the young gentleman.

"Indeed," the man answered, with a nod of his narrow, fine-featured face. "I drive by your home each day. The Boulders estate, isn't it? What a project. I am fascinated by the work you are doing."

Papa dipped his chin. "And you are?"

"Edward Close," the man said, offering his gloved hand to Papa. "It's a pleasure."

"Edward Close, the pleasure's mine. I'm Charles William Post. And this here is my daughter, Miss Marjorie Merriweather Post."

At this, Mr. Edward Close turned and fixed his cool, gray-blue gaze on me, his full lips curling upward into the hint of a smile. His lips, my eyes rested on his lips. And then, with the slightest arch of his eyebrow, Mr. Close said, "Oh, Miss Post, then you are the young lady who's truly in charge, from what I hear?"

I blinked, skimming my thoughts for some quick reply. "You hear correctly," Papa interjected, wrapping an arm around my shoulder and giving it a light, affectionate squeeze. "My Marjorie here is capable of running anything twice as well as I can. Why, when I was first getting things started in the family business, I didn't let a box of cereal out of my sight without

Marjorie's seal of approval. You could maroon this girl alone on a desert island and in a few days, she'd have the grains of sand organized. So the same went for our new house plans. My Marjorie here has an eye for these things." I felt my cheeks grow warm, but then Papa shifted on his feet and continued: "I'm a curious man, Mr. Close, so I've got to ask: Just where did you hear about us?"

"Greenwich is a small town," Edward Close answered as if he and Papa were old confidants, and as his body leaned close, I couldn't help but note the fresh scent of him, the hint of mint and tallow from his shaving soap.

"That right?" Papa offered a satisfied tilt of his head.

Edward Close nodded. "So, the Posts moving in and then preparing to build the largest home in the area—that was big news for our bored Four Hundred."

I knew to what Mr. Close referred in his quip about the Four Hundred, the elite of East Coast high society, a select clique of families comprising the Astors and the Whartons, the Stuyvesants and the Roosevelts. Entry into the Four Hundred was granted based not on net worth but on pedigree. The Vanderbilts had more money than all of them, but lacking the lineage, those railroad millionaires had been notoriously snubbed, denied entrée by members of the Four Hundred. The Closes, then, must have been some of the East Coast's oldest money.

Papa seemed unfazed. "It's going to be quite a place when it's done, Mr. Close."

"Oh, please, sir, call me Ed."

"Well, all right, then, Ed. You and your folks are welcome to stop in anytime you'd like to see what we're doing. Report back to these . . . Four Hundred . . . on the place."

"That would be wonderful, Mr. Post. Thank you," Ed answered, genuine interest lighting his patrician features as he looked from Papa toward me. I folded and then unfolded my hands, wishing I had a glass or a plate of hors d'oeuvres in my grasp, anything to provide some sort of distraction.

"What's got you so interested in buildings, Ed?" Papa asked. "Are you a builder yourself?"

"No, sir. The law, actually."

"That right?"

"Yes, sir," Ed Close answered. "I'm currently studying at Columbia." Again, Ed Close stole a quick glance in my direction. I returned his gray-eyed gaze this time, offering a partial smile.

"Well, I'm a food man myself," Papa declared, thrusting a hand into his pocket. "Don't know too terribly much about the finer points of the law, other than the fact that it's best to keep on its good side." Ed Close laughed at this. I did, too, grateful for the ease with which Papa could speak to anyone.

"Please, Mr. Post, Miss Post." Ed Close looked at me for a long moment, and I felt the hastening of my heartbeat against my stays. "Might I bring you both something to drink?"

"No, thank you, son," Papa replied. "My daughter and I were just about to get a bite to eat. But I do mean it: stop in and see the place next time you're passing by."

"I will, sir. Thank you. I would like that very much." Ed Close kept his eyes fixed on mine the whole time he was saying it.

After dinner, I left Papa in a small clutch of cigar-smoking New York businessmen and slipped out onto the back terrace, eager to get some air and escape the constant scrutiny of so many curious eyes. Papa seemed to relish the attention, the way our presence so evidently ruffled this staid, tight-knit gathering, but I was young and shy, and I found it daunting. Many of the young men had looked at me with an appraising sort of interest throughout the evening, but then, their eyes slanting toward my father at my side, not one had asked me to dance. Nor had a single young lady left her small huddle of satin and pearls to cross the room to make my acquaintance.

Outside on the terrace the night was cool and dark, the space illuminated only by the puddles of light that seeped through the windows and the open glass doors. I could see that a pair of girls a few years older than me stood whispering on the far side. On my approach they erupted in conspiratorial giggles and made a quick retreat back indoors. I stood alone, wishing I had a shawl to drape across my shoulders.

The sound of the music spilled out from the bright dining room, mixing with the evening chorus of crickets and peepers. Greenwich was a sylvan stretch of countryside in the full throes of late summer, tucked against the Long Island Sound and stocked with soaring old trees; a light summer wind rippled those leafy oaks and elms and maples now. I looked up at the sky and breathed in the night air, thinking back to the Battle Creek stars. How Papa used to point out the shapes they made across the sprawling backdrop of black. In the summers of my girlhood, Papa had rented a house for us on the shore of nearby Gull Lake, where I learned to swim and would invite my friends out for evening bonfires. On nights when it was too warm for a fire, we'd spend hours chasing lightning bugs, which we'd store in empty jam jars and release at dawn.

A voice behind me interrupted this reverie, signaling that I was no longer alone on the terrace. "Is that Miss Post standing out here in the dark?" It was a smooth voice, low but tinged with the softness of velvet.

I turned to see Ed Close approaching, his stride long-legged and relaxed. Smiling, he took the place beside me at the terrace railing and held me with his gray-eyed gaze. He was the only young man so far that evening who had not seemed to look at me like I was some strange, foreign specimen. "Indeed it is. Hello, Mr. Close," I answered, staring sideways at him. I realized then that those were the first words I'd spoken to him.

"Would you please call me Ed?"

"Oh? All right. Ed."

"Has our assembly so quickly bored you that you've been forced to come out here and count stars?"

I let loose a quick, quiet laugh. "Not counting," I said.

"Then what?"

I breathed in slowly before answering. "Simply admiring. Where I live—in Washington—we don't have such a clear view of the night sky. I live on a busy street filled with homes and streetlamps."

"Which street is that?" he asked.

"M Street. Are you familiar with Washington City?"

"Not as familiar as I am with New York City, I must confess. I really ought to visit, get to know the place better. It is our capital, after all."

"Well, you certainly should not visit this time of year," I declared.

"Why is that?"

I shuddered. "Terribly hot. A thick heat. The swamp waters. And the mosquitoes! No, no. Papa and I had to get away. That's why we are up here."

He nodded at this.

I looked back out over the evening. "When I was a girl . . . well, before Washington really, I loved summer evenings."

He pressed his hands on the railing and fixed his stare squarely on me. I met his gaze. Candlelight from inside flickered through the windows and out onto the terrace, catching the glint of his blond hair, casting a pleasant glow over his attentive face. "And where was that?"

"Battle Creek," I answered, aware that it must have sounded like a remote backwater to Mr. Close of Connecticut, a law student from Columbia and a member of the Four Hundred. As an afterthought, I added, "It's in Michigan. Battle Creek, Michigan."

"Ah yes. Cereal City," Ed said, a good-natured grin rippling his features.

"Yes." I narrowed my eyes to study him—was he mocking me? But his smile was earnest and wide as he said, "And your father is its mayor, from what I hear?"

I laughed at this. "Only informally."

"Is it true what they say about Dr. Kellogg?"

I tilted my head sideways, cocked an eyebrow. "What do they say about Dr. Kellogg?"

"Is he as stiff as he sounds?"

"Oh yes. More than stiff. Cold. You'll make me shiver thinking about him," I said.

"I wouldn't want that." Ed put his arms around my bare shoulders, a quick, playful gesture meant to ward off my shivers, but my body startled at feeling such sudden and intimate contact with his. Within an instant he had remembered himself, and he dropped his hands and stood straight beside me once more, a proper distance between our two bodies. But I could feel the whirl of my heartbeat.

Ed, appearing far more at ease than I felt, flashed half a smirk as he tipped his head toward me and said quietly: "For what it's worth: I favor Grape-Nuts over Kellogg's Corn Flakes."

I fixed him with a playfully stern gaze. "Then you're a man of good taste."

"Exquisite taste," he declared with a decisive nod.

"Good. Otherwise I was ready to tell you that this conversation was over."

"We can't have that," he said, gently nudging my shoulder with his. We looked at each other a moment, neither one of us speaking. I wanted to take him up on that earlier offer of a drink; it felt like a night for champagne. Eventually, he spoke: "I must confess, when I heard the words *cereal heiress from Michigan*, well, you were not what I was expecting."

Now I could not help but laugh. I cocked my head to the side. He had *heard* of me? He had heard enough that he was *expecting* something? With my heart at a gallop, I managed to force some cool Alice Roosevelt poise into my voice as I said, "I'm not certain I fully grasp your meaning, Mr. Close."

"Ed," he gently corrected. I arched an eyebrow, indicating he should go on. "I only mean . . ." He puffed out his cheeks a moment before letting loose a slow exhale and running a hand through his light, neatly combed hair. "I don't know. Simply to say that . . . well, you are entirely surprising, Miss Post."

"Marjorie," I said. He raised his brow, challenging me with his expression. I grinned, leaning just a fraction of an inch closer. "Come now, if I can call you Ed, then you may call me Marjorie."

"All right, then. Marjorie." The skin around his eyes creased as he smiled, and I felt my pulse quicken once more. I liked the way my name sounded on his lips. And now I could not seem to pull my gaze from those lips; I found myself wondering what it would be like to be kissed by them. But Ed saved me from completely embarrassing myself with my gawking as he continued, "And I am glad that Washington is a swamp."

I looked at him in silence, confused. He went on: "I'm glad that those inhospitable mosquitoes drove you north. Here. To Greenwich."

My cheeks flushed warm. I turned from his gaze toward the grass as I cleared my throat and said, "Ah yes. Well, Greenwich seems lovely. I am . . . I'm happy to be here, as well."

"Say, Marjorie, we can't hear the music quite so well out here."

I offered a gentle shrug in reply. I did not feel like going back inside and dancing. Not with everyone looking on. I preferred it out on the terrace, and I was enjoying Ed Close's company more than I cared to admit aloud.

He was staring at me, and his voice was low when he said, "How about a dance right here, then? That is, if you can fit me onto your dance card?"

I inhaled a quick puff of breath, grateful for the darkness that hid my too-wide smile. "Let me check," I said, lifting my card, the entire thing blank. "I am not otherwise promised."

"Good," he said, extending his hand. Even though we both wore gloves, a jolt ran through me as he took my fingers in his own and I felt his grip closing around mine. He pulled me close toward his tall, lean frame. I inhaled, and with our bodies so near, I noted that fresh scent again—his shaving soap mixed with the aromas of champagne and crisp country night air.

As we listened to the faint music and he led me through the slow, fluid steps, I reminded myself that I knew how to dance. Papa had insisted I take all of those lessons at Mr. Hinman's studio. I was suddenly grateful that he had, that he'd been aware that there was a whole world outside of Battle Creek, one in which a young lady needed to know how to dance a decent waltz so that when a young man as charming as Ed Close asked her for a dance, she didn't make a complete fool of herself. The same wide world that Mr. Hinman's daughters had gone off to explore—that had taken me east to Mount Vernon and then north from the capital to this green, coastal town. All of that had led to this moment. I'd come to the club that night hoping to dance. I'd stepped out onto the terrace looking for lightning bugs and fresh air and stars. But I felt in that moment as though I'd found something so much more exciting.

ED CLOSE APPEARED at our Greenwich home, The Boulders, the next day. He arrived several hours after breakfast, looking cool and relaxed in a crisp suit of immaculate cream-colored linen, a straw boater on his fair head, and a small spray of white petals in his lapel. I was sitting on the porch, and Ed offered a theatrical bow, removing his boater as he approached. "Miss Post, good morning."

"Mr. Close." I lowered my book and rose from my wicker chair, trying to temper the beam that threatened its way across my features. Taking in a deep breath, I forced myself to summon what I hoped looked like cool composure, a task made all the more difficult as I noticed how the morning sunshine fell on Ed's head of neatly combed golden hair. Goodness, he was even more attractive than I remembered. "How are you?" I asked, descending the porch stairs.

"Never been better." Ed arched an eyebrow, grinning as he looked up at me. "You see, I had a hearty breakfast of Grape-Nuts this morning. That put everything on the right path for the day."

"Glad to hear it," I said, rocking back and forth on my feet, patting down my skirt. I was in a lightweight day dress of pearl-colored silk, with a casual scoop neck and pale blue embroidery around the waist and sleeves. I hoped I looked relaxed and bright, even if my nerves suddenly felt in a tangle.

Ed cleared his throat. Was he awaiting my invitation to sit on the veranda? Or perhaps we should walk? Golly, I knew nothing about entertaining gentlemen callers. It would have helped to have grown up with a mother who spoke to me about these matters. But then, Mother and Papa had known each other since childhood; I doubted they had ever experienced any of these awkward encounters of an early acquaintance at the start of a courtship. If that was what Ed was even doing—was he there to court me, or simply for the house tour that Papa had offered? I was hopeless. But one thing was certain: I would not be caught dead asking Leila for advice on any matter of the heart—or any other topic.

Ed spared me having to suggest any activity when he said: "I've come for the tour. The tour your father was kind enough to propose when we spoke last night at the club."

My heart sagged. So then he wasn't there for me. Of course not. I was just a sheltered sixteen-year-old girl from Battle Creek, and he a Columbia law student, tall and blond, a member of the Four Hundred. Ed Close probably had half a dozen blue-blooded debutantes to whom he would pay visits of courtship before even thinking of me in that way. I squared my shoulders, forcing a neutral tone as I said, "I do apologize, Mr. Close, but my father is out this morning."

"Ed, remember?"

"Oh. Yes. Ed." I shifted on my feet.

Ed looked out over the grounds. A mourning dove cooed in the nearby elm tree, its body hidden in the branches that hung thick with leaves. Then Ed turned his light eyes back on me, saying, "I'm afraid I've come all this way, and I was rather hoping for my promised tour."

I swallowed.

"Can't you lead it, Miss Post? Please? You are, after all, mistress of the place, are you not?"

My heart lifted. "Marjorie, remember?"

"Marjorie." He pressed his palms together in a posture of exaggerated supplication and then winked. "Would you be so kind?"

"Oh, all right, I suppose I can do it." I bit the inside of my cheek, forcing myself to move slowly down from the porch and toward him. "Here, let's start in the garden."

The property was immense, and we were still working on the place, but Ed would be able to see the shape it was taking. The grounds were in the full bloom of summer, and the gardens spread before us green and leafy, the ancient elms and oaks stocked with bird life, and a stream cutting through our back lawn before rippling into a cheerful waterfall. Just past that, Papa had put in a golf course, and beyond that was a view of our horse stables and fresh-clipped fields for riding. "Papa plans to hire fifty gardeners just to take care of the grounds," I said. Not to mention the staff we would hire to clean, cook, drive our automobiles, manage our stables, wash the linens and clothes, and attend to the many other needs of the estate.

I turned and Ed followed suit, both of us looking up at the elegant home. The sound of the stream rippled in our ears, mingling with birdsong. The scent of summer roses and cut grass traveled on the gentle breeze. "I like those," Ed said, pointing to the striped awnings of green and ivory that hung over the house's two wings.

"Oh, they were my idea. For some shade," I said, trying my best to sound casual.

"It really is a splendid place," Ed declared, his voice quiet but earnest. "And your father was correct when he spoke last night."

Unsure of his meaning, I tilted my face sideways, so he added: "You have a good eye."

I allowed myself to smile at this.

He nodded once. "And remember, I warned you last night: I have exquisite taste." A playful grin, and I noted how his eyes took a quick glimpse downward, tracing a line from the scooped neck of my dress to my corseted waist, as he said it. I straightened, resisting the urge to fidget, to adjust my skirt or pat my hair. After a moment he turned and took my gloved hand in his, holding me with his gray-eyed gaze. My stomach tightened. Then he said, "You must be the happiest girl, Marjorie."

"Papa is very generous," I answered, resuming our slow walk up the lawn and back toward the veranda. He released my hand as we approached the house.

"It will be a fine home to come to when I finish school." My tone was bright, but in truth, even as I said these words, I felt a wave of discomfort wash through me. No, something more than discomfort. Terror. What I never would have dreamed of saying aloud to Ed was that I was terrified. Terrified of living in a town like Greenwich, a rarefied, impenetrable place. A place where I knew nobody, while everybody else here seemed to know one another, and had done so for generations.

And this house, if you could even call it a house, with its palatial sprawl—the house was lovely, to be sure, but what was I going to do with a mansion with a dozen bedrooms and a staff the size of a small army? Papa would come often—I knew that—but that meant that Leila would as well; I had no interest in being a third member of their party. And besides, Papa still traveled regularly to Battle Creek and New York and Washington for business, and many other places for recreation and pleasure. Mother was always off to some medical hospital or spa town seeking treatment for her lengthening list of complaints. I would be alone here more often than not. Perhaps The Boulders would be my home, yes, but what of the family to live with me in it?

It was fortunate that a lady was expected to wear gloves in public because the truth was that I had recently broken out in sores on the tops of my hands and had taken to scratching them to the point of rawness and bleeding. I had sores in my mouth as well. It was the stress—the impending question of where I would be when my final year of boarding school wrapped up. Where, and with whom. I had millions set to come to me when I reached my eighteenth year, but all the money in the world could not buy me answers to those most basic of questions.

In the recent weeks I had taken to spending unhappy hours before the mirror in my beautiful oversized bedroom, scouring my reflection, using tweezers to pluck wisps of silver that kept sprouting up in my honey-colored hair. My hair was going gray, at just sixteen?

I thought back to the previous night, the party at the club, and now I looked at Ed Close as he stood before me. My, how good he looked. But of course he did, for he was a creature of this habitat. He was so at ease here, with his pale linen suit and easy, suntanned smile. So settled, whereas my entire life stretched unresolved whenever I thought about the days past graduation.

Could he sense my sudden agitation? I wondered. It didn't appear so, because he angled his tall frame toward mine and fixed me with his golden smile as he said, "Well, now that you've been kind enough to give me a tour, I hope I might be so bold as to offer the same to you in return?"

This startled me. "Oh? What do you mean by that?"

"What I mean, Marjorie, is an invitation. Come out with me on my sailboat tomorrow. Would you?"

"I HOPE YOUR father will forgive me for running away with you." Ed smiled at me as he pulled gently on the tiller to steer the boat, its mainsail swelling with the breeze, his flaxen hair whipping around his face in a tousled, impossibly attractive way.

"Running away, are we?" I squinted and forced myself to look away from Ed toward the shoreline; to our right sprawled the green and golden coast of the Long Island Sound.

"We've crossed state lines," Ed said, pointing toward the land, where homes and docks, along with anchored sailboats and fishing craft, filled the view. "We are in Rye, New York. Perhaps we should keep going?"

"If we do keep going, where will we end up?" I asked.

He turned his suntanned face toward the water, skimming his hand over the top of its surface and creating five small wakes with his fingers. "New York City. Want to come back with me to law school?"

"I'm afraid I'm more interested in business affairs than law," I answered, blinking against the bright sunshine. The day was a warm one, but Ed looked cool and crisp in a collared shirt and short-cropped pants of cream and navy blue. I was in a light day dress of ivory and olive-green stripes.

"That's fine. Let's bypass New York City altogether, then," he said with a shrug. "Keep going. We can make it to Ireland if we go light on our rations."

"Ireland? Goodness. What if I get hungry?" I asked.

He shrugged again. "I'll fish for us. I don't need much. As long as I have you for company, I'll be happy." He made the comment as a joke, an offhand quip accompanied by a carefree smile, but I noticed how my heart tumbled in my chest as he did so. He'd be leaving for New York City soon, just as I'd be leaving for Washington and my final year at Mount Vernon. Would he write? I wondered. Or were there other girls in Manhattan, sophisticated and elegant socialites who were bound to be much more intriguing than I could hope to be?

"We'll plan for Ireland another time," Ed said. "I was thinking something a bit closer for today." He took the tiller back in his hand and angled the boat toward the shore.

"Oh?" I leaned back, stretching my legs long as the gentle sunshine poured down on us.

After a few minutes, we were bobbing in gentle waves just a few feet out from a beach of pale sand and wild green shoreline. "Lunch," Ed said, hopping below deck and reappearing a moment later with a large wicker food hamper.

"Here?" I surveyed our surroundings.

"A picnic." He leapt down and I laughed as his bare feet and calves splashed into the shallow water beside the beach. He ran the lunch hamper to shore in several long-legged strides before returning to the boat and dropping its small, heavy anchor. "May I be of assistance, Mademoiselle?" he asked, extending his hands toward me. I nodded and then he hoisted me in his arms, making me feel light as he held me high above the water and waded to the nearby beach.

There, a few paces back from where the small waves curled ashore, he laid out a checkered blanket and pulled a generous spread from his hamper: hard-boiled eggs, cold chicken, apples and cheese, olives, bread, and a jar of fruit preserves. "Hope you're hungry," he said.

"Quite the feast you've prepared here, Ed," I remarked.

"Just wait," he said, raising a hand and then reaching back into the hamper for one final item. I knew the box immediately, and I could not help but laugh. "Grape-Nuts." I nodded my approval.

"I told you I have exquisite taste," he said. "A few more boxes of this stuff and we would have been well provisioned to make it all the way to Ireland."

"I hope you got a good price. If not, I might be able to speak to someone."

"Marjorie, for you, I wasn't worried about the price."

I felt my cheeks flush with heat, and I dropped my eyes, my gaze making it as far as his lips before they lingered there. I wondered, again, about those lips—how it might feel to kiss their soft fullness. Goodness, but my dress felt hot in the summer sunshine. Had it really been the most suitable choice for boating and a picnic?

"But there is one more thing." Ed reached into the hamper and I could not help but glower as I saw the box of Kellogg's Corn Flakes. "This is for the fish," he said. He opened the cereal box and then showered the nearby water with a sprinkling of the tasteless Kellogg product. "That's all it's good for," he declared. "I'd never expect a human to touch the stuff."

I laughed, heartily approving. "Those could have come in handy if you needed to attract fish during our Atlantic crossing to Ireland," I noted.

"Exactly," he agreed. "But who needs Ireland, anyway? It's the company. As long as I have you, Marjorie Merriweather Post, I'm happy."

I allowed myself to smile at this, but I did try to conceal my blush by taking a bite of an apple and looking out over the water. The Sound was blue and calm, mirroring the clear cerulean of sky overhead. Summer was rolling too quickly through its final days, and if I were being entirely honest, I wouldn't have minded in the least if Ed Close had decided to spirit me someplace far away, just as he'd teased.

⁂

I HAD ONLY a few days before it was time to return to Washington and to school, and I grew increasingly agitated by the fact that I did not know what would happen between Ed and me when we both left Greenwich. Would Ed write to me? Was I simply a summer dalliance? A fun diversion before autumn and reality set back in? I was only sixteen, and Ed was five years my senior, on the cusp of becoming a Manhattan lawyer while I was still sharing a girls' dormitory in a finishing school hundreds of miles away. Ed was from Greenwich and the Four Hundred, while my money was new and came from cereal. Was I just a spree, a summer flirtation, an easy enough attachment to break off since I'd soon be leaving and so would he?

But then my mind would wander back to our moments together. The terrace of the Old Elm, dancing together in the warm summer darkness. His taking my hand on the lawn of The Boulders, his earnest gray-blue eyes holding mine. The beach and his picnic, his bright smile as he told me that I was all the company he needed. It couldn't all have been nothing to him, could it? True, he had not kissed me. Nor had he made any sort of romantic declaration. But surely he knew how I felt? Wasn't he, a gentleman in every sense of the word, thoughtful enough to spare my heart if he did not feel any genuine attachment?

In those final nights of August, as I noticed the sun dipping below the tree line earlier in the evenings, the days growing steadily shorter, I roiled, sleepless and agitated, under my bedsheets, seesawing back and forth: a conviction that surely I meant something to Ed Close, followed by a stern voice of censure telling me I was a silly young fool who knew nothing of love, and nothing of men like Ed Close or the ladies they married.

And then, just a few nights before my scheduled departure, on an evening when Papa was dining out in nearby Darien with Leila as I remained alone at The Boulders, I passed my worst night yet. I lay in bed as the hours ticked by, thinking about Ed and agonizing over my upcoming departure. The sound of wheels in the forecourt told me that Papa and Leila had returned, and I heard them alighting from the car and coming into the house. Muffled noises as they dismissed the last few servants for the night and retired to bed—in separate rooms or the same one? I grimaced; I knew the answer to that well enough. And suddenly the night grew even more wretched.

I awoke the next morning to a sunny day, mild without the drag of humidity, but I did not much care to enjoy it. I ate sparingly at breakfast, my stomach still tied in knots. Then later, as I sat alone on the back porch, something I had not expected happened: Ed Close approached on horseback. He came at a casual trot. I had been doing my best to distract my thoughts by writing out a packing list for my traveling trunks. But Ed's sudden, unbidden appearance pulled my thoughts away from all else. I lowered my pen as I drew in a long, fortifying breath. *Ed Close, you sudden and entirely disruptive summertime surprise*. My, but he cut quite a figure in that saddle.

"Marjorie, hello." Ed waved excitedly as he slowed his horse and hopped down, one of our grooms appearing to take the reins from him and lead the animal toward our stables.

I rose from my seat and walked slowly down the porch stairs onto the lawn, meeting him with my hand over my eyes to shield against the August sunshine. "Hello, Ed."

"Good morning," he answered. His cheeks were flushed and rosy from the ride and the morning's warmth. I longed to lean forward on my toes and kiss him right there. "Do you enjoy riding?" he asked.

"I do," I answered with a nod. I was comfortable enough atop a horse; at Papa's insistence I had grown up riding Western, both legs astride the saddle, hands clutched firmly around the horn, but I knew that the young ladies out here rode in the English tradition, perched in draped skirts on a modest sidesaddle, gloved hands primly gripping leather reins. It was a manner of riding that struck me as not at all practical, but perhaps that was part of the point.

Ed removed his hat, running his fingers through his golden hair with a sigh. His waves appeared uncombed, even a bit unkempt, which was something I'd never seen before, and he seemed to be struggling to choose his words, eventually saying, "Well then, next time we are together, we'll have a ride. How about that?"

My voice was quiet, my throat tight, as I answered honestly: "I'd like that." Because I longed, more than anything, for there to *be* a next time, regardless of the activity.

Ed looked me squarely in the eyes, his lovely features showing an uncharacteristic strain. "Marjorie . . ." But then he appeared to lose the thread of whatever it was he had intended to say.

I shifted my weight from one foot to the other, my body tilting involuntarily toward his. "Yes?"

"I . . . I have to leave tomorrow, to return to New York City."

I nodded slowly at this, feeling a tightening in my shoulders.

"Law school," he added.

"Yes," I said. I hadn't known when exactly he'd leave, but I had known it was coming.

"When do you leave?" he asked.

"Day after next," I answered.

"Yes," he said, glancing down toward his leather gloves. "I . . . you see, I couldn't . . . well, I didn't want to go, Marjorie, without seeing you one more time."

"I appreciate this visit, Ed," I said, swallowing. "I am happy to see you as well."

A puff of his cheeks, and then an audible sigh. "There's something I need to tell you," he said.

I wasn't sure my heart could take much more—it felt as if it might beat right through my rib cage. But I forced a steadiness into my voice as I asked, "What's that?"

He leaned toward me, taking my hands in his, and I let him do so, meeting his stare. And then he said: "You have enchanted me, Marjorie Merriweather Post."

I could have wept with relief to hear this, to hear Ed explain that I meant something real to him, just as he meant something to me. That I was more to him than simply a silly girl and a summertime dalliance. I smiled, my eyes drifting down to the ground, and I fought back against the needling threat of tears.

Ed squeezed my hands in his own, angling his tall frame toward mine. I caught the whiff of him, shaving soap and sunshine and saddle polish, and I noted how my vision went a bit blurry. "Marjorie, I know this is rash. It's so unlike me. . . ." His voice had an urgency that I understood—because I felt the same thing. "My dear girl, you've taken me completely by surprise, and the thought of being away from you just tears me up. Marjorie Merriweather Post . . . I wish to marry you. I do." He laughed, and then he went on, his entire face flushed, and I knew now it was not due to the August heat. "I wish to go to Mr. Tiffany's and buy you the biggest diamond he has. To stun you, just as you've done with me."

I let out a raspy laugh. I had hoped to hear that I meant something to Ed Close. That I had been more than a mere August flirtation. But this—love? Marriage? Before I could speak, he leaned forward, surprising me with the kiss I had been thinking about since the first night of our acquaintance. He pulled me closer, wrapping his arms around my waist as our bodies met, and then all thought of words flew right out of my head as I kissed him back, relishing the perfect softness of his lips. The warmth of his body so close to mine, the clean smell of his skin. I could easily have stood there all morning, kissing Ed with no regard for what was proper or who might be scandalized to see us, but Ed remembered himself, gently pulling back after an embrace that was shorter than I wanted. His eyes told me, however, that he desired more, that he longed for another, longer kiss just as fiercely as I did. But Ed Close was a true gentleman. He was likely worried that Papa, somewhere in that massive house beside us, might look through a window and see.

Papa. I'd never in my life made a big decision without my father's advice or blessing. But as I blinked now, dizzy from the heat and the sunshine and the lingering taste of Ed Close's lips on mine, I said the words without any hesitation: "Yes, Edward Close. Yes, I'll marry you."

Chapter 8

I WAITED A DAY TO SHARE MY NEWS, UNTIL AFTER ED HAD LEFT Greenwich and returned to Manhattan. Papa reacted as I'd expected he would, the reaction for which I had braced and prepared. "Now, Marjorie, let's just hold on and get our heads straight for a minute here." We sat in the bright breakfast room, our bowls of cereal growing soggy between us. I had told Papa that Ed had proposed and I had accepted his hand, and Papa was taking a while to find words with which to respond. Eventually, his face scrunched in what looked like the expression of a man taking the final steps of a steep mountain summit, he said, "You are much too valuable a prize for anyone to run in and hurry off with." He was managing to keep his voice level, but his blue eyes were aflame as he went on: "Much less a man we saw for a few days this summer and who presses you as he's leaving town."

I bristled at this on Ed's behalf. The idea of Ed's behavior being anything but upright and courteous seemed preposterous to me. "He's not pressing me, Papa." I looked down at my cereal bowl, mostly because I needed a break from my father's eyes in order to collect my own thoughts. I had expected Papa's resistance to my news. I knew how rash it seemed—Ed proposing after such a short acquaintance. But then, Papa had known Mother for most of his youth before he'd proposed marriage to her, and look how that had turned out. Didn't that show that when it came to matters of the heart, there were simply no set answers? I loved Ed and he loved me. What more was there to it? But I didn't voice any of this to Papa just then; instead I tried a different tack: "I thought you liked Ed, Papa."

Papa looked down at his mug of Postum, sloshing the drink around but not taking a sip. "I do. He's a fine young man. I like him very much.

But—" Papa paused to consider his next words with care. "But you must be very sure that your heart tells you that Ed is the one. A marriage without love—why, it would simply wreck your life. . . ." His words tapered off, but we both knew where that thought led.

I took a bite of my cereal but noticed that I tasted nothing. Papa inhaled and started a new thought: "Budgie, you're only sixteen."

"But you've always said it yourself," I interjected. "You've raised me right, with a better head than your average young lady."

"That may be so." Papa propped his elbows on the table. "Look, Budge, I'm with you in anything that'll make you happy. But can't you wait? Finish school and see at the end of the year?"

I considered this unexpected tack for a moment. In truth, I *did* want to finish school. I'd made it this far and was so close to my diploma at this point. Papa saw his opening as I chewed on his words and he pressed on: "If he is worthy, he will keep. There's no need to rush up the aisle." But then his face darkened, and his voice was gravel as he continued: "There is *not* any reason to rush up the aisle, is there, Marjorie Merriweather Post?"

"Papa! Of course not!" I gasped, feeling my cheeks flush with heat, mortified that he could even think I might have been so reckless. Or that Ed would be such a cad!

"Well, that's good," Papa said, sitting back in his chair, eyes fixed firmly on the tablecloth. "Didn't think so. But you know, as your daddy, I'm only making sure."

We resumed our breakfast in a strained silence. I could tell that Papa sat on tenterhooks, eager to see me consent to wait, at least until after my diploma was in hand. I *did* agree with his reasoning, even if I refused to reveal that fact in my posture or facial expression. It would be good to finish school, I admitted to myself. It could be good to make Ed wait just a bit. Why, we were both so young. There was no need to hasten marriage by a matter of months. I was about to tell Papa as much, that I would agree to wait until after I had finished school, when I was interrupted by a sudden waft of sugary, vanilla-scented air, followed by Leila's throaty voice at the threshold of the breakfast room: "There you are." And then she stiffened. "Oh, Marjorie, hello."

"Hello, Leila," I said, my voice toneless.

She glided uninvited into the room and stood near to where we sat, close enough for the cloying scent of her perfume to rankle. "Are your trunks all packed, dear?" she asked.

I nodded.

She looked at Papa, then back to me, saying, "I can hardly believe the summer is over and it's time for you to go already."

I pushed back from the table, entirely done with breakfast. Leaning close to kiss Papa on the cheek, I whispered, only for him to hear, "I'll think about it, Papa," and I left the room.

I had told him I would think about it, but in reality, I had made my decision the moment I had risen from that breakfast table. I'd marry Ed Close as soon as I graduated, and I'd start a family of my own. And hopefully, once I was established in a household with my own money and my own husband, I'd be done sharing a roof with Leila.

Autumn saw me unpacking my trunks and settling back into the brownstone of the Mount Vernon school. As it was our final year, Helen Hibbs and I had the pick of our lodgings, and we chose to room together. I was a dedicated pupil who studied hard and made fine marks; I knew Papa would not have abided anything else. And so even though my mind now swirled with thoughts of Ed Close and the Greenwich summer we'd shared, I completed my assignments on time and I answered my teachers with respect. But I was much less interested in schoolwork now that Ed had entered my life.

He wrote dutifully, every week, telling me about his law classes and his weekend trips out to Greenwich, reaffirming in his measured but affable manner that his commitment to me remained resolute. I found myself whispering about Eddie to Helen in the darkness at bedtime. I found myself penciling his initials in my notebooks during classes, daydreaming about changing my own name, and then practicing the letters: "Marjorie Close."

If Papa thought that perhaps the time and the distance would be enough to dampen my feelings or change my mind, he was wrong, but he did try to persuade me to reconsider. "You're so young," he wrote. "You've not been seriously courted by anyone, including Ed, and I don't know that you're ready to make such a momentous decision."

I ignored these written warnings, instead filling my responses to Papa with long descriptions of my schoolwork in the hopes of convincing him that I was a serious pupil and responsible young lady. But as autumn cooled to winter, he kept at it: "Marjorie, you've got millions to your name. There's no need to rush into any marriage until you're certain you've found the one for you."

I knew that Papa loved me, and I appreciated his protective efforts. But where were these efforts to protect my heart when he'd abandoned my mother? When he'd made his unspoken shift toward that woman, Leila, as his mistress? *No, Papa, you are not fit to lecture me on matters of the heart.*

All I knew was that suddenly, thoughts of my life after school and graduation no longer filled me with panic. I no longer had sores breaking open on my hands or searing the inside of my mouth. Eddie was in my life now, a lovely man, a charming man, a steadying ballast.

Where is my family?

Who will be with me when I am done with school?

Eddie was the answer I had been seeking to those questions.

PAPA ARRIVED AT Mount Vernon for my graduation ceremony, and to my horror, he had Leila on his arm. I felt my stomach clench as I watched them approach, Leila's youthful figure sheathed in a snug dress of peach taffeta, a large-brimmed hat fixed on her head at a jaunty angle, decked in ribbons and beads and horribly massive silk flowers.

Mother arrived shortly after, her skin matching her simple gray day dress, and she seated herself alone in one of the chairs set out for the ceremony. I couldn't help but glower as I looked at them each in turn: my mother was so beleaguered by melancholy and her constant headaches that she looked far older than her middle age, whereas Leila appeared fresh and lively, stylishly turned out from tip to toe in brand-new clothes, which Papa had undoubtedly ordered custom for her from New York City.

The ceremony was long, and the hot sun poured down on a sticky Washington morning. I felt myself sweating through my light dress of cream chiffon. Afterward there was a celebratory luncheon with cakes and punch, and then Papa escorted me back into the school, its thick stone walls providing a welcome refuge of cool air. There, Helen waited to bid me a tearful farewell, as she and her family were scheduled to depart that afternoon for Newport. We took our leave with long, affectionate hugs and many promises of letter writing. "And you'll have to let me know as soon as there is news with . . . you know," my friend said with a wink. She'd heard enough about Ed all year long to know that there'd be news on that front soon enough.

Papa and I were scheduled to leave Washington the next day for Greenwich, while Mother was bound for St. Louis to take a rest cure. Fortunately Leila departed by train that afternoon following the ceremony. That night would be my last at Mount Vernon and in the capital I had called home for the past few years, and Papa asked me if we might have supper alone at a nearby restaurant. I met him there after a brief nap and a change of clothes, feeling a bit sad about my parting with Helen, but excited that I now had my diploma. I felt eager and ready for all that lay ahead, particularly my upcoming reunion with Eddie up north and my conversation with my father about my plans.

Papa did not bring up Eddie's name as we settled in to our table and ordered our dinners, but I knew him well enough to see that he wanted to. It was why he had asked me to dinner, alone; he knew, now that school was done and I'd be moving up to the finished Boulders, that it was time for me to share my decision. And indeed, I *was* decided—I was going to marry Eddie.

At least, that was what I thought Papa wanted to speak about. That was what I had prepared to speak about with him over dinner. What I was *not* prepared for was what Papa did in fact bring up as we awaited our meals. Something entirely different, beginning with the words: "Marjorie, there's something we need to discuss."

"Yes." I nodded, swallowing a sip of chilled water. *Here it comes.*

Papa looked away, down at the table. I noted that a sheen of perspiration had pearled across his clean-shaven face. "You're a woman now, my dear. You've finished school. And I sure am proud of that. And happy for you."

"Thank you, Papa."

"It's a big thing, that diploma."

"Yes."

"A time of big change for you, too."

I nodded.

"And now, well . . . I'm going to be making a change, as well."

This was unexpected. I shifted in my seat. "A . . . change?"

"A big change."

"What do you mean, Papa?"

"You know that your mother and I . . . well, that our lives have gone in different directions."

I nodded again, saying nothing.

He leaned forward, landing his elbows on the table. "Well . . . I'm going to be remarrying. Soon."

Silence. The only sound that of the blood whooshing between my ears. The clatter of the restaurant—silverware, plates, patron chatter—had all receded to a distant thrum.

Papa getting remarried?

He fixed his eyes on mine, and I suspected that, had I not been seated, I might have folded over my legs. Leila was to become my stepmother? My heart twisted as it all clicked into place, one piece stacking neatly on top of the other: Papa hadn't asked me to join him here at dinner, alone, to celebrate my diploma or ask me about my plans or seek out the decision of my heart. The decision that he had asked me, almost a year ago, to delay. Did he even remember that he'd asked that of me? Did he even care what my decision was? No, Papa had brought me to dinner tonight to tell me that he and Leila had made a decision of their own. Together, the two of them. And now I was to receive and accept this news. The words I'd studied in French class popped to mind: *un fait accompli*. It was a done deal.

Papa went on and I listened, dizzy, his words sounding like a gramophone whose record was scratched and unpleasant; they would be married in the fall in Battle Creek. Now that I was done with school, Leila wished to move back there. The Boulders could be entirely mine, so I'd have room for a family of my own. Oh God, would Papa and Leila have a baby? She was, after all, only a few years older than I was. Was I to be replaced by a son or daughter from that woman?

Papa and I had never spoken long or candidly about my heartbreak over the divorce. Or my deep dislike of Leila. But he knew. Surely he knew. He was the smartest man I'd ever met. And what's more, Papa was the closest person to me in the world; there wasn't a single important memory in my life that did not involve him in some way. And yet, in spite of that, or perhaps precisely *because* of that, I found myself entirely unable to tell him now that he was breaking my heart.

And it was not only my heart he was breaking: Mother had been a withering husk of her former self since the divorce, and yet my father, a man whom I'd always known to be nothing but kind, would deliver this fresh blow to her in marrying such an unworthy successor? And he would allow Leila to look on my mother's suffering, smiling and gloating, decked in her custom couture? How was it that Papa—a man who saw everything, even what others did not—could be so blind to the tragedy he was writing for our entire family?

By the time we arrived back at the front steps of the Mount Vernon brownstone, I was decided: Papa was going to marry, and he had sought neither my opinion nor my blessing. Papa, therefore, had no right to dictate whom I should marry. He had made his choice; he had done this to our family. He would wed Leila.

Fine, then. I would marry Eddie.

Chapter 9

Greenwich, Connecticut
Fall 1905

I THOUGHT THAT A SMALL WEDDING WOULD MEAN ONLY A SMALL parcel of cares and concerns. I was terribly mistaken.

It turned out that the length of the guest list mattered not at all when it came to the woes of planning a wedding, because the only two people I cared about attending—Papa and Mother—refused to be there together.

Papa, who was paying, would not attend unless Leila was invited. I shuddered to think of her introducing herself to my guests. *Mrs. C. W. Post, so lovely to meet you*. And Mother had declared that she would be there only if Leila's name was left off the guest list. The two were at an impasse, and I erupted in tears as I surveyed the stack of invitation responses that trickled into The Boulders, tempted to toss them all into the fire and elope with my groom to Atlantic City.

Eddie looked on with an expression of rueful concern. "Is there anything I can do?" he asked.

"I don't know, Eddie," I answered, sighing. "I don't know how we see our way out of this mess."

In the end, after a series of tearful entreaties on my part, both Papa and Mother agreed to come and put on their smiles. Leila would be invited, but she would sit apart from my parents. And we would offer no celebratory luncheon to our guests following the church service—I could not trust my folks to keep the peace. "I'm so sorry, Ed," I said one Friday afternoon a few weeks before Thanksgiving, grimacing at the fact that my groom was seeing such discord in my family. I was accustomed to it; but what must he think?

"It's just as well, Marjorie. All I care about is walking out of that church with you." It turned out my groom had family troubles of his own, though in his calm, understated way Eddie barely spoke of them. His father, also named Edward, had already passed away, and so it was just his mother who would be attending, but Mrs. Emma Close had survived a terrible stroke a few years prior and could barely walk. When I met the woman who would be my mother-in-law, for a formal lunch with Ed at the Metropolitan Club, she was scowling and unspeaking for most of the meal, and I did not know if that was the effect of her injury or if she was simply unhappy with her son's choice of a Michigan bride with new money. Or perhaps a bit of both.

But there were plenty of reasons to feel happy in the months leading up to our wedding, too. Edward kept his word and bought me a diamond ring from Mr. Tiffany's in New York. We also designed our wedding invitations there, cards of thick creamy stock, our embossed names curling around each other. Soon enough those names would be joined, and I'd be Mrs. Marjorie Close.

Because Eddie came from one of New York's preeminent Knickerbocker families—those finest of Anglo-Dutch clans, his having been the original owners of much of lower Manhattan since before the American Revolution—we would be married at Grace Church on southern Broadway. My future husband's family had gifted the valuable acreage upon which the storied church now stood.

And there we assembled on a cold morning in early December, me at the top of the aisle of the historic church, its pews filled with members of the Four Hundred, along with my stolid mother and my simpering stepmother, the two women doing their best to avoid any eye contact.

I pulled my thoughts away from both of them, turning my focus down to inspect my gown one final time. Even if I lacked the pedigree of Edward's set, I had the wealth to make up for it, and so I'd dressed the part that day. My gown was a custom-made confection of creamy satin, handstitched with *point d'angleterre* detail and glistening with delicate beadwork of pearls and crystals. My new diamond earrings were a wedding gift from Papa, and my diamond choker was a wedding gift from Eddie.

The music began, first Bach and then Keble. The chapel smelled of fresh orange blossoms and countless expensive colognes and perfumes. Papa stood at my side, looking dapper in his coat and tails, a spray of fresh-cut white roses on his lapel. When he saw me studying him, he flashed me a quick sideways smile, and then winked once. As soon as I'd told him of my official engagement, he'd ceased all warnings and efforts to dissuade me from marrying Ed. And now, as he looked me in the eye, I could see in his intense, blue-eyed stare that he was holding back a deep well of feelings.

"Budgie," he whispered, as the string melody at the front signified it was time for us to begin our walk up the aisle. "My girl, I am with you in anything that brings you happiness."

"Thank you, Papa."

The music grew louder; it was our time. As I glided up the aisle, my dress unfurling in radiant reams of satin behind me, I kept my chin raised and my shoulders squared, a posture that would have garnered the approval of even the staunchest of the Mount Vernon Seminary etiquette teachers. As we neared the front of the church, my eyes fell on my future mother-in-law, Emma Close. I smiled at her, but just at that moment she was turning to the young woman who stood whispering at her side—a second cousin of Ed's, I remembered, even if I could not recall her name. I heard the lady speak to my groom's mother as I passed: "Well, she's a cute enough kitten, I suppose. Considering who she is and where she comes from."

My frame stiffened. Did Papa feel it beside me? I wondered. I knew what some in my groom's family might think. What members of their patrician set might believe: That I was new money, securing Eddie with my cereal millions even though his social station was so far above my own. That we Posts were provincial and unrefined, lacking the high pedigree of the Close clan.

I pulled my gaze away from Emma and her chattering companion and stared forward, fixing a determined smile to my face, my focus landing on my bridesmaid, Helen, standing at the front of the church. And then my eyes slid and rested on my groom, who stood with a calm, self-assured smile as he watched my approach. Eddie. He waited there in his long coat and tails, a spray of white petals bursting from his lapel, his smiling blue eyes fixed only on me. The man who had chosen me. Eddie, who was not only lovely and well educated and impossibly handsome, but also a gentleman, gracious and steady.

Eddie had never made me feel simple. He had chosen me; he loved *me*. What had he said? *You have enchanted me, Marjorie Merriweather Post.* There it was. I would be worthy of him. I'd make him happy that he'd picked me, and I'd prove to everyone in this packed church that Ed Close had been brilliant—and damned fortunate—in his choice of Marjorie Merriweather Post.

Chapter 10

Hot Springs, Virginia
December 1905

EDDIE AND I STEPPED OFF THE TRAIN IN THE POSH SPA TOWN OF Hot Springs, where we arrived at our hotel to find a pile of waiting packages that bore Papa's familiar handwriting.

"Mr. Close, Mrs. Close, welcome to the Homestead Hotel. These packages have arrived for you." It took me just a startled instant to realize that the hotel concierge was speaking to me. The concierge raised an eyebrow, staring with an amused expression. "Mrs. Close?"

"Mrs. Close," Eddie said, sidling up behind me, his arm weaving around my waist as his breath skittered over my ear and neck. "I rather like the sound of that, my dear."

The concierge smiled indulgently and looked away as Eddie's long, lean frame curled around mine, this well-trained man no doubt familiar with the halcyon glow that enveloped so many of the honeymooners who frequented his luxurious establishment.

"Wonderful," I said, shrugging my husband off with a playful smirk and nodding toward the front desk, accepting my packages. "Yes, I am Mrs. Close. Thank you." I patted down the skirts of my fashionable crimson traveling dress—custom ordered from Paris's House of Worth, like so much of my trousseau—and squared my shoulders, determined that I would look every inch the part of Mrs. Edward Close, even if it was taking me a bit of time to *feel* like the part was indeed mine.

I looked down at the packages. All from Papa, of varying degrees of thickness. What could they be? The sight of my new last name scrawled in his familiar handwriting created an odd, tugging feeling deep in my belly.

"Marjorie dear?" Eddie cleared his throat. The porters waited politely before us.

"Yes, ready." I gathered up the packages and followed the porters and my husband to our suite. Once settled in, Eddie having tipped and dismissed the men who had lumbered under my luggage, I plopped down into a plush embroidered chair and tore at the paper around the packages. The first parcel contained a receipt of deposit. I gasped when I took it in, in spite of my familiarity with Papa's boundless generosity. "Ed, can you believe this? Papa has given us one hundred thousand dollars as a gift." In truth the sum had been given only to me, in bonds bearing my new married name, but I said *us* in that instant, not knowing why, only thinking that I did not wish for Eddie to feel that he had been left out.

"Goodness. That sure is bully," my husband said from across the room, whistling as he slipped off his high button shoes and poured himself a scotch.

"And these," I said, jangling a loop of brass keys. "The Boulders is to be entirely ours." Again, the note said that The Boulders was to be entirely *mine,* but now that I was Eddie's wife, didn't that mean that the house was *ours*? I swallowed. "Papa won't stay there with Leila, not even in the wing he planned for himself," I said, masking the disappointment I felt. True, I had no interest in living there with Leila, but had it been only Papa, as originally planned, it would have given me great joy to share the estate.

"Well, I hope you know he can visit anytime he'd like," Eddie said, walking toward me and wrapping his arms around my shoulders. "We'll welcome him as if it were his home."

A smaller parcel carried a note, also from Papa. I tore the seal and read it, my eyes quickly misting, the words blurring as a thin screen of tears made them dance before my gaze:

Dear Little Sweetheart,

Well, the small toddler who has been over the road so long with Daddy is now a grown woman and a small toddler no more. It naturally brings a tinge of sadness to realize that the little girl with whom I had so many good times has faded into the past, but I am more than comforted with the splendid young woman grown from my small pal of years ago. Daddy feels well repaid for every effort he has made for you, my sweet daughter, and now I feel very sure you are going to be happily married and I find myself liking Ed as I would a boy of my own. Always remember that Daddy is somewhere close, and that he loves you always, sweet daughter.

Yours,
Daddy

I lowered the paper and saw that he had enclosed an additional message for Eddie:

Dear Ed,

Be tender and kind to my little girl. She is the only one I have. I have full confidence you will.

With all best wishes,
Yours truly,
C. W. Post

Eddie hugged me as I cried, telling me how much he admired my father. And even though I missed Papa, and felt the depth of the emotions behind his words and his gifts, I was thrilled to be with my husband, and grateful that the two men in my life felt such a mutual fondness.

We spent our days in Hot Springs wrapped in a peaceful daze of newlywed bliss and incredulity. Had we done it? Yes, we had. We were married. And now we were finally free of the crowds that had filled the church and the many details of planning the wedding, the fight to preserve the fragile truce between my parents, and we could simply enjoy each other.

In the mornings we slept late, taking our breakfast on trays in bed, as it was now my right to do as a married woman. On the first morning, when I was told by the kitchens that they did not offer Grape-Nuts on their breakfast menu, I grumbled and said, "I'll just have to tell Papa and Uncle Cal that they need to ship the Homestead Hotel some boxes."

Eddie laughed. "Won't poached eggs do, Mrs. Close? Or buttered rolls?"

"I've had Grape-Nuts for breakfast every morning since my girlhood. I don't see any reason to change that now."

"Now, now, Mrs. Close, do I detect a stubborn streak?" Eddie smirked, taking a sip of his coffee, and I smiled grumpily as I helped myself to a bite of his poached eggs.

We took strolls through the surrounding woods or sampled the curative spring waters that made Hot Springs such a popular destination. We read the newspapers or napped on the veranda, savored long meals, and Eddie enjoyed his cocktails while I sipped lemonade or iced tea.

Helen Hibbs had told me, years earlier, what the marital act involved. On the first night in Hot Springs, after we'd dined and returned to our suite, I took my time in the bathroom, brushing out my long hair and arranging my new satin lingerie over my pale, soft curves. I draped a delicate silk wrapper over my shoulders and dabbed my neck and wrists with a splash of jasmine eau de toilette, and then I rejoined my husband in the big bedroom, feeling both eager and nervous. Prior to our wedding, Eddie and I had never indulged in more than a few minutes of stolen kisses in a drawing room or a chauffeured car. I had loved kissing my fiancé, I had craved even more intimacy, but Eddie was a well-mannered gentleman who never would have dreamed of pushing things further than was proper.

Now that we were man and wife, this meeting in a dark hotel room and a big plush bed was entirely sanctioned. Eddie smiled, and then I did as well, as I sidled my body close to his under the covers. It was still early in the evening, but we were happy to fill the hours with long, uninterrupted kisses, Eddie making quick work of the few flimsy layers I had draped over my goose-pimpled skin.

I found it all to be pleasant enough, this indulgence in our new and total intimacy, but it was also the sort of thing that I suspected—and hoped—would grow more pleasant with repeated attempts. Eddie was not a passionate lover, but he was gentle and sweet, always ensuring that I was not uncomfortable. He bathed before and after our lovemaking, and he expressed his polite but resolute preference that I do the same. I didn't mind that; the bath was big and porcelain, and we filled it with rose-scented oil, taking turns scrubbing each other and laughing as our limbs became tangled.

Several nights into our stay, after a long dinner—and more gin and claret for Ed than I thought entirely necessary—I helped my unsteady husband back to our suite. Usually so discreet in his behavior and genteel with his manners, my husband, I was beginning to notice, did grow louder after vast quantities of drink, and so I shushed him as he sang his way down the hotel hallway: *"You're the flower of my heart, Sweet Adeline, my Adeline."*

"Ed! Shhh!" We were newlyweds and this trip was a celebration, so I did not find this bit of overindulgence too troubling, but I did worry about disturbing the other guests. Once situated in the privacy of our bedroom, I shut the door and exhaled my relief.

"To bed, Mrs. Close. To bed," Ed said, tugging on his shirt collar as he looked at me with listless gray eyes. He wanted to make love, I realized. I stifled the groan that nearly popped out; his present state of intemperance was not one I found attractive, but I reminded myself that we were newlyweds, and this was meant to be a week's worth of celebrating our love, so I assented.

That was the first time that I did not enjoy our intimacy, nor did I find Ed to be gentle and sweet as he moved on top of me. A few minutes later, seemingly satisfied, he let loose a grunt and then rolled off to his own side of the bed. "Too much damned vino," he muttered, his arm draped lazily over his sweaty face. "I was worried there for a moment I might not be able to see it through."

I did not reply. Ed lay beside me on his back, languishing in bed, which was uncustomary, given his usual propensity to hop up and bathe immediately following lovemaking. But that night he remained there, propped up on his pillow, pouring himself another glass of red wine. I wanted to ask him whether the refill was necessary, but I bit back my words, guessing that they might come off as ornery. When he spoke next, his breath was thick with the smell of the wine: "To think, we might have just made Edward Close the Third."

I flushed at that comment, pulling the covers a bit higher to my shoulders. He tipped his wineglass in my direction to ask if I wanted a sip, spilling some on the white sheets as he did so. I made a note in my mind to leave a larger than usual tip for the housekeeper the following morning and shook my head no to the offered wine. He sighed a moment, his fair hair falling unkempt around his splotchy face. "Of course, no wine for the pious *Christian Scientist,*" he said, a loose smirk sending his features lop-sided. "Thankfully the children will be Episcopalian."

I turned to face him, confused suddenly. By his tone, by the meaning of his comment. By how startlingly off-putting and unexpected his behavior suddenly was. All I could manage by way of response was an arch tone as I asked, "What?"

"Eh-pis-co-pale-eee-an," he said loudly, hammering each syllable as if I were hard of hearing. And then he smiled, his lips and teeth stained crim-son, as he added: "You do know that, right?"

I frowned. "I'm not sure where this is coming from, Ed."

"It is coming from the fact that we are going to have children, Marjorie. And that our children will be raised as I was. And what's more, it's impor-tant that we be united in that, Marjorie. It's a question of heritage: Closes are Episcopalians. You are now a Close. Which means I think you ought to become Episcopalian as well."

I narrowed my eyes, my rosy modesty of the previous moment quickly gone. "But . . . Eddie. You know that I'm a member of the Church of Christ Scientist."

Ed didn't look at me when he spoke next, his words slow, his voice drip-ping with an obvious derision: "What do you suppose our friends in Greenwich will think of that?"

Our friends. My first thought was: *They are* your *friends, not mine.* My second thought was: *Why would you not defend something that's important to your wife?* My father credited Christian Science with saving his life. And then mine. It had been the only thing I'd ever known to unite Mother and Papa. The kindness and generosity of Mrs. Gregory had been a credit to her faith, the very same faith that all in that household had leaned on dur-ing that dark Michigan winter.

I sighed, looking at my husband, seeing the crimson stain of his lips. The droop of his eyelids. It was just the drink talking, I reassured myself. He was not himself that evening. I hoped that we could both simply go to sleep and awake in a better humor the next day. He would apologize, I was sure of it. He'd be mortified once he looked back on this discussion with the clarity of sobriety and sunlight.

As I clicked off my bedside lamp and leaned forward to give him a chaste kiss, I spoke in what I hoped was a conciliatory, measured tone. "Ed, darling, I will go to the Episcopal church with you, if you wish. I'm your wife now, and I do support you. But you knew before you married me what my faith meant to me. So please, support me as well."

The next morning when we awoke, Ed said nothing of the previous night, save to complain of a wretched headache and roll back over to sleep. I decided to put off any reconciliatory chat and leave the room so that he might sleep. I rose alone and dressed hastily. I'd have breakfast downstairs and then take a walk, clear my head in the fresh air, I decided. But before I had left the lobby, I was informed that there was another package waiting for me at reception, this one from my dear friend Helen. She had clipped and sent along a pile of newspaper articles that had taken up the news of our wedding. I was stunned to see that these were not simply the New York and Connecticut society pages, where news of our marriage would be of local interest; journalists from as far as Washington, Chicago, and even San Francisco had filled their pages with details of our wedding.

Our marriage was declared the "preeminent union of the season, perhaps the year." Another journalist gushed: "The Closes will occupy a prominent position, for the bride is twice a millionaire in her own right, and the groom is a descendant of one of the finest, oldest families in the country."

There it was again: Eddie had the breeding, and I had the bank account. I read on, the next fawning words doing some good in softening my coiled nerves after the tensions of the previous night: "The bride, who has already attained a wide reputation for exquisite beauty, is probably the richest young woman in the United States, in addition to her dowry of youthful charm and grace."

I folded the articles, planning to keep them. I would show them to Eddie to remind him through his claret-soaked headache of the prize he'd secured in marrying me. I hoped that the other Closes were reading these gushing articles in their sunny breakfast rooms in Greenwich and Manhattan.

But most of all, as I read the accounts of our flawless wedding day, of the love that encircled us, of how our union stood out for its style and promise in even the highest levels of society, I hoped that the real thing would prove as magical as it all appeared when I read about it on paper.

Chapter 11

Greenwich, Connecticut
December 1905

EDDIE SCOWLED WHEN HE SAW ME ENTER THE BREAKFAST ROOM and take a place at the table, dressed only in my slippers and salmon-colored satin pajamas. The room smelled of coffee, and Eddie took a slow sip, gently replacing the china cup as he looked back down at his newspaper. After a moment, his voice quiet, he said: "Good morning. You do realize, Marjorie dear, now that you're married, you are entitled to take your breakfast in bed?" A tight, controlled smile replaced his frown of a moment earlier.

The footman appeared just then, and I nodded that I was ready for my meal. Eddie went on, speaking into his china coffee cup: "I'm quite certain Cook could manage putting some Grape-Nuts on a tray and sending it up."

I ignored the derision that tinged his tone, just as I'd ignored the comment he'd made to our butler when he'd first moved into The Boulders, giving his order that Cook was not to include Grape-Nuts in his own breakfast spread. He hadn't known I could hear: *I can't imagine starting the day eating birdseed.* Or had he?

Now, as I unfolded my linen napkin and accepted the warm drink of Postum that the footman poured into my coffee cup (I still drank only Papa's popular caffeine-free beverage), I did my best to assume a breezy tone as I answered, "I've been rising with the sun since I was a girl. Nobody else was going to collect those chicken eggs but me. In my experience, the only ladies who spend the morning in bed are those who work in a brothel or suffer from migraines."

Ed grunted and then tilted his head, taking another slow sip of his coffee. I noticed the way his hand trembled ever so slightly—too much gin again the night before, perhaps. I didn't know; I'd gone to bed hours before him.

When he spoke, his voice was cool. "In Battle Creek, perhaps, but this is Greenwich."

I was well aware that it was Greenwich; I certainly did not need his reminder. It was my house, after all, wasn't it? And twice the size of the one in which he'd grown up. I didn't hear him complaining about that. Even though the deed for The Boulders was in my name, I'd behaved as if the estate belonged equally to the both of us.

And yet, despite the fact that I'd given Ed the finest home in Greenwich—paid for by that birdseed, thank you very much—I was starting to sense that my husband, like so many among his clan, found me somehow lacking. As though I was uncouth or deficient in the necessary social niceties because I didn't stay up late with them, swallowing cocktail after cocktail, and then squander the morning snoozing in bed, only to ring a bell and have a lady's maid come in to feed and dress me as if I were a child or an invalid. No, I rose early with the sun and a clear head and got myself to the breakfast table as I'd done all my life. I knew no other way. Why, even Leila, for whom there was no love lost on my part, started her mornings early and with an air of purposefulness.

Ed was dabbing the corners of his fine, tight mouth with his napkin as he continued: "In Greenwich, dear . . . well, things are done differently." His gaze rested on my salmon pajamas, and I noted—not for the first time—how his calm, courteous demeanor seamlessly tipped into the realm of cool judgment, perhaps even disapproval.

"Never you mind, my dear," I said, forcing joviality into my voice. Perhaps I was only imagining things, being extra sensitive because others had made me feel common. I knew that my Eddie adored me. "We've got a busy day ahead of us, what with planning for the trip, and I figured I'd get to it. Can I do anything to help you prepare for the journey?" I was trying my best to be a warm and loving wife, even if I'd rarely seen an example of this in my parents' marriage. I was determined that our union would be different.

It would be our first Christmas as newlyweds, and we were planning to spend it in Battle Creek. It would be my first time seeing Papa since our wedding, and I was so excited about that fact that I was even willing to sleep under the same roof as Leila.

Ed, however, appeared less sanguine about the upcoming trip. "Christmas in Michigan. Never thought I'd say that." He drained the last of his coffee and folded the newspaper, making to rise from the table.

"Oh, you'll love it," I said. "The Christmas ham tastes so much better when you kill the hog yourself."

Ed's beautiful lips fell open in a gape. "I'm teasing," I added, trying to bite back my smile. "We're not *that* barbaric, my dear. I promise you, it's all civil enough in the Post residence. You'll see."

"I'm sure it is." He leaned down and gave me a quick peck on the top of my head as he prepared to leave the room. "I'm looking forward to seeing the home that means so much to you, my dear." He proffered a smile, and just like that, he was back to being my sweet Ed, courteous, bridled, even if his face betrayed a truth slightly different from his words.

MY ASSURANCES PROVED to be wrong, however, because the mood in the house felt far from civil. Being back in Battle Creek and under the roof of my childhood, only now with Leila as the lady of the house, rankled in ways I had not anticipated, and I found myself scratching my hands raw once more.

Eddie's discomfort at the informality of it all was blatant, even though he put forward his usual well-mannered demeanor. I could see in the way Ed looked around the rooms of our modest farmhouse, the way he topped up his gin glass first thing in the morning—he was in a foreign environment, and it was not one he enjoyed. We woke on our own and without a fleet of uniformed servants attending to us in our bedrooms. The expectation was that we were to make our own ways to a leisurely breakfast, often still in our pajamas. In Battle Creek the holidays unfurled without packed schedules of country-club luncheons or calling-card visits through old Greenwich estates. Even though the winter air outside was bitter cold,

Papa suggested activities like hiking the surrounding woods in snowshoes or skating across the frozen ponds. I appreciated keeping busy, and I enjoyed these wintry outings, except for when Leila came along. We'd come inside to thaw, passing lazy hours in front of the fire while sipping on mugs of Postum, listening as Papa and Uncle Cal shared stories from their youth. Our fanciest outing was the evening we rode the sleigh into town to visit at the Post Tavern that bore our name and to enjoy dinner with Shorty Bristol, my daddy's longtime friend and associate.

On our final night, after we'd managed to make it through Christmas Eve and Christmas Day without open conflict, through crowded visits with neighbors and old Battle Creek friends and even a church service of Christian Science, Papa planned a casual supper for the family at home, just the four of us. The family—hardly. But my focus was pulled from my irritation with Leila as I entered the dining room; I could see before he sat down at the table that Papa's blue eyes were aflame. No doubt he had some new topic about which he was eager to speak with us. I didn't expect what came next, however.

A servant brought out the roast with crispy potatoes and carrots. We bowed our heads as Papa blessed the food. After that, as he began to carve the meat, Papa looked down the table toward my husband and asked, "You all ready for your trip back east?"

Eddie accepted a serving of the meat as he nodded, all formal manners, even in this relaxed setting. "I believe we are, yes."

"We sure will miss you," Papa said, continuing to slice the roast before him.

"We'll miss you, too, Papa." I did not spare a glance in Leila's direction. "We'll see you soon though. When you come visit The Boulders this spring."

"Maybe sooner," Papa said, looking at me.

I arched an eyebrow, unsure of his meaning. Then he turned toward my husband and asked, "What do you know about Texas, son?"

"Texas?" Eddie held his fork and knife suspended over his plate, giving my father's question just the right amount of polite consideration, even though I could tell he was baffled by it.

Papa was done serving the plates, and he sat in his chair, still eyeing my husband as he went on: "I'm looking to Texas, son, as the way of the future."

"Why would you . . . ?" Eddie's veil of good manners slipped just momentarily, and Papa noticed.

Eddie cleared his throat, but before he could re-form his question, Papa interjected, "Come now, you don't have anything against Texas, do you, son? Why, your wife spent her early childhood there. Isn't that right, Budge?"

I shifted in my chair, nodding once. Papa propped his elbows on the dinner table. Eddie glanced to me, then back to Papa. "Of course . . . of course not. It's only . . . I've never been." Eddie chewed his food, saying nothing more.

Papa went on, a grand sweep of his hands as he spoke: "Then you don't know what you're missing out on." Silence stretched across the table, and after a few moments, Papa continued. "I want to establish my own village there. Already got the perfect name for it. We could call it Post, Texas."

I stopped chewing midway through a bite. "Papa . . . is that . . . done?" I asked, as surprised as my husband looked.

"Course it's done. Why, the Rockefellers are doing it in upstate New York as we speak. If you buy enough land, you can do whatever you want on it. I'm thinking it would be nice to have a place where we can create and invent, free from the thumb of some mayor or town council."

Eddie took a slow sip of his gin—how many had he had that day? I wondered—as he weighed some possible response. My husband's manners were so deeply ingrained into his being that he could not have been rude to Papa even if he had wanted to be. Nevertheless, I could see how flummoxed he was by my father's abrupt declaration. I was, as well. All Ed managed, eventually, in reply was a flimsy "Oh?"

Papa was undaunted. He hadn't let my mother put him off of fiddling with a rusty old corn toaster from Osgood's junk pile, and he wouldn't let anyone put him off this idea, either. "I'm considering some land down there, in the Panhandle. I was wondering if you two lovebirds would come with me. You know, to look things over?"

Ed turned toward me, wordless and pale, and I knew he was seeking my help. The clock on the mantel chimed softly. I did not know what to say. This was nothing new; Papa was always coming up with these outlandish schemes—brilliant gambles, to hear his admirers tell it, fool's errands if you asked his detractors—but Eddie clearly wanted no part in this one. My husband was a lawyer, Columbia trained, with a respectable practice in New York City and a predictable, comfortable life already plotted out in Greenwich.

And yet, Edward Close had married Marjorie Merriweather Post, and he'd married into the family of C. W. Post. Even as C. W. Post's only child and heir, I could not, as a woman, assume responsibility of Papa's ventures, and so the next best hope was that my husband might eventually wish to do so. Someday, if God blessed us with a boy, the entire Post empire could be my son's, but that would only be guaranteed if Ed agreed to step up in the interim.

Eddie was visibly uncomfortable with Papa's new proposition, however, and the silent room hummed as he grasped for some reply. All he managed to offer was a question of his own: "You wish for me to travel with you to Texas?"

"Indeed," my daddy answered, taking a bite of his roast. "The pair of you. We'll go to West Texas and then *across* it. We'll study the terrain."

Eddie looked down at his plate. "How would we travel?"

Papa clasped his hands on top of the table, chewing his meat. "Train as far as Dallas."

Ed made a face like he'd bitten into something sour. "And . . . and then?"

"Why, mules and chuck wagons. Just like I traveled as a young buck."

Eddie cleared his throat, shifting in his seat as he swirled his gin into a clear whirlpool; I could tell he wished to drain the glass in one gulp. But Papa was undeterred by his son-in-law's tepid interest. Perhaps even a bit entertained. "Come now, Edward Close, you ride, don't you? You fish? You hunt?"

"In Connecticut, yes. And on Long Island. But there, in Texas . . . well, I've heard about . . . Aren't they overrun with all sorts of creatures? Scorpions . . . copperheads, and the like?"

Leila sniggered and I wanted to toss my napkin in her direction. It was one thing for me to cringe inwardly at my husband's preciousness, but it was quite another for that woman to openly laugh at him.

Papa smirked, his tone one of good-natured teasing as he said, "What, you're not some fragile teacup, are you, Ed Close?"

Eddie shook his head, snorting out a short, guttural laugh. "No, sir."

"Come into my study, both of you. I'll show you the map. So much land, with great big reserves of oil underneath. And it can all be ours! I know an opportunity when I see one. You'll see what's got me all riled up."

I rose from the table and followed my husband and father into the study. Papa's desk was covered with papers—maps and land surveys, most of them. He waved us forward, pointing out places where he had marked up the plans. "Here's our spot." He drew a circle with his index finger around a vast stretch of land in the western part of the state. "I've got my eye on more than two hundred thousand acres on the frontier right here."

"Fort Worth," Eddie read the name of the nearest town, pronouncing the words as though he were listing an unsavory item on a restaurant menu.

"Yeah, a fine cattle town. But don't be thinking about the city," Papa said. "I'm looking here, to the country."

I read the names of the counties where he was pointing: "Hockley, Lynn, and Garza."

"That's right." Papa nodded, tapping the map enthusiastically.

"Never heard of the places," Ed said.

"And that's why it's got to be our spot," Papa declared. "That's where the opportunity is. Don't tell me there isn't some cowboy hidden under all that Connecticut."

Eddie rocked on his heels. My eyes roved over the map of unsettled West Texas land. I glanced at my husband, who nodded politely, even as his fine features were growing increasingly strained. And then I looked to my father, who went on and on about the fortunes to be pulled from that lawless, unsettled land of squatting ranchers and oil prospectors.

Papa was smart, I knew that much. He'd always seen opportunity where others had scoffed. And I thought it sounded like an exciting adventure, this trip to the West. What would we be missing back in Greenwich? Not much other than a few weeks of cocktails and golf at the club—

I knew that answer. But the harder question to answer was the one I wondered next: Could my husband get excited about a remote rural Texas settlement called Post?

IN THE END, Eddie agreed to go to see the land in Texas. In part because Papa was impossible to resist once he had set the sheer power of his will and enthusiasm behind something, and in part because he knew how much I wanted to make the trip. And more, he knew how much it meant to me that, for our family, for our future children, he take a role in my family's interests. As outlandish as it all sounded, Papa was a shrewd businessman who had made millions already on what many others would have called impossibly long odds, and we would have been fools to turn down an opportunity such as this, with hundreds of thousands of acres steeped in oil and cattle.

The plan was to depart by train together from Battle Creek. Leila and I accompanied the men as far as Fort Worth. Once their small party, including Papa and Eddie and a few guides and land surveyors, had set out from our Fort Worth hotel, planning to ride first toward Garza, Leila and I went our separate ways to await their return. We each occupied our own individual suite in the hotel, and there was no need for further interaction or meals together. Leila, as far as I could tell, spent her days and her money at whatever shops she could find on the wide cattle streets of Fort Worth, and at the card games they held in the grand lobby of the hotel in which Papa had installed us. I used the time to catch up on my writing to Helen and Mother, and to review the last of the decorator's figures and plans for The Boulders' new furnishings.

In that first week, the letters from Ed went from bad to worse. Papa saw adventures such as these as highly invigorating, just like his adventures with Uncle Cal back in their boyhoods; he found the spontaneity to be part of the thrill, and so he did not fixate too much on the minutia of the planning or itinerary. As they made their way west, Ed and Papa were staying each night wherever they had shelter at sundown—in rustic rancher camps, in flimsy canvas tents, in rock caves filled with the sounds of dripping water and other mysterious noises. Within a few days, Eddie found himself sick from the drinking water. The next day he accidentally sat on a barrel cactus, having never before seen such a plant, and having refused to wear the sturdy leather chaps that my father had offered him. Papa had hooted with laughter as he plucked the needles out of Eddie's backside, and Eddie lamented to me in his letter: "My God, why did I ever agree to this?"

But then Ed's letters grew even more dismal. One night, while they were making camp in a rickety cabin, a sky-blackening dust storm began to churn as a sudden cold front swept down the plains. As Papa and Eddie prepared to bed down for the night under a musty stack of woven wool blankets, the roof rattled under a clap of lightning. My stomach dipped as I read on: Just when my husband thought things could not possibly get worse, another spike of lightning hit nearby, and their terrified mules bolted. A minute later they heard shrieks—the mules?—followed by the yips of encircling coyotes. "I barely slept the entire night," Ed wrote, the outrage seeping from his primly written words. "Not until I saw the purple light of dawn did I feel sufficiently at ease to allow myself a brief doze." He awoke from those few hours of sleep to find that small vermin had chewed through his chow bag.

At last their tired party returned, lumbering dust-caked and ragged down the wide streets of Fort Worth. I'd never imagined my husband would be so relieved to be back in that cattle town, but after where he'd been, Fort Worth was a veritable metropolis.

I could tell as soon as I greeted the two men how drastically different their moods were: Papa sauntered into the lobby of the hotel appearing lively and invigorated—the sun and the adventure had colored his cheeks, and his blue eyes shone bright. It had all been a grand adventure, a reminder of the treks he'd enjoyed across the California mountains and the Great Divide. Eddie, who marched right to the lobby bar, appeared windburned and about ten pounds thinner, having spent much of the time sick from the water and the camp food. "Come with me," I said, looping my arm through his, noting how his hands trembled. "I'll draw you a warm bath."

"And a large glass of whiskey," he said, eagerly following me away from Papa and Leila and toward the privacy of our suite.

As my husband scrubbed off layers of dust in the big claw-foot tub, he downed glass after glass of the amber liquor, the sole Texan product that he seemed to appreciate. Afterward, we ordered supper to our suite and turned in early. He was too weary to make love, but we lay in bed talking. Having seen his face upon his return, I was not surprised to hear his words: "Good God, Marjorie, there is no way. I am never going back out there, let alone moving us there. It would be no place to raise a family."

I sighed, remaining close to Ed's body in the massive bed. I knew that Papa wanted my husband to be a part of his business ventures. That he had always wished for a son-in-law who felt like an obvious successor, even a surrogate son. But how could Eddie be that when he and Papa were so unlike each other? How could Eddie someday take over Papa's operations in Texas, all the way from Greenwich, Connecticut? I could not see it. But perhaps there was a middle road, and I tried to tread gently toward that. "Texas is not for us, Eddie. I agree with you. I was a little girl when we left here. I hardly think of it as home."

I could feel his body's exhale, could hear his lungs emptying in relief. I pressed on. "But what about . . . What would you think of being in Battle Creek?"

Eddie turned and faced me, his features draining of color. "Marjorie, you cannot be serious."

But I was entirely serious. I did not like Greenwich. I had finally admitted that to myself. After all, I'd had enough time alone in Fort Worth to think these things over, knowing before he'd even returned from the West that Eddie would never sanction a move out there. But I felt equally unenthusiastic about our staid Connecticut community; it was not my home. Battle Creek was. We could have a wonderful life there. Papa was driving as hard as ever, and his newest cereal, Post Toasties, had just been released, and it had been an instant sensation, clearing earnings of nearly $3 million in its first year. On top of that, our Grape-Nuts cereal and our Postum drink, both objects of Eddie's derision, were also bringing in millions. Everyone in America, it seemed, loved the Post name and wanted the Post products. We were far more popular than even the Kelloggs.

But Papa needed help. He wanted someone—a member of the family—to carry the Post company into the next generation. My husband was smart and well educated. Maybe settling a Texas village was not for him, but Eddie could be a great asset on the business side of things. Treasurer or vice president of the company? Someday even president, perhaps?

"Papa may have wild ideas," I conceded, "but he changed an entire country in introducing his ideas for breakfast. He's built an empire, and he wants us to keep it going. Think about it, Eddie. You and I could take up the mantle, really be a part of it. Together."

"Marjorie, you and I live in Greenwich. He built The Boulders for us." *In fact,* I thought, *he built The Boulders for* me. But I did not see how it would help for me to point that out. "That is our home," Ed declared.

"Yes, but—"

"Marjorie, dear, I am being as clear as I can be. Please hear me when I say that I want no part of Texas, or Battle Creek." As usual, Ed was civil enough with his words, but this time I could hear the steel beneath them; there was not an inch of give in his tone.

I breathed out slowly, feeling my body slacken in the big hotel bed. From outside came the sound of laughter and a lively piano tune, a group of cattlemen streaming out of one of the saloons.

A few moments later, the sound of my husband's steady breathing told me that Eddie had drifted off into an exhausted slumber. I remained in bed beside him but sleep evaded me; I passed hours in the dark, staring squarely at the truth that spread before us: If my marriage was to succeed, I would need to put my husband before the Post Cereal Company. Before my father's wishes. Even, it seemed, before my own wishes.

Chapter 12

Greenwich, Connecticut

WITH PAPA'S PLANS FOR BOTH TEXAS AND BATTLE CREEK FIRMLY ruled out for Eddie and me, I threw myself into making a life for us in Greenwich, so that The Boulders might start to feel like home.

Papa had accepted my announcement that Eddie and I would not be taking a day-to-day role in his Texas settlement or the Battle Creek operations of Post Cereal cheerfully enough. But he had a counteroffer, nevertheless. "Very well. But I'm not going to let you sit back with your feet up like those blue-blooded ladies of leisure, Budgie. You're too smart for that, and I trained you to keep busy. You'll manage The Boulders like the business it is—your employees depend on you. You're in charge. Your workers need their wages paid each Friday, and I want a balanced budget for the household each month. And I expect a portion of your budget set aside each month and invested for the future. You make your money work for you."

I was a new bride, only nineteen, now in charge of a huge staff and a sprawling estate with a large operating budget that had to be not only balanced but also invested. The task was staggering. Soon it all came to feel less like a gift and more like a burden—a load that I was grossly ill-equipped to bear; the weekly efforts of balancing the costs of the estate and paying out dozens of salaries proved harder than any of my school math lessons. Every meal became a source of stress as I'd look at my plate and then begin doing the figures in my head: Had I accounted for the costs of the food? The hands preparing it? The time required for its preparation? The laundering of the table linens?

* * *

"Dearest Budgie: See me in my room." I knew what this summons meant, and unlike the notes of my childhood, this one did not elicit joyful anticipation, but rather a thick bellyful of dread. It was the end of August, and Papa, who was visiting, wanted a full review of my accounts for the month. So when I joined him in his room, I submitted the fruits of my monthlong labor to him: my pile of household papers and receipts, with my lists of costs and expenditures. I sat there, nibbling my fingers, as he scrutinized my neatly penciled columns.

He spent several long minutes scouring every figure on the ledgers. Then Papa propped his elbows on the desk and looked up at me. I could tell he was not pleased. "This won't do," was all he said. My entire body wilted. I had worked so hard on all of those sums. I'd kept receipts and accounted for every wage and expense. I had checked and rechecked my math a dozen times. I'd been more fastidious in my household accounting than I'd ever been with any school assignment. "Why not?" I asked.

"Your budget is not balanced, Marjorie," he said, his voice wooden.

"What?" I leaned forward to peer over the columns. "By how much?"

His finger tapped the paper in front of him. "You're missing five."

"Five dollars?" But that was nothing.

Unblinking, he said, "Five cents."

Five *cents*? I sat back in my chair, mute. My mouth fell open. Surely he was teasing? But no, his face remained hard. "What is five cents?" I asked. A nickel! Why, I'd reach into my purse that very minute and gladly donate a nickel if that could set things to right. Only off by a measly five cents—wasn't my work pretty well done?

But Papa's lips were tight as he went on. "Marjorie," he said, his voice quiet. "Five cents is the difference between eating supper or going hungry to many a family." He sighed, then went on: "It's a question of having your affairs in hand. The greater the wealth, the greater the need for careful oversight. And you've got quite a bit of wealth. Why, if anyone in your employ were to note that you accepted unbalanced books . . . that you let money slip through, unclaimed . . . even just five cents . . . then the opening is there. Negligence, or worse, apathy, sets in by stages. You accept a missing nickel today, then what? Next month you'll accept a missing dollar? And then five? Go back into your columns. Review every transaction. And return to me when your business is in order."

Papa wasn't the only one who seemed to disapprove of my management of the estate. Eddie's small, measured quips of gentle disapproval were becoming ever more common. Such as when I decided to decorate my bedroom suite—Eddie and I each had our own rooms, as was the custom in our set—in bright silks and satins, much like the French style of Marie Antoinette and Louis XVI. I covered the walls with whimsical paintings of flowers and birds. My ceiling was frescoed with swirling rose-colored clouds. "I like pink," I said, admiring my pale rosewood end-tables brightened with figures of chubby cherubim, elaborate pieces that looked as though they could have belonged in the halls of Versailles.

"But isn't it all . . . I don't know, a bit much?" My husband grinned to soften the remark, but I heard the disdain nonetheless. Eddie favored a more traditional decorative aesthetic—rich mahogany paneling, heavy damasks of deep burgundy and hunter green. He wanted nothing that could be considered gaudy or flashy, and he certainly did not opt for winged angels frolicking on his furniture, or wispy pink clouds brightening his ceiling.

Eddie's favorite feature of the property was our golf course, and he often had friends over to enjoy it. When not golfing, he went to the club to play tennis, or he'd go riding with fellow members of the Greenwich sporting set. He also kept a law office in the city with several friends from Columbia, and so he spent many of his weeknights in Manhattan, when late hours of work and socializing demanded it.

On weekend days he was usually gone with friends: tennis with the fellows at the club often turned into cocktails, which then rolled right into dinner, and then more cocktails, which meant that Eddie often did not return home until well after midnight, at which point he'd collapse into his bed smelling of gin or scotch. I was seldom invited to join him on these outings, and so I was home on my own more often than not.

When I mentioned to Eddie that I would have liked to join him, to get to know some of his friends better, spend more time with him, he shrugged, joking, "But you can't stand firewater." I swallowed, taken aback by his casual but quick rebuttal. True, I had said that to him; too much wine made me woozy, and too much liquor left me with a headache. Papa had told me my entire life how important a healthy diet was, and the only thing worse in his mind than caffeine was alcohol. Eddie and his friends did not agree.

Eddie often stayed out late on Saturday nights, but on that summer evening, he came home even later than usual, and I was furious by the time I heard his unsteady footsteps out front. I had wanted to know exactly what time it was when he stumbled in, so I had dismissed the servants and locked the front door before retiring to bed; this would force my husband to knock in order to be let in.

Ed let loose a slur of profanity when he realized that our front door was bolted. I rose from bed at the sound of his knocking and looked at my clock. Fifteen minutes shy of three in the morning. I glowered, slipping a silk wrapper over my pajamas and descending the staircase to open the door for my husband.

"Is it the lady of the house herself?" Ed leaned across the doorway, bow tie undone, blond hair stringy around his face.

"Come in," I said, shutting the door quietly behind him so as not to rouse the entire household. "Do you have any idea what time it is?"

"Time for bed, my dearest wife. Time for bed." He kicked off a shoe and left it where it fell.

"Merry hell, Ed," I grumbled, leaning over to pick up the shoe. "You're going to wake the whole house." How mortifying for my maids and housekeeper to know that my husband stumbled home in this state, at an hour closer to dawn than dusk.

"I do love those pink pajamas," Eddie said in reply, as he sashayed across the front hall. I heard the scorn in his voice as sure as I smelled the liquor on his breath, and my stomach hardened. My voice was stony as I said, "Whiskey is a stupid substitute for your dignity."

Ed froze midstep. "Let me guess, one of Dad's many mottoes?" He smirked and then a hiccup jolted his narrow frame.

It would have been comical, had I not already been so irate, but seeing that silly hiccup only served to further fuel my anger. "Eddie, I've never witnessed a man so foolish with drink since being a girl attending a circus and seeing a wandering tramp begging for money outside the tent."

Eddie did not look at me as he began his slow, unsteady climb up the stairs, with one shoe on but no interest in grabbing the discarded one. And then, without turning, he tossed out his good-night farewell by saying: "Perhaps I should put on some rosy pajamas. They do exemplify good taste, after all."

I DID NOT know where to turn. Mother was sick so often, I could not add to her burden. Nor could I bear to tell Papa. For one thing, I couldn't stomach the idea of him sharing my troubles with Leila—the thought of her chirpy, smug gloating was enough to turn my belly sour. Papa wouldn't gloat, even though he'd cautioned me against marrying a man I'd known so briefly, but still, I couldn't bear to have him think I'd chosen wrong.

But it went deeper than that—I knew I'd let Papa down once before, when I'd refused his invitation to help run the Post family company, choosing my husband's happiness instead. Well, I couldn't very well let him down again by writing to him that my marriage was miserable, and that we were failing as husband and wife.

But even more than all of that, there was something else: I couldn't bear the thought of Papa losing respect for Eddie. And wouldn't that be inevitable if Papa were to learn the full truth of some of our quarrels? I knew that if Papa came to look at Eddie with disappointment or contempt, it would be just a short leap to my not being able to look at my husband with respect, either. And I needed to be able to respect Ed in order to love him.

A bright spot that summer came when Helen rang to tell me she was going to take the train down from Newport for a long weekend. I was thrilled at the news, eager for a chance to host my closest friend and savor her company. Ed had already made plans to crew a sailboat in a race up to Cape Cod that same weekend with some of his pals. "I'm disappointed that you won't get to see Helen," I remarked, as I watched him set out shirtwaists and trousers for his luggage.

"I know. But think of the sunny side, my darling," Ed answered, pausing to offer a quick peck on the top of my head. "Now you and Helen have the place to yourselves. It'll be good for the pair of you to have some hen time."

"No, you're right. Of course it'll be wonderful to see Helen. I only wish the two of you—"

"Say, my dear, any idea where my boater's gone off to? The straw one with the white band?" Ed looked around the room.

"I believe I saw it downstairs earlier," I answered, "in the dining room."

Ed snapped his fingers. "That's right! My goodness, would I be lost without you." He leaned toward me for another quick kiss. I managed a smile, and my husband, believing it, dashed out of the room in search of the hat.

I went with the chauffeur in the Ford to fetch Helen from the train depot. She stepped out onto the platform looking impossibly chic, a mint-green traveling suit sheathing her slender frame and a matching cap perched at a jaunty angle atop her head. "Mrs. Close, as I live and breathe!" she exclaimed, pulling me in for a hug before stepping back to make an exaggerated sweep with her eyes up and down my figure. I felt homely opposite her, wearing a suitable and wifely day dress of pale linen with lace detailing around the modest neckline. And the sound of my new name pronounced by Helen's familiar voice caused me to shift on my feet.

"No stork and bundle on the way quite yet, from the looks of it," she said with a wink, pinching my still-narrow waist. "Hell's bells, Marjorie, it sure is good to see you. A married woman." I didn't know why, but I squirmed under her appraising gaze, worried at what she might discover if she looked too long or too deep.

I brought Helen home to The Boulders. It wasn't until we were walking arm in arm around the lovely grounds of the estate that I felt my body soften a bit, the entire place unfurling green and fragrant around us in the late-summer afternoon. Helen was all easy chatter at my side, her voice familiar as she marveled at the stables and insisted on a round of golf. On Saturday afternoon we took a picnic hamper and blankets to the beach, where we swam and collected shells, watching the waves bob almost until sunset.

But it was on Sunday, over breakfast, that Helen reached for my hand across the table and fixed me with a serious expression. "Now, Mrs. Close."

I could tell by her voice that my friend was not going to let me slip out of whatever it was she intended to discuss. Perhaps I'd even been bracing for it all weekend, ever since I'd seen her step onto the train platform. But I tried to keep my own tone light as I replied, "Now, Helen."

"My train departs in a few hours."

My shoulders slumped. "I wish you could stay longer."

"I know, dear. And I was sorry to miss that husband of yours."

I turned my focus down toward my breakfast, stirring my bowl of cereal in a slow circle. Ed would be back later that evening.

"I'm just delighted that I got to see this beautiful home." Helen took a sip of her tea. "If my parents only knew—they'd be even more glum over my old-maid status."

I nodded, forced out a laugh. My home was indeed lovely; on that I could agree.

"But there's something that I simply cannot sort out," Helen said, her eyes boring into my face, even if I was avoiding her stare. She went on: "And that is . . . why aren't you happy?"

Now I met her gaze, my spoon falling to the table. Helen shrugged, gesturing around the room with a wave of her hand. "Your home is the tops. You're married to the man you love. Together you have just about anything a pair of honeymooners could ever ask for. Why . . . why don't I feel like you are yourself?"

At that, my resolve unraveled. "Oh, Helen." I folded over the table, the hot tears coming unbidden to my eyes. "It's not . . . it's not all as grand as you think."

"That I can see, dearest. Oh, don't cry. Now you're making me weepy." She squeezed my hand. "But whatever is the matter?"

"It's . . . it's Ed. And me, too. He . . . there's such a distance between us. All he ever wants to do is go out. But not with me—with his friends. And every week . . . he just . . . I don't know. . . ." I couldn't bring myself to say more aloud, to give words to the true depth of my disapproval and disappointment. Of how lonely and out of place I felt in his world. But Helen's eyes traveled toward the liquor cart in the corner of the room. We had these carts stocked in nearly every room of the ground floor, and in the bedrooms as well.

"You know, my dear," Helen said after a pause, folding her napkin and placing it gently on the table before her, "the two of you came into this marriage from wildly different backgrounds."

"Don't I know it," I said, my tone wry, even as I tried to fight back more tears.

"And the drinking . . ." Helen said, her eyes filling with warmth. I was so grateful to her for knowing me—for saying aloud what I myself hadn't been able to. She went on: "It's simply a part of his lifestyle. It's just the way these gentlemen are; they tip the bottles. They're social, you know. And you're not accustomed to it. But the two of you will figure out your own way."

"Helen, the drinking. I can't see how I'll ever grow accustomed to it."

"There, there, dear. He's young. His friends move in a fast set. But it's not like he's a bad sort. It's all in good fun. You'll get used to it in time, trust me. It's the same in Newport."

"It was not like that in Battle Creek."

"Naturally. But you're in Greenwich, my dear."

"As if I need to be reminded."

"Marjorie, my darling, the two of you are fresh off the starting block. In time, he'll settle. You'll see. And remember, you catch more bees with honey. If you keep things happy on the home front, that husband of yours will come to realize, in time, that he doesn't need to step out every night. It's an adjustment period, is all."

I frowned, and yet I nodded, taking in my friend's advice. Helen, after all, had grown up in a world much closer to the one Ed and I now occupied than I had. Perhaps I did simply need to give us time. It was worth a try. And really, what other choice did I have?

⁂

AS SUMMER FADED, making way for the crisp, golden cool of autumn, I hoped for quieter days and more time at home with Eddie. With golf and tennis mostly done for the season, perhaps he'd settle in a bit more at The Boulders. Perhaps we'd have casual dinners as a pair and retire to bed together as we'd done in Hot Springs and Battle Creek. Wake up beside each other and enjoy breakfast trays together under the covers. We may have been experiencing lifestyle differences, but the love between us was strong enough to bridge any such rift. That was what I believed, and with the right attitude, I was sure I could show Eddie it was so.

How wrong I was. It didn't seem like Eddie wanted me to even try to join his lifestyle. That fall, with the country clubs turning quieter after the high summer season, Ed started visiting Columbia friends and Manhattan colleagues for house party weekends in Newport, the Hudson Valley, and on Long Island. "It's for business," he'd say, kissing me on the top of the head before motoring off in my chauffeured auto for those weekends away. "All legal talk with the gents and cocktails into the night. You'd be miserable, my dear."

I asked him, after his return from a late-September weekend trip to Long Island's Gold Coast, if I might accompany him the next time he went out. "I've told you, Marjorie dear, you'd think it was all bunk. You wouldn't enjoy yourself."

"I know you say that, Ed. But . . . but I want to spend time with you."

He frowned at that but he didn't reply, and so eventually, after a moment and an intake of fortifying breath, I gathered the resolve to voice what I had so far been too afraid to ask: "Are you embarrassed by me?"

He turned, holding me in his unsmiling gray gaze. After a long pause, his voice quiet, he replied, "No, sweetie. It's that you're embarrassed by me."

IT WAS A rainy Friday afternoon in October, and Eddie was home from the office for the day. I'd had one of the footmen build a fire in our drawing room, and I sat before it, reading the latest issue of *Collier's* as Eddie fidgeted in the armchair across from me. His only entertainment since we'd finished lunch an hour earlier had been his scotch, it seemed. I forced back the bitterness my tongue was tempted toward, instead summoning a jovial tone as I lowered my magazine and turned toward him. "Everything all right, dear?"

"Dandy." His fingers tapped his glass. "Just bored, is all."

I rose from my chair and crossed the room toward him. "This is absurd."

"What is?" he asked.

I raised my arms. "Look around. We have the most beautiful home two people could ask for. We've got a beautiful life. We've got our health." He looked at me with a pale eyebrow lifted, unsure of my point. I went on, "We are not going to spend another afternoon quarreling. We love each other." With that, I threw myself into his arms and brought my lips boldly to his, assailing him with a kiss. I felt his body tense, and then soften. He might have been inclined to call my actions undignified, but he was loose from the liquor, and I was offering him something that very few men can turn down, no matter how refined their breeding.

He laughed, an exhale that smelled of liquor, as he settled me into his lap on the oversized chair. "That's the Marjorie I like to see."

In truth, I didn't know *what* he liked to see in me, but I wasn't going to press the point or risk an argument. Not right then. Not when he was, for once, eager to be with me; I would use that for the good of our marriage. We held each other and traded affectionate caresses right there in the plush armchair, not worrying about whether an unwitting maid might walk in. And then, after that had turned into delicious torture, we retired together to bed for the first time in weeks and made love.

And the next month, as I prepared the household for Thanksgiving, I had my own cause to be thankful because I had found the key, at last, to saving my marriage. I found out I was expecting our first child.

Chapter 13

Greenwich, Connecticut
Summer 1908

MOTHERHOOD SURPRISED ME. NAMELY, I WAS SURPRISED BY the fact that motherhood came so much easier to me than my marriage to Ed had. I think that was, in part, because I was not expected to figure out my new child entirely on my own—as had been expected with my new husband—but instead had many around to love the baby alongside me. And she certainly was a lovable thing, my pink little Adelaide Close. She arrived in the heat of late July. Papa came out for the birth and the early days of my daughter's life, mercifully unaccompanied by Leila. Mother also came, and the two kept to opposite wings of the house, splitting their time with Adelaide and switching off visits to the nursery with cool, cordial nods.

In spite of my own mother's troubles carrying a healthy baby to birth, Adelaide appeared to thrive from the start. She had a placid, steady disposition and was much calmer than I had been as a babe, my father declared. "Perhaps that's the Close in her," Papa said, and the remark pulled smiles to both Eddie's and my lips. I was thrilled to have Adelaide in our life—we both were. Holding her wrapped up tight in her soft, beribboned blankets so that only her little moon of a face peeked out, I would sing to her and tell her about the fun we would have together. I could not wait to travel with her, to teach her about the world and art and dancing.

Another welcome addition to the household came in the nurse I brought on, Miss Virginia Pearson. Miss Pearson was a natural touch. A middle-aged woman from Georgia, with a gentle drawl and an easy round smile, Miss Pearson never grew agitated by the baby's cries. She pushed Adelaide around the gardens in the pram or held her happily in the nursery rocking chair for hours, whereas I often found those long stretches of forced idleness to be wearying and tedious. Miss Pearson had never married, having lost her sweetheart to illness when she was younger, so she'd never had babies of her own, and thus "Pearcie," as I came to know her, poured all her love into my baby. With Pearcie's expert management of the nursery and loving care of the baby, Adelaide grew round and I made a happy adjustment to my new maternal role.

I sat outside on a pleasant spring day, looking out over the rolling green of our golf course. Our grand old trees were newly in leaf, offering just the right amount of dappled, cooling shade. Fresh-budded flowers spread bright color across the grounds, and I was taking my leisure on a cushioned chaise, enjoying the sound of our creek as it mingled with the lilt of birdsong. The window to the nursery was ajar, and I could hear Adelaide cooing and laughing happily with Pearcie after her nap.

Ed was out—riding, I believed—but I expected him home shortly. He'd fallen in love with Adelaide as quickly as I had. Whenever he was home he made visits to the nursery, eager for updates from the nanny and always trying his best to pull smiles from our daughter's round cheeks. "C.W. thinks she's got the Close temperament, but fortunately she got all her looks from her mother," I'd hear my husband say every time he introduced a friend to our daughter. On that day in early spring, I was excited for Eddie to return to The Boulders and hear my good news: though it had been less than a year since the arrival of our first baby, I was already expecting again.

But Eddie needed to come home before I could share this good news with him. As the hours passed, the sun dipped behind the tree line. The mild air turned chilly, and I retreated into the house as Adelaide had her evening feeding. Finally, just before our own dinnertime, Eddie returned.

When he leaned down to give me a quick kiss in greeting, he smelled of sweat-dampened tweed and something else—liquor. My stomach clenched, but I did my best to keep a pleasant, level tone as I asked, "How was your ride?"

"Fine," he said, loosening his collar. "I need to change."

"For supper?"

"No need to worry about me for supper, dear." He walked briskly through the room, his tall riding boots tracking a path of spring mud along our floor. "I'm planning on heading over to the club."

I shifted in my seat. "Eddie, I'd really like it if you'd stay and join me for supper."

"Oh? Why is that?" He paused and I could tell he was surprised by the insistence in my request; I'd stopped asking him, familiar as I'd become with his absences.

"I have news," I answered.

"Is Adelaide all right?"

"She's wonderful."

He arched an eyebrow. "Then . . . what is it?"

I smiled, my good news doing much to mollify my frustration as I said, "Adelaide is going to be a sister."

Ed looked down toward my flat belly, stunned. Thinking, no doubt, exactly what I'd thought when I'd noticed that my monthly courses, which had only just returned to normal, were absent once more. "How did that happen?" he asked.

I flashed him a wry smile, fairly certain that he did not need a biology lesson.

He ran his fingers through his tousled blond hair. "What I mean is . . . how, so soon?"

"It *is* soon." I nodded. "And yet, I think it's a straightforward formula. If you plant the seed, there's a chance the flower can grow."

"Well, that's marvelous," he said, and I knew that he meant it.

In truth, I'd cried when I'd first found out, feeling unprepared to do it all again so soon. Knowing the years it had taken for my parents to find their own hopes fulfilled, I had been stunned that Adelaide had come as quickly as she had; I'd never even considered that we would welcome *two* at such a pace. Adelaide was still so tiny. It would mean we would have two who were both babies. "So then, are you . . ." I hesitated. "Well, do you really think it's good news?"

Ed walked back toward me and knelt down beside where I sat. "I don't *think* it's good, Marjorie, my dearest." And then he took my hand in his and placed a soft kiss on top of it with his lips, those lips that I had loved from the start. "Why, I *know* it's good."

I softened at this, squeezing his hand. "I agree," I said, a tear blurring my eye.

"I only hope this one's as lucky, and also comes out looking like Mother," he said. Then, after another kiss, he rose and said: "I'll just go ring the fellows to count me out for dinner." With that, I was left alone in the room with a feeling of deep contentment. More than that: hope. Adelaide had brought us more joy and love than we'd ever shared before in our marriage. Wouldn't a second baby mean that much more?

SHE WAS A December arrival, our little Eleanor, and like her sister, she arrived strong and hearty. But unlike her sister, she did not stay that way.

Pearcie first came to me with news of the fever in the middle of the night, just a week after the baby was born. "Mrs. Close, I think we need to fetch the doctor. Immediately." I saw it in her face—Pearcie, my unflappable Pearcie, was frightened, and that sent me headlong into a panic. She went on: "It sounds as though the poor babe can barely breathe. . . . Her little lungs . . ." But a stifled sob kept the nurse from finishing her dreadful sentence.

I snapped to alert. Eddie had gone to supper at the club hours earlier. Of course he was not at home. I could have wrung his neck; his daughter was staring down grave illness, and he was not there for her—not there for me. I called a male servant to wake the chauffeur and sent him out into the night with two urgent errands. First, he was to fetch the doctor and bring him to The Boulders straightaway. Then he was to go to the club to find my husband and bring him home, dragging him by the coattails if necessary.

The doctor arrived within an hour, and Pearcie brought him up to where I sat in the nursery, rocking my baby. Eleanor had finally slipped into a restless but steady sleep. I gladly handed over her care to the doctor, with Pearcie urging me to return to my own room to try to rest for a spell. She'd fetch me as soon as the baby awoke. I knew I wouldn't sleep while my daughter was locked in such a struggle, but I did return to my own room to wait for Ed; I needed to speak to him when he arrived, without disturbing Eleanor's tenuous rest.

An hour passed and then another, and still no sign of my husband. Finally, as dawn was just beginning to purple the wintry view outside my window, giving the leaf-stripped trees the look of thin, brittle bones, I heard the crunch of gravel in the forecourt. I flew to the window and peered out, watching as Ed hurled himself out of the car and careened up the front steps toward the door.

Before Ed could make it up the stairs, a light, muffled knock sounded on my bedroom door. "Mrs. Close?" It was Pearcie. Her face was weary, but smiling.

"Yes, what is it?"

"The doctor wishes for me to tell you he has good news. He suspects pneumonia, but the fever has broken. Eleanor's breathing is now coming more easily. He believes we have every reason to hope that the worst has come and gone for our precious little one."

I flew to the nursery, not stopping until I stood over the cradle and saw, tucked there inside, my sleeping baby. She was breathing; though my heart galloped, I quieted my own panting breath so as not to disturb her. Somewhere in the house, I didn't know where, Ed was stumbling around. On most nights like this, I helped him out of his clothes and into his bed, mostly to spare him—or perhaps to spare myself?—the indignity of his being found by a servant the next morning, curled up in some chair in the rumpled clothes of the night before. But that night he would fall asleep in his dressing room or study. I didn't care. *Let him sleep it off*, I figured, and I'd speak to him about it once he was back in his right mind. As I stared down at my precious child, watching her chest rise and fall at a steady pace, I knew I didn't need Ed's slurred attempts at comfort. I had what I needed—the comfort of knowing my baby would survive. Even if I did not know whether I could say the same about my marriage.

Chapter 14

Greenwich, Connecticut
Summer 1911

"IT'S JUST LIKE MY DADDY ALWAYS SAYS: CHANNEL THE POWER of the mind. If you want to change your circumstances, then you have to change your attitude."

My younger girl, Eleanor, looked at me, and I could see in the wide blue of her eyes that she had no idea of what her mother spoke. *No matter,* I reasoned. I was saying it aloud for myself. I knew that I wished to change my circumstances, and I knew I would try my best to do so with a change of my attitude. If I was going to sit in my beautiful Greenwich mansion and feel melancholy, I would channel Papa's philosophies to overcome my doldrums, and I would do so by pouring myself into helping those who were less fortunate than I was. Like Papa, I would not abide self-pity, not when there was a world full of people who truly had cause for complaints.

I befriended a kindly Greenwich neighbor named Elsie Rockefeller, a woman about a decade my senior and well regarded in town, who invited me to join the leadership committee for the gala to support the United Workers of Greenwich. I was lonely a lot of the time, what with Eddie staying in Manhattan during the week and cavorting with lifelong Greenwich friends on the weekends, so I would keep busy by working on behalf of others. I joined the effort to raise money to save historic buildings from being torn down. I donated to local hospitals and schools. There was more to life in Greenwich, I decided, than just cocktail parties and country clubs, and I'd infiltrate the community by finding out those causes.

And I could do more than change my attitude, I decided—I could change my location as well. True, we had made our family's home in

Greenwich, but there was no reason, now that the girls were old enough, that we couldn't travel. Many in Eddie's set traveled—to Newport, Long Island, Saratoga Springs, London, and Paris. Why couldn't we do the same?

So the next winter found us waiting out the coldest months wrapped in the balmy warmth of Florida. Plenty of Eddie's colleagues and friends had fixed their interest on a wild stretch of the Atlantic coast where the railroad tycoon Henry Flagler had recently built a magnificent hotel on the barrier island called Palm Beach. He'd named his hotel The Breakers, and his first seasons attracted patrons like the Astors and the Belmonts, the Vanderbilts and the Fricks, and so, suddenly, it was the fashion to winter in Palm Beach. When I proposed we make a visit ourselves, Eddie lit up at the idea. It was the first thing we'd agreed on so easily in years.

Palm Beach was still only just developing, an outpost of chic luxury surrounded by thick jungle and untamed, mangrove-lined beaches. The shopping was still scant, the dirt roads ribbed and potholed, and that was precisely why I loved it. While Eddie visited with friends, sipping cocktails on the lawn of the luxurious Breakers or hitting golf balls off the terrace of our rented villa, I biked around the island, admiring the clusters of plump fruit trees and the tall, stately palms. Eddie and I loved to bask in the winter sun while the girls splashed with Pearcie in the surf. At night, after long dinners enjoyed outdoors against the background of the jungle noises, Eddie would knock on my bedroom door, and I'd welcome him with a warmth I hadn't felt since the earliest days of our marriage. Within weeks I felt contented and strong, my limbs golden from the sun and firm from my daily swims and beach walks.

Late in the winter, as our return to Greenwich approached, a knot of dread began to settle in my gut. I didn't miss Greenwich, and I did not feel ready to return to our staid, fixed life there. I liked it in Palm Beach, where the days were relaxed and so was my husband. Where the trees hung ripe with fruit and the tropical sun meant color and flowers all winter long. Society here was not codified; our hours were not allotted to the same sequence of monotonous and required activities. "What about building a home here?" I suggested one evening. Pearcie had taken the girls on an evening walk to look for sea turtles on the beach, and Eddie and I sat on the lawn overlooking the moonlit surf, its ceaseless procession of waves throwing a shimmering dance of reflected starlight across the horizon. "A winter getaway," I added, my voice filled with yearning as I rolled out my best pitch. "The girls love it here, and so do we. We could afford it, Eddie."

A cacophony of tree frogs filled the night air. And then I heard the ice clinking in Eddie's glass as he sloshed his drink, considering his response in thoughtful silence. Eventually he answered, "This is fine for a brief winter jaunt, Marjorie. But Palm Beach is not going to take off as any real destination. At least, not for our sort."

The night was wrapped in warmth, the nearby saltwater and humid air clinging to my skin, but now I felt a mist of perspiration begin to form as well—my body's bracing reaction to yet another quarrel with my husband. "What makes you say that?" I asked, shifting in my chair.

Eddie shrugged, already fatigued by the conversation. "It's a jungle outpost." He said it dismissively, and yet that was a large part of why I liked it. Eddie went on: "Have you seen the size of the mosquitoes?"

I could hear the resolve in his voice, just as I'd heard it when he'd ruled out Texas and then Battle Creek. But I didn't understand my husband's stubborn resistance this time around; to be sure, Palm Beach was not Greenwich, but it had the promise of adventure and variety, while also being part of the world of the Astors and Vanderbilts. It seemed like a place where both Eddie and I could get what we so desperately craved.

I was not ready to give up. "Just think," I ventured. "We could make a family home here. Do it entirely our way." But I knew as soon as it was out that such an argument would not fall on receptive ears with my husband. He did not wish to make his own way; nothing could have been less appealing to Ed Close.

He took a slow sip, sighing as he answered with a refrain I'd come to know so well: "It's just not done that way, Marjorie."

Chapter 15

Greenwich, Connecticut
Fall 1912

THE FOOTMAN KNOCKED WITH A TIMID, GLOVED HAND. I LOOKED up, my attention pulled from the guest list for a hospital luncheon that I was helping some of my Greenwich neighbors to put on. "Yes, come in."

The man entered and lowered his eyes to the carpet. My gaze went to the silver dish in his hands. "What is it?"

"A telegram for you, Mrs. Close."

"From where?"

"It's from Washington, ma'am."

Mother. I knew in an instant—Washington meant Mother. But news in the form of a telegram was not likely to be good. I accepted the paper from the servant and turned to read it with trembling hands.

Eddie was sitting opposite me with his newspaper. He looked on as I scanned the message. "What is it?" he asked. I met his gaze, feeling as if the blood had stilled in my veins. "Is everything all right?" he asked.

"Mother . . ." I shook my head. "She's . . . she's gone."

Ed's face drained of color, and I could see my shock reflected in his expression. "Gone?" he repeated.

I handed Ed the telegram, unable to offer any more words. As he read, I folded my arms around myself and began to rock. A faint mewling was the only sound I could give to my shock as my mind reeled: *Mother dead?* But she had only just turned sixty. She'd suffered from migraines for years, yes, but nothing that would have taken the life from her. Her only other chronic condition had been her flattening melancholy, made far worse in recent years by my father's departure for another marriage. But dead? Gone forever? How could that possibly be true?

"How?" Ed asked, voicing my own bewilderment back to me.

There was only one explanation that I could offer in return. "Died of a broken heart," I said aloud, knowing it to be something that no doctor would ever declare, and yet knowing it to be the truth.

❋

I DID NOT want the girls to be at the funeral, so Eddie remained with them in Greenwich as I went alone to Mother's home on M Street. There, facing the task of packing up the remnants of her life, I spent a few stunned days, aching, driven only by a feeling that work, however tedious, would be my best sustaining force. So I rolled back the sleeves of my black mourning dress and I got to work, sifting through drawers and boxes, through closets and trunks, through journal clippings and jewels. Faded photographs from my childhood. Articles detailing my wedding announcement, and notes I'd sent her from Hot Springs, Fort Worth, Palm Beach, and The Boulders. And then the earliest photographs of my Adelaide and Eleanor—with Mother's slanted handwriting naming each girl, detailing their birth dates and weights. From a few years later, a drawing of a pony that Adelaide had made for Grandmother and mailed to her. Through tear-streaked eyes I read Mother's faded journal entries from Battle Creek, written in Mrs. Gregory's upstairs bedroom, the one we'd shared on so many cold nights while Papa had lain, groaning, in the next room.

Papa joined me in Washington after a week. I didn't speak to him much; I didn't have much to say. Or perhaps I had too much to say, but lacked the strength to voice it. He seemed to understand, and he didn't force it. Together, dressed in our somber black, we set about planning Mother's final trip, a train ride back to her birthplace in Springfield, Illinois. The place where Ella Letitia Merriweather had grown up loved, raised by affluent and upright parents. Where she had been courted by and wed to her childhood friend, C. W. Post. How, I wondered, had her life turned so very sad?

"Budgie." Papa pulled me in for a hug on our last morning in Washington. For the first time since his arrival, I collapsed into hot, throat-choking tears, unable to speak. Unable to set my mind to the task of packing up the last of Mother's personal items. Tears pooled in Papa's eyes, too, as he leaned forward to wipe mine. His voice quiet, he said, "We are so small in this world, Budge. There's a greater power, and we're just a small part. Your mother . . . well, she is finally at peace."

I didn't say anything as he held me. I was so angry with him, I could have railed that he had been the source of Mother's heartbreak. But I let my body speak only through my tears, through the shudders that heaved me further into his comforting hug. In truth I knew that Mother's melancholy ran far deeper than just the loneliness of her final years. It had plagued her for much of my childhood. And what's more, I needed Papa in that moment. He was the only parent I had left.

I returned home after the funeral and resumed my life in Greenwich. Life without a mother. The hurt of her absence shifted, until eventually it was less a searing pain and more like a dull but persistent ache. The plain truth was that she had not been part of my daily life in years, separated as we'd been first by her illnesses and then by geographical distance. I missed knowing that she was alive, that she could be reached by letter or telephone or telegram if I needed her, but I had no choice but to carry on. I was still a mother, after all, and a wife. And a daughter. I settled back into those roles, not suspecting—not realizing—that it would all soon change again.

Chapter 16

Greenwich, Connecticut
Spring 1914

I WAS UNPREPARED. UTTERLY AND ENTIRELY UNPREPARED FOR the gutting shock that came on a mild spring morning, this time in the form of a telegram from California. The footman carried in the note just after Eddie and I had completed breakfast and sent Adelaide and Eleanor off to their piano lessons. I took the paper in my hands with a mild unease, but nothing could have braced me for what I saw. "I'm an orphan," I said aloud, staring numbly at my husband. Eddie returned my gaze, silent and confused.

"Papa," I managed to choke out the word. "He's left me." Just as Mother had left me. My father was dead. C. W. Post, the strong and dynamic man who had built an industry on his health and his indelible spirit, was gone. Papa had left this world. He'd left his empire at Post Cereal Company. He'd left his millions. He'd left me.

"I'm not even thirty years old, and I'm an orphan," I said, the words sounding faint and hollow as they slipped out. I was the only Post left. I was a very scared, very rich, and very sad orphan.

"NONE OF IT will be yours, Marjorie. Not if Leila has her way." Ed looked at me with a face pulled tight, his beautiful lips sealed in a straight line. He was concerned, and I knew he was correct to be so. For as long as I'd known her, Leila had set her sights on what was mine: my father, my family, my name, and now my inheritance.

Under the crippling pain of the fact that Papa was gone, there were searing layers of other unbearable agonies. First, there was the fact that Leila had declared her intention to fight me for the empire that my father had spent his life building, the brand that he had hatched with my little hand in his and Mother at his side. The empire that bore the name of my family, that Papa had first funded with the last pennies of Mother's dowry. All those afternoons of my girlhood spent stacking crates of raw wheat in the barn, gluing the labels onto the earliest batches, sampling handfuls of Grape-Nuts and Postum—Leila was fighting to steal it all.

But she would not win. I was a Post by birth; I was born of Papa's blood and mettle, and I was done letting that woman steal what was mine. "I'll hire the best lawyers in America," I declared. For once, Eddie did not scoff or argue with me. I would fight her with all of my energy, strength, and smarts. I had something she would never have—a lifetime of Papa's lessons. Papa's spirit had shaped me as a girl, and now that I was a woman, it helped to shape my every thought. I would not rest until Papa and Mother's legacy, my birthright, the Post Cereal Company, was in my hands where it belonged. Where Papa had always intended for it to be. That woman may have fashioned herself as Mrs. Post, but I would show her—and anyone else who needed reminding—just who the real Post was.

But then, even as my resolve hardened to steel and I braced for the legal fight, there came another blow. Worse by far than the telegram announcing Papa's death. Worse than the headlines outlining Leila's claims that the Post Cereal Company belonged to her, as C. W. Post's widow. And that came in the letter that Papa had written to me in his final moments—his suicide note.

My father was dead because he had taken his own life. C. W. Post, the man who had built his fortune speaking about the healing powers of faith and the supreme strength of the mind, had pressed a pistol to his own temple.

The scandal, the hypocrisy of it, sent me—and all of America—reeling. Newspapers filled column after column in every city with the sordid details. They called Papa's suicide a cowardly act. They roiled over the fact that C. W. Post would end such a glorious run with such an inglorious and selfish exit. They theorized that Papa must have lost his mind to have taken such a measure. They called him a fraud, mocking him for speaking about the quest for a healthy mind and body when behind the scenes he was a man of poor health and troubled nerves. As if they knew him. As if they had the right to pass their judgments on my daddy.

In truth, I was just as surprised and devastated as the rest of America. I'd been largely separated from him in recent years, as he and Leila had spent most of their time in California and Battle Creek. I'd ceded Papa's day-to-day presence to his young wife, what with Eddie and the girls and our life so firmly ensconced on the East Coast. My relationship with Papa in the later years of his life had been largely in the form of the regular letters we exchanged—letters in which he'd never let on just how much he was suffering, both in mind and in body.

Shock—swirling and tearful shock—blurred the words as I read the grisly newspaper reports of Papa's final days. Of course I would never have dreamed of asking Leila for details, so I got my news from the journals just like everyone else. And there was plenty to be had: Accounts of how he'd come down with a case of appendicitis in California. And then how, the papers panted, Papa had undertaken a "race against death" by private train to Rochester, Minnesota, to have the world-famous Mayo brothers perform lifesaving surgery, a procedure in which Papa, as a Christian Scientist, hadn't believed. When the Mayo brothers had finally pulled out Papa's bloated, rancid appendix, they had declared it "the worst looking thing you've ever seen."

The surgery had provided temporary relief, and Papa was soon well enough to travel home to the sunny climate of California. But then the excruciating pain in his stomach came back and, with that, a fatal dilemma: How could Papa sit idly by, allowing death to slowly take him—he who had claimed that he could beat pain and cure all ailments with his mind and his lifestyle? No, he could not let pain and rot win. He would not allow his failing body to gradually and painfully waste away. He would act out against it, seize control, as he had always done.

But Papa, I railed, *how could you abandon me, leaving me with this legacy of shame and cowardice?* These were words I would never have been able to speak aloud, not even had I been given the chance to stare into his bright blue eyes one final time. Papa was gone, and once again, he'd left me not understanding. Feeling like a fool because all of my life I had thought that all of the answers could be found in his beautiful, indelible spirit.

Eddie and I took a New York City train bound for Chicago and then Battle Creek. Across the country, my father's body was loaded onto a train in Santa Barbara, coming back to our midwestern hometown in the company of that woman.

Brilliant blue skies, a color not too far from the hue of Papa's eyes, marked our arrival in Battle Creek. Uncle Cal was there to meet us at the train depot, pulling me in for a slow, wordless hug, and I held on to him for longer than usual, reluctant to let go. "How are you doing, Uncle Cal?" I asked, swallowing against the tight squeeze of my throat.

He shrugged, his eyes red, and answered, "Probably about the same as you, Budge."

I pulled back my shoulders, but then, unable to fight off the impulse, knowing that this might be the only time in my life that I might pose this question, I breathed out the words: "Why, Uncle Cal? Why did he . . . ?"

Uncle Cal took in a slow, ragged breath, his eyes falling to the ground as he answered, "He just . . . Well, no man can expect to hold up the entire world."

It was my first time back in years, and the town was covered in its own black mourning garb, with the streetcars stopped, the storefronts and factories shuttered, and crowds lining the streets, half a dozen people thick. Hundreds of Papa's workers formed an honor guard, with a dozen of his men joining Uncle Cal to bear the walnut coffin along the route and through the wide front doors of the Independent Congregational Church. Inside, the church was packed with flowers and people, and hundreds more crowded outside to stand their own vigil. A large portrait of Papa presided over the altar, beneath American flags and a massive arrangement of white flowers made to look like our white barn.

As we buried Papa at Oak Hill Cemetery, I thought back to that frigid winter evening when we'd first stepped off the train in Battle Creek: Papa,

Mother, and I making our way to Mrs. Gregory's home with the last of our hopes and savings. This city had changed Papa, transforming him from a cripple to a giant, and he'd gone ahead and changed the city—and indeed, the world—right back.

As I turned to leave the cemetery, feeling simultaneously empty and also leaden with weight, I met a familiar face. "Hi there, Budgie."

I inhaled a quick breath; age had drawn a brush across the man's withered skin and weary features, but I knew him in an instant. "Shorty Bristol," I gasped, leaning into a hug. My father's right-hand man from the earliest days of the white barn, Shorty now stood before me with a sad, smiling face. Shorty looked, well, shorter, and I saw that a nurse stood nearby with a wheelchair at the ready. Goodness, this man who had once been Papa's constant companion, once the image of vigor and health, a faithful steward of Papa's hopes and successes—how had time caught them both with such a ruthless reckoning?

As the initial shock of his suicide settled, America seemed to join me in mourning, in bidding farewell to the man who had forever changed how we started each day. Telegrams poured in, heaps of flowers, letters and cards written by Teddy Roosevelt, William Howard Taft, Henry Ford, members of the Rockefeller and Vanderbilt and Carnegie clans. In a welcome contrast to the articles that had gushed with gory details, now the newspapers spoke about how admired and beloved Papa was. I focused on those pieces, vowing never to read another negative word about my father. What's done was done; I could not change it.

Instead I could choose to remember my daddy with all that was worth celebrating about him. And there was so much of that; I wept as I read about how Papa had created an industry, how even his business competitors had respected and liked him. How he had represented the promise of America's new century, how he'd been the one-man symbol to so many of hope, hard and honest work, and opportunity. How his generosity had known no limits. And how he had loved his country, his work, his employees, and yes, me, his only child, the blue-eyed girl whose image had so closely resembled his and who had graced the labels of his earliest products.

* * *

But the battle for whether I would be the heir to all of Papa's good and all of Papa's millions was just beginning. I had never trusted Leila, even in my girlhood, when she'd been all smiles and honeyed confidences—and I'd been correct in my dislike.

"She plans to fight you for it," Eddie said, sitting with me in our Greenwich drawing room after we'd returned home to the girls. I was still in my head-to-toe black, and I fiddled restlessly with my skirt, picking at a piece of loose thread in the stitching. Ed went on, "You're not the only one who has hired lawyers."

I looked up, meeting my husband's pale eyes. "What could they possibly be saying?" I asked.

Ed frowned as he showed me one of that day's headlines: POST MILLIONS LIKELY TO CAUSE FAMILY FIGHT!

I glowered. "That woman is no family of mine."

Eddie cocked his head. "But her attorneys assert that your father's final will bequeathed fifty percent of his millions to you and . . . well, fifty percent to—"

"To that woman?"

Ed nodded. "Your father split the Texas land evenly between the two of you. He intended for everything in Battle Creek and California to go to Leila. He left you The Boulders."

Land in Texas and California and even Battle Creek, that was one thing. But then Ed went on: "It's not just the matter of the land or the money, Marjorie." I didn't like his tenuous tone.

"Then what is it?" I asked.

Ed puffed out a long sigh before saying, "Your father, well, he split the Post Cereal Company between the two of you, as well. Right down the middle, half the stock for you and—"

"*Half* of the company for Leila?"

When Ed nodded, my stomach curdled, and I lifted a weary hand, imploring him not to go on. It was an outrage. Papa, Mother, and I had started Post Cereal together in our backyard, with Mother's money getting it all going. Both Mother and Papa had told me all my life that it would remain in our family, in *my* family's hands in particular. All the talk of Papa's being sick in both body and mind in his final days was making a grim sort of sense; how else could he have considered leaving half of our family's company to *her*?

With my heart more bruised than I could even admit aloud, I turned to anger, white-hot coils of searing anger. Anger toward Leila and her team of scavenging lawyers. Anger toward Mother for her years of melancholy—why hadn't she fixed things better so that I might have been spared just one battle resulting from her and Papa's antipathy?

And anger toward the pair of men in my life as well: Papa and Eddie. Had Eddie been a more attentive son-in-law and an adequate heir, Papa would have had no misgivings about bequeathing his empire to us and the future generations of our Post family. For all Papa's talk of raising me to be strong and educated, we had always known a man would have to someday run the company, and I had always believed that man would be my husband. But Eddie had ruled that out, and Papa had had no choice but to give up that hope. And Papa. *Oh, Papa, why have you once more let that woman snake her way between us?*

Sensing my heartbreak and perhaps, too, my rage, Eddie roused on my behalf. "I'm going back to Battle Creek," he told me one June morning not long after our return home. My husband had appeared in my bedroom looking freshly shaved and alert, already dressed in his sharpest lawyer's suit. "I'll be your representative there. Sort this out. We won't let Leila steal this thing, my darling."

"Thank you, Ed." I kissed him with relief. By lunchtime he had boarded a train west.

As my surrogate in Battle Creek, Ed spent hours, days, scouring all of Papa's papers in his study at the farmhouse. Leila no longer lived there, having set herself up in a posh brownstone closer to town.

I received a telephone call from the farm several days later and immediately told the operator to patch it through. Ed's voice sounded ebullient, even if far away. "I've got it, my dear. I've got it."

"What have you got?" I asked, sitting down on my bed in Greenwich.

"It's all sorted, dearest. Or at least, it shall be—and soon. You see, I've located the first contract from 1895, signed by both of your parents."

"Probably written up in the white barn," I said, swallowing hard. "With Shorty Bristol and Uncle Cal as witnesses."

"That's it, my dear. The paper establishes the Post Cereal Company and declares that all family shares shall pass from your father to you. Marjorie, the company has been intended for you since you were a girl. You already knew that. But now we've got the founding charter to prove it."

I could have wept in relief. Ed went on: "The law is on our side." He sounded triumphant, even as the telephone line from Battle Creek crackled. Now I just longed for him to return to us, contract intact and in hand, so that I might wrap him in a grateful and exhausted embrace.

"Now it's just a question of how long Leila wants to fight it," Eddie added. "But the good news is that I've got the paper, and you've got me."

AS WINTER ROLLED in, I woke one morning just before Christmas to a fresh fall of snow and a newspaper article that finally brought good news, the best possible news to make our holiday season joyful and our New Year celebratory. Leila had called the papers the day before with her announcement, and I read the resulting headlines:

POST SCANDAL: NO LITIGATION IN SIGHT
HUSBAND'S MEMORY TOO DEAR FOR MRS. POST
TO OPPOSE HIS DAUGHTER

I let out a whoop from my bedroom. Eleanor came bounding into the room, her eyes wide. "What's happened, Mother?"

"It's glorious news, my little darling. It's glorious news!" Leila had finally quit. She'd keep the land Papa had given her, the buildings, the millions, and she'd retreat into more wealth than she could ever spend. But that was all fine; I just wanted her to stay out of my life. *Husband's memory too dear for Mrs. Post.* I scoffed at it; it was an outrage that she had his name. But at least she would not have his company. My company.

I was suddenly and finally free of Leila, and richer than any young woman had a right to be, particularly a lady still years shy of her thirtieth birthday. And it was time for me to show the world just who Marjorie Merriweather Post intended to be.

Part Two

Chapter 17

Greenwich, Connecticut
Spring 1916

I WAS PAPA'S HEIR, AND THE ONLY MEMBER OF OUR POST FAMily still alive—the only *true* member of our Post family, though Leila would of course have argued that—who'd had a hand in the founding of the company, and it was time I had a say, even if that meant I had to get creative.

Because I was a woman, and therefore could not sit on the Post board of directors, Eddie would stand in for me at meetings. With Papa gone, we decided to establish a cabinet, an unofficial assemblage of the company's top leadership, and I asked Uncle Cal to become the chairman of the board. My uncle, along with his longtime right-hand man within Post, an honest and friendly man named Colby Chester, would now manage the major decisions that Papa would have previously overseen. Eddie would keep me apprised of matters within the board. Uncle Cal would also seek my counsel and input, I knew, out of respect for Papa and our family, and so I could serve as a leader of the company, albeit in an unofficial capacity.

"I want to be in New York," I announced one morning in early spring. It had taken me years to realize it, and then another while afterward to gather the courage to say it aloud, but there it was; Greenwich did not feel like home. Not to me, anyway. And with Eddie in the city so often during the week, it felt like the right thing for the girls and me to make our primary residence there. And so, with my assurances that we'd keep The Boulders for summertime and weekends and other extended visits, Eddie begrudgingly agreed.

Because Eddie wanted space and a yard, we bought a brownstone on Ninety-second Street, in the posh Upper East Side quarter nicknamed Millionaire's Row. I was content to accommodate this wish, as the neighborhood was less heavily trafficked than farther downtown, and we had a spacious garden for the girls to play in with their new puppy, Woofie, who shadowed them everywhere. We put in a rose garden as well as a small circle for the children to ride their bicycles. Our neighbors were the Astors, the Carnegies, the Woolworths, the Carlisles, and the Guggenheims—families that had enjoyed wealth for long enough to garner Eddie's approval.

In Manhattan my life settled into a pleasant rhythm. I'd complained in Greenwich that I'd had few friends and few activities to fill my calendar; that was not the case in New York. I met the other women in our neighborhood, befriending them over walks along the East River or play arranged between our girls, and suddenly my days were filled; invitations trickled in for tea with Elsie Rockefeller at the Ritz-Carlton, luncheons with May Carlisle in the big bright room at Delmonico's, where the society dames feasted as much on the gossip overheard from the surrounding tables as they did on the tiered plates of oysters and smoked salmon. Dinner at the Metropolitan Club with Edna Woolworth and Consuelo Vanderbilt. There was always another art gallery opening or some traveling exhibition that could not be missed. Woofie and I would accompany the girls when they went horseback riding along Central Park's Bridle Path or else to feed the ducks in the lake. There were outings to the shops along Central Park and Fifth Avenue or visits to the glittering counters of Tiffany and Cartier.

Manhattan evenings, too, unfurled with endless variety. Banquets sparkling with crystal and silver at the Savoy. Dances in the grand ballroom of the Waldorf-Astoria, with its soaring ceilings and tiered balconies. Galas at the Plaza where the women ogled one another's diamonds and the men compared notes on stocks, golf, and real estate. Broadway's Great White Way ablaze at all hours, performances along Theater Row, and the new behemoths of the Public Library, Metropolitan Opera House, the Olympia, and Carnegie Hall rising up from the wide, noisy avenues.

Whereas I found it all to be dazzling and wonderfully diverting, Eddie found it all to be a bit flashy—and he wasn't wrong. The patrons of these locales and the company we kept at these events were largely what my husband called "new money," families that had made their millions in just the previous generation in railroads or the banks of Wall Street, or by finding gold or iron out west. Eddie, a stolid scion of the Old Guard, looked down on this newer, brighter, faster world.

But I couldn't help but see the hypocrisy in his criticisms. "Money coming from Wall Street or gold mines, what a faux pas," I said, responding to Ed's most recent grumble as we sat side by side in the back seat of our car. It was a dark winter night, but the scene before us was dazzlingly bright, with theater façades aglow and streetlamps casting a flickering halo over the throngs of people who darted along the sidewalks, to and from dinners, shows, concerts. We were being driven from our townhouse to the opera. "The only thing worse would be money coming from midwestern cereal factories." I shuddered into my fur stole of pristine cream-colored mink and then flashed my husband a wry smile.

Ed looked out the car window and ignored the comment, just as I largely ignored his gripes against anyone whose blood was not of the purest blue. I could have reminded him that our *new money,* though it came from cereal and from farther west than the Hudson River, financed our full-time staffs. Our beautiful mansion in Manhattan with its soaring ceilings and crystal chandeliers. Our sprawling estate in Greenwich with our stables, tennis courts, and golf course. The girls' expensive tutors and his late nights at his clubs filled with card games and cocktails. Even this new Rolls-Royce in which he now sat beside me, scowling.

❋

THE NEXT MORNING I received my new friends Edna Woolworth and May Carlisle in the sunlit breakfast room of my Upper East Side mansion. Over tea, Edna filled us in on the plans for her upcoming wedding. She was marrying a man named Frank Hutton who was kind and well liked, even though he was—shudder to say it aloud—new money. I'd met Frank with Edna several times at the theater and dinner parties and had instantly warmed to his open smile and approachable demeanor.

"This blessed event has gobbled up all of my time and attention," Edna said, taking a demure sip from one of my Sèvres porcelain teacups. "I am so looking forward to having it behind me. Though"—she lowered the cup to the saucer and her gaze with it—"I can't imagine what I will do when it's over."

"Sleep," I said.

"If your new husband allows that," May quipped. We all laughed. May scooped herself another serving of sugared strawberries.

"I do mean it, though," Edna said after a moment. She looked at me, sitting up prim as a rose. "Right now the details of arranging the wedding, ordering the trousseau, and setting up the household consume me all day," she said. "What . . . what do wives do? After they are married and settled? To . . . to fill their time?"

As if on cue, the ormolu clock on my mantel chimed. Just beyond the tasteful wooden doors of the room in which we sat, a servant was cleaning dishes in the kitchen, and we heard the muffled sounds of the busy staff, reminding us that household chores, though seemingly endless, were certainly not among *our* requisite daily activities. I reached across the table and took Edna's hand in my own. "I understand your meaning perfectly well, Edna, my dear," I said. "Tea with you ladies is lovely, of course. Shopping on Fifth Avenue is nice. But . . . there's got to be something more, right?"

A faint smile curled Edna's lips upward. I went on: "How about this, Edna? Once you are through with the wedding and happily settled in as Mrs. Hutton, you will join me and May. We will throw ourselves into some purpose, ladies. A new hospital, perhaps? A school? There just has to be . . ." I glanced around the lovely room once more, heard a peal of laughter from a maid in my kitchen. "I know that we'll find some important purpose."

I COULD HAVE cursed those words when the news ripped across Manhattan only a few weeks later: war had crossed the Atlantic Ocean in the form of sinister German U-boats and an underhanded telegram to our neighbor Mexico. Armed conflict was washing ashore on American soil. And not just any war: they were calling it the Great War.

For several years I'd felt a stubborn niggling within; I'd yearned for *purpose,* to use my wealth to serve a cause larger than myself, and suddenly here it was—a worldwide war that had already claimed millions in Europe and now threatened to steal American lives as well. I'd craved some meaningful mission, and it looked as though the mission had come, and so I threw myself into work with a drive and a passion that surprised even me.

Overnight, America was forced to change and adapt to the overwhelming reality of war, and so the Post Cereal Company would do the same, I decided. The federal government now needed to feed and support a wartime army, and to do so, they would require much of the country's food materials. This meant that wheat, oats, corn, grains—the very ingredients that we needed in order to make our bestselling cereals and drinks—were no longer available to us.

This was terrible for the Post Cereal Company, and either Uncle Cal or Colby Chester called me several times a week, predicting that the new rules would ruin us. "I swear, Marjorie, our storehouses will be empty by the end of the year," my uncle declared. Rarely in my life had I heard this kindly man sounding so ruffled. He shared his brother's—my daddy's—optimism. But I could hear the tremor in his voice, carrying all the way from Battle Creek to Manhattan.

I frowned as I stared out my wide window, looking down at a Ninety-second Street draped in American flags. "Well, Uncle Cal, if America is changing with the war, then the Post Cereal Company will have to do the same."

"What do you mean, Budgie?" my uncle asked, slipping in my daddy's old nickname for me.

I smiled, pausing a moment before I answered: "We will need to try cooking with new materials. The soldiers need to eat, but America's fields are as fertile as ever. I don't see why we can't make this work. Let's get word to the board: we need to come up with new products and substitute recipes. Kafir, nuts, maize. We will raise our own storehouses and mills; we'll grind our own corn. We won't throw anything out or allow anything to go to waste. Stuff that can't be used for our cereals, we'll use it to make animal feed."

An audible exhale on the other end of the telephone line. My uncle's voice sounded less harried when at last he spoke: "You know something, Marjorie?"

"What's that, Uncle Cal?"

"Your daddy earned his success because he never let anything—or anybody—get in his way. You are his daughter. And you're absolutely right."

I drew in a quick pull of air, noticing the way my chest seized.

"I'll tell the board about your ideas," my uncle went on. "But it sure is a shame that you can't tell them yourself. It'll be your smarts, after all, that will keep us afloat."

There was work to be done closer to home, too, right there in the city where I'd chosen to raise our girls. I'd tossed out to Edna the idea of supporting a hospital, and now I found my chance to do something even better—becoming a volunteer at the Red Cross in Midtown. I went there every week and helped pack up surgical supplies, balance the ledgers with the donations that poured in, and roll gauze. Any free time that I had while sitting with the girls in the evenings beside the radio or in the mornings as I had my hair brushed and set, I'd knit socks, gloves, and caps for our soldiers overseas.

That spring found me working harder than I ever had in my life, and I was happier than I'd been in years, as well. Perhaps my sense of satisfaction came from Uncle Cal's gentle but sure words of support. Perhaps it was kindled by the smiles of the Red Cross nurses I came to know, the women who served with quiet but capable expertise. Perhaps it was from the lively spirits of the two strong young girls I was raising.

In those busy but meaningful days, I began to understand, truly, the fierce and formidable power of women. Though we could not enlist and take up arms, I felt that I, and the many women around me, could have a direct hand in supporting this war abroad and keeping this country free at home. Though I could not vote for the president, though I could not even sit on the board of the company that bore my family's name, I began to hope that, by the time my girls were older, these facts might change.

* * *

Late May found Eddie, the girls, and me back in Greenwich for a quick weekend trip. They were giving an early summer dance that night at the club, and so Eddie and I set out for the evening, leaving the girls at home with Pearcie for their supper and bedtime.

A waiter approached our dinner table a few hours into the party. "Mr. Close? Mrs. Close?"

"Yes?" Eddie lowered his glass of gin, seeming to note, as I did, the man's tense expression.

"We've had an urgent telephone call from The Boulders. Your auto is being brought round to the front. It seems . . . a fire . . ."

Eddie and I bolted out of our seats. "The girls," I groaned.

"To the car," Eddie said, the tails of his coat flapping as his long-legged stride made directly for the nearest clubhouse door.

Our car raced along the dark country road, our chauffeur slowing only once we arrived back home to see The Boulders roiling in orange flames and smoke. "Dear God," Eddie gasped. I didn't wait for the driver or my husband to open my door, but grabbed my long skirts in my fists and charged directly into the melee.

The firemen had already arrived. I nearly collapsed in relief when I saw where Adelaide and Eleanor stood on the lawn, their little bodies huddled against Pearcie, shivering in their white nightgowns. Woofie sat dutifully between the girls, and he barked as I charged toward them. "Girls!" I pulled them into my arms, feeling the trembling of their soft bodies.

"Mother!" They had been crying. I pulled back to examine them from top to bottom; they were unharmed—but terrified.

Beyond them, the scene was chaos: the usually pristine lawn was littered with debris, a small mob of inquisitive neighbors watching as the shouting firemen scaled the three stories of our flame-licked house. Eddie was talking to someone, a neighbor whose face I recognized but whose name I couldn't recall. I blinked, my eyes watering from smoke and shock as I tried to make sense of the mess around us. "Mrs. Close." The chief of the firemen came toward me where I stood with the girls.

"What happened?" I asked the man, turning from the mayhem to look into his bloodshot eyes.

"Everyone is out and safe."

"All the staff? The entire servants' quarters?"

"All accounted for, ma'am."

"Thank goodness," I said, offering a weak nod. "And thank you." I breathed in a gulp of the ashy night air and then immediately regretted it as a cough racked my frame. Once I'd cleared my throat, I simply stared, my focus blurred by my watering eyes, by the scrim of warm smoke that hung all around us, by the dazed, helpless feeling that filled me. "But the house . . ." I didn't need to complete the sentence. The house was destroyed. Especially my daddy's end, which looked like it was taking the worst of the flames.

"It was an electrical explosion," the fireman explained, pulling my focus back with his hoarse voice. "Defective wiring in the master suite, from the looks of it."

I met Ed's eyes across the lawn as the words settled over me. *Defective wiring in the master suite.* All the money in the world—the fortune required to amass antique furniture and hand-painted frescoes and every custom comfort—and yet my beautiful mansion had been built on botched wiring. I could have laughed at the cruel, scorching irony of it.

But before I could laugh, I began to cough. The crowd around us had grown, and several people now looked at me in concern. I avoided their stares; I could barely stomach the thought of meeting the eyes of my stunned neighbors. "Oh, Marjorie, my dear girl." A familiar voice: I turned and saw the earnest face of my friend Elsie Rockefeller, who stood among the group of observers. "What a horror. I am so terribly sorry." With that, Elsie leaned forward and picked up the nearest piece of debris that littered my lawn. I gasped—it was a piece of lingerie, an article from my bridal trousseau. Just one of the hundreds of personal items lying scattershot on the grass, on full display for anyone to see, along with brassieres and corsets, lace slips and stockings.

Inside the burning frame of the house, firemen were shooting their hoses and vaulting our precious personal items through the shattered windows as if they were bailing a sinking ship—our dinner china, Eleanor's baby portrait, my jewelry, Adelaide's dresses. It all came falling from the sky, landing all around us. I leaned over and with quivering fingers picked up one of the many letters from Papa that I had saved. Beside that were the singed remnants of an old family photograph from Battle Creek, Mother and Papa standing behind me on what looked to be my fifth birthday.

The firemen were valiant, but within hours, The Boulders was nothing more than a pile of ash and scorched beams. And what of my life in Greenwich? What was there to rebuild? Mornings on the lawn sipping iced lemonade, watching the men play golf, gossiping about people and then seeing those same people that evening for dancing and cocktails at the country club—why rebuild for more of that? It felt futile to put all of that back in order. Papa had planned this house during the collapse of his own marriage; he'd intended for it to be a home that he and I would enjoy together, and that had never happened. Then it had been intended as the home where I could start my own family as a happy bride. But had I ever been truly happy at The Boulders? It was like the firefighter had said: the wiring there had been bad from the start.

Chapter 18

New York City
Summer 1917

I WOULD NOT BUDGE, AND I WOULD NOT HEAR EDDIE'S SUGgestions to the contrary: I sold The Boulders property, and we made the mansion on Ninety-second Street our home. If my husband wanted space for the children to run and greenery to offset the commotion of city life, then space and greenery we could arrange. I bought the home next door and connected the two properties so that we had ample space both indoors and outdoors. With the added lot, we doubled the size of our garden, and the girls enjoyed roaming, climbing the small trees and digging in the dirt until their fingernails and petticoats turned a nice, filthy brown.

Refusing to lose any more time in regretting the loss of so many priceless and personal treasures that had gone up in smoke at The Boulders, I threw myself into refurbishing and decorating our New York City home. I ordered all new furniture for our family living rooms, custom from Paris. I found antique chandeliers and Gobelins tapestries to brighten the dark-paneled walls. I purchased cheerful Sèvres and Limoges porcelain, antique ormolu mantel clocks, and rich hand-carved end-tables topped with marble.

"I just hope it's not . . . Only, I would hate for it to seem . . . gaudy." That was the way Eddie reacted when I showed him a new suite of Louis XVI oak chairs and their matching table, freshly arrived at the house. With the help of several footmen, I was excitedly arranging them among the settee and sofa pieces in our drawing room. I shrugged off the barb; it would have been just as easy for me to retort that his family would never have been able to afford half of these gaudy pieces, regardless of their old Knickerbocker name, but what was the point? I had stopped agonizing over his approval, probably because I sensed that I would never get it. At least, not without giving up so many of the pieces of myself that I was determined to hold on to. And since we had lost so much in the fire out at The Boulders, I did not see the harm in replenishing our Manhattan home with the sort of timeless pieces that would make me feel happy and comfortable.

And besides, unlike in Greenwich, in Manhattan I was beginning to enjoy the warmth and favor of friends of my own. Edna Woolworth Hutton had become a dear friend. May Carlisle and Alice Roosevelt had become regular companions for tea and gossip. Even the Rockefeller and Vanderbilt ladies—perhaps remembering that their own clans had been dubbed "new money interlopers" just a few decades prior—consistently offered me their steady, even if a bit reserved, esteem when I saw them about town, which was often.

Though the Great War had already encroached on our lives through the changes we'd weathered at the Post Cereal Company, and through the volunteer work I'd taken on with the Red Cross, it touched us even closer to home when Eddie got called up. "France," he said, his features ashen as he broke the news to me. It was a clear spring afternoon, and I'd been surprised to see my husband return home so early from his office. He had heard just hours earlier: he'd be heading to the European front.

I shuddered as I absorbed the news. I'd read about the horrors of the French battlefields. Total war, they called it. Battles in far-off places with foreign names like the Somme, the Marne, Verdun—conflicts that had resulted in little land gain for either side but death tolls too staggering to fathom. I could not envision Ed in a filthy, rat-infested trench. I reached for him and took his hand in mine, noting, as I did so, that it felt cold. We may not have enjoyed the most tender of affections in recent years, he and I, but he was still my husband. Father to Adelaide and Eleanor. And now we would be forced to send him off to war.

Ed would go quietly and dutifully, that much I knew, no matter how he felt inwardly. He didn't share his private thoughts or feelings with me in the weeks leading up to his departure. But for as long as I'd known him, Ed Close had been a man who minded above all else how things were done. And when war broke out, able-bodied young men were called up to serve, and they went. That was how things were done. So that was what Edward Close would do.

I was almost envious that my husband had been called to the conflict. Not of the rat-infested trenches, the thickets of barbed wire. But I did still feel that unquenched yearning within, that pull to do something more. To feel that I had some worthy and guiding meaning to my life. I'd felt this way for a while, but now, with the war on and my husband bound to join the effort, the feeling piqued with a new potency: there had to be more to life than redecorating a drawing room and fitting my daughters for expensive new riding skirts. It rankled, equal parts restlessness and a vague droning of guilt; I saw myself as energetic and capable, and yet useless.

Daddy had never raised me to believe that, because I was a woman, my life would simply be that of a society hostess, with a prize opera box and a full dance card at the most exclusive galas. In fact, he'd always made it clear that he had quite the opposite in mind for me. And yet here was the plain truth of it: I couldn't enlist; I couldn't vote; I couldn't even run my family's company. But there had to be some way that I could use my energy and my wealth for good.

So I marched to the Midtown Red Cross office and declared myself ready to assist their efforts in a larger way. "What do you most need?" I asked.

I saw the head nurse's eyes go wide, first with excitement and then with relief. "Hospitals," she declared after a brief, thoughtful pause. "We are in desperate need of hospitals, Mrs. Close. Not here. But over there."

I swallowed. She wished for me to go to Europe?

"Not that you need to be there," she hastened to add, perhaps reading the confusion on my face. "But you could support the medical care."

I drew in a breath, relieved that Adelaide and Eleanor would not need to bid farewell to both their mother and their father. And then I nodded. "Well then, let's get to work." I resolved, with the Red Cross's input, that I would finance a hospital close to the worst battlefields—in France, because that was where so many of our American soldiers were being sent, including the father of my two daughters.

Chapter 19

New York City
Summer 1917

IT WAS A CLOUDLESS, STIFLING-HOT AFTERNOON IN LATE JULY, and I stood with my two girls on the dockside of New York Harbor, Eleanor and Adelaide huddling close to my skirts as so many uniformed men shuffled past. Eddie's massive transport vessel bobbed before us, its exterior painted in blue gray to camouflage its passage through German-patrolled waters. Eddie would be crossing the Atlantic to France aboard the SS *Saratoga,* and so would my new traveling hospital and its fresh staff, a venture that had cost me nearly $100,000. I was funding not only the facilities and medical equipment but also the personnel, and so scores of nurses, physicians, and other staff were boarding the SS *Saratoga* along with my husband and the troops.

Eddie scooped our girls up into one final hug. His pale eyes blinked rapidly, perhaps fighting back tears, but he forced a taut smile as he turned toward me. "I'd ask you to take care of things while I'm gone, Marjorie, but I know you will."

I opened my arms, wrapping them around Eddie as he continued to hold our girls. "We will miss Daddy, won't we, girls?" I asked. We held our tight family huddle for a long moment as all around us a noisy, chaotic scene unfurled: the steady clomp of boots up the gangplank, the seagulls arcing down and up in irregular loops, family members offering final tearful farewells as stoic officers urged the men to hoist their denim sacks and get moving. I fixed Eddie with a long, silent look and planted a final peck on his clean-shaven cheek. "I'll take care of our girls, Eddie. You take care of yourself." A barely perceptible dip of his chin, a nod, and then he stood to his full height, his golden hair catching the glint of the morning's bright sunlight as he winked down at Adelaide and Eleanor.

With one low, droning whistle, Eddie's ship steamed away from the docks and out toward the open water, gliding away from hundreds of waving hands and fluttering flags, plying its path through the harbor toward the Statue of Liberty and the wide blue ocean and, beyond that, a bleeding continent.

A few days later, a muffled knock at my bedroom door stirred me from deep sleep. "Yes?" I blinked, groggy. Was it Adelaide, eager to crawl into bed with me after a bad dream? Or Eleanor, worried about her father? No, it was my household secretary. "What is it?" I asked, the surprise evident in my woolly voice.

"News of the *Saratoga,* Mrs. Close."

I sat up ramrod straight in bed, no longer groggy. "Eddie?"

"Mr. Close is safe, ma'am," the young woman said, her voice barely a whisper in the dark bedroom. "But there's been a . . . rather an unfortunate occurrence."

I hopped from bed, not caring that the woman was seeing me in my state of undress as I fumbled to wrap my dressing robe around myself.

"The *Saratoga* was struck by another American ship," she said. "It was an accident. Everyone aboard made it safely to the lifeboats, but the ship . . . well, it sank, ma'am."

"Goodness." I sighed. "And what about all of the medical equipment?"

"Gone, Mrs. Close. I'm sorry to say, but when the ship sank, so did everything on board."

I sat down on the bed with a loud exhale. I was dizzy with relief that Eddie and the rest of the passengers had been saved, of course. Eddie would continue on to France, I presumed, as originally planned. But nearly a hundred thousand dollars' worth of medical materials, the entire outfit for a much-needed war hospital, was drifting at that very minute toward the bottom of the Atlantic.

The secretary hovered at the threshold of my bedroom, awaiting some order from me, no doubt. After a moment I stood back up, noticing how my eyes had adjusted to the darkness of the room. My voice was steeled with resolve as I said, "Then we will send another ship. I'll tell my accountants to approve the funds immediately. We're not giving up. Not when others are giving their lives for the cause."

"Yes, ma'am," the secretary said. "Will . . . will that be all?"

"Yes. Now, you try and get some sleep. I'll do the same. We can sort all this out tomorrow."

"Yes, ma'am. Thank you." She left the room with a quiet click of the door.

The following week, a fresh boatload of hospital provisions was bound across the Atlantic. I saw the SS *Finland* off with a very urgent entreaty that the crew might exercise all caution to arrive safely. And yet, it wasn't a friendly mishap this time that threatened to derail my efforts but those horrid German U-boats. I'd heard how the enemy haunted the ports of Europe, wolf packs prowling the deep, and they found the *Finland* just as the ship was entering French waters. But for the intervention of some nearby Allied battleships who fought off the submarines and escorted the *Finland* safely to shore, I would have lost another ship's worth of critical lifesaving supplies.

I whooped with glee and relief when the next telegram came in, this one informing me that all of my cargo and hospital personnel had arrived safely to Savenay, France. Within weeks my white stone hospital, previously a school building and now Red Cross Base Eight, was open and ready to start saving Allied lives.

Ed wrote regularly and reassured me that he was safe. He disliked the weather and the food, and he longed for the girls, but his encampment was far from the worst of the front. That was the gist of what he wrote, perhaps because that was all that was likely to make it past the censors. Back home, I'd never been so busy—or so content. Under Uncle Cal and Colby Chester's stewardship, my plan for the Post Cereal Company to explore alternative recipes and ingredients was seeing marked success, and we had recovered our initial wartime losses. While Eddie was serving in France, neither Uncle Cal nor Colby Chester had to keep up the pretense that their Post Cereal Company dealings were with my husband. Now, as Ed's surrogate, I could deal directly with them, and I loved it.

My Red Cross hospital was quickly recognized as a hugely necessary and well-run venture, and I made the staff know through my regular letters and telegrams that I intended to support them until the war was over. We steadily expanded to meet the growing need for care throughout France, and my contacts who worked at the Red Cross in Manhattan informed me that it was soon their biggest medical base in Europe.

⁂

"NOW, GIRLS, LISTEN to me. A tablespoon of this cod liver oil for each of you, and then I promise you can get back to your playing."

"Mother, not that horrible stuff again!" Eleanor wrung her hands, the bow in her golden curls askew, her cheeks flushed from her constant running and leaping.

"Yes, this horrible stuff again," I said, attempting a stern tone as I poured the thick golden liquid onto a spoon and stared down at my two girls before me. "As if the Great War isn't terrible enough for this world, now we have the Spanish flu killing millions. And thousands right here in New York City. The doctors all tell me it's absolutely critical that you take your cod liver oil. We all must."

Adelaide, my older girl, dutifully accepted a spoonful, grimacing but swallowing nonetheless. "There's a good girl," I said, nodding approvingly. Adelaide, at nearly ten, was tall like her father and willowy in her build, with thoughtful blue eyes and dark blond hair. She was a lovely girl but quiet and mature beyond her years, and I found it hard to pull a smile to her lips or any lighthearted banter from her.

Eleanor was the opposite. I often wondered if perhaps my second daughter was a throwback to my father in her cheerful self-confidence and her ability to make friends in any room. "But this stuff makes me burp. And the burps taste like fish. Fish breath, fish breath! Step right up for your fish breath!" Eleanor hollered.

"Eleanor Close, you mind your manners!" I chided, biting my cheeks to prevent my smile. Eleanor pushed her lower lip out in a pout, looking to Adelaide, who, with a tilt of her chin, urged her younger sister to submit, and eventually, she did. "Good. Now run along. And mind you don't track mud through the entire house," I said. And with that, my girls were off, Eleanor darting ahead as Adelaide skipped behind.

With my role for the Post Cereal Company expanded and my efforts for both the New York Red Cross and my base hospital in France keeping me busy, I had more than enough to fill my hours, but my priority remained my girls, who were budding into young ladies seemingly before my eyes. The girls had a huge home, a nanny who had adored them from birth, and a big oaf of a dog in Woofie, and Eleanor was the self-appointed President of the Mischief Club, always getting in trouble, while Adelaide functioned as her personal attorney, always coming to her defense.

While I had never had a sibling's friendship to enjoy, my daughters were fiercely devoted to each other, and I wanted to ensure that their childhoods were filled with happiness. They had a stable full of ponies and horses, and I indulged them in their desire to take riding lessons in Central Park. Once I saw how their affection for animals extended beyond horses and dogs, I let them establish a miniature menagerie in our large urban backyard; we had ducks, rabbits, kittens, and a koi pond stocked with swirling fish that provided no end of confusion to poor Woofie. There was also a feisty family of pygmy goats, and on cold nights I allowed the girls to bring the babies into bed with them and feed the goat kids from bottles of warm milk.

But it wasn't all laughter and play: the girls had personal tutors to teach them history, math, French, art, literature, dance, and piano. Now that they were old enough, I loved taking them on outings to study the scientific exhibits in the Museum of Natural History or to enjoy musical shows on Broadway or concerts in the splendid Carnegie Hall. Often, after the girls joined me for a musical, they would come home determined to reenact the performances themselves, and so our drawing room would be converted to a makeshift theater, with Woofie, Pearcie, and me playing the part of rapt audience members.

Because the girls were so lively and boisterous, filling the home with the sounds of music and giggly mischief from the moment they sat down to breakfast each morning, it struck me as odd when I returned home to a quiet house one day the following autumn. I'd been out at the Red Cross station all morning, unloading crates of cod liver oil that I'd donated for the nurses to take over to the tenement houses along the East Side of Manhattan. Those neighborhoods, overfilled with immigrants from Italy, Ireland, Hungary, and elsewhere, were facing the contagion of the Spanish flu like a wildfire, and it shattered my heart to hear the stories. Back home, the house was quiet and cool, a sanctuary. I paused as I entered the foyer, handing my shawl to the butler and taking a moment to collect myself, to calm my addled nerves. "Eleanor? Adelaide?" No answer from within. The butler shrugged as if to tell me he was unsure of their whereabouts. "Girls?" My voice echoed throughout the large front hall. "Pearcie?" No reply.

I climbed the broad staircase toward my bedroom. There, at last, I heard muffled giggling. Then the thunder of Woofie's bark. "Adelaide? Eleanor? Where are—" I gasped, following the sound of their riotous laughter into my bathroom, where I found both girls splashing in my bidet, drenched and giggling as if they were having a romp in a garden fountain. "Girls!" I stalked toward them, outraged, but before I could reach them to turn off the faucet, I slipped on the damp marble and went skidding across the room. This only sent Eleanor into further peals of defiant laughter.

Just then Pearcie charged in. "Girls!" she bellowed, taking in the wet, messy scene. I was prepared to turn toward the governess with a stern chiding and a piqued question as to how, precisely, she had let the girls get into such mischief, but I could tell by the woman's expression that she had some reason for her absence. Her face was as flushed as if she had a fever. "What is it, Pearcie?" I asked, slowly rising from the slick floor.

"Mrs. Close, we've—" Just then we heard the clamor outside. Church bells ringing from nearby Holy Trinity. *At this hour?* Then an explosion like gunfire, or perhaps it was fireworks.

"News from Europe, Mrs. Close," Pearcie continued, her voice thick with feeling. "The Great War—it's over at last. We've won."

I looked around the drenched bathroom, suddenly completely unconcerned with the gushing bidet, the slippery tiles, my dripping daughters. The Great War was over. The fight was over, and we had won. Europe would be delivered from the scourge of the kaiser and the worst conflict to tear across its land in a lifetime. Peace would return to its ravaged people. Our American soldiers would come home.

Eddie would be coming home.

It was all such wonderfully welcome news. It was what we had hoped and worked and prayed for since the earliest days of the conflict. Why then, I wondered, did I not feel overjoyed?

Chapter 20

New York City
Fall 1919

"DON'T YOU THINK IT'S A BIT"—EDDIE LOOKED AT ME IN THE mirror's reflection as I sat before it, scrutinizing the rubies on my new earrings, their glimmer on perfect display thanks to my upswept chignon—"I don't know . . . excessive?"

I touched the jewels at my ears. "What? You don't like the rubies?" I turned to face him, my body draped in a lightweight dress of white, a sapphire necklace and matching blue bracelet adding bright bursts of color. These earrings were the final touch to make my attire red, white, and blue.

"No, I mean outside." Eddie gestured toward the window and the garden beyond. "The bleachers you've had erected in our backyard."

I tilted my head sideways, pulling my eyes from him. "More than four million young men served over there, including my husband. Excessive?" I shrugged. "Perhaps. But the war is won, and you deserve a grand party."

I looked at Eddie. He was inspecting his own appearance in the full-length mirror, and I rose to cross the room to him. I touched the decoration on his jacket lapel, awarded to my husband by the French Legion of Honor for his service. He raised his hand and gently nudged me away, disinterested in my adjustments. "It's not *my* grand party," he said. "I think you like any excuse to put on a lavish affair." With that, my husband offered me a tepid smile and left the room.

The Great War had ended months prior, and now our victorious General Pershing was back home in the States and leading his army on a grand parade, starting at the northern end of Manhattan and marching all the way to Washington Square Park. Because we could see the spectacle from our garden, I'd had my landscapers build a raised platform where we would gather and watch the festivities. Coloring my garden were fresh-clipped heaps of red roses, arranged throughout the space in the shape of red crosses to support our wartime work. But while peace had been restored to war-ravaged Europe, the détente that hovered over our home felt fragile.

It was odd: my husband and I rarely raised our voices or traded harsh words. If anything, that might have been preferable. The discord between us was more of a widening chasm, resulting from the increasingly obvious fact that we shared so very little in common. There was no warmth or tenderness, no laughter or understanding. I shuddered at the fact that lately, I was reminded more and more of the frosty remoteness that I'd spent so much of my childhood observing and mediating between Mother and Papa.

And though my husband was home from war, *home* meant something very different to him than it did to me. Eddie wanted to be in Greenwich; I was insistent that we remain in Manhattan. He wanted a wife who was happy to sit at home and graciously receive a set rotation of society ladies in her drawing room, or else to step out to visit with those very same ladies for tea or luncheon; he did not want a wife who was constantly hurrying out the door for work at the Red Cross or some meeting to fundraise for the immigrant-aid societies or Spanish flu relief efforts. And he certainly did not want a wife who supported the Women's Suffrage movement. Being too outspoken on anything rankled Ed Close, but a social cause as controversial and divisive as the women's right to vote was particularly out of the question. "Marjorie, it's just not how things are done," he'd said after he'd come home from Europe and discovered, to his horror, that his wife had become a supporter of the suffragettes during his absence, one whom President Woodrow Wilson knew of by name.

It's just not how things are done.

"According to whom?" I'd asked, not bothering to hide my pique, and he'd simply shaken his head and left the room. Perhaps to pour himself a drink. Or perhaps feeling as weary of our distance, of our misunderstandings, as I myself felt.

But I could no longer listen to that refrain without finding it very difficult not to grimace. The Eddie with whom I'd fallen in love had been tall and handsome, with smiling blue eyes and immaculate manners. He'd been gallant and kindly, with an understated charm and a way of looking at me that made my heart tip lopsided. Perhaps Eddie was still all of those things. I knew he was still a good man. But I was no longer the timid, sheltered teenage girl whom he'd first asked to dance during her high school summer break. I was no longer a girl at all—the fact of the matter was that now I was a woman, and as I'd grown up, our love had grown cold.

For a while I considered that perhaps we should simply live apart, so that we could spare everyone the pain and scandal and maybe even both get what we wanted. Ed could be in Greenwich where he wanted to be; I'd stay with the girls in New York. Since his work so often brought him into the city, he'd get to see them regularly. It had been the arrangement my parents had turned to when they found they could no longer live together.

But then, considering that, I'd feel my stomach curdle. Such a course was untenable, a fool's delusion. It had been the arrangement my parents had turned to indeed, and look how that had served them; it hadn't truly spared anyone any pain, had it? No, I would not live the way my parents had. I would not simply bide our time in a loveless union, a family in nothing more than name. I would not put our girls through that.

I heard Ed in the next room, asking one of the servants to bring him a gin. Farther away, in the front hall, I could hear the sound of the girls giggling, excited that their friends would be coming over and that there'd be a parade and lemonade and heaps of sweets. I squared my shoulders and glanced in the mirror, giving my appearance one final sweep of scrutiny and bracing to start the party. This was a day for celebrating, and I would not let things between Ed and me cloud our good time.

It was a lovely September day, the mild weather cooperating with our weeks of planning for the garden and doing much to lift my mood. Church bells rang out. Crowds had gathered by the thousands to line the entirety of the parade route. As my guests filed in, their smiles brightened by the good weather and the excitement of the parade, my servants milled throughout the garden, offering chilled champagne and small bites of smoked salmon and deviled eggs.

I'd invited May Carlisle, Elsie Rockefeller, the Astors, the Vanderbilts, and I greeted my guests cheerfully. My smile went even wider as I saw my friend Edna Woolworth Hutton arrive with her husband, Frank. Beside them entered another couple, a pair so smartly dressed that they looked as though they'd just stepped out of a fashion advertisement. "Marjorie, dear, please meet my darling sister-in-law, Blanche Hutton."

I looked into the pretty face of a brunette with high cheekbones and wide, dark eyes. "Blanche, thank you for coming. It's lovely to meet you."

"And you, Mrs. Close," the woman replied, the smell of her fresh floral perfume filling the air around us. "I've heard such wonderful things from Edna."

I turned back toward my friend and Edna smiled, then she turned with a droll look toward Blanche's husband, saying, "And this is Frank's brother, my rogue of a brother-in-law, Edward Hutton."

I turned to the woman's husband. Another Edward, but I couldn't hold that against him. "Delighted you could join as well, Mr. Hutton."

"Somebody had to hold Blanche's purse for her," Edward Hutton replied, winking at me, and I found myself shifting on my feet. As Edward Hutton wove his arm gently around his wife's narrow waist, pulling her close with a gesture of casual, unselfconscious intimacy—a gesture that Ed Close would never have dared display in a group setting—I stole a closer look at the man. Edward Hutton was undeniably handsome, with a thicker frame than my own Ed's and a straight, strong jaw. His dark blue eyes and light hair were not as fastidiously groomed, but that gave him an ineffably dashing quality.

I swallowed, forcing my gaze back toward the lady at his side, smiling as I searched for some cordial conversational morsel that I might offer her. "Blanche, I truly envy you. I love our Edna. I wish I could call her my sister."

"Oh, I know," Blanche said, blinking her long, dark lashes as she nodded. "I didn't decide to marry Edward until after I'd met his sister-in-law. She made my decision easier."

I laughed, feeling my cheeks grow warm. I had said I was jealous of

Blanche in her choice of sister-in-law, and it was true. But as I took a sip of my cool lemonade, I noticed how it tasted bitter in my mouth. And that was, I realized, because I was also a bit jealous of this woman for the easy warmth and casual caresses that her adoring husband offered her.

After my parade party, I stayed home to oversee the dismantling of the stands, directing the servants and chatting with the girls before their bedtime. Eddie went out with some of his Columbia friends to continue the celebrations. I was not awake when he returned home, nor did I know what time that was. We had not shared a bedroom since his return from France.

The next morning, I joined him at breakfast. I noticed how his features sagged, pale and weary, no doubt made so by a night of countless gins and scotches. How, as he sipped his coffee, the china cup trembled in his unsteady hands. I glowered. *Should I say something?* Oh, but what was the point? I wasn't going to change Ed Close, no more than I was going to allow Ed Close to change me. Once more, I could not help but think back to the slow and winnowing decay of my parents' union. How I had always been put squarely in between them. And then, when they had finally split, I had been a young woman about to embark on my own life and my own romantic relationship—it had been the absolute worst time to see their marriage, and my family, fall apart.

I would not do that to my own girls. I would not dwell in resigned apathy, no longer feeling that words even mattered. I would not ask us all to endure years of frosty unhappiness—a false peace—not when I already knew where it was headed. I'd cut it off now, while they were young and I could protect them.

Divorce. I'd once been so shattered by the word. So cowed by how big and ruinous it had seemed. And yet, here I was, choosing it for myself. For our family. That morning, not touching my breakfast, I sucked in a long gulp of fortifying breath, and I told Ed Close that our marriage was over.

Sadly, quietly, but with his cool, somber, well-bred dignity, he agreed. He'd known, just as I had, that this was coming. He packed up a suitcase and he and his valet left, checking in to a suite at his club. Now it was up to our attorneys to work out the details.

I willingly offered him a generous sum in parting. Was it to assuage my own guilt? Perhaps. I would keep my home with the girls in New York. "Where will you go?" I asked him, but I already knew the answer. He would finally be able to return to Connecticut. I felt no pang of envy at his taking that territory as his own; Greenwich had always been Eddie's domain, the domain of Mrs. Edward Close. I was Miss Post once more.

Nevertheless, it did sting when I heard, first through my daughters and then even more through the gossip of the society pages, how quickly Ed began stepping out with someone else. We'd only just signed the attorneys' papers, but already the newspapers were filled with the details. Who was this new lady in my ex-husband's life? Her name was Elizabeth Taliaferro, and she was a brown-eyed beauty from Texas. *Texas!* I could not help but gasp, recalling the image of my husband sitting on a cactus, groaning: *My God, why did I ever agree to this?*

My daughters met this lady after a weekend trip to their father's in Connecticut, and they reported back that Miss Taliaferro had been perfectly nice, arriving for the introduction with sweets and a new doll for each. Well then, she seemed serious about Ed, I noted, if she was also willing to pay court to his eleven- and nine-year-old daughters. I smiled good-naturedly as they told me about her, as they giggled about the way that their father had held her hand when they walked as a foursome down the sidewalk in Greenwich, on their way from the Episcopal church toward Sunday brunch. I was adamant that my pain did not become theirs.

I was stunned anew when, after the briefest of courtships, Adelaide informed me over the telephone that her father had become engaged to this Miss Taliaferro. It hadn't served him well the last time, marrying a girl he'd known so briefly. *I'd* certainly learned my lesson, but it seemed that he had not.

Oh well, I wished him nothing but happiness in his second time through. He was, after all, always going to be the father of my two girls. And he was a good man, Ed Close, even if not the man for me.

But I was even more determined than before to avoid Greenwich. The new Mrs. Close would no doubt be presiding over society out there in no time. *Just as well,* I thought. I, Miss Post, had never liked it there. I had considered the destruction of The Boulders to be a sort of blessing.

Botched wiring from the start—in the house, in the marriage. I was building anew and excited to do so. The end of the marriage even brought with it a feeling of relief, of a burden sloughed off. Now I answered only to myself, and as myself. I didn't see any appeal to remarrying. That was what I believed. That was what I told myself. Oh, how wrong I was.

Chapter 21

Palm Beach, Florida
Winter 1919

A WARM WINTER BREEZE RIPPLED THE PALM TREES, CARRYING with it the scent of saltwater and perfume as Edna approached me with a tall, good-looking man by her side. I could see through the dim light of the stars overhead and the lanterns strung along the deck of the yacht on which we stood that it was not her husband, Frank Hutton, though the resemblance was immediately noticeable.

Edna greeted me with a smile as warm and balmy as the night air. "Marjorie, my dear, you remember my brother-in-law, Ed Hutton?"

Ed Hutton. I knew the name, and hearing it immediately quickened my pulse. *Ed Hutton*. I narrowed my eyes to see him better and noted that, yes, he was the man I'd met at my victory party in New York City. The day of General Pershing's parade. I summoned a look of cool calm as I extended my ungloved hand in greeting. "Of course. Lovely to see you again, Mr. Hutton." *Blanche,* I recalled in that instant. His beautiful brunette wife was named Blanche.

Ed Hutton brought my hand to his lips, rippling my skin with gooseflesh as his light eyes fixed on mine and he said, "And you, Mrs. Close."

I winced at the name. "Now it's just Miss. Post. Or better still, Marjorie."

Edward Hutton cocked a golden-blond eyebrow.

"Ah, yes. You've both become unattached since our last meeting," Edna interjected, her tone as light and airy as if she were remarking on the state of the weather. And yet, with that one statement, my entire body stirred;

the night was a warm one, but I found I was suddenly shivering. Just then Edna's gaze slid across the large yacht. "Oh, excuse me, I need a refill on my champagne." Off she went.

You've both become unattached since our last meeting.

How convenient, I thought. Both Edna's quick exit and the revelation she'd just dropped between us. Ed Hutton, no longer married. But I was stunned to hear it: Blanche Hutton had seemed like a lovely enough woman. And they'd seemed happy on the afternoon through which I'd watched their warm interactions. Had we both braved the specter of social banishment to go through with divorces?

"Sadly, my wife is no longer with us," Ed said, perhaps reading the confusion on my face. His charming smile flickered momentarily, a candle sputtering in a breeze.

No longer with us? But then, Ed Hutton was a widower?

He continued: "The Spanish influenza."

I brought my hand to my mouth. "Oh, Mr. Hutton, I am so sorry to hear it." And I was. As attracted as I was to the man, I would never have wished such a fate on anyone, that flu that had cost more lives than even the Great War, reaping its harvest from poor and privileged alike.

"It has been a difficult year," he said, rocking on his feet.

"I can only imagine."

"At least I have our boy." At that he smiled, the skin around his blue eyes creasing with genuine feeling.

"Then that is a positive." I nodded. "Mr. Hutton—"

"Please, call me Ed."

"I will do nothing of the sort," I answered, and then I saw by the sudden rise of his brow that he was confused by my remark, so I explained further. "I am sorry to say it, but my husband was Ed. My former husband. I don't want another Ed in my life. I'd say my appetite is rather gone for the name."

He leaned close and I breathed in the scent of him, shaving soap mixed with the faint hint of cigars and the brine of the ocean air. I held the boat's railing, suddenly a bit dizzy. I watched his lips as he spoke next, his voice low: "Then call me Ned. Those who are closest to me do so."

"Flattered to be pulled in so quickly to your inner circle," I said.

"Well, I have no interest in being any sort of second serving of Ed for you."

I pressed my hand to my chest with exaggerated gravity. "You, a second serving? Never."

"Speaking of appetite," he said, leaning forward to rest an elbow on the boat railing, "you're the cereal gal, aren't you?"

"Is that what they call me?"

"Oh, they call you all sorts of things."

I tilted my head to the side. "That right?"

"All good things," he said. "Don't you worry."

"Such as?"

"Oh, let me think. Well, beautiful, for one. Intelligent. Charming. Like I said, all good things. And true things."

The blood pounded between my ears as he angled his frame so that the two of us stood facing each other, our bodies nearly touching, our attention fixed squarely between us without a care for anyone else on the deck. Ordinarily my eyes would have skimmed the remainder of my surroundings, looking out for others I might know, but they were locked on the man before me, unwilling to be pulled away. I cocked my head to the side, smiling at him in surprise and delight, and I noticed how his blue-eyed gaze swept my figure, pausing a moment to appreciate the bare skin of my shoulders. I was bronzed from the sun, my hair streaked with wisps of gold. I was thirty-two years old, single, and happier than I'd been in years. Parting ways with Eddie had been without a doubt the right choice. And now Ned Hutton and I stood together on this gently bobbing boat, both of us unattached, and I thought it preposterous that I had told myself I'd never love again.

Our faces were so close that it would have been the easiest thing in the world for our lips to touch. But Ned spoke quietly next: "If I tell you a secret, promise not to rat me out to all these Yanks?"

I nodded.

He leaned even closer, whispering into my ear: "I'm from the Midwest, too."

"Oh?"

"Ohio. Have you ever heard of it?"

"Once or twice."

"Then you're probably the only one here who has."

"Michigan," I said.

"Yes, I know." He fixed me with an appraising grin, and I felt my cheeks grow warmer. Just then, a footman approached bearing a tray of bubbling champagne. Ned took two flutes and offered me one, which I accepted with a clink of cheers. Then he went on: "There's more that we have in common, from what I hear."

"That so?" I asked, taking a sip of the cold drink, feeling the bubbles travel down to my belly and send a burst of giddiness throughout my body. Or perhaps my proximity to Ned Hutton was responsible for that.

He nodded, then said: "My old man passed away when I was young. Ten years old."

"I'm sorry to hear that."

"He left us with nothing," Ned continued.

"That must have been difficult. For your entire family. You especially, being so young."

He shrugged, mumbling a passing "yes," and I noted in silence how we'd both endured tragedy at a young age. The loss of parents, and in his case, the loss of his wife on top of that. Having lost both of my parents by the end of my twenties, I felt that there was a certain strength that couldn't help but be forged through those harshest of life's early fires—and a bond that inevitably resulted between those who'd been burned in that same kiln.

"So I got a job when I was just a youngster, working a mail room. I had to support Mother. I put myself through college and then business studies. I got my first job in a Cincinnati bank. My second in San Francisco. Then after I lived through the earthquake out there, I decided to move to New York City to open up a shop of my own. And now my firm on Wall Street makes millions."

It didn't seem like boasting, the way he said it all. It was simply the truth. He was a self-made man who'd pulled himself up from tragedies and losses with nothing more than his own smarts and grit and determination. He reminded me of another self-made millionaire whom I'd known and loved. He felt, already, familiar, even though this was the first time we'd spoken at any length.

I smiled at Ned, raising my champagne glass and clinking it once more to his. "Well then, here's to you."

He returned my look. "And here's to you."

We each took a sip of our champagne, standing side by side a moment in a silence charged with both excitement and somehow an easy, companionable comfort. The faint lap of the ocean water against the belly of the boat sent us up and down in a lulling, gentle rhythm. *Would it be wrong for him to kiss me, right here, in front of everyone?* I didn't really care.

"Goodness, Marjorie," he said after a moment, his voice pulsing with some deep feeling. "It feels nice to feel good again. What with everything that happened . . . it's been . . . well, it's been quite a year."

I turned to face him again, meeting his blue eyes. He went on, saying, "It was a surprise seeing you here tonight, but I'm glad it happened." He ran a hand through his thick golden hair, looking out over the ocean as he sighed. "How long are you here for?" he asked.

The truth was that I had plans to leave Palm Beach the next weekend—my return train ticket was already booked for New York. But my answer came quickly: "Oh, I'll be here for a few more weeks at least."

Ned Hutton smiled at me. "Me, too," he said, holding me with his gaze. And then, a moment later, he added: "I'd like to see you again, Miss Post."

"I agree," I said. "With all of it." It *had* been a difficult few years for me as well. It had been a surprise to see him there, on that boat, that night. But I was glad I had, and I knew that I wanted to see him again.

I DID NOT leave Palm Beach the next weekend as planned. Nor the weekend after that. I should have been hesitant about falling in love again and even more reluctant to think of marrying again. A divorce was a scandal that few people were willing to invite one time; a second would be unthinkable.

But I did not let that concern me, because, in truth, all I wanted to think about was Ned Hutton. For the next few weeks, as I remained in Palm Beach, I did little else but see Ned. Dinner at The Breakers hotel overlooking the ocean, as the setting sun turned the wispy clouds overhead into rose and sherbet lace. Ned singing me Marion Harris songs as we walked, arms linked, up Worth Avenue. Dancing at Bradley's until my feet hurt and Ned insisted I remove my heels as he carried me home in his arms, giggling and barefoot. He'd taken a suite at the Everglades Club for the winter, and soon enough I all but abandoned my rented villa and decamped to his place. The best nights were the ones when we never left his room at all.

I'd never been intimate with a man before Ed Close, but now that I had decided to go to bed with Ned Hutton, I realized that I'd never in fact been intimate with anyone, ever. There was a closeness with Ned that I'd never known—never even imagined—to be possible with a man. The way Ned loved me, it was as though my body was some delightful gift to be unwrapped and savored. As though my pleasure was his greatest challenge and his only goal. Ed Close had been cool and courteous—Ned was fire, and it was fire that he stoked in me as well. A fire I hadn't previously known existed. With Ned, it was a mad, fast, intoxicating love. Less a choice than a compulsion—I needed to be with Ned Hutton; it was a fact so much larger than anything I had the power or the desire to resist. And Ned, to my dizzying delight, felt exactly the same way about me.

The girls were happily settled in New York with Pearcie and their tutors, so I remained with Ned a few more weeks, until the end of his stay. Finally, as the season came to its close, I decided to rent a private railcar for the journey north from Florida to New York so that we could travel home together, continuing to bask in the rapturous joy of our new and all-consuming love affair even after we'd bidden farewell to those balmy Palm Beach nights. I'd never known rail travel to be so deliciously enjoyable; the only problem was how swiftly it passed.

When our train did roll into Penn Station and we stepped back onto New York ground, as it was time to part ways—Ned toward his rented bachelor apartment in the Plaza hotel and me toward my mansion uptown—we both paused at the threshold of the station. My sleek chauffeured car waited at the curb. "I don't want to say goodbye," I said, feeling ridiculous as I said it, and yet knowing that he'd understand. I'd see him soon—we had plans to dine at Delmonico's the next evening, but already that seemed too far away.

"How about we don't?" he suggested, looking at me as we stood there, our breath misting between our faces. All of late-winter New York City roiled around us, but I didn't hear anything other than those words.

"Don't what?" I asked.

"Don't part ways," he answered, the cloud of his breath merging with mine. "I don't want to. You don't want to. How about you marry me? And then this . . ."—he waved his hands between us—"this never needs to end."

I gasped out my yes. Yes, I would become his wife. Mrs. Edward F. Hutton. I couldn't feel anything but giddy, all-consuming joy—Ned was my happiness after more than a decade of loveless days.

I DIDN'T WANT another church affair, a spectacle for hundreds of guests and grasping journalists. We'd both done that once before, a fact I didn't feel eager to spotlight. So Ned and I exchanged our vows in a private, modest family gathering at my home the following summer, while the girls were off from school and before Ned's son, Halcourt, was due to start his studies at Yale. We ate lunch together immediately afterward and toasted with cake and champagne. Of course the newspapers caught wind of it as soon as we signed the marriage license, and the journals churned the next day with the news of my marriage to the "handsome Wall Street millionaire."

The girls were off to Greenwich shortly after that to spend a few weeks of their summer break with their father, so all I wanted was to enjoy my new husband in peace. We decamped from crowded, sticky Manhattan to Ned's Long Island estate. I loved the calm, easy days out there. We'd sleep late and take our breakfast on trays in bed. By late morning I was outside, wading in the surf, pulling up fish and turtles and small crabs that I brought home and put in bowls of saltwater to keep for the girls. Ned and I went for leisurely horseback rides through the woods surrounding his estate or long walks through the sand. On clear evenings we'd rig up his sailboat and pack a picnic hamper, then go bobbing in the Atlantic surf, making love with nothing but the sweep of the ocean and the summer evening as our backdrop.

Ned's son joined us out there in the final weeks of summer before he was due in New Haven. Halcourt was a dreamboat of a young man, tall and blond just like his father, and I suspected that both of my girls harbored giddy crushes on him, even if he was their stepbrother. I couldn't blame them—he had the same good looks and easy smiles that had pulled me so quickly to his father. If anyone knew how irresistible a force the Hutton charm was, it was I.

I was gloriously in love with Ned and thus very willing to love Halcourt like a son. Just as Ned treated my girls with the warmth of a father. And since Halcourt no longer had a mother in his life, there was no awkwardness for me. I had only ever wanted the two girls, but now I had three children suddenly. That was perfect. In my thirties, I was still young enough to feel vibrant and beautiful with my new husband, and yet I did not feel the need to endure another pregnancy or childbirth.

Ned had whispered to me, in the quiet of our bedroom as we lay blissfully spent and entwined in each other's limbs, that he'd be happy to have another baby. I'd considered it, but I'd quickly decided that it was not what I wanted. I would rather we just enjoyed each other, I told him. Enjoy the growing children we already had, who had matured past the difficult years of infancy and constant, unpredictable needs. With Ned and the three of them, our little family was all I would ever need.

What I *was* interested in was a new project. A new building project, to be specific. Ned's Gold Coast estate was lovely enough, with woods where the fellows could ride and hunt, with a gracious sweep of beachfront and a comfortable enough house. And yet, I was jealous of the fact that Blanche had been this home's first mistress. It was she whom Ned had first carried in his arms across the threshold of what was now our bedroom. She had hosted Thanksgiving at this dining room table and Fourth of July fireworks in the backyard. She had hired this staff and decorated these rooms, and thus, even though Ned gave me no cause to feel anything but absolutely adored and desired as his new wife, I nevertheless felt her presence everywhere. I wanted Ned and me to start fresh, to build together a new home for our new family.

With the help of a New York City broker, I found a generous parcel of lush land on Long Island's North Shore in the town of Brookville. There was not yet a house on the property—which was precisely how I wanted it. I took Ned to walk the forested land one afternoon in that late summer. "How many acres is it?" he asked.

"Just under two hundred. Plenty of woods for you to ride," I said.

"And then some," Ned agreed, looking around. I could see from his face that he liked the spot—the gentle hills, the thick forests, the smell of the nearby ocean, and the clean country air. "But no house," he said, turning to me, weaving his arms around my waist, allowing me to breathe in his scent and go entirely dizzy.

"Leave the house to me," I said.

"Oh?" He cocked an eyebrow. When I nodded, he went on: "A penny for your thoughts, Mrs. Hutton?" and then he laughed, adding, "Or in this case, I'd venture it'll cost quite a few pennies."

"I was thinking a brand-new mansion done in the English country style. A lovely garden, a tennis court, a pool. The beach nearby, of course. We could call it Hillwood."

"Hillwood," Ned said, considering the name a moment before answering: "I like that."

"Good," I said. "Then it's settled."

And just like that, I had my new project.

⁂

IT WAS A golden morning in September, just days before Halcourt and the girls were set to return to their schools, and Ned walked with his son toward the stables. "How about we ride over to the new property?" Ned suggested. "Check on the progress?"

Halcourt agreed and Ned gave me a kiss on the cheek before they left. The girls had gone out for a swim, and I sat on the veranda, enjoying the view of gardens and grass and beyond that, the ocean, thinking that the spot really was quite lovely, even if I was excited for what would soon be our new views at Hillwood.

Sometime later, a commotion pulled my attention toward the house, where I saw one of the kitchen maids approaching. "Mrs. Hutton?" I could see panic in the young woman's eyes, in the patchy splotches tinting her cheeks.

"What is it?" I asked.

"We've just had a call on the telephone. From the new estate. It was Mr. Hutton."

My heart plunged into my belly. "Ned?" I asked, rising from the chair.

"Mr. Hutton was the one on the phone, yes. But he had news of Mr. Halcourt."

"What news?"

"There's been an accident while they were out riding. A terrible fall. Mr. Halcourt . . . well . . . he's . . . he has been . . ." At that the girl broke into a sob, barely able to finish the sentence. But nevertheless, I heard the word on which she choked.

"*Killed*?" I gasped in disbelief, my body dropping back into my seat. I blinked a moment in mute, stunned silence, eventually managing only to say: "Halcourt . . . dead?"

The girl just nodded once. I could see how she fought to compose herself. Ned's son dead. That golden boy, so full of vigor and humor and promise. That boy who had filled the house with laughter as he led the girls in sliding down the banisters. The boy whose scent still lingered in his bedroom, in the drawing room, in the front hall. The boy whose footsteps still echoed across the house; memories of his stepping jauntily into the breakfast room. His jovial raids on Cook's sweets in the kitchen, excursions after which he'd always share his bounty with my blushing girls. Set to depart for college. *Dead?*

My vision swam, my mind traveling back to long-buried memories, glimpses of Eleanor's earliest days, how my feverish baby had almost perished in my arms. How I'd felt certain that the death of my child would be a blow from which I would never recover. Ned had already lost a wife. And now this fresh blow. A blow to our home, to our entire family.

⁂

WE FOLLOWED BEHIND Halcourt's coffin in a silent, somber procession, Eleanor and Adelaide clutching my hands as we hobbled along in our heavy black garb, and Ned keeping his distance, cloaked in a blackness entirely his own. A dark and unspeaking figure, though his mottled face showed the extent of his brokenness.

Ned wished to bury Halcourt near Brookville, beside the sea and the wife whom he'd lost there, and so after the church ceremony, we walked in silence to the cemetery. By that time, the crisp fall air had just begun to brush the world around us, tinting the lush green trees with the first hints of reds and golds, but those of us there that day wore only black crepe and pale, ashen faces. I took Ned's hand in mine when the priest said the final blessing over the coffin, but his fingers were limp, and his eyes did not meet mine.

Back at the house, after I'd said the final farewells to Frank and Edna, after I'd kissed the exhausted girls in their beds, Ned and I sat alone on the veranda, staring out at a dark surf rippled with moonlight. The same place where I'd been sitting when I'd heard the news of Halcourt, I realized with a shudder. I looked sideways at Ned. Save for a few words, my usually irrepressible husband had been silent for hours, days even. Ever since he'd witnessed the horrific accident that had taken his boy's life.

An hour passed, or maybe three—I couldn't tell. I could hear the muffled sounds from within the house, where the maids and footmen were clearing the final china dishes and folding the last of the stained linen for the laundresses. I made to rise, to leave Ned in his silent vigil, but as I stood, he reached for me, gripping my hand in his. He'd been so inaccessible for so long that this sudden urgency gave me pause, and I stared into his face. I noticed, with a slight jolt, that his eyes were aflame. "Marjorie," he said, his voice sounding choked.

"Yes, my love," I answered, kneeling beside him. I raised my hand to touch his cheek.

"Don't," he said, and then he erupted into sobs, his face crumpling onto my shoulder. "Don't leave me. I can't . . . not you, too. I couldn't bear it. What would I do if I lost you, too?"

His body trembled, and I wrapped my arms around him. "There, Ned. There, darling. I'm not going anywhere. I'm here." I rocked him like a child, and to my relief, he let me. "I'm here, Ned." I said it over and over, my words a low, soothing vow, as my husband wept.

I knew it then, with leaden certainty: I would never be able to take away Ned's pain. I would never be able to bring back his son, and thus I would never be able to give him the thing he'd most need and want for the rest of his life.

But there was one thing I could do: I could give Ned another one. My husband had told me, in the first days of our marriage, that he'd love for me to have his baby. So that, I decided, was what I would do.

Chapter 22

New York City
1922

NED TROOPED INTO MY BEDROOM, AND I COULD TELL FROM THE glimmer in his eyes that he had something pressing to tell me. It was good to see him smile again. A welcome glimpse of sunlight after a thick and impenetrable cloud finally slips aside.

And it was surprising to see him looking so fresh, so full of vim that morning: we'd been out late the night before, dining with the Woolworths, the Vanderbilts, and the Morgans in the massive ballroom of the Astors' Waldorf-Astoria. I was still in bed, even at this uncharacteristically late morning hour.

Ned sat down, perching beside me on the edge of the bed. He was impossibly good-looking in the suit he was wearing, all crisp folds and dapper lines. He leaned forward and ran his fingers playfully along the neckline of my loose blue silk dressing gown. "Mrs. Hutton, I have news for you."

"And what is that, Mr. Hutton?" I wished he'd shut the door and join me in bed. But apparently he had *other* business on his mind, as he went on: "I've set a new personal best today."

"Oh?"

"Yes," he said with a nod. "This is the first time in my life that I've made a million dollars for my wife between breakfast and lunch."

My mouth fell open in a gape. Ned went on, "That's you, wife." He beamed at me as he cocked a light eyebrow and leaned closer on the bed. "How about a kiss?"

"It sounds like you've earned one." I leaned toward him and obliged, my fatigue suddenly forgotten as I tasted his lips. Outside the window came a clamor of noise—taxi drivers in some dispute on the street below us—but it felt like a world away from where we were.

The kiss was over too soon, and I groaned when Ned pulled away, his expression bright with excitement. I could tell he was on fire, too, but he had something other than what I had on the mind. "Marjie, there's just no stopping us at Post."

Under Ned's expert business guidance, we had recently taken the company public on the New York Stock Exchange. Uncle Cal was older now, well into his sixties, and so I had given my wholehearted approval to his suggestion that Colby Chester should prepare to take the reins of the company as president, with Ned coming on as chairman of the board. Not only had my new husband jumped at the opportunity to join my family's company, but he had also taken no time to show us all that he was doing a damned fine job. He loved the work, and I loved him all the more for that.

Ned smiled as he rose from the bed, eager to get back to business, pausing only at the door to flash me one final grin and the promise: "I'll tell you this much, boss: The Post Cereal Company . . . we are going to continue to shatter records. And expectations."

We weren't the only ones who felt these stirrings of excitement and promise at the start of the 1920s. Society had cracked wide open during the Great War: young men who had survived the barbed wire and poison gas of Europe had come home eager to make merry, and young women who had found their voices while working through the war were unwilling to step back into the stifling confines of the corset or the role of society hostess. The Four Hundred no longer held their undisputed lock on *how things were done*. Ned and I were new money, to be sure, but we had so much of it. Manhattan was our playground—a playground where suddenly it was less about one's name and date of entry into the *Social Register* and more about youth, beauty, and money; those assets we had in large supply.

My social circle broadened with Ned at my side, since he, unlike Ed, was always eager to meet interesting new people, regardless of their pedigree or gentleman's club affiliation. Gone were the staid nights of dancing quadrilles and the Viennese waltz in some stuffy country club. Now it was the Charleston and the foxtrot, the shimmy and the tango in crowded speakeasy basements, the music loud and the laughter loose and champagne-soaked. New York City was scintillating, the streets of Broadway haloed in new lights. We met and befriended the famous movie stars Mary Pickford and Billie Burke, as well as Billie's charming cad of a husband, Florenz Ziegfeld, who reigned as Broadway's leading man with his *Ziegfeld Follies*.

With the girls now at Mount Vernon for school, Ned and I decided to decamp to warmer climes for the winter season, so we rented a casita at the Everglades Club in Palm Beach. It was where we'd first fallen in love. And unlike Ed, Ned felt quite at ease in Palm Beach; he'd made millions as an investor for so many of the people who wintered there—Charles and Nelle Pillsbury, Consuelo Vanderbilt, Anna Dodge, the Astors, the Barclays. Ned and I had friends there all winter long and no shortage of invitations. We would dine out on Worth Avenue, ordering Oysters Rockefeller and champagne at the exclusive Alibi Club. We'd dance the hours away in the splendid Breakers ballroom, its floor-to-ceiling doors opened out over the ocean, or overlooking the rolling green of the palm-lined golf course at the Everglades Club.

During the days we'd swim and ride bikes along the Intracoastal, or Ned would drop a line off the breakwaters to fish, as I'd plop happily beneath a cabana and write to the girls or drift between napping and reading.

"What are you reading?" Ned asked me one afternoon as he sauntered up from a round of morning golf and found me sprawled on a lounger, consumed by my book. I showed him the cover. "*The Great Gatsby,*" he said, reading the title aloud. "Sounds intriguing enough. Who is Gatsby? And why is he so great?"

"More than intriguing," I said, breathless, eager to get back to it. "It's delicious, and it's just about the only thing that I'd be willing to shoo you away for. So, be gone, Mr. Hutton, and I'll let you have Mr. Gatsby after I'm through with him." What I did not tell Ned in that moment—what astounded me most about the book—was that, as I read it, I felt that *The Great Gatsby* could have been written about my husband. So much so that the more I read, I truly began to wonder if perhaps Scott Fitzgerald, whom we'd met with his wild southern wife, Zelda, on several raucous nights in Manhattan, had based his Jay Gatsby on my husband: a handsome, smart, driven man who rises from nothing to climb to the top of the ladder. A romantic man, a generous man. An impossibly wealthy man. Only, unlike Jay Gatsby, my husband was open with everyone he met—loved by friends and all who knew him. And unlike Jay Gatsby, my husband had gotten the girl.

I RETURNED HOME one afternoon after tea and bridge at Billie and Flo's place. Our house was quiet and cool, with the windows opened to allow in the pleasant cross-breezes of salty ocean air. I found Ned reclined on a lounger on the back terrace, his eyes shut to the sweeping vista of afternoon surf and brilliant blue sky. *Let him sleep,* I decided; he'd had a late night out the previous evening, gambling at Bradley's Beach Club. I sat down on the lounger nearest him and looked out over the yard.

Several gardeners were at work a few feet away, sweating as they clipped our fruit trees. I watched the man who stood nearest, noticed how his shirt was lined with dirt and perspiration. Inside, the household staff was already bustling about with preparations for dinner. The house was full from the moment we awoke each morning until after we settled into bed—we had servants to clean our bathrooms, press our linens, clear the dishes from which we ate, wax our motorcar, and water our flowers. We came down for a brief and glorious season, Ned and I, but these staffers lived in the area all year. Of course they did; this wasn't a vacation destination for them. While we were here to make merry, they had no choice but to work.

I glanced toward my husband, still asleep. It was in that moment that I began to feel those familiar stirrings, that bothersome malaise that always threatened to sprout up amid such seasons of excess and revelry. Happy as I was with Ned, I could not deny the nagging thought that there just had to be more to all of this than the dancing and dining and golf and gossip. I leaned closer to him. "Ned?"

My husband stirred, starting slightly when he saw me seated beside him on the terrace. "Oh! Marjie. Hi." He sat up, blinking.

"Hi there," I replied.

"How was . . . Where were you?"

"Billie's."

"That's right. How was that?"

"Nice," I answered. "She says hello."

"Did you win at bridge?"

"Of course I did," I answered with a wry smile. But then I sat up a bit taller, my mind turning elsewhere as I listened to the clip of the gardener's shears. He was trimming the branches that grew heavy with guava and avocado, beautiful clusters that he would nurture and then harvest, plucking them at precisely the right moment for the kitchen staff. Cook would then prepare an array of colorful dishes with these rich fruits—meals that Ned and I would enjoy. I fidgeted in my chair. "Ned, I have a question for you."

He yawned, his eyes still sleepy. "What's that, my dearest girl?"

I raised my hand, swept it out over the grand view of blue and green that unfurled before us. "What is the point of all of this?"

Ned ran his fingers through his golden hair. "All of . . . what?"

Another wave of my hand. "This."

"Well, if we're going to be getting all philosophical, wifey mine, I'm going to need a cup of coffee."

"This beauty, Ned. This wealth. I just mean . . . if we don't use it for good." An idea had begun to form in my mind. Billie had been talking just that afternoon about her husband, Flo, and his frustration that getting to the nearest hospital required a trip all the way to Miami. *We need a hospital closer to Palm Beach,* Billie had griped, taking a sip of tea.

I could not stop thinking about that as I sat there on my terrace that afternoon, the hired workers sweating just feet away from us, my husband still looking at me with his beautiful face full of confusion. A hospital. A medical facility in town that would benefit our wealthy friends, to be sure, but that would also mean improved care for those who lived here and worked here year-round. Those who could not afford a car and chauffeur, and had no way to get to Miami for treatment. Those who lived in the shanty villages just over the Intracoastal, in the significantly less prosperous town of West Palm Beach.

I felt my entire body thrum with excitement at the idea: we would raise the money to open a brand-new hospital. We'd throw a grand gala, a party so stunning it would be the most sought-after ticket of the season. We'd raise all of the funds for the entire facility in one glorious night. It would be a monumental task, but with Ned's and my energy and the help of our friends, we could do it.

That night at dinner I continued to chatter excitedly about the idea, laying out more of my thoughts to Ned, who nodded slowly, seeing that I was determined to move forward with the plans. "We won't build it in Palm Beach," I said.

"We . . . we won't?" Ned frowned. "I thought that was the idea."

"No." I shook my head. "We'll build it in West Palm. So the poor have access." I snapped my fingers, another idea sparking. "Flo and Billie know how necessary this is. We'll get them involved."

"Absolutely," Ned said, catching the wave of my enthusiasm. "We can have Flo work something up like one of his *Ziegfeld Follies*. Dancing, songs, costumes. Stage props and sets, too. It'll feel like Broadway, but with a distinctly Palm Beach flavor. The brighter the better."

"I love it," I said, rising and planting an excited kiss on Ned's lips. "And I love you."

"Love me or not, Marjie, I can already tell that you're going to put me to work."

"That's the truth. Now, if you'll excuse me, I need to go ring Flo. We have work to do."

Over the next few weeks and months, I threw myself enthusiastically into the planning of this hospital benefit. With Billie Burke and Flo Ziegfeld on board as early supporters of my cause, word spread quickly about the Huttons' ambitious goals, about the fact that Flo Ziegfeld would be giving a grand *Follies* right here in Palm Beach, specifically aimed at raising funds to open a local hospital. Soon enough, our friends began asking how they could help and how they could get on the guest list.

Flo, a dear, agreed to loan us not only wardrobe pieces and sets but also several actors from his Broadway productions. I paid to get his actors down to Florida, and Billie and I agreed to make cameos onstage as well. As the night of the performance and gala approached, I tried on my costume, a risqué bodice of bright purple rhinestones that showed plenty of leg and décolletage. On the night of the show, my French lady's maid, a pretty young girl named Renée, plumed my hair with crystals and ostrich feathers. "You look like one of our cancan dancers in Paris, Madame," she said, smiling as she applied a final dusting of rouge to my cheeks.

The sun set that evening over a mild, clear night—the perfect sort of weather for hours of dancing and revelry. The dinner was a lavish banquet of fish and fillet, champagne and oysters, fresh fruit and a dozen varieties of fine cheeses. Those guests who were not dressed for parts in the stage performance nevertheless came decked out in their brightest and merriest attire: floor-length gowns of shimmering jewel tones, blinding necklaces and earrings, headdresses of feathers and bright tropical flowers. One of Flo's most famous singers, Harry Fender, had made the trip down for the show, and when he was done with his set, he pulled me up onstage for my cameo. The crowd roared with approval as I danced alongside Harry. Ned looked on, beaming.

As the guests kept dancing, the servants kept refilling champagne flutes and dessert plates. Our friends packed the large space with laughter and song, so many people telling me on their way out that it was the best party they'd been to all winter. They begged me to make it a repeat event; they vowed to write even bigger checks the following year. Multiple Palm Beach hostesses asked me how they could ensure that next year, they'd get a part on the stage.

By the time the musicians had packed up their instruments in the faint gray of the coming dawn, Ned, Billie, Flo, and I stood at the front table and marveled at the fact that we had brought in over $100,000 in a single night. I wished my friends a triumphant farewell, thanking Flo with a big kiss on the cheek for all that he and Billie had done to help us. As Ned counted the checks and money one more time, ensuring that we were correct, he looked at me with a bright smile.

"Will it be enough?" I asked, my feet aching from dancing but my heart soaring after the night's success.

"I'd say so," Ned answered.

Our driver waited just outside the door. Ned yawned as he wrapped his arm around my waist. "Now, shall we go home, Mrs. Hutton?"

"I'd say so," I said with a nod, taking his arm and walking beside him toward the car. "Goodness," I said as we sat together in the back seat, our bodies leaning toward each other. "I've got a new appreciation for what those Broadway stars go through each night. This thing is uncomfortable." I gestured toward the tight bodice I'd been wearing for more than twelve hours. "I need to get out of this rhinestone contraption the minute we get home."

"I think I can help you with that," my husband said, giving me a sly, sideways smile as he placed a kiss on my neck, stealing an appreciative peek at the overspill of my décolletage. *Yes,* I decided, *the night was a success in every way imaginable.*

Chapter 23

Gold Coast, Long Island

THE PRESS HAD GIVEN THESE YEARS A NICKNAME: THE ROARING Twenties. The description was appropriate, particularly in our Hutton household. Ned's career had been marked—and made—by seizing opportunity and molding success for himself. It was an outlook on life that felt right to me; it felt like home. That was precisely how Papa had taught me to live. Having achieved wealth beyond anything that a poor, fatherless boy from Ohio or a scared, penniless girl in Battle Creek had ever dreamed possible, we governed our marriage with an attitude all about enjoying life to the fullest.

Since Ned's appointment to the position of chairman at the Post Cereal Company, we were doing better than ever before, earning millions every year. As long as Americans continued to eat breakfast, the money would continue to pour in—more money than we could possibly spend. And believe me, we spent plenty. While Ed's recurring censure during our marriage had been prompted by my propensity for the lavish—what he'd shuddered to call gaudy—Ned saw nothing wrong in enjoying our wealth. He applauded as I ordered custom gowns dripping in fringe and silk and crystal beadwork. Necklaces from Cartier with diamonds as big as grapes, bracelets from Tiffany with sapphires and amethysts.

Life as Mrs. Ned Hutton felt as though we were always driving at top speed, as though somehow Ned Hutton made the world spin around us, full and bright. Ned loved cars, and even though we had several chauffeurs on staff at all times, he learned how to drive for himself, and I loved nothing more than those golden afternoons when he'd knock on my bedroom door, leather driving gloves and goggles on, mischief tugging on that impossibly beautiful face as he said, "How about a drive, Mrs. Hutton?"

As the lush Long Island countryside unrolled before and around us, we'd laugh with delight as Ned sped the automobile down the dusty back roads, parking when we found pleasant and private clearings, and there, with the windows down and the seabirds cawing across the sky overhead, he'd make love to me. After years of trying, I'd yet to have luck in conceiving, but we were certainly putting in our best effort, and we were still young enough to believe it would happen.

Life together settled into a hectic but joyous rhythm. We'd ring in the New Year in Palm Beach, where we had quickly established ourselves as popular mainstays of the winter season. Spring found us back in New York City just as the tulips began to line Park Avenue. As spring warmed to summer, we would decamp with the girls to our new mansion, Hillwood, on Long Island. Fall found us back in Manhattan. I soon learned that, even as we changed location with the passing of the seasons, many of the faces remained the same. At every gala, show, or house party, we'd see the Ziegfelds and the Vanderbilts, the Rockefellers and the Hearsts, the Dodges and the Pulitzers. Our neighborhood on Long Island was labeled the Gold Coast by the press, and with good reason—our neighbors had gold aplenty.

That spring, there was a party every weekend, and Ned never wanted to miss a single one. When it came time for us to host at Hillwood, I set my focus on planning with all the care and attention for which I'd become so admired in Palm Beach. "I've decided on a theme," I declared to Ned several weeks before our event.

"Oh? And what shall it be?" he asked.

"Versailles," I said, showing him the creamy stock of the invitation I was working on, its letters swirling in gold-embossed cursive. I needed to post them within the next few days to get the party on everyone's calendar.

"Versailles," Ned repeated, looking the invitation over. And then, with a lopsided smile, he kissed his fingers and said: "Let them eat cake."

In the days leading up to our event, I filled my home with potted trees and hothouse orchids. Our groundskeepers erected a massive white tent on the lawn with a wooden parquet dance floor, and we ordered long mahogany banquet tables and hundreds of Louis XVI chairs from New York City for the dinner. Silver candelabra festooned the tables as lanterns twinkled overhead. I made sure our small ponds and fountains were teeming with new multicolored fish.

On the evening of the party, with the house astir and the meal and the grounds nearly ready, all that remained was for me to put on my costume. With the help of my lady's maid, Renée, I dressed with care in a custom gown of rose-colored silk à la française, a froth of pearls and ribbons lining the bodice. A pannier hoopskirt gave my figure a wide bell shape, and Renée spent over an hour powdering and teasing my hair until it soared over my head in a vaulted pompadour worthy of Marie Antoinette herself.

I scrutinized my reflection in the mirror one final time as I prepared to go downstairs and greet my guests. I certainly looked the part, from my powdered and jewel-trimmed hair all the way down to my dainty pink silk heels.

Especially lovely, I noticed, was the natural flush that colored my cheeks. I smiled to myself, my entire body feeling soft with joy. I had just noted that morning that my monthly courses were a week late. This was not something that ordinarily happened to me, and thus I felt very confident that I was carrying Ned's baby. I had yet to tell him; he'd been out all morning playing golf, and then we'd both been so harried with the final preparations for the evening and the three hundred guests we were poised to welcome. I wanted to tell him in private, when we could be alone to relish our joy. *Tomorrow,* I decided.

As I left my bedroom and descended the stairs, I realized that I had not seen Ned in hours, and I wondered if he was dressed and ready. That thought, however, was interrupted when I noticed that there, at the bottom of the stairs, stood my daughter, just home from school the day before and right on time for the party. "My darling girl!"

"Mother!" Adelaide looked lovely in a gown of lemon-yellow silk, her own hair powdered and teased. I gave her a kiss on the cheek as we giggled together, admiring each other's elaborate attire.

"Is it true that there will be fireworks?" Adelaide asked.

I leaned close, pressing my finger to her lips. "Shh, it's a surprise. But yes. After dinner." Adelaide squealed in delight. And then she saw her friend arrive by chauffeured auto into our forecourt, and she pulled me by the hand to the front door. "Mother, this is my friend Dorothy. Dorothy Metzger."

"Nice to meet you, Dorothy," I said. "Glad you could join us this evening."

"So nice to meet you, Mrs. Hutton," the girl cooed in reply. As she and Adelaide chattered excitedly about the night ahead—my daughter's first time attending a Gold Coast evening party, but not Dorothy's, from the sound of it—I studied the girl. Dorothy Metzger looked barely seventeen years old, and yet she was dressed provocatively, with her fulsome décolletage on full display as it overspilled her scarlet gown. A decorative beauty mark had been propped alluringly on the mound of her left breast, a risqué touch that went with the theme of Marie Antoinette's court, even if it seemed perhaps a bit precocious for such a young lady. Whereas Adelaide looked festive and sweet, a prim doll dressed for a costume party, Dorothy looked like she was channeling the aesthetic of one of Louis XIV's bawdy mistresses. And where were the girl's parents? I wondered. Off on the Italian Riviera, perhaps. Or yachting up the East Coast. Not minding their lively young daughter on what would undoubtedly be a raucous night of cocktails and dancing.

As the guests began to stream in and the party got under way, my servants bustled about in pale silk uniforms designed especially for the evening, resembling the livery of Versailles, and they offered chilled champagne, gin, and canapé plates of caviar, lobster, and pâté. I'd hired an orchestra for the evening and had arranged with the help of Flo and Billie to line up some of his best tenors and sopranos to sing for my guests before the formal seated dinner that would take place under the twinkling tent.

Throughout the course of the evening, as ever more bottles were uncorked and popped, as ever more gin was poured and caviar tasted, my brightly costumed crowd became looser and louder. The night darkened overhead as the lanterns and candles cast a warm glow over our garden. I opened the dance floor with Ned, who looked comical in his silk overcoat and breeches, a long wig of white Louis XVI ringlets bobbing with his dance steps. I had been sipping water rather than champagne for most of the night, and so it was with a clear view that I watched and laughed as my guests wobbled out to the dance floor to join us in tipsy, giggly pairs. Something about the Versailles attire made everyone look even more ridiculous.

"Are you enjoying yourself, Your Majesty?" Ned asked. He seemed to be quite thrilled with the merriment of the evening.

"I am, sire," I answered. But then my laughter turned to a sharp gasp when I spotted Dorothy Metzger, Adelaide's guest, holding forth amid a group of men in the center of the dance floor. The nearest man, whose sweaty head was topped with a lopsided wig of flamboyant orange ringlets, was pawing her as he pressed his silk-breeched groin against her hoopskirt.

"Ned!" I pulled my husband closer. "Look at the Metzger girl!" At that moment, another man was plucking rolls of money with his teeth out of Dorothy's ample, nearly-exposed bosom. "Ned, that's Adelaide's friend. We should do something."

Ned looked on and laughed, taking a swill of his gin. "Like what?"

"I don't know . . . but her parents aren't here. The girl needs to be told . . . I'll go find Adelaide."

"Marjorie, dear. You invited our guests to a night at Versailles." Ned raised his hands, sweeping them over the scene before us. "You got what you asked for."

NED DID NOT come down to breakfast the following morning, and I did not see him until it was nearly time for lunch. I sat outside on the terrace reading the latest reports on the Post Cereal Company's figures that Colby had sent over. I had selected that morning as the time to tell my husband the good news about the baby, but when I had come down and seen the absolute havoc of our gardens, my mood had turned sour, and I no longer felt like the time was right.

"Morning," Ned said when he eventually appeared, planting a kiss on my cheek, reeking of liquor even though he was dressed and freshly shaved. From the way his straw panama hat tipped low over his eyes, I could tell his head felt a bit tender. He did not comment on, or notice, the mess of our backyard.

"Morning," I said.

"How long you been up?" he asked.

"Hours," I said. "Shall I ring for your breakfast? Or lunch?"

"No." He grimaced, shutting his eyes as he sprawled out on a sun-soaked lounger.

Was he really going to go back to sleep, when he had only just awoken? "Ned," I said, with a noticeable chill in my voice against the backdrop of the warm morning.

"Yes?" He blinked one bloodshot eye partly open, staring at me sideways.

I put my papers down, sitting up. And then leaning toward him, a hand raised, I asked, "Have you noticed the garden?"

He took a moment to respond, glancing for the first time out over the bedraggled grass. Chairs were smashed in the middle of the dance floor. Shattered bottles of costly French Bordeaux stained our goldfish ponds. My nearest rosebush wore a wig of white ringlets. Articles of couture clothing floated atop the swimming pool like rotten algae, remnants of when several of our guests, including Dorothy Metzger, had decided to strip out of their French finery and jump nude into the pool shortly after the fireworks.

"Oh," was all Ned replied. Then he shrugged. "Albie will have the place put to rights in no time," he said, naming the head of our grounds crew.

I glowered at this, but Ned didn't notice, because he'd closed his eyes once more. "Last night . . ." I tried to collect my thoughts. "Looking around this morning, it feels like a colossal waste."

"Of what?" he asked.

I considered for a long moment before I answered: "Of my time, my energy, our money. What was it all for?"

"It was all in good fun."

"Yes, but did you not see the group standing over by the pool, rolling their tobacco in banknotes? Those folks were literally burning their money.

It's absurdity. And I did not like that girl with Adelaide. That Dorothy Metzger."

Ned chuckled. "I thought she was entertaining."

"Ned, you cannot be serious. The girl had men picking money out of her bosom with their teeth."

My husband shrugged, rubbing his fingers over his fresh-shaved cheek. "It's good for Adelaide to spend time with some people who can kick back and have fun. She's so damned solemn all the time."

I was hardly in a mood to concede, particularly on the point that Dorothy Metzger was anything but a vile influence on my daughter. "I just . . . I found the whole thing to be rather off-putting, especially when—"

But Ned interjected: "Marjorie, dear, you're sounding like the prig. It was hardly the wildest party we've ever witnessed. They were just behaving in character." Ned offered me a rueful smile. "Versailles was a place of excess, after all. And you invited them to Versailles."

I bristled at this, but inwardly, I had to concede that he had a point. It *had been* my own idea; I had selected the theme of Versailles. But, merry hell, look at what had happened to the people there just a few years later.

Call in your level head, Budgie. Papa's words pulsed through my mind in that moment and I felt a shiver run through me, even though the morning air was warm and bright. I looked around once more, blinking as I surveyed the debauched scene. Papa would have seen this mess and told me that I was absolutely correct to feel disappointed in myself. To feel like a fool for inviting guests to waste my money and carry on like boors.

It was time to put on my good head, I decided, drawing in a fortifying breath, rising from the chair determined to start cleaning up before the entire thing was left for my staff. I turned toward my husband to enlist his aid, but then I couldn't help but frown: Ned was snoring on the lounger.

WEEKS LATER, I awoke shortly after midnight to searing cramps gripping my belly. I groaned, reaching across the bed to wake Ned. "What is it?" he asked, his voice woolly with sleep.

"I think you need to call for the doctor," I said, my words little more than a strangled whisper. I'd told Ned about the baby just shortly after I'd gotten over my frustrations with the Versailles party. He had been ebullient, sharing my joy with a childish giddiness. But now something felt terribly wrong. "It's my stomach," I groaned. "What if it's something with the—" But then I shrieked when Ned pulled back the covers and we both saw the bedsheets smeared a flaming red.

"A baby boy," the doctor declared, his features ashen as he told us. I had been three months along in carrying my son. Our son. When Ned heard the pronouncement, he covered his face in his hands and fled the room. I curled up in my plush bed and shut my eyes, too weak, too carved out and emptied even to cry. I ordered Renée to draw my thick drapes, encasing my room in black, and for several days I sent tray after tray of food back to the kitchen, untouched.

It was the strangest thing: after feeling certain that I did not wish for more children, once I'd decided to have another baby, with Ned, I had become desperate for one. I longed for that third child, the child that would be ours together. And after years of trying, I'd almost gotten it. "Why don't we try again?" Ned asked late one evening as he joined me in the dark bedroom, attempting to cheer me up. It didn't work, as I was hardly in any mood for romance.

I knew that my window was closing, now that I was well into my thirties. I wanted desperately to have a baby with Ned. But I began to feel more and more certain that our lifestyle was contradictory to carrying a healthy child within. Our pace was so frenetic, our schedules so exhausting. Late, booze-soaked nights. Hours of chaos and dancing and cigarette smoke. Always on the move, trains and cars, always packing up and going here and there. "I think we need to find another place," I said to Ned one morning at breakfast. I hadn't slept well, and my head felt mottled, but on this point at least, I had found some measure of clarity. "Someplace . . . other than here."

Ned raised an eyebrow, questioning my meaning. He loved Long Island; he'd always known me to love it as well. And I *had*. I'd picked this land myself, designed the home and the grounds with care so that every inch would be in accordance with what we had wanted. And yet . . . "I need a change, Ned."

Ned considered this, nodding slowly as he took in the full impact of my appearance, and I could see in his expression what he saw: my drawn eyes that had been crying far more than usual of late; my complexion pale because I no longer spent my days enjoying walks through the sand and swimming in the ocean; my hair limp, whereas before I had always styled it with such care. "Let's take a trip," he said. "To a spa town. Saratoga? Or Vichy, if you would prefer something overseas."

I shook my head no. "I don't mean simply a trip. I mean a new place we can call home. New faces. New scenery. A slower pace."

Ned breathed out. Eventually, he answered. "That's fine, Marjie. You know that for me, wherever you are is home."

I SET MY sights on two hundred acres in the wilds of the Adirondacks. The girls were getting older—who knew how many more summers we'd have with them?—and I wanted to make a place where we could spend our summers as a family, free of the excesses of the Gold Coast with its gin-soaked parties and money-rolled cigarettes.

Because it was entirely my vision, I wanted to bring Ned around to the idea, and so I proposed a name that I knew was sure to please him: Camp Hutridge. "Wait until you see it, Ned," I said, as we stepped off the sleek wooden Hacker-Craft boat and stared at the splendid swath of property that surrounded us. It was a crisp, clear fall day, the sort of day that made the water of Upper St. Regis Lake shine like a mirror, reflecting the rich green of the mountains all around us.

As Ned and I toured the wooded lakefront on foot, he did not need much convincing to fall in love with the place: a tranquil ridge covered in virgin forest of white pine and birch, a waterlocked camp hemmed by the Upper St. Regis and the two Spectacle Ponds. "This could be a refuge for us, Ned," I said, already enjoying the calm of the place, noting the way my body felt softer, my breath slower and easier after only a few hours there. "Peace and quiet."

"It would need a lot of work," Ned said, looking around the compound, the notched-log cabins and scattering of buildings in various states of disrepair. "The buildings are barely livable. And because it's waterlocked"—he paused, glancing out over the water—"everyone would have to be ferried in by boat. The work crews would have a hell of a time getting everything in, not to mention the horse-and-cart teams that would have to haul everything up to the ridge before we could start building. It would be some job to get this place up to your standards, Mrs. Hutton."

"A lot of work," I agreed. "Sounds like just the job for me," I said, folding myself into his arms. "Please?"

We stood together a moment, looking out over the calm, gray-blue lake. "It smells clean here," Ned said. I nodded, smiling. As if on cue, a loon let out its low, mournful song, and a gentle breeze skittered off the water, carrying the scent of pine and birch and a distant campfire. I felt Ned draw in a deep breath, and then he spoke: "All right, Marjorie. You say you need a refuge. And I say that I need my wife to be happy. So, if this'll make you happy, then let's do it. Let's become woods folks."

With Ned's blessing, I threw myself into the renovations of the camp, determined to make it a place where everyone in the family could be happy. I never felt more enlivened than when I had a large, all-consuming project that demanded my time and energy, and that is what Camp Hutridge became for me. Ned had remarked that the buildings needed work, and he had been correct. The dock and the boathouse would need to be entirely rebuilt. I'd have to hire a full staff to clean and then furnish the place. But, once it was all finished, there would be boating and hunting for Ned, waterskiing, hiking, and swimming for the girls and their friends. Clean mountain air and slower days with the people I loved.

With the expertise of a local architect, I planned the camp around a central lodge, with rustic wooden beams, birch wallpaper, and a large stone hearth. A dozen surrounding guest cabins would offer plenty of lodging for family and friends to visit while still affording everybody space and privacy; every guest building would have a dedicated butler and housekeeper. Our boathouse, I decided, would be remodeled in the traditional Adirondacks style, fashioned of gnarled tree roots and curling trunks of cedar, but the gleaming wooden motorboats housed within would be top of the line in luxury. "We may be in the forest, but we can still live in style. And comfort," I said.

I approached this project of building Camp Hutridge with a zeal I had not previously felt. It truly felt like the first home that Ned and I were establishing together, untainted by death or the shadow of a lost loved one. I paid attention to every detail, from the morning gong that sounded across the grounds announcing breakfast to the decks of antique Apache cards my guests would shuffle during their after-dinner games.

Hutridge was to be our family's fresh start, and our first summer there was exactly what I hoped it would be, full of gentle northern sunshine, crystalline lake water, and peaceful rest. We'd sleep with the windows open all night, allowing in the cool breeze of the pine-tinged forest, the gentle sounds of the lapping lake and the nearby loons. By morning the air would be chilly, and Ned and I would find each other's bodies, soft and warm, under our Navajo blankets.

I was correct to believe that summertime in that place would bring us contentment, for as soon as our first season there was complete, I had cause to celebrate. Ned and I left our Camp Hutridge idyll feeling rested, healthy, and eager to welcome our new baby.

Chapter 24

New York City

We hoped for a boy. We told everyone that we wanted a son together. Having already birthed two daughters, I was certain, as my condition progressed, that this time felt different. That this time it would be a son, and we would call him Ned, Jr. We could not believe how wrong we were.

Our little girl came out plump, strong, and pink, with startlingly blue eyes and downy wisps of golden hair. She arrived in the last few days of December, one final and best Christmas present, a gift for the whole family to carry into the New Year.

Since we had already planned to call the baby Ned, we decided to name her Nedenia, and the family nickname quickly became Deenie. I loved all of my girls madly, of course, but I had to admit that this third daughter of mine was exquisite, her rosy little face such a lovely blend of mine and that of the man I adored—she was ours, she was the product of our love; only with nature's brilliant improvements. I was infatuated, and so were Ned and the girls.

While we were still basking in the glow of our growing brood, our family was also preparing for another meaningful birthday: the Post Cereal Company was marking its thirtieth year, and it continued to soar. The next New Year's Eve found us toasting our most successful year yet, with our company president joining us for a private dinner at our home. "Colby," Ned said, "we owe you our thanks. And Marjie, my dear, here's to 1925."

It was over his postdinner cigar and brandy that Ned laid out his ambitions for the coming years. Custom dictated that I should have excused myself from the dining room, leaving the men to their drinks and business talk at the table while I retired to the drawing room for the proper and ladylike postdinner tea or sherry. But both Colby and Ned knew that I wanted to be part of the company conversation, and in fact, it appeared as though my husband wished to enlist my opinions. "Marjie, it's been thirty great years since your daddy changed breakfast for America."

Colby and I both nodded, agreeing.

"We are now so much more than just breakfast," Ned went on. "And we are poised to grow accordingly." I liked how he said it—I liked that he said we would *grow*, to be sure, but also how he said *we*. Ned truly thought of my company as his, as well. We were a partnership, with my Post family legacy not a source of frustration or even embarrassment—as I'd so often felt it to be for Ed—but *his* cause also. Why, he'd given up the control of his own firm, resigning from that post in order to make my company his purpose, and he'd taken to it with mastery.

Ned exhaled now, a fragrant wreath of tobacco smoke encircling his relaxed smile as he said: "I'm thinking a veritable food empire. More than cereal, more than the Postum drink. We've conquered breakfast—let's take on the other two meals of the day, too."

I leaned forward in my chair. Ned was an intrepid businessman, but this . . . Was this realistic? Colby seemed to think so. He propped his elbows on the table and said, "Now's the time. It's about finding something the people not only want, but need, as well. You find something they need, then there's no stopping you."

"That's it, Colby." Ned nodded, gesturing with his cigar. "People need food more than they need oil or skyscrapers. Rockefeller started with oil, and look how he's grown. Carnegie started with steel. No one in their right mind would claim that food is any less important—or profitable—than either of those." Ned took a pull of his cigar, the cinders at the tip flaming bright orange, and then he turned to me, asking: "What do you think?"

Both Colby and Ned looked at me, waiting, as I considered it all. My mind swirled with cigar smoke and New Year's champagne and memories. Thoughts of Papa and Uncle Cal and Shorty Bristol. Our Battle Creek warehouses, raking the warm wheat myself all those afternoons following school. And then my mind traveled to one particular Battle Creek morning. Papa and me walking, waving to the overworked mothers who had to hurry indoors with their daily milk jugs. Papa telling me that the American woman shouldn't have to spend hours laboring over breakfast each day. And then, as if Papa sat there in the wood-paneled dining room with me, the thought skittered across my mind: Who was to say she didn't want the same convenience for lunch and supper as well?

"If we're going to think about lunch and supper, then I want to think about how we can make it easier for the American family to prepare it," I declared, the newly formed thoughts moving quickly from my mind to my lips. "And not just with convenience in mind . . . Let's think about how we can help the American woman get meals on the table with foods that make her family healthier." I noted how both Ned and Colby sat back in their chairs as they listened. I went on, my tone as animated as I suddenly felt: "Papa started this company with those exact goals in mind. Most women do not have all of this"—I gestured around our grand room and over the long table still covered in our Sèvres dinner dishes, then toward the door that swung into my staff kitchen—"all the support I do, particularly in feeding her family. What does such a woman need? What does she want? Let's think about it. Meals that are already prepared. And packaged. Let's not cut the quality of the food, but let's cut the amount of time it takes to prepare it."

Ned raised his glass and drained the remnants of his brandy, smiling at me as he did so. "Marjie, my girl." He hopped up from his seat, sailing toward me and pulling me up into his arms. "You're right! You're absolutely right. And you're brilliant, to boot!" Colby Chester laughed as Ned swept me across the room in a makeshift waltz. "Here's to the New Year. And to the Post Cereal Company!" Ned said.

Colby heartily agreed.

"And most of all, to my wife."

So, with my blessing and my money, Ned and Colby went to work finding foods that would make it more convenient for families to cook and eat. Over the next couple of years, we bought dozens of new products and brands to fold into the Post Cereal Company. We bought companies called

Jell-O, Minute Tapioca, and Hostess, which meant that suddenly we would be offering premade desserts. We bought another company called Log Cabin, which gave us product lines like syrup and sauce. We bought a company called Hellmann's, bringing us into the market for new and ready-made condiments such as mayonnaise and other spreads. Seeing how popular ready-made drinks were also becoming, we bought two companies called Kool-Aid and Tang. And then, even though I detested the stuff—just like my father before me—I came around and signed off on a check to buy Maxwell House Coffee.

Ned was right: we were so much more than simply breakfast. And we kept on buying; we kept on growing. We snatched up companies to make premade cakes, laundry detergent, instant rice, baking powder, kitchen soaps. If it was going to make the mundane chores of life easier and quicker, then we would make it available to the masses. And, we suspected, people would buy it. And buy it they did. Within just a few years, our sales had surged to nearly $60 million in a single year.

Ned was ebullient, and so was I. He had a favorite refrain that he'd declare on his way out the door each morning, kissing Deenie and then me as he headed to our new Post headquarters on Park Avenue: "With my luck and your brain, Marjie, the world is ours." That was how we felt. It was the Roaring Twenties. America was rich, and we were the richest. I, Marjorie Merriweather Post, had the golden touch of Midas and the youthful vivacity of Marie Antoinette.

The only thing I lacked was the foresight to see that both of those figures eventually brought about their own dooms.

Chapter 25

Gloucester, Massachusetts

"CALL ME CAPTAIN HUTTON." MY HUSBAND SLIPPED THE CAPtain's hat atop his dark blond waves, and when it settled over his carefree grin at a rakish angle, the stubble of his three-day beard darkening his suntanned cheeks, I would have called him anything he wanted.

"You may be captain," I said, a wry smile tugging on my lips. "But just know that this first mate is not going to eat canned foods at sea." And with that, I turned and looked back over the bobbing New England coastline.

We'd bought a yacht, a gleaming schooner with the power of six hundred horses and the comfort of a fine floating hotel, with plenty of room on board and half a dozen spacious stateroom suites. Ned and I had decided to spend the summer with Deenie on the water, setting off from New York and pulling in for stops at all the quaint, salt-stained harbor towns from Cape May up to Bar Harbor.

It was during that summer, while dreading the occasional nights that we had to spend away from shore, away from clean restaurants with fresh, healthy food, that I had a new idea. "Ned, why don't we think about frozen food?"

"What?" Ned looked at me askance.

It was an overcast day, and we were skimming the gray Atlantic somewhere near the fishing town of Gloucester, Massachusetts. I could see a scattering of redbrick buildings and a squat white lighthouse on the coast, the seagulls cawing overhead as they made their loops, scanning the rocks for food. I turned back toward my husband as I said, "I heard the idea from Chef, while he and I were meeting to plan our next few days of meals."

"*Frozen*?" Ned looked as if the word itself tasted rancid in his mouth.

But I went on: "Yes, frozen. There's a fellow who lives out here, a local fisherman by the name of Clarence Birdseye. He has a factory where he freezes fish. Just a local guy with a modest outfit, sells to the people in the area. But I'd like to see his operation."

Ned looked disinterested. Overhead a seagull cawed, then plunged into the water right before us.

"Come on, Ned. It's a cloudy day anyway. Too cold to swim. Let's go visit this Birdseye fellow. Perhaps we can buy something to bring aboard for supper."

And so we did, taking a small skiff into the cove and paying an unannounced house call to the local facility known as Birdseye Frozen Foods.

Clarence Birdseye was a friendly, unassuming man, with ruddy weathered skin and a rolling manner of speech that surely came from the many years he'd spent up north in Canada, fishing through frozen waters and hunting for wild game in the ice and snow. Mr. Birdseye didn't react with any particular interest when I introduced myself, but his quick nod told me that he recognized my name.

It took me less than ten minutes to conclude that Clarence Birdseye was a man who knew what he was doing. As he toured us through his small but efficient operation, I asked him all sorts of questions. How had he gotten started? Why frozen foods? Why here? He told me that he was a fisherman by trade, and he had come to Gloucester because of the abundant supply of cod, bass, and haddock. Previously he'd lived and traveled throughout the frozen north, where he'd learned the science of frosting and defrosting foods from the locals up there, the Inuit hunters and fishermen who survived because of their knowledge of this process of freezing and thawing whatever food might be available. Then, back in the United States, he'd determined that our new technology known as the assembly line was his best means of mass production.

I listened and nodded, growing more impressed with this Mr. Birdseye, and with the operation he was running entirely on his own in this modest town of Gloucester. Then I had another question: "Mr. Birdseye, would it be possible for you to grow this operation? Higher quantities of what you're already doing, and perhaps some new frozen products as well?"

He didn't blink before answering, "Of course, ma'am." But then he wavered just a moment. "That is, I could apply this science of freezing food to just about anything. The only trouble is, I can only do so much by myself. Someone has to catch the fish. Pick the vegetables. Work the assembly lines. Sell the food. I could expand, yes. But I would need more hands."

"It's a lot to do," I said, nodding as I surveyed his tidy but small operation. When my eyes landed on his massive coolers lining the walls, each one packed with pounds of fish that would keep for weeks—months even—another thought struck me. "Mr. Birdseye, don't you think that we might be able to eliminate a lot of hunger if we had a stockpile of frozen foods? We could freeze in times of plenty, in order to have a ready supply for times of scarcity?"

Mr. Birdseye nodded decisively. "Indeed, Mrs. Post—er, Mrs. Hutton. Not to mention giving everyone choices for food all year long. Just think of it: drinking a glass of lemonade in January. It sounds impossible. But it's not. I can do it."

Just think of it. That's precisely what I did. And the more I thought about it, the more fervently I decided that I liked what he'd said, and what I'd seen. I liked Clarence Birdseye; I knew implicitly that Papa would have liked him as well, what with his kindred drive to succeed, to serve, to think creatively. Solving a problem, meeting a need, and helping out your fellow man in the process. Not to mention making money—and the potential for lots of it.

"We should buy Birdseye, Ned." We were back on the schooner and sailing out of Gloucester's cove under the cover of thickening gray clouds. The water churned with a chop of whitecaps, and the skies threatened rain, but I was more concerned with the dark glower on my husband's face. His lack of a response—either he hadn't heard me, or he had chosen not to answer.

"Ned? That was an impressive operation. With us taking it over, Birdseye could really be something."

Ned shook his head as he finally answered me: "Nobody wants frozen food, Marjorie."

I pressed my hand to my hip, piqued at such a decisive dismissal. "I'm not so sure about that," I said. "Have you asked a single housewife? Think about how frozen foods would reduce her work. This is a real opportunity, Ned, and one we can't afford to pass up."

Ned braced himself against the yacht's railing as he stared out at the receding New England shoreline. "You know what people think of when they think of frozen foods?" he asked. "They think soggy. Frostbitten. Tasteless. Besides, you're not even thinking of the storage problem. How would these housewives of yours keep their frozen foods?"

"Cooling refrigerators," I answered with a shrug. "Just like Clarence Birdseye said."

Ned laughed, a derisive sound. "You think every woman in America wants a refrigerator in her home?"

"If it means she can keep food fresh and plentiful," I answered, "then yes, I think she would."

Ned waved his hands, shooing away the thought like a tedious fly. "No one wants to have to buy a refrigerator. Not a grocer and not a housewife, either."

"Ned, they would do it. I'm telling you. It would mean a change in the way food is stored and prepared, sure. But isn't that what we do?"

My husband turned and stared at me, his handsome features drawn tight as his eyes seemed to search mine. I refused to fidget, refused to break from his probing gaze. When he finally spoke, his voice was one of willed patience, tinged with the hint of exasperation: "Marjie, my dear, do I tell you how to run a dinner party? Or what necklaces to buy? Please, my darling, can you quit telling me how to run the business?"

I narrowed my gaze, stunned and stung. And so, in that moment, I stung back: "I was learning this business at Papa's side before you knew anything about it."

Ned raised his hands before his chest. "Now, no need to insult me, Marjorie."

"Same goes for you, Ned." It was unlike him, and a side of him I didn't like seeing. A moment later, Ned sighed. I turned and looked out over the water, white fists wrapped around the railing, my stomach choppier than the rough waters our yacht now plied. Just then the ship rocked, sending a spray of cold ocean water onto the deck, misting us where we stood. I gripped the railing tighter. I was not going to be the first one to walk away, to back down from this exchange.

When Ned eventually spoke, his voice was quiet, and I could barely hear it over the roil of the surf: "Listen to reason, Marjie. Frozen food? It would mean a disruption to everything we currently think about food. Not just in preparation, but in storage, in cooking. What makes you think people would want that? It's an errand likely to cost you millions and end in failure. Why on earth would you take something like that on?"

"Because, Ned, that's what we have always done."

NED RESISTED ME. For over a year. We fought about it so regularly that Adelaide and Eleanor began to roll their eyes, taking Deenie's hand and leaving the room whenever the topic of Birdseye came up. "Here we are, in the Birdseye of the hurricane once more," they'd say.

Ned would scoff, insisting that it would require too many changes for the middle-class household. That no reasonable man wanted to keep a freezer in his own home. That it would be too difficult to oversee a fleet of trucks conveying frozen food. That it would be a hassle to try to maintain the quality and safe handling of the food. That nobody wanted the many headaches that would come with a frozen food industry, nobody from grocer to housewife, and least of all Ned Hutton.

But I refused to relent. I ordered Colby to keep giving me reports on Birdeye's progress. His operations in Gloucester continued to thrive, but it was clear that he needed more money and more personnel to truly grow. He needed what only we, the Post Cereal Company, could give him. Eventually, when the value of Birdseye kept going up, and I saw that this wasn't some passing trend, I went directly to Colby. "Ned doesn't like the idea. But it's my checkbook and my name on the company, not his. And I can't put this one out of my mind." It was an early spring morning, and Ned was out hunting on Long Island. Deenie and I were in Manhattan, set to join him later that afternoon, but I wanted this business tended to first.

"Marjorie . . . er, Mrs. Hutton." Colby looked at me with an expression of visible discomfort. "You and Mr. Hutton have decided on this . . . ? You've . . . you've changed your minds on the topic of frozen foods?"

"No," I said, shaking my head. "I haven't changed my mind at all. I've liked Birdseye from the beginning. Now, Colby, I'm not asking you to do anything squirrelly or dishonest. I know that Ned is the chairman of your board. I'm not saying we ask Mr. Birdseye to get married. First, let's just see if he'd like to dance."

Colby's brow was crumpled in confusion. "Meaning . . . what, exactly?"

I crossed my arms. "Meaning, let's see how much he'd ask for his company."

Mr. Birdseye proved to be as shrewd and ambitious as I'd always suspected him of being, and he quoted us a high price for his operations—$22 million. All for a business he had started in an ice hut in Labrador with a few frozen fish. But we could afford it. And besides, I knew a thing or two about betting on plucky men who started businesses with nothing more than a good idea and the intention of changing the way people saw their world.

We announced the acquisition of Birds Eye Frozen Foods that summer. I was relieved it was over and happy with the purchase; Ned was not. But I forced myself not to falter. He hadn't wanted the man's company, and he certainly hadn't wanted to pay $22 million to get it. *Well, it's my money*. I didn't need to say it aloud, but the thought arose. Time would prove me correct, I knew that. I just hoped that my husband would be all right when it did.

My husband needed a win, and I knew it. So when he suggested a name change for the company, even though it would mean giving up Papa's original mark on it, I listened attentively.

"We are so much more than just the early Post Cereal products now," Ned went on. "We've got drinks, desserts, condiments, detergents and soaps, and even Birds Eye Frozen Foods." Birds Eye Frozen Foods, already one of our biggest earners. It turned out that American cooks and shoppers *did* appreciate frozen foods—the convenience, the variety, and yes, even the taste—as I had suspected they would. I bit my lip to quell a smirk.

And Ned didn't notice, as he was excitedly laying out his thoughts on the matter at hand: "We should have a name that is more versatile. Something inclusive."

I nodded, thinking for a moment. "Post Foods?"

But Ned shook his head. "That doesn't encapsulate the volume we have. It has to be something . . . broader."

"More general," I mused aloud, still thinking it through.

"That's good!" Ned snapped his fingers, a spark of inspiration lighting his features.

"What?" I asked.

"That's it. More general. How about General Foods?" Ned suggested.

I considered it. *General Foods.* Nowhere in that label was the Post name featured. But it was simple and it was accurate, and it gave us room to continue to grow. "General Foods," I repeated, trying it out for myself. We needed a name as broad as our company. The Kelloggs could continue to nip at us with their corn flakes—we now covered every meal of the day. "General Foods." I nodded slowly. "I like it."

"Good. I do, too." Ned pulled me in for a kiss, and I felt his frostiness giving way. My only question was: Would this thaw last?

Chapter 26

Palm Beach, Florida

"EXQUISITELY BEAUTIFUL." THAT WAS HOW THE JOURNALISTS described me as I showed up, night after night, at the best parties, dressed in the wildest costumes and the finest gowns, with Ned—dapper Wall Street financier turned unstoppable General Foods chairman, always the most commanding man in any room—at my side.

The postwar years danced along with all the breathlessness and verve of the Charleston, a decade fueled by champagne and jazz and rising hemlines, and Ned and I found ourselves at the center of a constant and raucous circus atmosphere. When we decamped to Palm Beach for the winter season, the world's wealthiest and most powerful people queued up for invitations to our dinners at home and on the yacht. We palled around with celebrities like the beautiful divorcée Consuelo Vanderbilt, the young American heiress turned English duchess, and now an infamous international social fixture. We befriended the dashing White Russian playboy Prince Sergei Obolensky, former confidant of the murdered Romanovs. We mixed with a constant stream of de facto American royalty, people like Alice Astor and Mary Pickford and of course our closest friends, Broadway and Hollywood golden couple Flo Ziegfeld and Billie Burke.

On board our yacht, things could be especially relaxed, and so Ned and I loved to sail past Key West to Cuba and the Bahamas and from there take off throughout the warm turquoise waters of the Caribbean. The Ziegfelds were our constant companions; the men would fish for grouper and tuna while Billie and I would lounge on the deck, laughing over the stories about us in the society pages as we admired the lush and colorful scenery.

Our itinerary was loose as we passed the winter floating through the

Caribbean, zigzagging from one island to the next, and our nights were often haphazard. Each time the yacht brought us into a new port, Ned would rally us to dress in our finest and take off in search of the lively local nightlife, particularly the tropical casinos and dance clubs.

I was not entirely comfortable with how regular it was becoming, during our stops in these island ports, to make a beeline toward the nearest casino. I had never been a gambler. I saw Flo's telltale influence behind my husband's increasingly risky appetites, but I didn't wish to be the only spoilsport; Billie didn't seem to mind in the least. I knew that Flo and Billie, as wildly successful artists and performers, lived a lavish lifestyle; a man like Flo could not have created the *Ziegfeld Follies* if he wasn't given to brilliant flights of flash and excess. And besides, Ned so often supported me—in the management of my family's business, in the parties I wished to give, in the friends I sought to host, in the travel itineraries I charted for our lives and the homes I managed—that the last thing I wanted to do was scold him in front of our friends. So I bit my tongue as he and Flo threw away my money, night after night, port after port.

And yet, there were times when even my mad love for Ned, my desire to make him happy, could not keep my frustrations bridled. Like one horrible night in Havana. We pulled into port and disembarked to have dinner in the old town. The air was warm and balmy, and it smelled of tropical pleasure, a heady swirl of floral perfume, ocean breezes, and the crackling chicken skins being cooked in the colorful restaurants that lined the narrow streets.

We began with cocktails at the American Club before moving on for dinner and dancing at a raucous spot called La Casita Roja. As I enjoyed the conch and colorful slices of fruit, sipping moderately on my island punch over the course of the meal, I watched with dismay as Ned swallowed glass after glass of the local amber rum.

A band played near where we sat. Billie didn't seem to notice, or care, but I saw that women with warm brown eyes and sprays of colorful hibiscus in their hair were in plentiful supply throughout the club, including the few who were hovering around our table, serving our men drink after drink. By the end of the meal, I could hear that the words coming out of my husband's mouth were warped by the liquor. "I'm ready to get back to the boat," I announced to the table. A server was clearing our plates, and I had to shout to be heard over the din of the music and the dancers.

Ned sat across the table smoking a cigarette, watching the lively dance floor as the beautiful young couples moved in time with the jaunty beat. "Ned, darling, did you hear me?" He turned toward me, his pale eyes unsmiling. "I'd like to get back to the boat," I repeated.

He shrugged, taking a pull of his cigarette. "Not me. One doesn't turn in early in Havana."

"But . . ."

Before I could finish, my husband leaned to his side and slapped Flo on the back. He whispered something just to Flo and then, to the table, declared, "Come on, let's get more of the giggle juice, what say-o? Señorita!" Ned lifted a hand to summon a nearby young lady for a refill of his rum.

"I'm tired, darling," I said, leaning toward him as I pressed my palm gently to his arm.

He looked me squarely in the eye, his face matter-of-fact as he said, "Then go to bed."

I sat back, stunned. The drums were vibrating throughout the whole club, and I could feel them rattling my chair. "Aren't you going to come with me?"

"No," he said.

I stared at him, noting the slick of perspiration along his blond hairline. For a moment, silence stretched across our table, even as the raucous noise of the instruments and singers, the dancers and diners, roiled all around us. Billie emptied the last of her punch. Flo clapped his hands together, breaking the tense silence. "I'll keep him company, Marjie." Flo's face had a rosy flush, and the top few buttons of his shirt were undone. God, it was humid there.

Then Flo cracked a smile, a slack expression that perfectly demonstrated just how many rums he'd swallowed. "Come on. The man's not one of your Caribbean lobsters, held by the claw of his lady."

Ned laughed at this, nudging Flo with an elbow as he said, "Oh, but she'd like it that way."

"Hardly," I said, stiffening in my seat.

"I'll come back to the boat with you, Marjorie," said Billie, taking my hand.

"There," Ned said, looking from Billie to me. "It's settled. Billie can obey . . . I mean, *accompany* you."

I sat across from my husband in fuming silence, staring at him. Willing him to stop this foolish behavior, even if it was the drink talking. When he refused to speak or acknowledge me further, I felt my body go cold in spite of the tropical heat. All around us the crowd was giddy, the music coming like wave after wave of ecstatic noise. After a long pause, my voice low and joyless, I said, "Do see that you make your way back to the boat tonight, Ned, dear. I'd hate to have to leave you in Cuba when we push off tomorrow."

Ned offered me half of his blue-eyed grin, taking another sip of his rum as he replied, more to Flo than to me: "Is that a threat—or a promise?"

BACK IN OUR stateroom, I didn't sleep a minute. As the ship bobbed gently in the calm Caribbean current, I watched the hours tick slowly by on my bedroom clock, growing increasingly irritated. Still, Ned did not return. Finally, when the first hint of dawn was slipping its way over the water, I rose from bed, too furious to feel fatigue.

I skipped breakfast, making my way alone up to the quarterdeck, where I sat, looking out at the calm water. Billie might have woken, might have taken her breakfast, but I did not seek her out. I sat on a lounger with a pile of magazines I'd packed, but I did not read them as the morning moved steadily on. It was full daylight when I finally saw two figures approaching, wobbling on the dry land as if they were already on board a roiling ship.

I did not say anything as they stepped onto the deck. Ned saw me seated on the chair and approached. He leaned toward me, arms outstretched, pulling me in for a sloppy kiss. I grimaced, stiffening as I tilted away. He reeked of cigars and liquor. This was Cuba, after all, but I loathed the smell and hated the further evidence of my husband's debauched night.

"Do you have any idea what time it is?" I managed, my voice low. He looked like hell—hair tousled, shirt collar stained some bright rum-punch pink. I did not want to appear the harpy, and I would not make a scene, particularly not in front of Flo, but Ned seemed determined to try my patience. He lifted a hand as if he were swatting a fly, and then, without another word to me, he turned and went unsteadily below deck.

Flo remained behind, looking only slightly less worse for the wear. He probably had nights like this more often and thus was less beat up once the sun rose. "Don't be too rough on him, Marjorie."

I exhaled a puff of air, forced a wan smile, but then I looked away, out over the water, so that Flo would not see how hard I was fighting back the tears. I would not try to speak. Flo went on: "He was trying to earn back his money so he wouldn't have to tell you about the bill."

"The bill?" I had thought I could not possibly be angrier with my husband just a moment earlier.

Flo nodded.

"And how much was that bill?"

Flo hiccupped, shaking his head. "I'm sworn to secrecy."

I left Flo on the deck and marched below and right into our stateroom, pushing the door wide open. I noticed that the room, too, now reeked of rum and cigars. Ned, sprawled facedown on top of the bed, did not stir. I walked to the bed and nudged his shoulder. "Wake up." No movement. "Wake *up*."

He roused after a minute, confused, as he let out a pungent exhale. "Marjorie? You startled me."

"Before you fall into too deep a sleep, I want to know what you lost at the gambling tables."

He blinked, rolling onto his side and curling into a fetal position. A groan. "Please, can I just sleep for a bit?"

"Ned, tell me."

"Can we discuss it later?"

"How much?"

He shut his eyes. "I can't quite remember. But it wasn't too much. Please, let me sleep."

"That's not what Flo said."

He brought his hand to his tousled hair. "I'm tired, Marjorie. Can't this wait for just—"

"Ned, tell me right now. How much money did you burn through last night in the casino?"

He sighed, rubbing his ragged face with his palm. After a long pause, he said: "Marjie, let's just put it this way—not more than some of those diamond necklaces you buy."

My breath caught, my throat tightening in rage. When I spoke, my voice was low and hoarse: "Ned, those are investment pieces that I will have for the rest of my life. Not the same as getting pickled and throwing money away on cards or green chips."

My husband said nothing in response.

I pressed on. "I want to know. How much?"

"Fifty-five."

"Fifty-five dollars?" My mouth fell open in a small puff of a laugh. That, at least, was a relief, even if I was still furious with him. But this was silly. Though I never would have lost fifty-five dollars on any bet, it was a pardonable sum. I exhaled, my body softening with a wave of relief.

But then Ned said, simply, "No."

"No, what?" I asked.

"Not fifty-five dollars."

"Fifty-five hundred?"

He groaned, and then shook his head.

Was that the boat suddenly rocking, or just the loss of my legs? I raised a steadying hand and braced against the wall. "Fifty-five *thousand* dollars? In a single night of gambling?"

The blood throbbed in my ears; I thought it might very well rupture my veins. When my husband said nothing, I went on: "You might as well have set a fire and lit that money ablaze."

Ned looked as if he wanted to shut his eyes and put the pillow over his head. "Marjorie, I have a wretched headache. Please. Can we discuss this later?"

"Fifty-five thousand dollars," I repeated with a gasp, still unable to believe the sum. "Why, think about how much good we could have done with fifty-five thousand dollars. We could have endowed a new hospital, a new library. Fed a family for a year—several families."

Ned rubbed his temple with his fingers in a slow, rhythmic motion. I was pacing the room at this point, needing some action through which to vent my anger. When, finally, he did speak, his tone was acidic, and so were his words. "Please, Marjorie. Go look in your wardrobe, your jewelry chests, and tell me how many starving families could live off of your necklaces alone. You are a fine one to preach to me on frugality."

This blow was intended to hurt, and it did. Not only because of the way my husband deflected all blame right back onto me, but also, I suppose, because it was true; I did love luxury, and I did treat myself to indulgences with regularity. But in my deepest core, buried as it might be under layers of grape-sized diamonds and custom silk, I still thought of myself as the Battle Creek girl who had grown up next door to a barn. The daughter of a man who had seen it as his mission not only to succeed but also to do good for other people. I was his steward, the heir to that legacy just as much as I was the heir to his millions. And I didn't want anyone to see me otherwise, least of all my husband. But it was clear, after a comment such as that one, that he did.

Ned was not done. "I'd have no problem spending my own money on such things. But, oh wait, I had to give it all up. So someone could run your old man's business for you."

My vision swam. I had nothing to say to this, nothing more to say to him, so I left our stateroom without another word. I found my lady's maid hovering in the corridor at the threshold. "Madame, is there anything . . . ?" Renée lowered her eyes.

"No, thank you." I blinked back the sting of tears, touched by her warm loyalty after my husband's callousness. Or perhaps it was the fatigue of the sleepless night finally catching up to me, but there was no chance I would be getting in bed beside my husband. "Actually, Renée, there is one thing. Please make up the Rose Suite for me. I think I'll rest for a bit." But first, I marched straight to the captain. "Back to Florida," I said, my voice rougher than the waves breaking on the nearby coastline.

"Mrs. Hutton?" The captain looked at me, confused. "I thought we were heading next to Nassau?"

"The plans have changed," I said, shaking my head. "The holiday is over."

Chapter 27

Palm Beach, Florida

BY THE TIME WE RETURNED TO PALM BEACH, NED AND I HAD settled into a tenuous truce, the forced civility of superficial pleasantries and tiptoe walking, but I was determined to restore the peace to our marriage. No more aimless floating through the Caribbean, I decided. No more nights in casinos, Flo twirling our cash through the humid, rum-soaked air. Those cruises through the Caribbean were a quest to go find trouble—too many casinos, too much booze, too much riotous revelry.

Ned and I had always been happy in Palm Beach together. It was where we had started. And it was there that we would double down and set things to rights. What we needed was a new project, something to bring us together as the dynamic team we were, a shared sense of purpose for our family and our life. After much thought, I had an idea for what that might be. "Let's build something really special here," I said over breakfast one morning in late winter. After years of rentals and temporary homes, it made sense to put down permanent roots here, in this place that brought us both such joy.

Ned considered the proposition, sipping his coffee in silence. I pressed on: "We can find some land on the water."

"Ocean property means hurricane nightmares" was all Ned offered in reply.

So then, he was in the mood to argue. But I was undaunted. "Then we'll find a place that's protected from storms."

He thought about this. After a moment he said: "The only hurricanes we want are the ones *we* start." He was right that we were quarreling more often, more than I would have liked, but I could see that he meant this as a joke, even an olive branch of sorts, so I laughed.

⁂

"HOW ABOUT MAR-A-LAGO?" I proposed. "Sea to Lake. We could call the place Mar-a-Lago."

I made the suggestion as Ned and I sat with our architect, Marion Wyeth, who'd already made a name for himself as society's preeminent builder, designing luxurious properties from Manhattan to Palm Beach and everywhere in between. We had purchased twenty acres of lush jungle on the ocean, not far from our friends who frequented Mirasol and The Breakers and the Everglades Club. I loved the property because it not only boasted sweeping views of the Atlantic but also abutted Lake Worth, stretching from sea to lake.

"Sea to Lake. Mar-a-Lago," Ned said, trying out my suggestion. "I like it." Then he looked at Marion. "You'll soon learn, my friend, that Mrs. Hutton's suggestions are more like orders dressed up in polite finery. Best to say yes and keep her happy." Marion laughed at my husband with a knowing tilt of his chin.

And yet, this premier builder was not keeping me entirely happy—at least, not with the building plans he had proposed so far. "Too traditional," I said as he and I pored over his latest designs. "All these Spanish villa drawings—just like all the other millionaires down here. I don't want to follow a trend; I want to create one."

As the weeks passed and I gently but resolutely rejected more and more of Wyeth's meticulous sketches, Ned grew frustrated. "What more can he do, Marjie?" Ned asked me one night. "You say you want to defy the trends, build something wholly inventive, unlike anything else down here. But Wyeth needs more direction than that."

"I like what we have at Hutridge," I offered. "The camp layout."

Ned looked at me askance. "You're going to tell Marion Wyeth to build you a compound of log cabins overlooking the Atlantic? What'll he use—palm trees?"

I glowered. "Not that *look* . . . but that same *idea,*" I said. "One central building and a series of outdoor terraces and patios leading to surrounding buildings. So it can feel like a home, but also a place where we can host and entertain."

Wyeth was not enthusiastic about the plan, but Ned did not want to fire him. "How about we ask Mizner to join the team?" he suggested. Addison Mizner was another sought-after Palm Beach builder, popular for his sprawling palazzos that lined the ocean.

"No," I replied, without a moment's hesitation. "I don't want just another Mizner mansion. I want something different."

Flo was over, since he and Ned were about to leave for a fishing trip—and God only knew what other activities—off of Key West. He had been listening to this exchange, and now he interjected: "How about Joseph Urban?"

Flo was an expert at spending my money, and I rarely agreed with his choices, but this time I was desperate enough that my interest was piqued. "Who is Joseph Urban?" I'd never heard the name, but in this case, that worked in the man's favor.

"I hired him to do the stage sets for the *Follies,*" Flo said. "The guy is a genius. He built for Emperor Franz Joseph before the Great War. Grew up in Austria-Hungary. Built for the other nobles, too. Even the royals in Egypt. He's eclectic, but top-notch."

"Eclectic is good," I said. "I want eclectic."

And the man, I soon saw for myself, proved as colorful in his personal appearance and mannerisms as in his background and building aesthetics. I flew Joseph Urban down to Palm Beach the next week to tour the property with me and hear about my hopes. He was a massive bear of a man, weighing nearly three hundred pounds, I guessed, whose small bow tie seemed fairly ready to pop off his thick neck. He huffed and sweated as we traipsed around the untamed property, speaking fast in his guttural Austrian accent as he stepped over thick roots and ducked under dense fruit trees and mangrove branches. Standing there in my work boots and my rubber gloves, I threw everything at him: I wanted something entirely original. I wanted a camp-like layout with a gracious main building and a complex of surrounding outbuildings. I wanted to draw out the natural beauty and whimsy of the lush tropical jungle in which we were building. I wanted to enjoy sweeping views of sea and lake. I wanted to be protected from hurricanes. I wanted it to be a place for intimate family visits *and* grand, lavish parties. I wanted it to be the most thrilling thing that Palm Beach society had ever seen. At the end of our interview, Urban nodded slowly, silently, as if absorbing and assimilating all of the facts I'd just thrown at him.

The next morning Joseph Urban came over for coffee and laid out his response to my architectural riddles. "Madame Hutton, I can do this for you."

I laughed at his plain, matter-of-fact self-assurance. Unblinking, chin tilted down as if he were bracing for some ride on an unbroken stallion, Urban went on: "I see influences from the Spanish and the Mediterranean that are so popular in this area, but let's pull in Baroque and Gothic and Arabian details as well. I see a central building with a soaring tower. If this is your palace, then that is your keep. Terraces and cloistered patios will link to other buildings. You want to entertain, yes? You have a big family? We'll need many rooms. And this land! Madame Hutton, we don't just tame this jungle; we work with it. We'll have lovely lawns that go right up to the water. The best vistas. We'll have fruit trees, and a golf course, and fountains. We'll have gardens better than anything the Moors built at the Alhambra. We'll have arches like a Venetian palazzo, and we'll have friezes like an ancient Greek temple."

As Urban spoke, his words clipped by his hard-hitting Teutonic consonants, his hands gesturing wildly with pencil poised between thumb and pointer, I nodded enthusiastically. Everything he said sounded outlandish, but the man was artistic and inventive, and certainly not afraid of doing something wholly new and different. By the end of our conversation, I had something to tell him: "I want to hire you, Mr. Urban."

He pressed his hands to his waist, eyeing me like a stern governess, a reaction far different than what I would have expected, considering the massive job I was trying to give him. Then he frowned, tucking his pencil behind his ear. "There is just one small thing we must discuss, Madame Hutton, before I can accept this job."

"What's that?"

"Your budget."

I'd told Urban I was prepared to spend $1 million on the construction of Mar-a-Lago. Now it was my turn to look like the stern governess. "Yes, Mr. Urban?"

Urban shook his head, his lips thinning as if he'd bitten into something sour. "It will not suffice."

I stared at him, arching an eyebrow, unsure whether to receive his candor with admiration or offense. Unvexed, Urban squinted into the bright sun, sighing as he looked at the sparkling surface of the Atlantic. "It will be the most beautiful place you've ever seen. A work of art, Madame Hutton. But we will need more—how do you Americans call it?—cash."

I exhaled, looking out over my untamed, sprawling oceanfront property. Already I could imagine the masterpiece that Urban had spoken of. I could see it rising up between sea and lake. I yearned for it, and I knew that it could be ours. The man who could give it to us was standing in front of me, the man who had given Austria its imperial façades and Broadway its dazzling *Follies* stages. But there was only one answer for the moment: "I'm going to need to speak with Mr. Hutton."

AFTER MUCH DISCUSSION—A few of the discussions growing more heated than I would have liked—Ned agreed to let me bring Urban on board. Wyeth would stay, though, as well, and I got the sense that Ned saw Urban as my man on the job and Wyeth as his own. "Otherwise, this lovely *cottage* that you're building us is going to send us to the poorhouse," Ned said. He had good reason to fear Urban's influence on the project: the man wanted every fixture in the house made custom and hewn of solid gold.

The project took a full year and then a second one, the bills quickly soaring past our million-dollar allotment, and even I began to grow frustrated as we continued to stay in rented properties for multiple winter seasons. Ned's frown grew more deep-rutted with each check he wrote. But both Urban and Wyeth reminded us that the project was so colossal, so innovative, and so complicated that it was more important that we get it done correctly than that we get it done quickly. I begrudgingly agreed.

Finally, after three years, they did finish. The main mansion, the outbuildings, the gardens, the terraces, the beach, and the lakefront—it was all ready. Mar-a-Lago stretched from sea to lake as a breathtaking compound boasting Spanish, Moorish, Venetian, Egyptian, and even classical European influences. The place was right to every last detail, from the moment one rolled through our front gate onto a lane hemmed by stately palms. I'd wanted eclectic, and that was what the home was, with its salmon stucco walls, Moorish archways, hand-painted tiles, and whimsical parrot and monkey drainpipes. But the best aspect of the property, in my opinion, was how the home blended so seamlessly with the stunning beauty of our natural setting. In every room, tall glass doors opened out onto the grounds, where palm-dappled sunlight shone in the day and golden Spanish lanterns twinkled at night. The gardens burst with fragrant tropical plants: orchids, lemons, oranges, kumquat trees where parrots perched, adding their bright colors and music to the surroundings. Thick hollyhocks climbed the columns of the stone patios. Fountains gurgled as fish pools flashed with the colorful Caribbean specimens stocked within.

We'd held Urban back from all that he'd recommended, but in the end he was correct: even with Ned watching the budget and approving every one of my decisions, the price tag was many times more than we'd hoped it would be. Ned was exasperated, especially when he had to sell some of my General Foods stock in order to keep the project going. But it was worth it, I countered. Palm Beach had never seen a private home as grand or original or creative.

When we were finally finished, I threw open the doors and announced that I was at last ready to welcome the ravenous members of the press for a visit to Mar-a-Lago. All the major magazines sent photographers, as did all the newspapers. They moved with me from room to room, a swarm of flashbulbs and questions, and I couldn't help but chuckle to myself as the representatives for *Vanity Fair* jostled with writers from *The New York Times* and *Town & Country*. I stood before the grand new fireplace in my living room and gave them my best smile, happy that I'd had the vision to set out on this project, and deeply relieved that it was over. I'd begun the building with the intention of breaking all molds and setting society tongues to wagging. I'd done just that. I'd shown them all that Marjorie Merriweather Post did not follow trends—she set them.

Chapter 28

New York City
1929

FALL FOUND US BACK IN MANHATTAN, WHERE I AWOKE ONE chilly morning to stare through my picture windows and see Central Park's trees tinged with shades of bright amber, gold, and orange. I took a slow sip of my Postum and felt a warm sense of contentment. Ned had already left for the office, and I could hear Deenie, now six, laughing in the hallways as she played chase with her nanny.

My little Deenie. The child continued to be the delight of my life, having traveled throughout England with Ned and me over the summer and delighted in the chance to join us for a private audience with King George V and Queen Mary. There, to my stunned surprise, the queen had even congratulated me on our completion of Mar-a-Lago, saying she had read all about the home and she was eager to see it.

The air in New York was getting cooler, and soon we would decamp to Palm Beach. Since we had finished our construction and I had convinced Ned to forgive me for the price of it, things had been harmonious for our scattered family. General Foods was soaring, and we'd soon make back the money we'd spent on Birdseye's company. My Adelaide, recently married, was living in a lovely apartment close by with her new husband, Tim Durant, and she was expecting—my first grandchild. Eleanor, just shy of her twentieth birthday, was finished with school and back in New York City, a charming young lady with no shortage of men giving suit for her time and attention. Yes, things were quite all right in the world, I noted, smiling to myself as I rang my bell to dress.

Later that day, after I'd caught up on letters, after lunch and a walk with

Deenie through the park and a quick trip to Bergdorf's for a new pair of autumn gloves, I picked up the newspaper, wondering what they'd have written about me in the latest columns. Although, these days, there was just as much interest in my Adelaide and Eleanor as fixtures of the Manhattan social set, a fact that displeased the former and delighted the latter. But before I could even skim the front page, a sound at the bedroom door pulled my attention up, and I stared at the threshold to see my frowning husband as he burst in. "Ned, dear?" We had plans to leave with Deenie for the Gold Coast that evening, but not for several more hours. What was he doing home?

My husband said nothing as he strode into the room, his face in crumpled and inscrutable disarray, his skin the color of ash. I put the paper slowly to the side. "What is it?"

He looked up and into my eyes as if he had only just realized I was in the room. I noticed the quiver of his hands. And then, finally, with a voice thin and hollow, he said simply, "They are calling it the Great Crash."

THEY WERE ALSO calling it Black Thursday. And then Black Friday. And then Black Monday. And then Black Tuesday. The worst days in Wall Street's history. The largest and cruelest loss of wealth in our nation's history. The economy had not simply crashed—it had cratered. After a decade of runaway profits and risky credit and recklessly optimistic excess, we were plummeting uncontrollably toward a ruthless reckoning. It would be not only a recession, but far worse. A depression. A very great depression.

I sat back in stunned silence, the breath catching in my throat as the radio droned on. It felt absurd that in just the few months prior I had been dining with a king and queen in London. Fretting over Mar-a-Lago's golden light fixtures. Ordering an entirely new season of custom gowns from Paris and London. Dressing for dinner parties wearing precious jewels as big as eggs.

Each day brought fresh news of horror and loss. Grown men hurling themselves from their Manhattan office windows. Droughts and food shortages stretching from the Midwest to California that would leave millions starving. This, when I'd just spent millions building myself a palace in Palm Beach. Millions more on clothing and parties and yachting and travel. The past decade had been a time of ravenous, reckless consumption, but now America stared down a new decade that promised to bring deep and punishing hunger of a very different sort.

Like most everyone else in the country, I was poised to lose profits, but I myself would never go hungry. I would never be desperate. I would continue to enjoy wealth and privilege beyond what most others in the world could even imagine. People would always need to eat, and thus General Foods would continue to do fine business; in fact, our affordable and ready-made foods would do a fair bit of good for those who suddenly lost access to fresh crops and more costly seasonal produce. And so I heard Papa's voice as clear as if he stood there in the room with me: *Time to put on your good head, Budgie.*

If I was to live amid such splendor and enjoy such wealth, I would use it for good. That had always been the point of our Post wealth, and that philosophy was needed now, perhaps more than ever before. As Papa had taught me to do as a young girl returning home from school to a white barn that smelled of wheat and molasses, I would roll up my sleeves and I would get to work.

I locked my jewelry and gems into a vault; what good were precious stones when men were hurling themselves from their Wall Street windows? When mothers and children were queued up around the block, shivering in the cold wind, waiting hours for watered-down soup and a square of hard bread?

I was forty-two years old, but I still felt young, enlivened with a newfound sense of purpose, and I threw myself determinedly into public service. I filled my calendar from morning until evening, organizing benefits for churches and soup kitchens and the Salvation Army. I gave dinners in my home for hospital workers, teachers, police officers, and firemen. I made a gift to my Mount Vernon Seminary so that they could continue to pay teachers' salaries and keep the facilities in good repair, even as they struggled for lack of funds. I paid to transport the entire New York City

Circus troupe down to Mar-a-Lago by train, elephants and all, for a charity benefit to help children who'd lost their parents.

But I wanted to make sure that my help served those closer to home as well: I made it known that any staffer of mine who was facing troubles, from the Adirondacks to Manhattan, from Long Island to Palm Beach, was to come to me immediately. I did not expect recompense, and I did not need credit. I would not have those closest to me feeling desperate in these times, not if I could do something about it.

And yet, in spite of this, I felt like I needed to do more. Something that could extend beyond just my own two arms and hands, beyond just the limited scope of the needs I could see in front of me. My wealth would become a burden on my soul—I could feel that—unless I found some way to truly share it with those who needed it most.

"It's got to be food," I declared to Ned one gray winter morning, as I stared out over a snow-covered cityscape. I couldn't help but think of the many who were standing out on those bleak streets at that very moment, huddled in a line for something warm to eat. "Food, not just for their bodies," I continued, "but for their spirits, too. I want to open up a public kitchen."

❧

"THANK YOU, MRS. Hutton," the woman said, her chapped hands trembling as she clutched a young child with each one. "Oh, God bless you. But how can we ever thank you?"

"Now, no need to thank me until you've tasted the food. I just hope it's good. Come in, come in. It's so nice to have you." And with that, I ushered the woman and her two little ones indoors, out of the bitter wind and toward a clean waiting table. I'd opened the Marjorie Post Hutton Canteen on New York's ravaged West Side, in the neighborhood known as Hell's Kitchen. Immediately, they had arrived at our doors: mothers with hollowed-out cheeks and cardboard for shoes, men whose dignity had been worn as threadbare as their old work suits. Immigrants who barely spoke a word of English and native New Yorkers who'd woken up one day to find themselves in a hostile city they didn't know, even though they'd lived there all their lives. *Come to the Marjorie Post Hutton Canteen and be fed,* I said. *Come and be warm. Come and be safe.* And so they came. By the thousands they came. There, I spent hours on my feet ladling thick soup and clearing dishes, hugging the tired young women and coaxing smiles from the shy little ones, listening to the tales of my adopted hometown's many heartaches.

Because these folks deserved a few hours in a comfortable, clean space, I'd hired a full staff, and I made sure that every table had a starched linen tablecloth and a glass vase of fresh-cut roses. I hired men who were out of work and outfitted them with white gloves and crisp blazers. I asked them to shave, and I paid them to serve as my waiters. I reviewed every menu, making sure the folks who came in would be getting healthy food—and as much as they needed. Gone were my banquets of gold and mahogany; now I fixed my exacting hostess's eyes on every detail in that canteen. And when they left, I saw them off with hampers and baskets of more food, healthy rations that I hoped might help lighten just the smallest portion of their heavy loads. If a young lady's clothes looked too thin or her child's clothes showed rips, I sent them home with clean sweaters and warm wool slacks, items I'd pick up each month at Bloomingdales.

Before long, the locals throughout Hell's Kitchen were calling me Lady Bountiful. These people, thousands of them, saw me as their patroness, but they did not guess how much they gave me as well. Not since the Great War had I felt such a deep stoking of purpose in my belly. After the delirious recent years of distraction and decadence, I felt that I was finally living in a way that aligned with what Papa and Mother had taught me, that I was finally using my wealth in the service of something larger than myself.

Everywhere we looked, there was need. Farther downtown, Ned opened a public kitchen of his own near the neighborhood known as the Village, and I loved him for it. I pressed my fortunate friends to join our efforts, too, calling on them as I raised money for the Salvation Army. I held a gala for the Samaritan Home for the Aged and hired opera singers to entertain my well-dressed guests. I gave teas and dinners to raise money for medical clinics. I served as a chair for the Unemployment Relief Fund and even stood by myself out on street corners to make my case to passersby, urging them to donate either time or funds.

Reporters and journalists had always been ravenous for details of my life, and so I decided that I could now use that for some good. I invited them to tour the Hoovervilles around the city with me. I invited them to visit my canteen. I invited them to see the shelters and the breadlines that had seeped into the landscape of our city streets. "Why, Mrs. Hutton, you've got more money than all of these poor folks out here combined," one reporter remarked as we walked side by side down Manhattan's ravaged Tenth Avenue.

"That may be so," I said, looking the young man squarely in the eyes. "And that's why I aim to keep it moving. I make it work, make it create, make it do good, and make it help in many hundreds of ways."

I didn't do any of it for fame or recognition. But of course I appreciated it when it came, nevertheless. Particularly when the First Lady, Eleanor Roosevelt, invited me to the White House so that she might thank me in person. Ned was not overly fond of her husband, President Franklin Roosevelt, and I knew that our First Lady was at odds with her cousin, my longtime acquaintance Alice Roosevelt, but I did not bring any of that up when I met the kindly lady at the White House. Instead I smiled and returned her thanks, noting with surprise that Eleanor Roosevelt seemed a bit shy, perhaps even a bit insecure. "It's wonderful, what you are doing for people, Mrs. Hutton," Eleanor Roosevelt said.

"Well, the feeling is mutual, Mrs. Roosevelt." The First Lady smiled, that wide, toothy grin I'd seen on so many newspaper pages, and then we turned together and posed for the swarms of photographers, alongside her other guests, including Amelia Earhart and Charles Lindbergh.

Closer to home, another Eleanor was also demanding my attention. That spring, my daughter, my lively and lovely Eleanor, stunned me by eloping with a man she'd only just started seeing, a divorced stage writer by the name of Preston Sturges. I didn't mind that he was divorced; I wasn't that much of a hypocrite. Nor did I mind terribly that he was so much older than my girl, who was barely more than twenty. I didn't mind that Eleanor had chosen him even though she had countless suitors and could have had her pick of any number of suitable, respectable—and respectful—men. Men who would have shown the decency of first asking for her hand and then marrying her in a church in broad daylight. What I *did* mind was that this man, who was not wealthy and yet was known as a wild spendthrift at speakeasies and other questionable night spots, had talked my girl into running away with him to the Catskills to do the thing quickly and in secret.

Many of my friends, aghast and heartbroken at the news, asked me if I would disown my daughter. I couldn't. As hurt and disappointed as I was, I loved my girl with the very same ferocity that had gripped me on that night some twenty years earlier, when I'd held her new body, tiny and febrile, and prayed that she would not be taken from me. I couldn't disown my Eleanor, no more than I could slide the bone out from under the skin of my arm. No matter the husband she'd chosen, I wanted my daughter in my life. I wanted to know her children, if and when she had them. I *did* cut off her trust and stop her allowance, but that was as much for her protection as it was for her punishment. Eleanor was bad enough with finances—she went through cash as if it were water—and I wasn't going to have her money falling into the hands of Preston Sturges. But I would not disown my beloved President of the Mischief Club. I had been young and foolish once, as well. I had been impulsive in love and had married the wrong man. What right did I have to punish Eleanor for doing the same, even though I knew how it would end?

Chapter 29

Winter 1934

IT WAS A DIFFICULT TIME TO BE IN AMERICA. IN AN AGE WHEN half of our country's families couldn't manage to put supper on the table, my wealth stood in cruel contrast, and I was as aware of that as the many reporters who continued to trail me, ravenous to snap my photograph and report on my comings and goings.

I had been as horrified as the rest of the nation by the harrowing headlines of that poor Lindbergh baby. The small boy snatched from his nursery crib while his parents slept just down the hall. I recalled that tall, square-jawed young pilot, the fair-haired man who'd smiled beside me as we'd accepted our honors from Eleanor Roosevelt. If such a thing could happen to him—a crime committed by a desperate villain demanding money as ransom—then couldn't it happen to my girls as well?

In spite of the ravages of the Depression, General Foods was not only surviving—it was thriving. Ned was a skillful steward at the helm, and people still needed to eat; our products made that easier and more affordable for them, especially our Birds Eye. The money continued to come in, millions each year, more money than we could spend.

And yet, as much as I put my money to work helping others, I felt the need to get away for a bit, lest I become a target. I put honest, competent people in charge of my charities, and I paid them well to do good work. Our canteens continued to employ and feed hundreds of people a day, and now safe, clean beds were also available for up to fifty women and children a night. And so, with these management positions filled and funded, and with both of my older girls married and settled in households of their own, Ned and I decided to pack up Deenie and board our ship, sailing out of New York for a bit.

I would never have said it aloud, but I hoped that the trip to sea would do some good where I needed it the most—specifically, in my faltering marriage. It was our inaugural journey on a new yacht, one that Ned had designed, named the *Sea Cloud*. I saw the ship as a sort of peace offering to Ned, a gift of goodwill, though I made sure to explain that we had bought it together, with money that was *ours* rather than mine. It was only fair—he'd given me the reins to build Mar-a-Lago to my liking, and wasn't he responsible for many of the millions that I had, the profits that kept climbing, allowing me to enjoy our luxuries?

Ned loved being on the water, and so did I. I hoped that, together with our Deenie, we could take off on new adventures. The *Sea Cloud* was a behemoth floating atop the seas, stretching over three hundred feet long, which meant it was grander than any of the luxury vessels belonging to the Vanderbilts, the Morgans, even the Windsors and the rest of the royals of Europe who plied the waters with their imperial yachts.

With custom furnishings in the French style of Louis XVI and a staff of more than seventy on board, we could travel the world with all of the luxury of Mar-a-Lago or Hillwood, while enjoying the spontaneity of our own whims. Ned liked to enjoy his drinks in the bar lounge or his cigars in the smokers' saloon. When not swimming off the deck, we could keep active or enjoy massages in our state-of-the-art exercise rooms. Ned could get a shave while I had my hair washed and set in the salon. Deenie relished the private screenings in our onboard movie theater, accompanied by her full-time tutor and nanny, a firm but capable woman by the name of Mrs. Tytler. The kitchen staff served our meals on our custom *Sea Cloud* blue-and-white china. And thanks to Birds Eye Frozen Foods and the coolers we'd installed in our cooking galleys, we did not lack for good meals—everything from our vegetables to our desserts could come from the very menu that General Foods had made available to the public.

That first season aboard the *Sea Cloud,* we crisscrossed the seas from Martinique all the way to France and then Italy. Deenie delighted in everything—cooking with the staff in the crew galley, counting the dolphins that crested the waves along the bow, swimming in the warm waters of the Caribbean while massive turtles lolled beside her. She and Ned would spend hours fishing together, him showing her how to drop her line over the deck while I sat in a lounger nearby and enjoyed the gentle warmth of the sunshine and their laughter.

Those carefree months on the seas had all the makings of blissful happiness. Ned loved being a captain at sea. Deenie loved the ship. I loved my family. We should have been nothing but content as we relished the joys of an exciting and picturesque voyage together. And yet, even though the winter sun poured down on us, bright and brilliant; even though I had the people I loved most right beside me; even though my body was strong and healthy and I had blessings around me beyond counting, I could not ignore the fact that a frostiness had taken hold of my marriage.

One morning that winter, as we were anchored off the coast of southern France, I sat on the deck finishing my breakfast against the colorful backdrop of the port city of Cannes. White gulls circled overhead as the softest of breezes rippled the turquoise of the Mediterranean, and I felt the stirrings of hope. We were in France, one of my favorite places on the planet. The weather was balmy, and the view of the sea crashing against the cliffs was divine. Could we put things to right? I certainly hoped so. I would certainly try my hardest.

Ned and I had quarreled the night before, just after dinner. He'd made a comment to Deenie during the meal, calling me a spoilsport when I'd declined his suggestion that we head to shore and visit some of the nearby Riviera casinos. I'd managed to bridle my tongue in front of our daughter, but after Deenie had gone to bed, I had let him hear it; I'd had enough of him painting me like that—to our friends, to his business associates, now to our daughter. He'd said nothing in defense or apology, he'd simply skulked off to the bar lounge aboard the ship, not returning to sleep in our stateroom.

But today, I reminded myself, was a new day. I would apologize for how angry I'd gotten. Perhaps he'd apologize for his infantile name-calling. We could take a swim with Deenie in the Mediterranean, perhaps motor to shore in one of the skiffs for a relaxed lunch under an umbrella at one of those colorful beachside bistros. It would be a good day for all three of us, together.

As Ned and I had slept in different bedrooms, I hadn't yet seen my husband or my daughter, but I was ready to get our day started. I had decided that I would surprise Deenie by telling her and Mrs. Tytler that they could have a day off from lessons. After lunch we could rig up one of the smaller sailboats and Ned could steer the three of us up the coast, looking for a pleasant cove where we could fish and swim.

Just then, the sound of footsteps on the deck, and my lady's maid appeared. I made to rise from my chair. "Ah, Renée. Good morning. Have you seen Deenie or Mrs. Tytler?"

"No, Madame."

I patted down the skirt of my light-blue dress, making a note that I'd need to pack a bathing suit for our outing. "Very well. And how about Mr. Hutton?"

Renée's gaze flickered, only for a moment, before she answered: "Mr. Hutton . . ." She blinked against the bright sunlight, or perhaps she was avoiding my eyes. "I saw him going ashore, Madame Hutton."

Now it was my turn to blink, surprised as I was by the news. "What?"

"I saw him in one of the skiffs. Heading toward the port."

"When?" I asked.

"An hour ago, perhaps." Renée folded her hands together before her waist.

I looked out over the deck and toward the shore, as if I might find Ned's distant figure against the outline of the mountainous coast. But of course I could not. "Was he . . . alone?"

"Yes, Madame. Driving the small boat himself toward the port."

I sat back in my chair, my hopes for the day pierced. Ned had already left, gone to shore on his own. I had so many more questions, but I knew Renée could not provide me with their answers. No one could, other than my husband. *Why, Ned? What are you doing?*

He'd been distant for weeks, disappearing for hours at a time even though we were contained together aboard a ship surrounded by seawater. But with the yacht being as massive as it was, it was surprisingly easy to lose track of each other. He could be in the movie theater, in the exercise rooms, in the lounge, with the barber. When I found him—sometimes half a day later—and asked him where he'd been, he'd shrug and tell me he'd been fishing, or swimming, or getting a shave.

But leaving the ship without even telling me—going ashore on his own into a harbor city, one that he knew I wanted to see and visit with him—that was a first. Was he really so angry with me because of our quarrel the night before? Should I commandeer a dinghy for myself and go look for him? But that felt foolish. I didn't know which café or fishing cove he'd be in. He'd come back, I reasoned. He was simply trying to teach me a lesson. *Fine,* I thought. *Let us both cool off.* I wasn't going to chase him like some naughty dog off his leash.

The morning warmed and brightened to afternoon. The hours passed as the white sun arced across the sky and then began to dip over the Maritime Alps, stippling the coast in soft hues of rose and gold, and still Ned did not return. Nor was he back when Deenie and I met up for supper on the deck.

I sat there with my daughter, poking my plate of fresh-caught bluefin tuna, doing my best to look at ease even though I had very little appetite. When Deenie asked, "Where is Daddy?" I forced a smile from my strained features.

"He went to explore Cannes a bit."

Deenie frowned, confused. "Why didn't we go with him?" she asked. It was the natural question.

At that I became slightly flustered, but I did my best to stammer a credible reply: "He . . . he wanted to scout some good fishing spots. To . . . to take you. Tomorrow."

Deenie accepted this, turning back to her dinner plate. I looked out once more over the water and, beyond that, the shimmering coastline of the Riviera. Daylight had given way to the glimmer of candlelit cafés and colorful dance halls. I could hear the faint echoes of their music. Where was Ned amid all that activity? And when would he come back?

"Any word of Mr. Hutton?" I asked once I was back in my stateroom, Renée helping me undress for bed. The French girl simply shook her head, lowering her eyes as she turned away from me and crouched low to return my shoes to the wardrobe. I sighed and got into bed, but I did not sleep much that night.

Ned did not return the next morning. Or the next afternoon. I had Cook prepare dinner for the three of us, certain that Ned would have returned by then, but he did not. As Deenie became more confused, I went from feeling frustrated and guilty to being just plain furious. "Where is Daddy?" she asked again. I mumbled something about business that he had to tend to onshore, and she accepted my answer, but we both settled into an uneasy quiet for the remainder of the meal. Finally, after we had finished dinner and I'd sent Deenie off to watch a movie with Mrs. Tytler, as I stood alone on the deck, I saw a small light blinking toward us from the coast. The humming rasp of a small, far-off boat engine and the faint smell of petrol. One of our dinghies. *Ned!*

I groaned aloud, a mixture of relief and anger, as I braced for his return and the confrontation that I knew would come. The night was dark, but I saw the outline of his small dinghy getting bigger as he approached, and then I saw his figure steering the small craft.

Ned pulled up alongside our starboard side as several crew members scrambled to help him aboard. I felt ill as I watched him fumble with the rope to tie off the dinghy, and I knew instantly that he was in some state. My relief at seeing him hardened to fury. As he clambered up onto the yacht, he looked disheveled and unsteady on his feet, and I guessed it had nothing to do with the gently rolling surf. He saw me standing there, watching, and he didn't attempt to hide his grimace. His hair was ragged, his cheeks ruddy with sunburn and God knew what else. Eyes red-rimmed, as if he hadn't slept in days. Which, I assumed, he hadn't. "Where the hell were you?" I demanded, hating the desperation that was so evident in my voice. But bother that, I decided; I'd waited two days for answers, and now I'd have them.

His breath was terrible when he answered, "Well, hello to you, too, my dearest Miss Post."

I ignored his sarcasm, repeating my question: "Where, Ned?"

He shrugged, pointing toward the bright coast, and then turning back to me, he said only: "Ashore."

"How dare you?" I leaned toward him. The servants, I noticed, had scrambled off, leaving us alone on the starlit deck with nothing but the beautiful Mediterranean night and our ugly, seething anger.

Ned leaned on the railing, eyeing me sideways, his blond hair drooping over his glassy expression as he said, "What, am I one of your servants now? I failed to punch in for duty, that it?"

"No, you are my husband," I said, my voice sharp against the lovely sounds of rolling water and wind. "You are my husband, Ned, even if you . . . even if you refuse to act like it."

"What does that mean?" he asked, looking me squarely in the eyes for the first time. A challenge.

What *did* it mean? I wondered in silence. And did I even have the courage to say it aloud?

Chapter 30

Hillwood Estate, Long Island
Spring 1934

"POOR BILLIE," I SAID, READING THE NEWSPAPER WITH A FROWN. The society articles regularly roiled with insinuations of Flo's liaisons, but recently his outings with his golden-haired stage star Marilyn Miller had gotten so regular and flagrant that Billie had an all-out scandal on her hands.

Ned responded with a vague grunt, not looking toward the newspaper spread before me. I cleared my throat, pressing on: "I know that Billie turns a blind eye, but don't think for a minute that I'd do the same, Ned Hutton." I attempted to keep my tone light as I said it, as if it were a mere hypothetical quip I was tossing out, but inside, my heart clamored. *Answer me, Ned. Tell me I have nothing to worry about.*

But instead, Ned simply rose from the breakfast table and left the room in silence, leaving my heart not only clamoring, but aching as well.

Billie had kept quiet in spite of an abundance of evidence, but the truth was, so had I. Now there was no longer any denying what I had for so long trembled to admit, either aloud or even silently to myself: my husband, whom I still adored madly, certainly seemed to look—and behave—like a man on the stray.

Had I been blind? Perhaps even willfully so? And if so, for how long? For years he'd declined to accompany me when I'd take my brief trips away to Saratoga or Newport for spa weekends, but he rarely gave me much detail when I returned and asked him about his time. Then he'd started slipping away for fishing excursions with more frequency, trips with the gentlemen only, long weekends to Montreal or Atlantic City, never inviting me. And of course, when we were at sea, there'd been many a night when I'd returned to the yacht for bedtime with Deenie but my husband had chosen to stay ashore. "One more drink," he'd say, all innocent smiles as he leaned on a beachside bar, only to return many hours—or sometimes even days—later.

I'd noticed the way Mrs. Tytler blanched when he entered a room, averting her eyes and finding some excuse to quickly leave. Many of the maids did the same, especially Renée. Was it so bad that even my servants pitied me and reviled my husband? Even my maid knew what I had yet to admit to myself?

But because I had never been confronted with anything amounting to cold and hard evidence, I'd stanched that nagging and perfidious voice of suspicion, stuffing it deep within my belly, willing my mind to scrub it out of my thoughts. When the doubts had refused to relent, I'd leaned on my faith, begging God that my husband might prove me wrong. Or, at the very least, that he'd change. And then I'd waited; I'd given him chance after chance in the hopes that these were just passing moments of weakness—perhaps even elicited, in part, by my combative behavior—rather than part of a perennial pattern. I'd redoubled my efforts to be the loving and lovable wife, hoping that if we could only turn the corner in our marriage, Ned would no longer see a reason to stray from it.

The fact of the matter was that I just loved Ned Hutton. I loved the man desperately. I longed with every beat of my heart to keep our marriage intact because I simply did not want to imagine life without Ned Hutton as my husband. I longed to keep him with me and Deenie, the daughter to whom he was such a loving father. Those desperate, indelible desires had allowed me to delude myself for months, and then years. The only alternative would have been to leave him—and that, I was unwilling to do.

So I didn't leave.

And I didn't confront him.

Until, finally, it became so brazen that I began to wonder if perhaps Ned wanted me to see it.

IT WAS A mild, overcast day in early spring. We were at Hillwood for the weekend, and I thought it would be nice to take a walk with Ned down to the beach. Deenie was out for a riding lesson, so I went alone to my husband's bedroom. There, to my surprise, I found the door to his suite locked. I knocked gently. No answer from within. I pressed my ear to the heavy oak door but could not hear anything other than the clamor of my own heartbeat. I turned to leave, angry with myself for the silly jealousy that had pricked upon my discovery of the locked door. *Such foolishness,* I thought. What good would such suspicions serve anyone?

But then, just as I was turning to walk away from my husband's bedroom, I heard it. A laugh, Ned's. And then another noise—faint rustling—followed by soft steps on the wooden floor. Someone rising from the bed. And then laughter again—not Ned's. The low but unmistakable sound of a lady's laughter.

The world went blank before me, and I thought I might faint. Wobbly, leaning against the wall of the corridor, I made my way back to my room. Once there, I knew that only some frantic and busy activity might keep me upright, so I threw open the lid of one of my traveling trunks. Without any awareness of what I was doing, I began to toss my personal items into it—gloves, stockings, shirtwaists, undergarments.

I rang the bell for Renée. I would leave. I'd go back to New York City. I'd take Deenie and we would leave without telling him. I'd have the locks on the door changed, and I'd keep him out. I needed to get out of there, fast.

I rang again for Renée, this time more insistently. I was too addled, too dizzy with rage and anguish to pack, and I needed her help. But she didn't come. I rang a third time, pressing down on the bell's button angrily. But still no sign of Renée. For three quarters of an hour, she did not come. Finally, as my trunks were bursting with rumpled and unmatched clothing items, she appeared at the door to my suite.

I turned to face her, seeing the surprise on her features as she noticed my trunk. "Where were you?" I snapped, venting the anger I felt toward my husband on my poor, unsuspecting lady's maid.

"Seeing to the"—she looked around the room—"bedding, Madame." Renée folded and then unfolded her hands before her waist. "To change the sheets."

I felt a sudden surge of blood to my temples. "Bedding?" I looked at her empty arms.

Renée swallowed, saying nothing. I narrowed my eyes, studying her suddenly with a prickling feeling of discomfort: she looked prim and tidy as always, but was that a tinge of flush on her cheeks? And did her hair look as though it had been just recently brushed, more recently than when she had dressed that morning? She smelled of her fresh rose water, but why would she have reapplied it in the middle of the afternoon? And where were these bedsheets she had been fetching?

I shook my head no. Surely not. My own lady's maid? *She would never.* He *would never.* But then I knew it: yes. I felt it like a tug within my breast, my heart's immutable response to my head's attempts at reason—and denial.

Yes, he would.

And now there was no way to unknow what I had seen in the bright and stark daylight of the truth. My heart felt as if it might rupture, and I plopped down on top of my trunk with an audible sigh. *Bedsheets. Bedsheets, indeed.*

That was it. To continue on in such a manner would have driven me mad. But how to proceed? How does one go about getting a divorce—a *second* divorce—from the man she still loves? The man who runs her company and manages her millions. The man who adores her, *their,* beloved daughter. The man who would no doubt fight to keep all of these things.

Ed Close, though he'd been deeply disappointed by my request for a divorce, had accepted my decision with his customary civility, the same cool resignation that I'd found so infuriating at so many other points in our marriage. Divorce was not *how things were done* in Ed Close's world, but if we were going to do it, he wanted it done swiftly and quietly, with no whiff of scandalous discord to further add to the unpleasantness, not a single morsel of gossip to set society tongues to wagging.

Ned would be different. Ned, as I knew all too well, was a man of passions. Our love, like our fights, had been mad and fiery, and I already knew that he would oppose a divorce if he found even the slightest opportunity to do so. And Ned Hutton never shied away from a fight. If I wanted to do this quickly, my dignity coming out intact, I would need to be smart about it. I would not ask Ned for permission; I would present him with my decision as a fait accompli.

But according to the law, I would need proof of his infidelity in order to do that. Only if I, as a woman, could *prove* to the court that the man was a philanderer would I have the right to sue him for divorce, with my custody of Deenie assured and no possible claims on my company or my money. And so I would get it, I decided. And my husband, by carrying on his dalliances right under our own roof, had just given me the best way to do so.

I may have been Mrs. Edward F. Hutton to my staff, but the fact of the matter was that the servants had their generous salaries from my bank account, and they worked for me. And so the next day, while Ned was out, I summoned his valet to my suite.

"Mrs. Hutton, you asked for me?"

"Good morning, Clip. Yes, I did. Shut the door, please," I said, waving him into the room. "I have something you can help me with."

The proof came in the shoe prints—two pairs of distinct shoe prints, crossing my husband's bedroom and leading into the bed. I'd asked Ned's valet to carry out the plan precisely: on my direction the man had sprinkled the wood floor and carpets of Ned's suite with the thinnest layer of mineral powder. Not enough to see with the naked eye—certainly not if one had other, more pressing matters on the mind when crossing that suite.

When I hired a private detective to come in and check two pairs of shoes against the suspicious prints that led into my husband's bed, we got a perfect match—Ned's and Renée's.

Chapter 31

New York City
1934

"YOU'RE WAY OFF THE MARK, MARJIE. I DON'T EVEN KNOW THE girl."

"Her name is Renée, Ned, and you know her quite well. At least show her—and me—what little respect you can in this dreadful business."

"Aw, Marje, this is crackers. Why would I dally with your servant?"

"It beats me, Ned. I was hoping you could explain that one."

"Goddamn it, Marjorie, you've got it all wrong! You know I love you. More than anything!" He huffed, indignant, trying to deter me with this show of righteous outrage.

But I was not a fool. At least, not any longer. I squared my shoulders and stared him directly in the eyes as I went on: "I don't do anything by half measures, Ned Hutton. You should know that by now. When I set out to discover if you were an adulterer, I did the work, and now I have the proof."

I saw his entire frame sag at this, as if the air had been pulled from his lungs, and with it his will to fight. He looked at me as if he did not know me, as if I were no longer the woman he had held in his arms so many times. Just as I had never thought it possible that he would stray, he had never thought it possible that I would leave. And now here we both were, staring down the final lessons we'd teach each other in this wrecked and ravaged union.

I cleared my throat, summoning steel to my voice even though all I wanted to do was weep. But that would have to come later. For now, I had to act. "Here is how it will go, Ned: You'll give me the divorce. I'll keep

Deenie with me. You'll get her for visits over the summers and holidays. I'll pay you what's fair, but you won't take my homes. I'll keep them all. You'll step down from the board of my company."

"Marjorie . . . please. Can we discuss this? Let's both just slow this down a bit. . . ." His voice was choked. "This is my *life*. You are going to ruin my life, do you hear? My daughter. My work. My home. Everything that you and I have—"

I raised my hand. "Ned, there's nothing more to discuss." I just needed to get this out, and then he would not take anything more from me, least of all my dignity. "My life is ruined, too. Don't you see that? The only difference is that I'm not the one who decided to ruin it."

SUMMER GAVE WAY to fall, and then, somehow, it was winter. We celebrated a quiet Christmas and then a subdued New Year's together, me and my girls at home in Palm Beach. For months, I had felt too melancholy to do much more than simply rise from bed and then sit, alone, in my bedroom. Knowing that it was a crushing heartbreak for Deenie, too, I knew better than to weep in front of her, but Eleanor and Adelaide were with me, mercifully. My youngest, fortunately, had just been enrolled at Mount Vernon that fall. Deenie would, I hoped, have plenty at school to keep her mind off the heartbreak that filled the home she'd just left.

Colby Chester took the reins of General Foods without a moment of hesitation, vowing to me that I would not need to worry about the company during this transition from Ned's leadership. The company would be all right. My Deenie would be all right. My family would be all right. Everyone told me this, and yet I found it nearly impossible to believe.

The truth was that I had been in a state of mourning for quite some time, long before the divorce papers had been signed in court and then splashed across the news journals. I'd taken years to reckon with the unwanted possibility that the husband I adored was betraying me. That my marriage was careening toward its disastrous end. But still, it felt like a death for which I could never have braced.

* * *

Nor could anything have prepared me for what came just a few months later. Less than half a year after the signing of our divorce agreement.

Ned had told me that he still needed me. That he loved me as wildly as he had on the day we married. That his life would be ruined if I left him. And yet, shortly after the New Year, while reading the society pages of the New York papers to see what I might have been missing during my quiet respite in Florida, I saw a photo that showed quite a different story. It may have been black-and-white, but it exploded before me in a stunning barrage of colorful details.

Ned, smiling.

Ned, accompanied by a beautiful young girl.

Ned . . . planning to marry again.

Hell, I couldn't look away in time; I could not help but read the article. And as I did, I noted that I recognized not just Ned's face, but hers as well. A young divorcée, about the same age as my Adelaide. The caption spelled out her name: Dorothy Metzger.

I blinked, my memories shifting and swirling violently in my mind. A girl not yet in her twenties, out and about without her parents. Adelaide's guest. A summer party at my home on the Gold Coast. The theme: Versailles. The costumed guests behaving like a crowd of fools. A brazen young girl with wigged men pinching cigarettes and dollar bills from between her breasts.

Dorothy Metzger. Ned was going to marry *that* girl.

The memories shifted again as my vision swam. I was no longer a jilted ex-wife or a scandalized mother on the Gold Coast but a smiling young girl, still in finishing school, popping in for a surprise visit to my father, only to stumble on the scent of cherry perfume and a scattering of inexplicable divorce papers. And then I heard him in the next room with that woman, that woman who was not my mother.

Oh, Papa.

Oh, Ned.

Oh, Marjorie Merriweather Post, you fool.

How could they have done this to me? Both of them—these twin betrayals. A pair of cuts so deep that they could never truly heal. Why had the two men I loved most proven to be the worst men of all?

Chapter 32

Palm Beach, Florida

ALL THAT HAD ONCE BEEN BEAUTIFUL AND BRIGHT, EVERYthing in my world that had seemed to me lovely and joyous, pure—fair and right—all of it went black. Grief and shock and embarrassment bled together in a blotting brushstroke that darkened everything I saw. Everything I had known.

Melancholy. That's what Papa had named it. Others called it malaise. World-weariness. Doctors now had a term of their own for it; they called it depression. They could call it whatever they liked; I knew of the menace that lurked all around me, an inheritance bestowed on me not only by Papa but by Mother as well. It was grief, plain and simple; crippling, blackening grief, and it threatened to swallow me whole if I did not fight with everything I had to keep it at bay. *Depression*. Great in its enormity, terrible in its depth. America was in the midst of it, and so was I.

Not since Papa's death had I felt such a consuming pull of grief that made it hard to emerge from under my thick covers. But even then, when I'd lost Papa, at least I'd had a fight into which I could pour myself—the fight with Leila for my family's company and my daddy's legacy and fortune. This time, what was there to rise and fight for? Where would I find the strength to claw my way out of this primal morass of heartache?

The answer came, as always, from right within my own home. My girls. Yes, they were older. Yes, Adelaide and Eleanor were both married in households of their own, and Deenie was off at boarding school, where she was changing from girl into young woman, growing less dependent on her old mom with each passing day. And yet their hearts still needed me. I was, and would always be, their mother, and they would turn to me as they navigated their own respective swells of joy and pain.

And for my Adelaide, one such swell loomed that winter as my eldest girl faced the indisputable fact that her own marriage was doomed. After years of discord, Adelaide had finally accepted a hard truth of her own: that her husband, Tim, was an unrepentant philanderer and spendthrift. She wept to me that she longed to sue for divorce. What could I do but hold her and reassure her that she was correct in her decision? Promise her that her life would go on. That she was not a failure simply because her marriage was over. That she, somehow, would manage to survive. Not only survive but, someday, stitch back together all of the pieces that suddenly felt so fractured and lost to her.

The truth was that I needed those words then more than ever, particularly as I began to read every few days in the society pages about Ned and the brand-new Mrs. E. F. Hutton. I read about how eager Dorothy was to start a family. I read about how Ned Hutton couldn't keep his hands off his glamorous young bride while they danced all night uptown at the Cotton Club or swallowed down steaks and martinis at The "21" Club.

Men. Even the good ones turned out to be rotten. They hurt me, and they hurt those I loved most. I loathed the thought of bumping into Ned or Dorothy. I dreaded the thought of seeing friends and acquaintances around town, even the most well-meaning among them. Such run-ins were inevitably accompanied by whispers behind gloved hands. The darting of eyes and lifting of eyebrows when I entered the room. Even the sympathetic grimaces of people who wished me well—I wanted none of it.

So, that winter, I remained in Palm Beach, where I could lose myself in Mar-a-Lago's lush embrace. Where the sounds of surf and birdsong could distract my listless thoughts, and sunshine and warmth could nurse my bruised heart. Ned had griped about all the money we'd spent—*my* money—to build the place, but now look at how things were fixed: he was gone, but the house remained. And in that sorrowful season, it was my refuge.

I didn't much feel like playing the society hostess that season. I kept Mar-a-Lago's gates shut and remained largely cloistered within the sprawling grounds of my waterfront retreat. I slept. I swam. I walked the beach. I studied the landscaping and the flowers with my gardeners, picking the mangoes and oranges that went into my breakfast and lunch. I turned to my faith, finding some comfort in the belief that there was a higher power that understood the mad way of things, even though I myself could not. I spent quiet evenings at home, accompanied by the moon and the ocean, calmed by the sounds of the tree frogs and the doves as the water lapped my shores with its rhythmic and timeless lullaby.

Perhaps it was the period of prolonged rest; perhaps it was the gentle sunshine and the fresh air, the tender and protective presence of my household staff; but by the end of winter, I began to feel the stirrings of hope once more. I began to feel that my heart had healed enough to brave some small outings past the gates of my own personal cloister. I began to telephone Colby Chester more regularly, to check in on board meetings and keep abreast of the company's updates. On one of those calls, Colby paused at the end of our talk. Silence pulsed on the long-distance line, and I could tell there was something more he wished to discuss before we hung up, likely having nothing to do with business. "Marjorie?"

I curled the cord around my fingers. "Yes?"

"If it's not too forward . . . if you don't mind my asking . . . how are you doing? Really doing?"

I sighed, considering my answer. After a long moment, I said, "You know what, Mr. Chairman? It hurts like hell. In fact, I felt like I was in hell there for a while. But I'll be damned if I'm going to let any devil get the best of me."

I could make out the sound of Colby laughing from hundreds of miles away, and then his reply: "I sure am glad to hear that. That sounds like the old Miss Post."

"No need to go calling me *old*—"

"Oh, Marjorie, you know what I mean."

"Colby, you've known me long enough. I'm not going to let anyone knock me down for too long. I'll always get back up to go another round."

When Colby spoke, his voice had turned wistful, and I could tell he was smiling as he said, "You sound an awful lot like someone I once knew."

I nodded, not saying anything.

After a moment, Colby added: "Well, Miss Post, it's good to have you back."

"Thanks, Colby. It's good to be back."

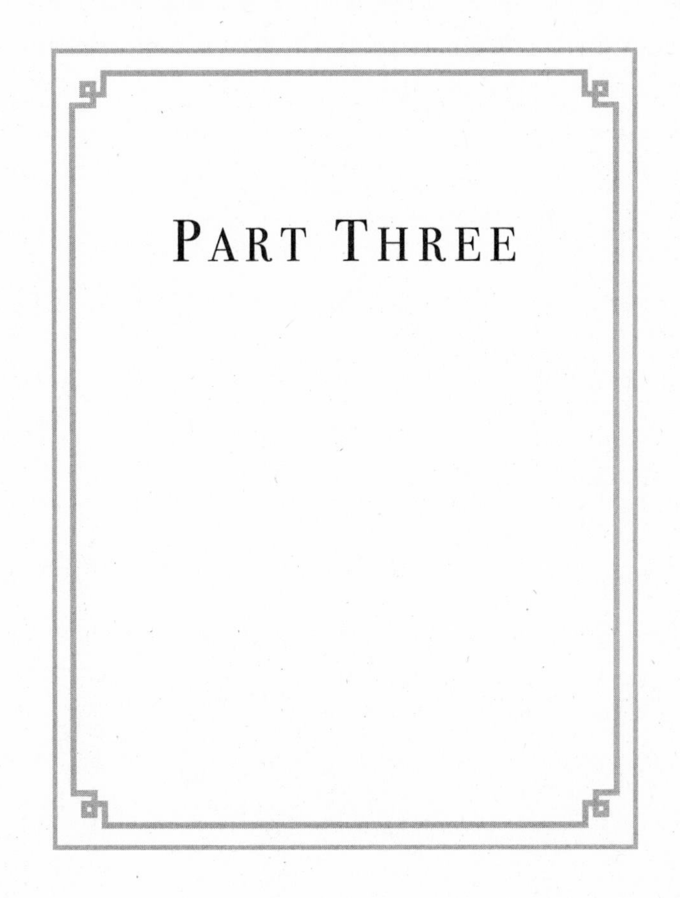

Part Three

Chapter 33

Palm Beach, Florida
Spring 1935

IT SOUNDED LIKE A SIMPLE ENOUGH INVITATION, A SMALL GATHERing with my old friend May Carlisle. "It'll be just a casual dinner *chez nous,* Marjorie, dear," May promised when she telephoned me from her home a short distance from South Ocean Boulevard. "Jay and I are having a dear friend who is in town from Washington. We'd love to have you." A pause, and then: "I've missed you."

"I've missed you, too," I answered, my voice quiet. "Oh, all right. One dinner. I can't see the harm in that."

So I pulled myself together. And as I scrutinized myself in the mirror I noticed that, for the first time in months, I liked what I saw in the reflection. The sun had kissed my cheeks, turning them a soft, rosy hue. My hair, freshly washed and swept loosely from my neck and face, was streaked with gold. My body was lean—too lean, as I'd had absolutely no appetite lately—but my muscles were firm from all the swimming and gardening, and my blue eyes had regained some of their glimmer as I looked forward to a night in the company of an old and caring friend.

May's welcome put me at ease as soon as I arrived, reassuring me that I had been right to make my first and gentle foray back into society at her side. "My darling Marjorie. I'm so delighted you made it!" May greeted me with a kiss on each cheek and a full smile, her arm sliding around my waist. "But my goodness, look at you. Slim as a chorus girl."

"Well, it's a wonder what heartache will do for the waistline," I answered, my tone wry.

"Oh, honey, I know." May leaned toward me, giving my arm a conspiratorial squeeze. A gesture that felt more like support than pity, which I appreciated. May went on: "What a cad he turned out to be. I'm not even going to speak his name aloud. I'm just glad you are out, rather than pining away at home. He's not worth your tears, Marjorie."

"Thank you," I answered, fearful I'd lose my fortitude if I said more.

May straightened beside me, looking effortlessly lovely in a flowing dress of lemon-yellow chiffon with a large floral print, her hair pulled back and accented by a single spray of hibiscus. "Well, I'd offer you a stiff drink, but I know you'd just turn me down. Come say hello to Jay. He's been asking after you all winter."

I saw where her husband, Jay, stood across the candlelit terrace—but he was not alone. "Who's that?" I asked, my steps halting as my eyes landed on the gentleman involved in conversation with May's husband. The man was tall and slim, with dark hair and, from the looks of it, a strong opinion on whatever topic he was discussing.

"Oh, that's Joe Davies," said May. "Our friend from Washington. Didn't I tell you we have a houseguest this weekend?"

"Yes, but when you said a dear friend of yours, I assumed it was . . ." I studied the man a moment longer, noticing the expressiveness of his dark eyes, warm and wide set, as he spoke. Just then he said something that made Jay erupt in laughter.

May's features creased into a coy expression as she turned back to me—the face that one makes when she's just been struck by a brilliant idea. That, or when she realizes that her brilliant idea has been taken up by her confidante. "He is a dear friend, Marjorie." And now May's voice was low and conspiratorial. "And not only to us, but to President Roosevelt as well. Remarkable man, really."

"He's from Washington?" I asked.

"Yes."

"Well, I'm just glad to hear that he doesn't come from Wall Street."

"Far from it," May said, laughing.

I went on: "And hopefully that means he hasn't read all about my scandalous divorce." It would be nice to meet someone and not feel as if they already knew all of my dirtiest secrets.

"Oh, I doubt he has," May answered, shaking her head. "Joe is concerned with matters of more consequence than the gossip rags, my dear. He's a lawyer, but the word is that Roosevelt keeps trying to pull him into his administration. Or else convince him to run for the Senate."

"Ah," I said, nodding.

Now *that* was something unexpected. I'd sworn off men—not only Wall Street bankers, but all of them—and yet, as I stood there on that pleasant, starlit southern night, I could not entirely deny the urge I felt to meet this man, this Joe Davies from Washington. So I was delighted when May leaned close and whispered, "Let's sit down to dinner. I hope you don't mind, but we're terribly informal tonight. I didn't even bother with place cards, since it'll be just the four of us." I did not mind at all.

May guided me toward the table, speaking in a hushed voice: "I'll put Joe to your left." Did I imagine the playful lift of her brow as she smiled at me?

The table was small and tastefully decorated on the terrace overlooking the water, with a crystal vase of fresh-clipped orchids at its center and a small flute of champagne set before each place. Jay, our host, gestured toward his dark-haired friend as he introduced us. "Marjorie Post, please meet Joe Davies, in town to visit us for the weekend. We're trying to convince him there is more to life than just politics."

"It's lovely to meet you, Miss Post." Joe Davies turned his dark-eyed gaze on me, and I felt a shiver across my skin as he extended a hand to help me into my seat. When he tucked in my chair, his fingers lightly brushed past my shoulders. *What was that sensation?* I wondered. *Delight? Attraction?* Whatever it was, it had been months since I'd felt anything like it, and it was not entirely unwelcome.

"And you, Mr. Davies," I answered. "I've heard nothing but the most wonderful things from May."

"That so? I had no idea May was such a liar." Joe Davies took his own seat at the table with a smile. The moonlit surface of the ocean rolled gently behind him. I shifted in my chair, reminding myself not to stare. And to take in a big breath of the warm, salty night air.

"Well, Joe is a particularly welcome guest tonight, because he comes from Washington with some terribly juicy gossip," Jay said, sitting back casually in his chair as a server appeared on the terrace with the first course.

"What's that?" May asked, her features brightening. "What a considerate houseguest you are, Joe, coming with a gift like that."

Joe Davies demurred, lowering his eyes to the table, so Jay willingly carried on, clapping a friendly hand on his guest's shoulder: "Turns out our friend Joe Davies here needed this brief respite in the sun even more than we knew, because things are about to get a lot busier for him."

May and I exchanged an inquisitive glance as Jay continued, "Roosevelt has finally prevailed upon his pal Joe to leave the comforts of his fabulously lucrative private practice and take up the work of our government."

Now I, too, was undeniably intrigued. "In what capacity?" I asked.

Joe cocked his head to the side, accepting his plate of salad as he answered: "It'll be a posting with the State Department, in all likelihood."

"Now, Joe, no need for all this modesty when you're among friends," Jay interjected, and then, leaning toward me, he added, "Pretty soon, we'll all be calling him Ambassador Davies."

"An ambassadorship," I remarked, taking a small sip of my champagne. "How exciting. To where?"

Joe poised his fork above his salad plate as he fixed his dark eyes on me. "Not sure yet," he said. "But most likely England or France."

I nodded, forcing myself to take a small, measured bite. "London or Paris," I said. I could hardly imagine anything more exciting. "Do you have a preference?" I asked.

"No." Joe shook his head. "As I told the president, I wish simply to serve, and—"

But Jay cut in before Joe could finish that thought. "Marjorie, do you know what Roosevelt calls himself?"

I looked toward my host, answering no, I did not.

"FDR calls himself 'Joe Davies's sidekick,'" Jay answered. May laughed.

I turned back toward Joe Davies, my interest further piqued. "How did you become so close with the president?" I asked.

Joe spoke with less flair than Jay, but I found myself impossibly drawn toward him, eager to hear whatever it was he had to say. "I worked with Woodrow—er, President Wilson at the Paris Peace Conference."

I cocked my head. "After the Great War?"

"Yes," Joe answered. "Franklin and I became close as young men around that time. Back when we both had a bit more time for golf."

"Did you come from a political family?" I asked.

"Not at all. I come from a long line of dedicated drunks."

I couldn't help but laugh at this sudden and unexpected swerve, marveling at the man's candor. And humility. Joe went on, and I noticed, only vaguely, that May and Jay had speared off into a conversation of their own, leaving Joe and me to ourselves. "From Washington, though, I presume?" I asked.

He shook his head. "Welsh immigrants. My parents made their home in Watertown, Wisconsin."

I straightened in my seat, my entire frame enlivened as I replied, "Ah, and I come from Battle Creek, Michigan."

Joe's dark-eyed gaze glimmered. "So we are a pair of displaced midwesterners."

"It appears we are."

"My father passed away before I'd finished grammar school," Joe said, taking a bite of his food. I stole yet another sideways glance toward him as he did so, noting the fine cut of his pale linen suit. His impeccable posture. The strong, pleasing contours of his profile. This was a man who had ascended to the trust and close friendship of multiple presidents of the United States entirely on his own merit and work. Much like another man I had known.

Joe must have felt me staring, because he raised his gaze and met my eyes directly. And then his expression shifted suddenly, and he looked at me the way one might study some ornate piece of art. I sat back a bit in my chair. His voice quiet, Joe leaned close and said: "Your eyes are quite lovely, Marjorie. But I am sure you already know that."

I laughed at this, mostly to buy myself time to form some response, and then I answered: "Well, Joe Davies, I'd say you already have your political flattery down."

His eye contact flickered just momentarily, and I saw it sweep over the bare skin of my arms, my shoulders, before rising back to meet my gaze. "I'm not a politician, remember? I'm a lawyer."

"I'm not sure if that's better."

He grinned at this. "Regardless, I'll look away now, so you don't find me terribly rude. Otherwise I might just end up staring at you all evening." He did look away, but then he leaned toward me, and with a playful smirk, he gestured toward his salad plate and whispered, "It's a fine salad, but I do have to say—I'm partial to Birds Eye vegetables."

"Are you, now?" I asked, tilting my head sideways.

Joe nodded. "That was brilliant on your part, if I might say so. Those vegetables. And all of the other frozen foods. Why, I probably eat Birds Eye at least three times a week."

"I'm glad that I could be of service. I thought it was a good idea, too." I turned back to my own plate, noting that I was in fact quite hungry; for the first time in a long while, my appetite had come to the table. "So, Joe Davies, when do you head off to Europe for your assignment?"

"I'm not certain," he said, lifting his gaze toward me. "Why do you ask? Are you interested in a trip to Paris? Or London?"

"Oh, always," I said, managing a casual smile.

"Well, you have to promise me that when you come over, you'll let me know. Will you?"

"Won't you be entirely too busy?"

"For you? I doubt it."

I could feel my heart beating in my throat, between my ears, against my necklace. May and Jay were prattling on beside us, telling the servants to pour the wine and bring the next course. I turned my focus toward my plate again, stanching the urge to beam too brightly. A wave broke on the nearby shore and I heard the crash of all that churning water, felt the faintest misting of warm, sticky air on my skin, every inch of it rippling to life. *Oh, May, you are brilliant,* I thought to myself. I had wondered whether I was up for a small dinner party that evening. Now all I could think of was how grateful I was to have accepted the invitation. To have met this lovely man, Joe Davies.

Before the dessert was served, May rose from the table to make a quick trip to the powder room, and I stood to join her, eager to gush about my sudden delight in Joe Davies, eager to praise her inspired idea to introduce us. I noted how he hopped up to help me from my chair, how his eyes followed me from the table, remaining fixed on my retreating figure the entire way across the terrace. I waited until the door to the powder room had closed before I wheeled on my friend, my voice bursting as I exclaimed: "Oh, May! You are a darling."

May took my hands in hers. She smiled, but I could see some strange new tug of restraint in her features as she returned my gaze. "My dear Marjorie." She gave my hands a squeeze. But what was the meaning of her odd expression?

I didn't pause to ask. Instead I gushed on: "He *is* remarkable. His manners! And he's so very smart. And about to become ambassador to France or England? Goodness, he's something. And to think that he's managed to accomplish all this when—"

But May raised a hand, and my words ceased midsentence. "I expected you might find Joe Davies interesting," May said. "I thought you'd enjoy meeting him. Chatting. Perhaps even flirting a bit. But I never expected . . . well, *that*. The pair of you look like you've been pierced by arrows."

So I wasn't the only one who had felt it. I couldn't help but smile at this. I leaned closer to May as I said, "It's daffy to admit this, but I think we might have been."

Then why did my friend's features appear so taut? Why wasn't May happy that her setup had been such an inspired and immediate success? She blinked, her eyes falling to the floor. After a moment, her voice low, she said, "There's only one problem, my dear."

I felt my lungs tighten. "Oh? And what is that?"

May turned her stare back toward me, and I saw her entire frame wilt. And then, with a sigh, she said, "Oh, Marjorie. Joe Davies is a married man."

Chapter 34

New York City

HER NAME WAS EMLEN DAVIES. SHE WAS THE MOTHER TO JOE'S three girls. And very much still his wife, even if the pair had been, according to May, living separately for years. How embarrassing. But even more, how disappointing. To have met a man so attractive, so charming, so interesting—and who apparently had felt all these things about me as well—only to discover that he could never be mine.

I returned to New York City at the end of the spring, eager to see my girls once more but dreading a busy social season, my first one since the split from Ned. I was surprised on the Monday morning that first week back when my butler appeared in my sitting room to tell me that the operator had telephoned with a caller from the District of Columbia. "Deenie?" I asked. She generally only phoned from boarding school on Sunday afternoons or if something was wrong.

"No, ma'am. A Mr. Joseph Davies on the line," the man said, clearly unfamiliar with the name.

I rose and crossed to the corner of the room, where the nearest telephone perched on a round marble table. "I'll take the call in here," I said. The man nodded and shut the door.

I took a moment to compose myself, to clear my throat and force some calm into my voice. Then I picked up the receiver. "Hello?"

"Hello, Marjorie?"

It was Joe. My heart clenched at the sound of his voice.

"This is she," I answered.

"Marjorie—Joe Davies here."

"Hello, Joe." A pause as I drew in a breath. "This is unexpected."

"I . . . I know it is."

Silence.

"Marjorie?"

"Yes?" I was still there.

"I had to call."

I kept quiet, forcing him to fill the silence. Eventually, he did: "Marjorie, I haven't stopped thinking about you. Not for a minute."

So then I hadn't imagined it. "Joe, May told me. About your wife. Emlen is her name, isn't that right?"

"Yes." I heard Joe's exhale, his breath crackling on the line. "Emlen."

I swallowed, and then forced myself to go on. "I don't understand why you didn't tell me."

"I know, Marjorie. I . . . I should have. I didn't know how. You see, she's not . . . It's not really as though we are married."

"I don't understand."

"She's in London. We rarely speak. We rarely see each other. We have nothing between us anymore."

"Three daughters?" I asked.

"Yes, yes. I love my daughters more than anything. But, you see, they're all adults now. And out of the house, living their lives. And it's time that I . . . Well, Marjorie, meeting you was the kick I needed, and now I know."

I didn't say anything. After a pause, Joe said: "I'm going to London, and I'll tell Emlen it's over. It just has to be. So that . . . well, so that this, this between us, can begin. The right way."

"Joe, this is madness."

"That's exactly what it is. I'm mad for you, Marjorie. Was I the only one . . . the only one who felt it?"

The pair of you look like you've been pierced by arrows. That's what May had said. What was the point of lying? "You weren't, Joe. I felt it, too. But I just about wept right there in May's powder room when she told me you were married."

I heard another exhale. And then his voice again, more urgent. "Can I come up to New York City to see you?"

"No," I said. Silence on the line. "Not until your marriage is well and done."

"Please, just let me visit. Only to talk. We can meet in public somewhere. I just—"

"I won't do to your wife what another woman has done to me."

And I didn't want to see Joe as capable of that, either. That was no way to start a courtship. I didn't want something illicit with him. I wanted, I realized, a proper relationship. And then I wondered—was it a blessing or a curse, my heart's ability to contemplate love once more?

APPARENTLY JOE WAS thinking about love again as well, because from that point forward, I began to receive massive flower arrangements daily. The servants would blanch as they carried in the heaping bowers of rose and lily and peony and begonia. "Another one, ma'am, from a Mr. Davies of Washington."

He'd ring my home several times a week, though I always had my servants offer some excuse as to why I could not answer. He spent a fortune on telegrams that carried no news but snippets of Browning or Shakespeare: "Haply I think on thee, and then my state / Like to the lark at break of day arising / From sullen earth, sings hymns at heaven's gate."

He wrote letters in his beautiful looping cursive as well, but even to these I didn't respond. And yet, of course I read and kept the letters, just as I relished the flowers and delighted in giddy silence at the telegrams and telephone calls. I stowed his handwritten notes in my bedside table and returned to them in the evenings before bed, inevitably shutting my eyes with a pang in my heart. "Dearest Blue Eyes—Do you believe me, dear one, when I tell you how you hold my heart and my soul? There are so many places in my heart that cry out for you. The purest gift in this life would be to look into your beautiful eyes daily."

Though outwardly I remained resolute that we would not converse, that we would not meet, that we would not court in any way while he was a married man, inwardly I was hopeful as I had not been in years, perhaps ever. Joe Davies was a romantic, to be sure, but he was also a serious man. A mature man, an idealist who was about to do great things. To think what life could be like beside him, as his partner. This was not a man who would squander his—or *my*—energy and time at raucous parties. Who would throw my money away at billiards or gambling. After the disillusionment with Ed and then the heartbreak with Ned, to find a man, a devoted man, a self-made man, one who had risen from nothing to the height of power and brilliance and with such a passion for serving others, and to know that he cared for *me*—why, the thought of Joe's love was that much sweeter because of the bitterness that had preceded it.

Finally, that summer, I received the telegram for which I had been longing: "IN LONDON. JUST MET WITH EMLEN. MARRIAGE IS OVER. MY HEART IS YOURS."

The next day I received a follow-up: "SAIL DAY AFTER TOMORROW. STRAIGHT TO NEW YORK. TO MY BELOVED BLUE EYES."

A week later I bid farewell to Deenie, who was home from school for the summer but off to spend two weeks with Ned—and, I shuddered to think of it, Dorothy—down at his estate in South Carolina. Though it tortured me to think of my girl away with the pair of them, the one piece of good luck was that I was alone at home in New York City when Joe arrived, fresh from his Atlantic crossing. "Mr. Joseph Davies here to see you, Mrs. Post," my butler announced that afternoon.

"Thank you. Show him in." The attendant had the good taste to make a swift retreat from the drawing room before noting my flushed appearance. They all knew about Joe Davies, of course; everyone in my household did—about the flowers, the notes, the telegrams, the phone calls. Surely they had suspected that the day for this meeting would arrive. Only no one in the household, least of all me, knew how it would actually go now that Joe had knocked at my door.

I stood, pulling my shoulders back, fixing a calm expression to my features even as every inch of my skin suddenly pulsed with my hastened heartbeat. And then there he appeared, in my drawing room—Joe Davies. His tall figure and dark-eyed smile were even better than I had remembered. He must have changed before disembarking from the steamer, because his striped suit was crisp and immaculate, his brown hair neatly combed. In his hands was a bouquet of a dozen red roses. Best of all was the way he looked at me as he spoke, with an expression that showed both affection and desire. "Well, my dear. I went all the way to London and back for you. I told Emlen it was over. My lawyers have already completed the documents. Now may I finally tell you that I love you?"

I smiled, feeling as if molten silver rippled through my veins. "I suppose you just did."

With that, Joe swept me into his arms, for a kiss long overdue and yet worth every moment of the waiting as our lips finally met. Our bodies folded into each other's as if created for this embrace. But it was over too soon when Joe pulled away, glancing down at me as he said, "But there's just one more problem."

Dread pitted my stomach. "What now?"

Joe smiled, a lone brow lifting. "I hurried here in such haste, I'm afraid I forgot to book a hotel."

I laughed in giddy relief, taking the roses from his grip. "Now, *that's* a problem I think I can help you with."

Then I took his hand in mine and led him to my bedroom suite, blushing at the thought of what the servants would be whispering over their supper that evening. But I didn't care, not really. And I certainly didn't think anything more of my own supper that evening—there were other, more pressing appetites that Joe and I had waited entirely long enough to satiate.

Later, in bed, my entire body soft as I lay wrapped in Joe's arms, I asked him the question that I had been dreading, even though I knew it needed to be addressed. "How did it go?"

He sighed, his finger tracing a line up my back, sending shivers along my skin. "She was angry," he said. "If it were left to her, we would have gone on as we have for years. Not married, but not divorced, either. She keeps my name while we live our lives apart."

I nodded. I knew a thing or two about that sort of arrangement. It was what I had grown up with; it was what I had been so adamant to avoid in my own life.

"The hardest thing," he said, his voice taking on a strained quality, "is the girls. Of course they're not girls anymore, but you know what I mean. They are taking her side."

I swallowed, absorbing this. I tried to sound optimistic when I answered: "For now, they are upset. Of course they are taking their mother's side. It's natural. And it means you raised loyal girls. But they will come around, Joe, once they see what we share between us. I know they will."

He drew in a slow breath. "I certainly hope so," he said, his voice quiet. I turned to face him, tracing the contours of his brow, then his eyes, his perfect nose. When I reached his mouth, I let my lips take over for my fingers, and together we were swept back toward the sort of conversation that required no further words.

We had two weeks together in New York, and we spent them luxuriating in our newfound love. It was the strangest thing with Joe, an intimacy that felt both intoxicating in its newness, in the excitement of discovery and the zeal of untapped ardor, and yet entirely familiar, worn-in and comfortable, as if we'd always known each other, as if our bodies had always sought and loved one another.

Several nights into Joe's stay, I stood before the mirror and made a suggestion over my shoulder. "Would you like to go out tonight? Perhaps for supper, or a show?"

Joe sat in my armchair beside the window, casually skimming the day's newspaper. Beyond him, through the large picture window overlooking Central Park, New York City was awash in the golden light of a balmy summer afternoon. A few hours more and the restaurants would be overspilling with laughter, the theaters packed with their colorful offerings. We'd barely left my house all week save to pick up a few essentials for Joe's stay and to take some brief walks, and he was only there for another week; surely he wished to take in some of New York. Ed, from the very start of our marriage, had needed diversion outside of my company—I'd never been enough to keep his interest. And Ned—well, the man was more at home at raucous night spots or dancing his way through lively parties than at any of our own homes.

Joe flipped the page of the newspaper he was reading, casually glancing up at me with a shrug. "Only if you'd like, Blue Eyes. I'm happy as could be right here in this room."

I couldn't help but beam at this, crossing the room to fold into his lap and plant a kiss on his stubbled cheek. "But aren't you restless? Here you've come all the way to New York City, and you've got nothing but little old me to look at."

Joe's eyes narrowed, boring deep into mine. After a moment, a matter-of-fact look on his face, he said, "I didn't come all this way to see New York City."

I shifted in his lap, slightly tremulous at the intensity of his expression. He went on, his hand moving gently up and down my back as he spoke. "I came to see nothing *but* you, Marjorie Post."

On the final morning, just hours before Joe's departure, we sat in bed eating breakfast together. I wished he could stay longer—indefinitely—but reality had finally summoned us both with calls we could not refuse; Joe was scheduled to visit the president at his family home upstate in Hyde Park, and Deenie was set to arrive back home to me before her upcoming return to school. Our imminent separation was softened by the fact that I was planning to accompany Deenie back to Mount Vernon and then was scheduled to spend a week or so in D.C., where I could see Joe's life. Deenie didn't know this yet. How would she feel about it? Particularly coming off a two-week stay with the father she adored? But my musings were interrupted when Joe spoke: "Marjorie, this may not seem old-fashioned, how I went about this. But I can assure you that in fact I am."

I sat up a bit taller in bed, looking at him. "I am as well," I answered. I did not casually take up with men; I'd been intimate with two others in my life, and both of those men had been my husbands. I suppose I had guessed from the start that Joe wanted to ask me to marry him. And that I wanted to answer yes. But I was far too traditional to be the first one to broach that topic. Instead I said, "I shudder at what my servants must think," laughing as I took a sip of my Postum.

Joe looked at me intently, his dark eyes kindled by a thoughtful expression. After a moment, he said: "You know I will have to leave soon. I don't just mean to Washington. For London or Paris."

My stomach clenched. I had known he was leaving; of course I had.

From the night of our first conversation, I had known that he was preparing for an ambassadorship that would take him overseas. And yet, I hadn't wanted to confront the fact of that longer separation, one that would feel far more arduous than merely my being in New York and his being in Washington.

Joe went on: "It would be harder to travel like this, without setting tongues to wagging. I can't guarantee that State Department aides are as discreet as your staff." He waved a hand between us, indicating our casual companionship in bed, our state of unselfconscious dishabille. "So it sure would be nice if you'd marry me." He said it as an offhand remark, but there was nothing casual about his strained expression as he awaited my reply.

My heart fairly tumbled within my rib cage. Marriage! To Joe Davies. It was what I had wanted, and now here it was, being proposed to me. Marriage, for a third time. And yet, this time, with this man, it felt so entirely different, so entirely unlike the others, that it might as well have been a first for me. I cleared my throat, matching his nonchalant tone as I lowered my cup back to the breakfast tray and asked, "You'd like that, Ambassador Davies?"

"More than anything."

I allowed a beam to burst across my features. "Then I suppose we ought to do it."

At that, Joe leaned forward and kissed me, a firm, determined kiss, one that roiled with desire and the enormity of all that we had just agreed to. We put our breakfast trays aside, forgetting about the rest of our food.

Afterward, he lay beside me. "My fiancée. My own Marjorie." His voice had the giddiness of a youngster. "The girls . . . I told them. Before I asked you, I wanted to let them know."

I turned, angling my body toward his. "And what did they say?"

His beautiful face darkened. A slow exhale, and then Joe said, "At the risk of entirely ruining our celebratory mood, they told me they will do everything they can to break you and me apart."

I nodded, taking a moment to collect my thoughts before offering a reply. "Well, Joe, I'm happy to hear it."

His face crumpled in confusion. "What?" he asked.

I sat up, propping myself on my elbows, my voice resolute as I said: "I wouldn't expect anything less, and frankly, it makes me think that much more of them. I wouldn't have any use for a girl who felt differently. I only hope that, with time, I can show them who I really am, and what their father and I share."

Chapter 35

New York City

"THIRD TIME, I'LL MAKE IT STICK." I STOOD BEFORE THE FULL-length mirror in my bedroom suite, putting the finishing touches on my wedding gown, a velvet creation of pale pink with long sleeves and rose embellishments. Even though the tradition among society brides had been to wear white ever since Queen Victoria had set the trend, I was no virginal bride, and there was no pretending I was. I was a mother of three, marrying a divorcé who had three of his own, and since this would be my third time down the aisle, I had done away with the aisle altogether, Joe and I opting for a private, informal affair at my place, surrounded by just members of our families and a few of our closest friends, including, of course, May and Jay.

I'd had fun with the preparations, ordering a massive cake weighing over two hundred pounds, and I'd filled the home with more than a thousand fresh flowers. The winter morning dawned clear and cold. President Roosevelt sent us a telegram of congratulations. And Joe slipped me a note that arrived on my breakfast tray: "You are the best of me, and praise be, I am the best of you."

How was such a man mine? I had always yearned for love. Twice I had thought I'd found it only to see the specter shift before me without my ever really understanding how—or when—the rupture had happened. After those twin failures, I'd lost hope that a lasting love would ever truly be mine. And yet here he was. The best man of them all. My Joey. And because of what I had been through before him, I could appreciate it all the more. The pain had all been worth it to bring me to this moment, the start of my life as Mrs. Joseph Davies.

As the hour for our exchange of vows approached and our handful of guests began to trickle in, dressed in their lush sable coats and creamy satin gowns, word got out somehow that I was getting married inside on that cold day a couple of weeks before Christmas. Within minutes, a crowd began to gather on the street in front of my door. A few brazen reporters tried to enter, and when my butler declined to let them in, they decided to stand sentry-like, flashbulbs raised, ready to snap a photograph should Joe or I decide to glance out the window.

"Send them all some cake," I said, as I floated happily among my arriving guests.

Billie was there, and I smiled as I kissed her in welcome, asking how the preparations were going for her role as Glinda the Good Witch in the upcoming picture *The Wizard of Oz*. "It's coming along," Billie answered. "Judy is a lovely young girl. But speaking of lovely . . . Marjorie, I don't think I've ever seen you looking this happy."

At that my eyes slid across the small crowd to where my soon-to-be husband was greeting his close friend Stephen Early, press secretary to President Roosevelt. I turned back to Billie, taking her hand in mine. "That's because I *am* happy, Billie," I answered, squeezing her palm.

My friend returned my smile. "Then I'm happy for you, Marjorie, dear."

And yet, I could not claim that sentiment was shared by all who were gathered in our home on that cold day. "You sound like Marie Antoinette," Deenie grumbled as she stood at my side. "*Let them eat cake*." She waved her hands with a theatrically haughty look on her beautiful young face. She was in a sour mood, angry with me, I knew, for getting married to a man other than her father. Had she punished Ned like this on his remarriage? I wondered. But I didn't ask, because, really, what did it matter? That was between her and Ned. I was her mother, and I would do everything in my power to set things right between us, and between her and Joe as well. And I knew that she would come to love my Joey eventually. There was no way to know the man and not love him.

I put my hand to Deenie's cheek. It was soft and smooth, her entire face glowing with youth, her features pristinely beautiful, even if sad. "My darling girl," I said, "Marie Antoinette's groom may have been a king, but

I can promise you that he was not nearly as wonderful as that man over there. I hope you'll give him a chance."

We would depart on the *Sea Cloud* the next week to explore the Caribbean together as newlyweds. Deenie was scheduled to be with her father for the Christmas holiday and then back at school, so Joey and I would travel by yacht from our honeymoon directly to Palm Beach, where we would wait out some of the winter. From there we would go on to Washington, where my new life as Mrs. Joseph Davies awaited.

"MY DEAR, I can't remember the last time a new bride arrived in Washington to ruffle so many of these old vulture feathers. At least, not since my own wedding." Alice Roosevelt looked at me with a wry smirk over my Limoges china teacup. She was now, legally speaking, Alice Longworth, having married her beau, the Ohio congressman Nick Longworth, but she was still Alice Roosevelt to me. And she knew exactly what she was doing in coming to my house that day to join me for a cup of tea. She was showing her support for me, even as the rest of the Washington social set refused to acknowledge my existence.

"I don't know Joe Davies well, but I know *you,* Marjorie Merriweather Post Davies, and if he's good enough for you, then I trust your judgment. Even if he is a friend of old Feather Duster's." Alice used her well-worn nickname for her cousin, our popular president, even though he was no longer the bumbling boy with a childhood crush on her. But the venom between the Oyster Bay Roosevelts, sired by our former president Teddy Roosevelt, and the Hyde Park Roosevelts, the clan of the current president, was the stuff of an epic Greek drama, one that I had no desire to get caught in the middle of.

Fortunately Alice had plenty of other gossip fodder that afternoon, but the topic eventually returned to how hopeless my own social standing was in the capital. "The problem is that Emlen Davies lived here for decades," Alice explained. "Her family's been well regarded in the area for centuries, and she's got a lot of friends. Which means that you, Marjorie dear, have a lot of critics."

"I do see that," I said, frowning as I took a slow sip of my tea. Of course I'd noted how the parlor doors had consistently been closed to me when I'd paid calls to my neighbors just shortly after my arrival to town. How the well-dressed matrons in the restaurants and theaters would look away, brows knitting in censorious scowls, as Joe and I entered together. How whispers seemed to trail my wake as I walked along the streets or stopped in to browse the shops of Georgetown. "But it's not as though I'm an arriviste myself," I went on. "Why, I spent much of my youth here. I went to boarding school up the street. My father lived here for years. My mother lived here until the day she died."

"That's all well and good," Alice replied, shrugging. "But you weren't here as Mrs. Joseph Davies. Now you are, and you're the one they are blaming for Emlen's heartbreak."

I glowered at this. "Heartbreak, my foot. She was living apart from him and never cared to see Joey another day in her life."

Alice sat back in her chair, crossing her ankles as she flashed me an impish smirk. "Oh, but these ladies love a good scandal, and that's precisely what you've given them. Edith Wilson has put the mark of Cain on you."

"Lovely, just what I need. The former First Lady calling for my head."

"She's not the one you should be worried about, dearest," Alice said, leaning toward me. "The one you should be concerned with is Betty Beale."

I knew the name. "The newspaper reporter?"

Alice nodded. "Goodness knows my cousin Eleo isn't First Lady in this town when it comes to society. She's timid as a church mouse. Goes tongue-tied at the sight of a calling card."

Eleanor Roosevelt was notoriously shy and retiring as a hostess, even if I did remember her warm and gracious smiles when she'd welcomed me to the White House a few years prior. But I wasn't going to argue with Alice over her description of her cousin, and she was eager to say more: "If Edith Wilson is the District's first lady when it comes to society and hosting, then Betty Beale is its gatekeeper. Not a gathering occurs without that woman in attendance. And she always reports on who was invited—and who was not."

In the coming weeks, I saw Alice's insights prove all too accurate. Betty Beale used her pen to slice me up on an almost daily basis. Having weathered plenty of bad press already in my life, I didn't care all that much that she wrote about how I was barred entry to the regular teas given by Mary Borah—wife of the powerful and longtime Idaho senator Bill Borah—or that Edith Wilson had put the word around town that she would not attend any gathering to which I might also be invited.

What *did* bother me was the gossip having to do with Joe's and my relationship. That I had paid Emlen millions in order to cajole her into accepting the split. That Joe didn't really love me, but rather loved my money. That I had seduced Joe into a tawdry affair. That I had my eyes on FDR and was planning on using my politically connected husband to get all the way to the White House.

None of this, of course, was true. I'd never spoken to Emlen Davies; I'd never offered her a cent. Nor was Joe some shameless fortune hunter, marrying me simply to gain access to my millions; Joe had plenty of money on his own and had little interest in mine. And besides, I was mad about Joe. I did not have my eyes on any other man, and that certainly included the president.

It was mortifying to read all of this, however untrue it was, day after day. Joey and I were blissfully happy together, but we did not exist in a bubble. I'd loved the years I had spent in Washington in my youth, but this was a different time in my life, and I wanted friends. At the very least, I wanted to be able to walk down the street or into a restaurant without the droning of scandalized whispers in my ear.

Though Joe and I laughed it off when we read the papers day after day, if I was being honest, it troubled me how vehemently my new hometown had rejected me and my marriage. And there was more than simply my bruised feelings and wounded ego at stake; Joe's business and his plans to serve Roosevelt were political in nature. Being a social castoff could hurt any chances he had in his career. It was possible that, in marrying me, Joe had ruined his own future. How could I allow that to be the case?

I decided that if the Washington Old Guard did not want to offer me a place in their club, then I would make a place for myself. I was still energetic and capable, and I had resources at my disposal that made just about anything possible, if only I could ignore the muck and get to work. *Put on your good head, Budgie.* Business, I decided. I would turn my focus toward my birthright and my first passion—my family's business. And if I succeeded, I would surprise them all. Heck, I might even end up surprising myself.

"MR. COLBY CHESTER, it's me. Marjorie. How are you?" I had my longtime friend and the head of my company on the telephone line. It was a conversation for which I'd spent days preparing; but now, even though my tone sounded casual enough, it wouldn't have surprised me if Colby could hear my heart thumping across the line.

"Marjorie, hello. It's great to hear your voice," Colby said. "I figured you were off honeymooning somewhere."

"I was, but I'm back now."

"How is life in the capital as Mrs. Joseph Davies?"

"It's great," I lied.

"Any word on whether the posting will be Paris or London?" Colby asked.

"Not yet. We're still awaiting word from the president. But we should hear any day now."

"Do you have a preference?" Colby asked.

"I don't," I answered. That was the truth; either option would be a thrill, since France and England were both countries that I loved, and they happened to be our two most important European allies. "But listen to this, Colby. Until we go . . . there was something I wanted to speak with you about."

"Of course, Marjorie. You know I'm always here."

"I . . . Colby, I would like to join the board." I paused, drew in a breath. Then I went on: "I'd like to serve as a director." Silence pulsed on the long-distance line between us. Because I felt the need to fill it, I added, "At General Foods," and then immediately winced.

After a long pause, I heard Colby's exhale. And then his voice, emotionless, as he said, "It's certainly . . . an interesting idea. And not something that any of us have seen before."

I nodded, not entirely surprised by his hedging, but motivated to win his support. My own tone, in contrast to Colby's, was crisp and clear when I replied: "A woman on the board of one of America's largest corporations—I know it sounds momentous. But times have changed. Why, our First Lady does more for this government than many of her husband's cabinet members. And besides, speaking of cabinet members, there's a female in there now."

"Frances Perkins," Colby said. "Of course, Roosevelt's labor secretary."

"This country is clawing its way out of the Depression," I went on. "Women are working outside of the home every day to feed their families. They don't have time to waste on worrying whether it's ladylike. Let's do what makes sense. I ran one of the biggest military hospitals of the Great War from across an ocean. And I established one of the busiest canteens in the country. I employ more men and women in my various homes than most male business owners can claim to do anywhere in this country. And I know how to run things. Papa taught me well. I've been preparing for this role my entire life."

"You're absolutely right," Colby said, and I could tell that he was nodding into the telephone on his end. "Of course you're right, Marjorie. How does . . . Joe feel about it?" I understood the question and just how many layers it had. It was a question not only of how my new husband would feel about a wife who sat in on board meetings with a room full of men, but also of how my husband would feel about his wife putting aside her duties as hostess and homemaker to stay current on business and managerial matters. How my husband would feel about having a wife who wielded such power and independence. But even more, how my husband would feel about his wife taking those powers and responsibilities away from *him* in the process, since my representation on the General Foods board had always been by proxy, with my husband holding the Post family member's place at that table.

No more.

I spoke now with steel in my voice: "Joe isn't like Ed, and he's certainly not like Ned. He's perfectly comfortable with his wife going into business," I said. "And since Ned is out, I'll take his spot."

Betty Beale could put that in her column. It wasn't society gossip; it was real news: I would be the first woman to serve on the board of directors in General Foods history. Regardless of what the society dames in Washington might think of me, nationally it was received as a positive move. THE GALS ARE INCHING THEIR WAY INTO BIG BUSINESS, went the headline. *Fortune* magazine wrote a glowing piece on my appointment, while *The Literary Digest* praised me as a woman "thoroughly schooled in the corporation, and respected for her sound business sense."

The board appointment gave me so much more to focus on than the bitter gossip in Washington, and it required that I make regular trips to New York for the meetings. By summer, as Joe awaited word on his upcoming assignment, he was ready to travel north with me as well—up to the Adirondacks for a few weeks of rest. I'd scrapped the name Camp Hutridge after the split with Ned, settling on Camp Topridge instead, and I could not wait to show the place to Joe and enjoy our time away from the Washington swamp.

I got up to the Adirondacks a few days ahead of Joe's scheduled arrival in order to open up the camp and prepare for his first visit. The most pressing matter was changing everything over from Hutridge to Topridge. I'd been the second mistress of a home before, and the last thing I wanted was for Joe to arrive and feel as if he'd stepped into another man's domain.

With that in mind, I'd ordered new stationery for the bedrooms and new labels for our homemade jam jars, and had changed the monogrammed grates over the fireplaces. Anything that bore witness to Ned Hutton's onetime residence at the place had to go. That morning I was sitting with a few of the maids, and we were pulling the stitching from all of the towels embroidered with my former initials, MPH, replacing them one at a time with my swirling new initials, MPD. That's when I got the call, Cook finding me under a pile of bath towels in the main lodge. "Mrs. Davies? The operator has Mr. Davies on the line."

"Mumsie." Joe's voice crackled in the receiver, greeting me with one of his favorite new pet names.

"Joey, my love." All around me the waitstaff bustled throughout the bright great room, readying the furniture and sorting kitchen supplies for the coming weeks.

"How is Topridge?" he asked.

"Sublime," I answered, glancing out the floor-to-ceiling window at the lake, where at that moment the thinnest lacing of fog was settling over its smooth surface. "I can't wait for you to get up here. You leave tomorrow, right?"

A pause on the line. I shifted on my feet as Joe said simply: "Mumsie."

"Yes?" My pulse quickened. Nearby someone dropped a cooking pot, and I startled at the clamor it made against the wooden floor.

"I had the most interesting lunch today," Joe said, his voice sounding far away. It was, I reminded myself.

"Lunch? With whom?" I asked.

"With our president." A beat of silence. "At the White House."

I hadn't known he was having lunch with the president.

"He called me just this morning, so the whole thing was rather last minute," Joe said, perhaps sensing my confusion.

My stomach fluttered. "And?"

"He's officially offered me the ambassadorship."

"Ah." I leaned back in my chair. "So you won't make it to Topridge." Now I understood why he had been bracing on the line—our summer plans were derailed. But I wasn't going to get rattled by that; we had been waiting on news of this appointment for months. I was ready. "Well, we have a lot to do in that case. I guess I should arrange my trip back down to Washington. We'll have to prepare for our crossing. When do we sail? Is it London? Or Paris?"

"Blue Eyes, my love . . ."

"Yes?"

An instant of silence—and then it stretched longer. Too long. My throat went dry. "What is it, Joe?"

"He wants us to go to Moscow."

"What for?"

"To be stationed. Moscow, in Russia," Joe repeated, louder this time, in case the telephone connection was faulty.

"No, I know. I heard you. It's just . . . Russia?" I went silent. All I knew about Russia was the news of the revolutions there. How the Bolsheviks had grabbed power in a bloody fight and then shot their tsar and his beautiful young family. A distant and violent land, Russia, with bleak winters and far too much snow. "What happened to London? Or Paris?" I asked, my voice flat.

"He said Russia."

"Well, it can't be final, if he's only just suggested it today. Surely we could try for France or Britain? Why, you and he are so friendly. I'm certain that—"

"It's got to be the Russians," Joe said, his tone without a wisp of waver.

"Why?" I asked after a moment, my thoughts spinning.

"Roosevelt needs us there."

I still did not understand this sudden and unwelcome reversal in our fate. Joe went on: "The Reds have taken over. Lenin is dead, but Stalin has seized complete power. Nasty man. Shoemaker's apprentice turned dictator."

I nodded—that much I knew. But what I didn't understand was: "Why us?"

"It's good that it'll be us. Who can better represent America, and all of our promise, than my Mumsie?"

I could think of a hundred other ways to serve our nation and exemplify American promise. But in Moscow? After a long pause, Joe spoke again: "What do you think? You're awfully quiet."

I sighed. How could I answer that question? I'd known Joe was hoping for an ambassadorial post when I met him. I'd encouraged him to pursue it. Of course, I'd believed it would be in some place other than Moscow, but then again, so had he. Hadn't I vowed to support him, even if this was the furthest thing from what I'd expected, what I'd hoped for? At a loss as to what to say next, I offered: "It strikes me as a pretty bleak place."

Joe exhaled, and I could hear his rueful laugh on the line. "It is. But bleak or not, they've got millions of people. And we will need them as our allies pretty soon."

"The Russians?" I asked.

"Yes."

"Why would we want the Bolsheviks to be our allies?" I asked. They had murdered their tsar, along with his wife and children.

"Because Roosevelt fears there might be a second Great War. He says that Stalin is bad, but that the fellow over in Germany, Hitler, might turn out to be worse."

Chapter 36

American Ambassadorial Residence,
Spazzo House, Moscow
January 1937

MOSCOW, BLEAK AND WHITE AS A MOONSCAPE, COULD NOT HELP but make an impact. The bright-domed towers soared over Saint Basil's Cathedral, crimson and cobalt and gold, brilliant bursts of color against the pale backdrop of falling and fallen snow. Red Square sprawled before us, unimaginably vast, filled with hordes of bundled pedestrians who tucked their chins against the snowy wind and trudged determinedly from the buildings toward trams and trolleys. The minaret spears of the Kremlin, that fortress-town of former tsarist palaces and churches, pierced the iron sky with their defiant redbrick crenellations.

But our ambassadorial residence, Spazzo House, was downright underwhelming, with its wan exterior of chipped yellow limestone, its drafty interior of peeling ceilings and weary, uncooperative pipes. Even though I had come to Moscow with a determined enthusiasm, I said as much to Joe shortly after our arrival: "This simply won't do."

Joe frowned, his breath misting in a cloud of vapor as he glanced around the large, sparse front hall. "It certainly needs some work," he agreed.

Luckily, I had come prepared. I had read and studied up enough prior to our Atlantic crossing to understand that these revolutionary Russians hated or distrusted much of what we Americans stood for—democracy, capitalism, faith—and apparently they eschewed comfort as well, if our lodgings were any indication. Fresh, healthy food would be in short supply, I'd heard. "Joey, my dear, I may be living in Moscow," I said, as I looked around the large, dingy space that we were to call home, "but I plan to show them a thing or two about our American way of life. Maybe I can even win a few friends with some fresh vegetables."

"It sounds like as good a place to start as any," my husband said, hauling one of our many trunks up the wide stairway. He paused on the landing, his chest heaving as he caught his breath. "Mumsie, how many trunks did you say?"

"Thirty," I answered, stepping past him with a leather valise in my hand.

Joe's eyes widened. "*Thirty* trunks?"

"And fifty suitcases," I said. "I may not travel light, but I travel ready. You'll be thanking me soon enough."

The society columns and the D.C. Old Guard had been as vicious on my departure from the capital as they had been on my arrival, predicting that I wouldn't last more than a few months in Russia. So I'd arrived with a fierce determination to prove them wrong. Of course I would have preferred London or Paris, though I would never have admitted that publicly. Of course I'd been apprehensive about the bitter cold—I'd been spending my winters in Palm Beach for years—but did they forget that I was from Battle Creek? Snow was nothing new to me; I'd spent my youth tromping through the stuff. I'd do it for Joe. I'd do it for our president, who had sent us off with orders to make friends with these stolid, mistrusting Russians. And I'd do it for myself, to prove I was so much more than just a coddled society hostess. Sure, I didn't know a word of Russian. I did not have any credentials in politics or foreign service. I knew there were many who scoffed at these facts, and at us, from Washington to Moscow. Who was Marjorie Merriweather Post to think she could manage a job as important as this one?

Marjorie Merriweather Post just so happened to be the first Ambassadress to the Soviet Union that America had ever sent. Our government had only recently recognized the Soviet Union, and since Joe's predecessor, a competent and pleasant enough friend by the name of Bill Bullitt, had not had a wife, I would be making history. And—our president hoped—I would be making friends.

We were to be gracious and warm and hospitable, but not flashy. When it came time to pack, I had locked up all but a few pieces of jewelry in storage in New York and Palm Beach—I didn't want to remind the somber Soviet officials of their dead tsarina.

In opening our doors and inviting Communists into our parlor and our dining room, we'd be inviting them to glimpse the capitalist comforts of our American lifestyle; to that end, I packed our china for hosting banquets, our crystal stemware for entertaining, our linens and lace for elegant dinner parties. At Bergdorf's and Bloomingdale's, I ordered us an entirely new wardrobe for the Russian winters: heavy coats trimmed with fur, thick cashmere stockings, muffs and kid gloves and sable hats in the muted dark colors so often seen throughout the Russian capital.

Many in the Soviet Union were starving, the country having suffered from widespread famines in recent years, and winter would no doubt present the cruelest months of all. And even the food and drink that they *did* have available on the sparse store shelves seemed questionable at best. State Department aides had warned us before we departed that we should not drink the water without first boiling it, that to eat whatever raw fruits or vegetables were available would be a foolish idea, that meat and fish posed even greater risks, due to the widespread presence of tapeworms. Milk or cream would have been out of the question, but the country didn't have either in ready supply.

This, I decided, we could also use to our advantage. "Let's call it grocery diplomacy," I declared. I knew that, as ambassadress, I would be expected to host luncheons and dinners for large crowds regularly, and—even on the rare nights that we dined in, just the two of us—I was not going to endure months without fruits or vegetables, without meat or chicken, not when our own country had an abundance of it all year round, in large part because of my own company's ingenuity and success. So I'd packed dozens of coolers and iceboxes onto the *Sea Cloud,* cramming every inch with Birds Eye frozen fruits and vegetables; pounds of meat, fish, and poultry; cases of rock salt; frozen desserts; and tubs of frozen cream. I would welcome my guests as a generous hostess and dazzle those Commies with the extent and variety of our American plenty, brought to them by my very own General Foods Corporation.

* * *

We'd crossed a rough, roiling wintertime Atlantic aboard the USS *Europa* and then continued by train across the cold, snow-packed European continent, switching in Berlin and then again in Warsaw. Our snow-heaped train rolled through the border town of Negoreloye and, just after the New Year, during the most dismal time of the year, into Moscow. The weak Russian sun shone for just a few hours each day on run-down buildings coated in ice. But it wasn't just the gray and gloomy weather that I noticed; the people on the street had gray faces as well. Deeply lined skin and gaunt features pulled tight by cold or hunger or worry—probably all of the above.

Inside Spazzo House I decided not to waste too much of my time on moaning about the weather or the city's general state of disrepair. I couldn't control those things—so I'd focus instead on what I could. As Joe and I went room by room, unloading luggage and surveying the quarters and directing the household staff in arranging our items, I rolled up my sleeves and looked around the place with my keen hostess's eye and a fervent determination to scrub and decorate and improve as if our mission depended on it. To my mind, it did.

Spazzo House had been glorious once, that much I could see from its bones. Built before the Bolsheviks, the residence had originally belonged to a favorite of the tsar. Its lemon-yellow façade had probably been cheery and bright at that time, but I made a mental note that it was in desperate need of a fresh coat of paint as soon as the snows were done falling. Marble columns gave the place a stately feeling, and the large rooms—once dusted and enlivened with some new décor—would be perfect for our plans to entertain.

But in order to bring the inside of the home up to the grandeur that its original architectural designs deserved, we'd need to overhaul some of its sagging and threadbare features. For this I had also planned ahead: the *Sea Cloud* hadn't arrived with only my food; I'd also brought much of my household team—my cook, my butler, my housekeeper, and half a dozen maids to scrub and launder and dust and repair. As Joe and I settled ourselves in, my team got right to work unpacking much of our favorite furniture from Palm Beach and Manhattan, along with rugs, lamps, framed photographs, feather beds, and down blankets, even bathtubs and my favorite porcelain toilet.

⁂

"WHAT DO YOU think? Are the pearls too . . ."

Joe cocked a grin, scrutinizing my appearance as I searched for the right word.

"I don't know . . . excessive?" I asked.

"My dear, you will be a model to these Soviets of the best that America has to offer." My husband came close and planted a kiss on my rouged cheek. "And anyway, I think they'll be more stunned by the Jell-O, or perhaps the peaches, than your jewels."

"Let's hope," I said.

Word of our arrival in Moscow had reached the highest levels of the Communist Party, naturally, and our first week had brought with it our first two big diplomatic tests: an invitation to the Kremlin and a party in our own home that evening.

Our first official event as hosts at Spazzo House would, no doubt, prove full of unforeseen excitement, just as our trip to the Kremlin had a few days prior. We'd been invited inside the walls of that sprawling redbrick complex in order to attend a meeting of the leadership of the Communist Party, gathering at that time for their Constitutional Convention. With the American-Soviet relationship so newly restored, we'd been offered a prime seat in a diplomatic box in the balcony of the vast, high-ceilinged hall. Beneath us, nearly three thousand representatives from across the Soviet Union gathered and debated—Cossacks in bright wool tunics, Kazakhs with large brown eyes and ruddy cheeks, Ukrainians in military uniform, even white-shawled women with chic bob haircuts and ripples of finger waves. "Look, Joe!" I pointed at the lively array of delegates. "Women! Serving in government."

"Yes." Joe nodded, taking it all in, from the flag-draped walls to the front dais packed with suited, sober-looking men. "They do get that right here."

"Eleanor Roosevelt would be delighted to see a showing like this in

Congress," I remarked. My eyes continued to comb the packed, cavernous hall. "Who is speaking now?" I asked, my eyes fixing on the front podium, where at that moment a mustached man with small spectacles was holding forth before a massive red Soviet flag emblazoned with the hammer and sickle, gesturing animatedly toward the attentive assembly.

"That is the prime minister," Joe answered. "Or premier, as they would say. Vyacheslav Molotov."

Just then, another man entered at the front from a side door, and the hall erupted in deafening applause. Even Molotov turned and stopped speaking midsentence, the premier joining in the riotous clapping. His turn was clearly concluded as this new man, stern and squat, with features of blade-sliced granite strode assuredly toward the front. From my balcony seat I could just barely make out his thick mustache over dark, unsmiling lips. His gray military tunic nearly matched the wan shade of his skin. And amid the roar of the crowd's applause, a buzz of reverent whispers skittered across the massive hall.

"Joseph Stalin," Joe said, his voice low in my ear. "Leader of the politburo and the Communist Party. The sole ruler here since Lenin's death." When Joseph Stalin raised his paw-like hand and the entire assembly of thousands went silent in one obedient instant, I pulled my thick sable coat closer around my shoulders, feeling a chill run through my body, one that I was sure had nothing to do with the bitter Russian winter or the drafty Kremlin hall.

Now, back at Spazzo House, my focus was turned entirely to our hosting duties. "So who is coming tonight? Will that awf—" I sealed my lips before the thought could escape; I knew we were being listened to. Bullitt, our predecessor, had advised us that the residence was wired from floor to ceiling. He'd spent hundreds of his own dollars on hiring technicians to take out the pesky little recorders, but the electricians, of course, reported to the Soviet secret police, and thus could not be counted on. Besides, all of the locally hired household staffers, ostensibly provided as a friendly service by the Russians, were also spying on us and relaying everything back to the all-powerful intelligence services. There was no point in trying to combat the eavesdropping; they'd easily install new bugs as quickly as we could have them removed. Our only way was to watch our words with vigilance. And so that's what I did as I forced a neutral tone to my voice and posed a new question to my husband: "Will Secretary Stalin be honoring us with his presence this evening?"

"No," Joe said, the quick lift of his brow showing me that he appreciated my discretion. "Prime Minister Molotov, and his wife, Polina, will be here. She herself is a member of the government. She's been named Commissar of Cosmetics and Perfume, so she has business dealings of her own. Perhaps you'll find common ground with her."

"Wonderful. If I need any makeup while we're over here, I'll know whom to ask." I scrutinized my appearance one final time, looking into a gilded mirror from Mar-a-Lago, since the ones that had already been at Spazzo House were all cracked and dim. "How do I look?"

"Lovely," Joe said, admiring my cream-colored gown and simple strand of small but lovely pearls. When he leaned in to kiss me, I felt warm for the first time all day. As I raised my hands to pull him closer, the lights overhead flickered, and a moment later we found ourselves cloaked in sudden and total darkness. "The power just went out," Joe said, and I didn't need functioning lightbulbs to show me how on edge he was all of a sudden. We had hundreds of important people on their way to our first official dinner party, and the Russian night outside was bitter cold, not to mention black as ink. How could we possibly host with no power?

A servant appeared at the threshold of the room, bearing a candelabra that cast just enough of a glow for me to see his concerned face. "It's the coolers, Mrs. Davies. Our refrigerators are putting more of a strain on the electrical wiring than this house is up to."

I glowered. I knew a thing or two about botched electrical wiring. Half a world away, in another lifetime, it seemed, I'd seen my house burned to the ground, my girls huddled on a lawn in their nightgowns surrounded by the scorched remains of family mementoes.

"Turn on the generators," I ordered, grateful that I'd seen fit to transport several miniature units on my yacht, along with everything else. "And add it to the list—we'll have the electrical wiring overhauled from top to bottom." I'd pay out of my own pocket. And I'd ship my electrician over if need be.

Chapter 37

Spazzo House, Moscow

"PREMIER MOLOTOV, IT IS SO NICE TO MEET YOU." I EXTENDED my gloved hand for the handshake I had been prepared to expect, and Vyacheslav Mikhailovich Molotov, the top-ranking man in the Soviet Union, took it in his firm, viselike grip. He spoke his thanks, his Russian greeting passing to me through our interpreter as I took my chance to quickly study his features. Even though I had seen Molotov from afar just a few days earlier at the Kremlin, I was surprised by the impression he made up close—his face was not unattractive. In fact, with his big eyes and wide, apple-round cheeks, he looked almost boyish. Yet he gave off the unmistakable aroma of a heavy cigarette smoker and his teeth were the shade of a yellow onion.

His wife, at his side, was not a particularly beautiful woman, but she made a striking impression with her dark hair and thick eyebrows, her face a collection of large features—full, unsmiling lips, a prominent nose, and long, wide-set eyes. Polina Molotova was introduced to me through our interpreter, and then she handed me a parcel wrapped in clean cloth, with a bow tied around it. "Madam Molotova would like for you to open it, please, Mrs. Davies," the interpreter explained.

I did as Madam Molotova asked, finding a loaf of bread and a small cellar of salt in the package. "How kind," Joe said beside me. "A traditional Russian greeting—bread and salt. It is considered a welcome gift."

"I am so appreciative," I said, smiling toward our guests in turn. "Welcome to Spazzo House."

I had gone over every detail with my staff in exacting precision, and our evening began in a solidly American fashion: cocktails and passed hors d'oeuvres. My white-coated waiters stood poised to take and deliver orders, and both of the Molotovs asked for vodka, while Joe had a scotch and I sipped on a glass of club soda.

After that, Joe and I welcomed the Molotovs and our other guests into our circular dining room, where the table was spread with a colorful feast that could just as easily have covered my banquet tables in Palm Beach or Manhattan: shrimp cocktail, skewers of pineapple and chicken breast, meatballs, carrots glazed in maple syrup. My white table linens were crisp and freshly laundered; my crystal stemware glistened beneath the newly polished candelabra.

"Kak krasivo!" Polina Molotova surveyed the spread with her wide-set eyes going even wider. Then she turned to me, rattling off something that her translator quickly interpreted into English: "Madam Molotova hears that Madam Davies is the owner of a vast farm in America?"

"Something like that," I said with a smile. "My family business is in food and drink." I saw Joe engaged in conversation with Premier Molotov, whose unmoving features gave away little about the contents of their conversation or his opinions on it.

"Then you own many large warehouses?" Polina Molotova asked.

"Yes, we do have warehouses. And factories."

"Your workers are lucky," my Russian guest said, looking once more at the feast. "Once our winter passes, we will have all of this food as well."

My eyes went to the pineapple, the shrimp, the carrots, but I smiled politely and posed a question of my own: "I hear that you, Madam Molotova, are in charge of managing the cosmetic and perfume businesses here in the Soviet Union?"

"Yes." Polina Molotova nodded. "Lipstick, soap, perfume. We have everything you Americans have. Better than Paris and New York." Madam Molotova nodded once more, decisively, then she lowered her gaze to where I held my hands folded before my waist. She rattled off another quick sentence in Russian.

Her interpreter pointed to my finger. "Madam Molotova wishes to compliment your white stone."

I looked down at my ring, which had a large but tasteful diamond, a solitaire setting in a pear cut. "Thank you. It's a diamond."

"No, it can't be," Madam Molotova responded, shaking her head. "Diamonds only grow round."

"How about some food?" I offered. "I know I am hungry."

Later that night, before climbing into bed, Joe and I sat soaking in a warm tub. It served a dual purpose: we were cold all the time, so it helped us thaw out just a bit, and we'd heard from Bullitt that tapping a pencil or running the water were two of the best ways to thwart the recording bugs that filled every wall and light fixture. Since we wanted to discuss the evening we'd just had, the warm tub was a welcome haven.

"The Molotovs are an interesting pair. Polina Molotova was stern, but not unfriendly," I whispered. The room smelled pleasantly of lavender—one of our own imported essential oils—and the mirrors were steam-smudged. "She invited me out with her this weekend."

Joe's dark brows shot up. "Really?"

"Yes. For a drive and lunch."

"That's great, Mumsie."

"How was your end of the table?" I asked. "Premier Molotov looks as if he rarely gets excited by anything."

Joe splashed the water, leaning closer as he lowered his voice. "Don't let his dull expression fool you. He's a sharp one. He's one of the original Bolsheviks. He was right next to Lenin during the revolution. Now he's backed Stalin, and he was smart to do so. Molotov will continue to wield great power."

I lowered my head beneath the surface, savoring the embrace of warm, lavender-scented water around my face, my ears, my hair. When I emerged, Joe went on, speaking right next to the gushing faucet: "Do you know that Molotov is not his real name? He changed it as a young Bolshevik. Because the Russian word for hammer is *molotok*. And that's what he is: Stalin's hammer."

I nodded. Joe did not need to go on. In spite of the Molotovs' gifts of bread and salt, their smiles and chatter at dinner, we were under no illusions; we had been sent to make friends for Roosevelt in Moscow, but that was only because, as bad as Stalin and his lackeys were, Roosevelt suspected that Hitler and his Nazis might be worse.

As if on cue, we heard sleigh bells begin to jingle outside our windows, below us on the black, snow-covered streets. Joe looked at me, frowning, and I nodded. We both knew what that jingling sound meant: while it might have seemed merry enough back home, even part of some quaint Christmas carol, we had come to learn that here, at this midnight hour, it was the sound of one of the dreaded NKVD sleighs making a most undesirable house call. Just a moment later, a shrill burst of voices. A peppering of gunshots, more shouting—women's terror-stricken shrieks—a crying baby. And then worst of all, nothing. The streets blanketed in snow and quiet once more, only the bark of a distant dog and the receding tinkle of the sleigh. And the unspoken trembling of a city awoken by fear.

POLINA MOLOTOVA WELCOMED me into her roomy car, a sleek black limousine with four doors that looked an awful lot like one of our American Packards, though of course I saw a Soviet logo had been attached, a small hammer and sickle gleaming atop both its trunk and hood.

I took my seat next to Madam Molotova, as her interpreter attended us from the front seat. "Welcome, Madam Davies. Thank you for joining us," Madam Molotova said, her lipsticked mouth a tight, bright slash against her pale face. And then, gesturing to a woman seated on her other side, she added, "Please meet Madam Litvinova."

I extended my hand toward the woman beside Polina and was stunned when she addressed me directly, with a ready smile and crisp, perfect English. "Mrs. Davies, it is my pleasure. I'm Ivy Litvinova, wife to Commissar Maxim Litvinov. Really, it's so nice to meet you."

"Oh," I said, sitting back against the plush seat of the car, not sure what to make of her flawless, upper-class British accent.

Ivy Litvinova flashed a quick grin, nodding once. "Yes, I'm a Brit. I met Maxim in London, you see. Back when I was called Ivy Teresa Low."

"I see," I said, smiling at her, feeling as though, suddenly, I might have an ally in this bleak, foreign place.

But just then Madam Molotova rattled something off in stern Russian toward the front of the car, where the translator sat beside the chauffeur, and the young aide turned to me and said: "Madam Davies, Madam Molotova wishes to show you one of our new city attractions; it's called the Park of Culture and Rest."

"How lovely," I said, nodding gamely toward Polina and then Ivy. "Thank you."

"Let's be off, then," Ivy said, and Polina bobbed her chin in approval. I was relieved to see that both women had dressed much as I had—fur coat and hat, gloves, kid-lined boots over stockinged feet.

But while my companions within the spacious sedan sat warm and full-bodied, their cheeks colored with blush, I saw quite a different scenario as I looked out the windows.

There, in the dreary streets, women hunched forward, their brittle shoulders curling into postures of permanent and self-protective slouching. The men, some of them with noses tipped black by frostbite, carried hunger in their eyes that did not look as if it could be sated by food alone—though food was surely needed as well. Most of the people I saw around the city appeared pale to the point of grayness, their gaunt features pulled tight, their eyes weary but ever vigilant. I thought back to the night of my dinner party, and I couldn't help but feel a pang in my stomach at the memory of the plentiful spread I had offered. And then that feeling curdled into something even more dreadful with the recollection of the terror that had traveled on those soft sleigh bells. I couldn't help but shiver right there in that car as I looked out at the street and wondered: How many of the people that we now passed had lost a loved one?

But Madam Molotova's voice interrupted my gloomy musings just then as she pointed out the window, saying, "Ah, here we are. You see over there?"

I forced myself to focus, looking toward where she pointed her gloved finger. The car slowed to a crawl alongside a vast, flat, snow-covered field. On the far side, there appeared to be some sort of amusement park with rides. Though it must have been a few hundred acres, only a handful of people milled around the empty space.

"That's called a roller coaster over there," Madam Molotova explained through her translator. I nodded, choosing not to tell my hostess that I knew what a roller coaster was.

"And here, in the spring, is a large garden. People can read, play games, have picnics, bring children. Can you imagine such a place, right in the middle of our city?" A proud smile lifted Madam Molotova's large features.

"It's lovely," I said appreciatively. "It's like our Coney Island in New York."

"What is Coney Island?" Madam Molotova asked.

"A park back home, with a roller coaster like that. Only it's near a beach. My daughters love to go there. These gardens must be more like Central Park, where my daughters learned to ride their horses. But the roller coaster at Coney—"

"*Nyet.*" Madam Molotova shook her head decisively, and I did not need the translator to tell me that she'd said no.

Then she went on, and this time the young aide explained to me: "It is not possible what you say, Madam Davies. There is nothing like this outside of the Soviet Union, or anywhere else in the world."

I sat back in my seat, looking at Polina Molotova, who stared at me, unblinking, as though we were engaged in one of the childhood games that my girls had enjoyed, where the object was to be the last one to look away. Beside her Ivy Litvinova fidgeted in her seat, folding and then unfolding her hands in her lap. I swallowed, deciding not to argue. My job was not to dismantle the Soviet propaganda machine. My job was to make friends for America.

"HOW WAS YOUR lunch with Polina Molotova?" Joe asked that evening, after he had returned home from a day of meetings and we'd readied for bed. He tapped his pencil against his glass of water as he spoke.

I raised my own glass of water and tapped my ivory comb against it as I whispered my response: "A success, I think. It's interesting, though—her apartment was fine. But if that is the residence of the highest member of the ruling party, I cannot imagine how the common people must live."

"Oh?" Joe asked.

I nodded. "Threadbare furniture that looked at least a few decades old.

The place was big enough, but the rooms were dark. In the dining room, about half the bulbs of the chandelier needed replacing."

"How was the food?" Joe asked, knowing how seriously I took my menus whenever I hosted.

I grimaced, offering my answer with my sour expression. "Not a single fresh vegetable." And yet she'd been so proud, even boastful, of her luncheon spread. Of the venison slices and the steaming tureen of thin cabbage soup. Of the osetra caviar, oily mounds of red and black fish eggs beloved by all Russians but now available only to the highest and most powerful. We'd sipped not French wine or American soft drinks but Stolichnaya vodka and chilled Sovetskoje Shampanskoje, the Russian sparkling wine that I found overly sweet and thick.

You see? Polina Molotova had said to me, pointing proudly to her table as servants heaped our simple white plates with what looked to be unappealing globs of lumpy gray purée. *We have vegetables in winter, too.*

I'd eaten a bit from each dish, to be polite, guessing that the colorless mush must have been potatoes, or perhaps turnips—it was impossible to tell based on my tasteless bites. "And then there was something—a fish from the Volga River as a main course." I shuddered as I climbed into bed, still tapping my glass as I added: "You know what else I found interesting?"

"What's that?"

"The home was nice enough, but I did not see a single family photo. Nothing that appeared . . . I don't know, personal. Sentimental."

Joe shook his head. "That doesn't surprise me. The attachment is to the State. Not to something as fickle or transient as the family unit. You know what they say here? It's called Lenin's Rule; they have it drilled into every comrade, from the very first day of grade school and every day after that: 'Trust no one. Watch your wife. Watch your children. Report to the State on their activities.' "

I exhaled a puff of breath. After a pause, I said, "Well, sentimental or not, Polina Molotova has invited me on another outing with her next week."

Joe's dark eyes creased in interest. "Where to this time?"

"She said it's called a commission shop. I'm not sure what we'll be shopping for. But she seemed eager to show me."

"Wonderful." Joe planted a kiss on my brow. "I told the president what a smash hit you've been here, Mums."

I tapped my drinking glass with my comb one final time as I leaned close and whispered, "I went for a walk this afternoon, after the lunch, with Ivy Litvinova, who is a truly lovely woman. But you know what I saw? I think there was a pair of secret policemen following me."

"Of course there was," Joe answered.

I was about to express my outrage at this, but just then, there came a tap on the bedroom door. "Come in," I called. A young woman appeared, her pale eyes fixed firmly on the floor. She was a Russian member of the household staff, but her English was passable. "Ambassador Davies, Madam Davies, will that be all for the evening?"

"Ah yes, thank you," Joe said, dismissing her. "Good evening."

The girl left without another word, shutting the door timidly behind her. I knew her name to be Katya. Poor girl walked around all day as though frightened of her own shadow. Joe waited a minute after Katya's exit before leaning close. He tapped his glass as he spoke: "It's not just the secret police outside. Every single one of them is spying on us as well."

I sighed, nodding, picking up a pot of lavender cream and rubbing it into my hands. Joe spoke loudly now, no longer tapping his glass or whispering his words: "My Mumsie Blue Eyes." He spoke so that anyone listening would hear. "I am thrilled that your lunch with Madam Molotova was such a pleasant one. You are showing the Russians that the Davieses and, indeed, the Americans, have put good relations at the top of the agenda."

Chapter 38

Moscow
Late Winter 1937

POLINA MOLOTOVA'S BLACK LIMOUSINE CARRIED US OUT OF THE crowded city center and through a flat stretch of countryside populated by white birch trees, green-needled firs, and the occasional dacha or country farmhouse rising up behind a fence. Eventually, pulling off the wide, fresh-paved highway and into the lot of what appeared to be a storehouse or factory, we rolled to a halt, and I narrowed my eyes to stare through the heavily tinted windows. A massive, dilapidated building hulked before us. All around us, a vast lot loomed, empty of cars or pedestrians. "Where are we?" I asked, managing a blithe tone in spite of my unease.

"Commission shop," Polina answered, making to rise as her chauffeur opened the car door. "This one houses some of the works of Karl Fabergé."

"Fabergé?" I repeated the name as I emerged from the car into the pale winter sunshine. "As in Fabergé eggs?" I knew the name to belong to a Russian jeweler, the favorite artisan of the Romanovs.

"Yes," Polina answered with a nod, her red-lipped smirk showing that she was less than impressed by the man's reputation or intimacy with the murdered imperial family.

I followed her through a creaking double door and out of the sunlight. Inside the dank warehouse, the air hung unmoving and smelled of dust and concrete. "Fabergé's work is in *here*?" I asked.

"Some of it," Polina answered, leading the way, her heels clicking against the hard floor. "All those Romanovs and their kind fled faster than rats when the people came to power. Selling off their jewels and art. But what they left behind now belongs to the State, as it should. Think about all of the waste." A wave of her red-nailed hand. "How many millions of rubles went toward the tsarina's diamond necklaces rather than feeding her starving people?"

I nodded solemnly, assuming what I hoped was an inscrutable mask over my features. Polina continued: "Now we will sell it. To capitalists like you." Polina winked at this last remark, flashing a teasing smile. "Ah yes, here we are."

What she'd called a commission shop resembled a cavernous and run-down warehouse packed with overspilling crates and boxes, dustcloths and tarps sliding off piles covering nearly every inch of floor and wall. I suppressed the urge to gasp, instead breathing in a big gulp of the stale air as I surveyed the space before me: through the motes and the dim sunlight that seeped through streaked windows, I saw an endless sprawl of precious relics. But *relics* did not fully and accurately describe the scene: it was treasure. Treasure that the tsars and their impossibly wealthy nobles had spent centuries and fortunes commissioning and accumulating, only for it to now be left in disarray, the glistening spoils of a glorious and bygone dynasty, held in the grip of a new government that saw no use for such masterful skill or lavish splendor.

My eyes roved hungrily over the piles and rows that glimmered, brilliant, even in this gloomy warehouse: golden wine chalices, rich tapestries, jewelry forged of every precious gem, silver tea services, holy icons, diamond-encrusted ashtrays, crystal flutes brushed with gold, religious crosses made of egg-sized emeralds and sapphires. It was staggering to see—even the pens and letter openers were wrought of precious stones with masterful detail. Such treasure belonged in a museum! Not in some run-down warehouse furred by cobwebs and dank with water damage.

It was astonishing to think of the worth housed in just that one building alone. But I swallowed the thought, curbing my desire to offer such an observation. "What is this?" I asked, pointing toward the nearest object, amazed that I would be able to reach out and touch it if I were so inclined.

Polina waved one of the workers over, and he offered his answer as he took it in his grimy fingers and handled it—too roughly, I noted—like a pound of meat for sale on the butcher's block. Polina translated his disinterested answer to me: "An ashtray of diamond and lapis lazuli. It belonged to Prince Yusupov. He married a Romanov princess, and then he killed the charlatan Rasputin. Much to the dismay of the last tsarina, that . . . Alexandra." Polina spat as she finished speaking, the names of a murdered cleric and queen too sour on her tongue.

A chill ran through my body. Of course we Americans knew of the lore of Rasputin, rumored sorcerer and healer, much-maligned adviser to the final tsarina who, desperate to keep her hemophiliac son and heir, Alexei, alive, had allowed the mystic complete run of the imperial court.

"And this?" I made my way slowly, reverently, toward the nearest aisle, noting that there were thousands of pieces to examine; had I weeks to study each object, I still don't think I would have made it through the entire warehouse. And this was just one such building on the outskirts of Moscow.

"This was Catherine's tea set," Polina answered, referring to the revered Russian empress we in the West knew as Catherine the Great. "Ah, and this inkwell is made of diamond and amethyst. It was a gift from Catherine to one of her lovers, Grigory Potemkin. The woman was a notorious whore."

I nearly grimaced at the irreverence, at all of it. The way Polina spoke about her former rulers, rulers who, just a couple of decades prior, had been considered God's anointed vessels on earth.

"You want?" Polina asked, picking up one of the empress's teacups in her bare hands.

My mouth fell open. "Are . . . are you serious?"

"Yes," she answered, shrugging.

"How much?" I asked, still incredulous.

She handed the cup, once the personal possession of the world's most powerful woman, to the worker with a hasty Russian order. He weighed the cup nearby on a rusty scale that looked like something we would have used in one of our warehouses back home to weigh our livestock feed.

"You pay per gram," Polina told me. "One ruble, one gram."

"That's . . . that's all there is to it?" I asked, my tone no longer casual or indifferent, in spite of my best efforts.

Polina eyed me with a quizzical expression, answering: "Of course. We weigh it, we get price. Why would it be otherwise?" she asked, her voice flat.

Because of the history. The artistic mastery. The imperial provenance. But apparently to Polina Molotova and those of her ruling party, onetime ownership by an empress did nothing to add value; if anything, it took away from an object.

"We Russians know that these baubles are useless," Polina said, apparently guessing my thoughts. "The Romanovs were surrounded by jewels, and what good did it do them? Or any of us?" She looked around and shrugged again, as if to prove how little it all meant. "But if you think these things are impressive, we can look at more. The Kremlin has rooms and rooms filled. And all the old palaces now belong to the State. My Vyacheslav can get us in. We need to get rid of the stuff. I'll take you."

They needed our money, I realized. And they knew that these treasures would be impressive to us, seeing our sentimentalism, our capitalist inclination toward the unique and material, as a vein of weakness, one of the fatal flaws that would eventually bring about our undoing. But if they were willing to part with these treasures, then I was willing to buy them.

I blinked, stunned, as we stepped out of the dim warehouse and back into the mild sunshine. Clutching my set of priceless Romanov teacups in my hands, I walked with Polina toward the waiting car, feeling as though at any minute some guard would emerge from the warehouse and demand that I return these relics, insisting that there was no way I could simply pay a few dollars and take Catherine the Great's personal treasure home with me. But no one did. No one stopped me. And so, I decided, I wanted more.

As punishing as the Russian winter had been, spring burst across the city in equal measure, the larch and willow trees erupting in leaf, the Moskva River rising as the final floes of ice melted, the red tulips and purple lilacs cheering the city with their perfume and vibrant color. As the days grew longer and milder, I settled into a pleasant enough rhythm. Every morning I would walk a route past the Kremlin and along the Moskva. The people, I noticed, looked different in the spring as well, thawing like the earth beneath the gentle sunshine. Children laughed, their pale cheeks turning rosy. Some pedestrians even greeted me with fleeting smiles.

I'd return to Spazzo House most days in time for lunch. The house had been vastly improved since our arrival. I'd swapped out some of the old plumbing with new pipes, and I'd overhauled the electrical system. Fresh paint gave both the inside and outside of the house a cleaner, brighter appearance. And now our walls were covered in priceless objects of art. Whenever Polina invited me on an outing to a commission shop, I gladly accepted. I'd spent the winter and spring accumulating as much treasure as I could—dishes of silver and porcelain, pens crusted in diamonds, glittering holy icons, sable and mink coats, tapestries, paintings, vases, glasses, and of course all different types of jewelry. I now had a collection of baubles fit for a tsarina, Joe commented, but I wouldn't have dreamed of wearing the pieces until we returned to America.

Since diplomacy was our primary job, we entertained several times a week, hosting dinners for staffers of the American embassy and Russian government officials, or else delegates from other friendly countries like Britain or Canada. Joe spent much of his days closeted in his offices dictating memos for the president and the State Department. At other times he was busy meeting with members of the press corps, dining out with fellow members of the diplomatic community, and taking meetings with Soviet officials. As much as I had enjoyed my friendship with the commissar wives like Polina and Ivy, Joe was a great success with government members like Molotov and Litvinov as well. We had no shortage of invitations to ballet and opera performances at the famed Bolshoi Theatre, to dinners at restaurants frequented by the highest-ranking members of the politburo.

But as much as we were enjoying our time in this strange and colorful land—a place both hospitable and ominous, possessing a storied and vibrant past and yet fiercely hostile to such a past—I longed for home. Deenie would soon be out of boarding school for the summer, and I ached to see her. I longed to gather her, Adelaide, and Eleanor to me to hear without censor about their lives and to tell them about our strange Russian adventures. And not just the three of them—I wished to speak to my husband without the ever-present eavesdroppers. I longed to walk a city street without a secret police tail, to stare into the faces of those I passed and see something other than fear or mistrust in their eyes. I longed for the optimism and earnestness and plenty of our American smiles, our American tables, our American homes and homeland.

What's more, Joe had begun to suffer from sudden and debilitating stomach pains. Several times he had to cancel meetings at the last minute because the discomfort was too severe for him to be upright. He rarely found himself up to the task of eating a full meal. Sleep became difficult at times. After a few weeks of this, at the recommendation of Ivy Litvinova, I called a Dr. Dmitri Pletnev and asked that he pay us a call at Spazzo House. The doctor appeared several hours later, a kindly man with a warm manner and charming, even if broken, English. He spent an hour examining my husband in our bedroom.

Afterward, the doctor stood before me and my husband in the hallway outside our bedroom, his face rumpling as it shifted back and forth between gentle smiles and confused frowns. "Ambassador Davies, Mrs. Davies, do you have perhaps a doctor in the United States who is familiar with your whole history?"

"Yes," Joe said, clutching his side in discomfort. Standing like that was difficult for him.

Dr. Pletnev sighed, nodding. I wondered, in that moment, about all that the doctor was thinking, all that he could not say, given the fact that we were being listened to through probably a dozen different microphones. Finally, all Dr. Pletnev said was: "I suggest you see him." And so, as spring ripened toward summer, Joe and I asked the president for permission to take a trip home to Washington. Fortunately, permission was granted via a prompt telegram reply.

BEFORE OUR DEPARTURE, we decided to host a final dinner party. Nobody could accuse the Davieses of leaving Moscow in anything but the grand style for which we were now known. I planned to give the party in honor of Polina Molotova and Ivy Litvinova, in thanks for their generous hospitality, but we invited hundreds of other guests as well—the cabinet of commissars, ambassadors from nearly every European country, members of the press corps, dozens of high-ranking Soviet party members, even kind Dr. Pletnev.

The night of the party was a mild one, and with the gardens surrounding Spazzo House in bloom, I decided to throw open the French doors and light candles across our veranda, where small clusters of furniture were arranged and a makeshift bar stood ready and stocked with American cocktails and Russian vodka. I'd hired musicians for the night and asked them to play a mixture of Russian classics, including works by Tchaikovsky and Stravinsky along with American favorites like Porter and Gershwin. I dressed simply for the evening in a satin gown of pale rose, gloves to my elbows, with my ears, wrists, and throat bare of jewelry. My smile was warm and genuine as I greeted my guests.

Inside, the home looked bright and beautiful, thanks to new lighting and our décor, which included framed photos of our family mixed with priceless imperial art. As we gathered around the dinner table, a rich feast spread before us thanks to General Foods—and more specifically, Birds Eye—Joe made a toast to welcome our guests. Just a few minutes later, once we were seated and poised to begin our soup, Comrade Molotov raised his glass of vodka, asking whether he might also offer a toast. "Of course, Premier," Joe said, smiling.

The room fell silent as the premier tilted his vodka and looked in my direction. "Madam Davies, Ambassador Davies, for the first time, when I enter the American embassy, I feel a welcome that is worthy of your country." And then he nodded, and an aide appeared at my shoulder, delivering into my lap an immense package. Beaming, Molotov ordered Joe and me to unwrap the heavy parcel right there in front of our dinner guests. We did so, pulling out a pair of magnificent sable coats. "For President and First Lady Roosevelt," Molotov explained, as the table erupted in applause. "Warm, you see?" Molotov pointed a thick finger toward the glossy pelts. "Just like relations between our two countries, thanks to the Davieses."

The musicians played as our guests ate and drank for hours, lulled into relaxed cordiality by champagne and vodka and steak, the warm evening and our free, open hospitality. Later, once our guests had risen to begin dancing, I presented Polina and Ivy each with a small gift I had arranged—the film reel for one of our new American films, *Swing Time,* starring two of our own national treasures, Ginger Rogers and Fred Astaire.

Polina and Ivy had also brought a gift, and they presented it to me then. An uncharacteristically wide smile stretched Polina's lips as I unwrapped the stunning set of jeweled vases once belonging to the fabled Princess Anastasia. "We do know how you love your art," Ivy said with a wink. And then, leaning close, she whispered, "I'm so glad to see how you appreciate it, Marjorie."

Polina interjected, "You show us your American ways; we show you Russian ways."

"Indeed," I said, nodding warmly, thanking my two friends in turn for all of their generosity.

"You shall be missed, my dear," Ivy said, her smile flickering for just a moment before she fixed me with a cheerful grin once more. "Now, let's get you to the dance floor. I know that my Maxim wants a dance with our hostess."

Joe held tight to my arm as we stood in the doorway of Spazzo House and bid one final farewell to our last guests, a giggly Maxim and Ivy Litvinov, who had stayed until well past midnight and had enjoyed at least four glasses of vodka each. The air was still mild and the sky no darker than a velvety purple, these being the longest days of the year, and Joe's embrace was tender as we watched the commissar's car lights recede into the sideways shadows of the Russian spring night. "My dearest Mumsie," my husband said, pulling me inside and toward our bedroom. "You have been an unmitigated success. The beloved ambassadress and America's most irresistible asset."

I smiled at this, padding barefoot up the marble stairs. The night, like our diplomatic tour in the country, had been an unabashed triumph. Even Joe had found himself feeling well enough for the hours of feasting and dancing. We had shown the Soviets how happy we Americans were. And now I longed for nothing more than to go home.

Chapter 39

Washington, D.C.
Late Summer 1937

BACK IN WASHINGTON, I STARED INTO THE CONCERNED FACE of my physician, both of us thinking about Moscow. "Moscow Malaria," my physician declared, stethoscope draped like a necklace around his throat after a long and thorough examination.

I grimaced, but that only made my stomach hurt more. "What exactly is Moscow Malaria?" I asked.

"It's largely a mystery," the man answered. "Even to me. Like the flu in symptoms, but unlike the flu, it lingers in the body for months." And it *had* lingered for months, this discomfort and fever I'd been experiencing. Worst of all were the bouts of intermittent hearing troubles, as if cotton balls were being stuffed into my ears one minute, then plucked out the next.

"Time and rest," the physician said. "Stay in bed, Mrs. Davies. You've overexerted yourself in Russia. And now it's time to recover." I nodded, accepting his prescription.

In spite of my feeling ill, in spite of Joe's regular stomach pains, things had not been all bad in recent months. We'd left Moscow and cruised our way through Europe aboard the *Sea Cloud,* with stops in Vienna and Paris before a longer stay in London to attend the festivities of King George VI's coronation. As guests of our American ambassador to England, Robert Bingham, we kept a full social schedule. We went to dinner at the townhouse of a rising member of the government, a man by the name of Winston Churchill, whose sharp-tongued wife, Clementine, had me in stitches by the second course. We attended the glittering coronation ball presided over by the royal family, during which time I couldn't help but silently observe that my new Russian amethysts and diamonds were even more splendid than any of the other priceless pieces on display in the palace. And I spent a lovely afternoon strolling the flower-lined paths of Hyde Park with Sara Delano Roosevelt, the president's very proud and protective mother, who was also traveling abroad at that time.

It was after all of that, while boarding the *Sea Cloud* for the Atlantic crossing toward America, that I first started to feel the crippling pull of exhaustion. "I've simply overtaxed myself," I told a nervous Joe. First in Moscow and then especially in London. But after a week straight of resting in bed and keeping an empty schedule in my private stateroom, I had not recovered. I couldn't keep food down. Tired as I was, sleep evaded me because of the discomfort of chills and fever. The first thing I did when I arrived back home to Washington was summon the doctor.

And it was on his orders that I found myself in bed for the next few weeks. Deenie, home with me in Washington until she returned to school, remained faithfully at my side. As terrible as I felt, I did relish this time with my girl after such a long separation. She delighted in studying my new Russian jewelry and pieces of art. She listened with wide-eyed amazement as I told her about the fur-clad commissars, about the colorfully domed towers of Moscow, about my outings with Polina Molotova and Ivy Litvinova. At thirteen years old, Deenie really was a charming young girl, blooming and bright, just on the cusp of her teenage years. I wished I could freeze time and keep her cheerful and close like that forever.

The only time I saw a frown on her lovely young face was when Joe would enter my bedroom, interrupting our private time and confidential whispers with business of his own. "My Mumsie— Oh. Well, hello, Deenie," Joe said as he sauntered in one afternoon, finding Deenie and me huddled together under the blankets, laughing in my bed as I told her about Polina Molotova's confusion over Coney Island. Immediately I noted how Deenie's soft young frame stiffened beside me. I had hoped she would warm to my husband in time; I had understood all too well that there was bound to be some natural bitterness toward the man who had replaced her father in my heart and in our home. But neither time nor effort had done anything to soften my daughter toward Joey.

Joe, for his part, either didn't notice or didn't let it bother him. He swept into the room now without a knock, carrying a stack of something—photographs, I realized. "Hey, Deenie Doll, did Daddy Joe ever show you this picture?"

Deenie huffed an audible exhale to match her scowl. She loathed his nicknames; she refused to call him Daddy, as he'd asked her to. Mostly she just looked away whenever he entered a room, not speaking to or answering him at all.

Joe leaned toward Deenie over the bed, and I saw how she recoiled, but he stuck the photograph in front of her face so that she couldn't help but see. "I just had a whole pile of our photographs developed from this past spring," he said. "There's our Mumsie dressed for the coronation ball. Isn't she the most lovely woman you've ever seen?"

"Sure," Deenie said dismissively. Then she turned toward me. "Mom, I think I am going to go start packing for school."

I felt my heart drop; I'd been enjoying our afternoon together in bed.

"Ah, look at this one," Joe said, flipping to the next black-and-white image. "Here we are outside of Paris on our boat."

"Mother's boat," Deenie said, her voice toneless.

Joe looked from the photograph toward Deenie, his dark brow rising. "What's that?"

"You mean *Mother's* boat," Deenie repeated, her aquamarine eyes staring squarely into Joe's for the first time. "The *Sea Cloud* is my mother's boat. She and my daddy built it together."

The blood pounded between my ears as I looked from my beautiful daughter to my husband, noting how his olive skin now appeared pale. Even his lips looked lighter as he calmly said, "That's right, Nedenia. They did build it. Before I took over the registration. Now it's my name on the deed, if you want to be technical." He nodded once, a tight movement, before flashing a wide smile and adding: "Well then, off you go. Those school trunks won't pack themselves." Then, to my relief, Joe turned away, tucking the photographs under his arm and leaving the room before either of them could utter another word.

WITH DEENIE BACK at school, I gave up my efforts to rise from bed and took to my covers completely, the illness, this so-called Moscow Malaria, attacking my entire body. My ears still felt as if they had been packed with cotton, so hard was it to hear anything. Joe, too, continued to complain of stomach pains, but our doctors were confounded by our strange and persistent symptoms.

As the days shortened and the nights turned darker, so, too, did the news from abroad. Germany was growing ever more aggressive under Hitler, who appeared to have solidified his grip of total power through his fanatical Nazi supporters. That autumn he began railing about how Czechoslovakia rightfully belonged to the Germans. Italy had its own fascist dictator, a man named Mussolini, while another, Francisco Franco, looked poised to take control of all of Spain soon, and Japanese troops were plowing their way through China with disheartening speed and brutality.

At home, we faced hostilities of our own. The Washington rumor mill had once again turned on us, with the club gossips and newspapers salivating over a rumored feud between my husband and the leadership in the State Department. There were whispers that Joe had gotten his post only because of my money, that the president was favoring him as a friend over many other career diplomats who were better suited and more deserving. I frowned as I read it all, sick in bed. Columns claiming that Joe and I saw the ambassadorship as a chance to frolic across Europe, attending coronations and luxuriating aboard our yacht. They blamed me for the fact that Joe and I were at home in Washington, painting me as a coddled and domineering wife, a dilettante who had wanted the prestige of a Parisian assignment but refused to take up the Russian post I had been given.

"With friends like these, who needs enemies?" I grumbled, throwing down the morning's newspapers. "I'm starting to wonder whether the Commies like us more than the Americans." I felt dizzy, as was so often the case when I tried to rise from bed in the morning, but I knew I had to get up. There were too many things to do: Prepare for the upcoming Christmas holiday, during which time Deenie would be coming home.

Wrap the presents I was planning to send up to Adelaide and Eleanor in New York. And pack; I needed to start packing my trunks.

The truth was that Joe and I were remaining at home in Washington for the holidays, but we knew we had to return to Russia after the New Year. Ill or not, I was not going to supply more fodder for the papers that were claiming we had abandoned our post. That we'd bought ourselves the position and therefore didn't feel compelled to actually do the work. Even though I was still as sick as I'd been when I'd arrived back home for treatment, even though Joe's stomach still roiled with pain, we needed to get back to the Soviet Union. No one would accuse me of shirking my duty.

WE ARRIVED IN the dead of winter, February, to a new chill in both weather and relations. "Roosevelt warned me things would be different," Joe said, speaking to me outside of the car but before we crossed the threshold of Spazzo House, knowing that the instant we set foot back inside, our every word would be recorded. "Before, it was just the fear of a possible war. Now it is the inevitability of an armed conflict. Germany won't be stopped. But we have one important mission: keep Russia away from friendship with Germany. Russia should be our ally against Hitler, if only we can convince them to trust us."

It came as no small relief that, with time, the symptoms of my illness had in fact lessened. And when I did still feel discomfort, I did my best to channel Papa's old determination and push my way through. But elsewhere, Joe was finding that his own determination was running into resistance. After several weeks back in the Russian capital, my husband confided to me that Litvinov, such a warm friend during our previous stay, was proving aloof this time around. Now the foreign minister was declining Joe's invitations to lunch and failing to return his calls. Always civil enough when they happened to meet in crowds, but entirely inaccessible.

"I'll call on Ivy," I suggested, running the bathwater on a cold night. "I'll invite her and Maxim to the ballet with us."

"Good," Joe said, nodding. "Yes, a night at the ballet with my lovely wife . . . who could turn that down?"

And so I made the arrangements. The show we settled on was *Flames of the Revolution,* and Max and Ivy arrived at the Bolshoi bundled in sable, their faces pale and subdued. We greeted them in the lobby, escorting them to the box we had taken for the evening, but the Litvinovs did not return our easy, friendly chatter as we settled into our seats. Nor did they soften as the instruments in the orchestra pit completed their warm-ups and the theatergoers trickled in, all of them stealing glances upward toward us, the infamous Americans and our guests, the revered Commissar Litvinov and his British-born wife.

When the curtains lifted and we had no choice but to sit in silence and watch the dancers as they leapt across the stage, I breathed a sigh of relief to feel the awkwardness disperse. I knew why Ivy and Maxim were holding us at such a distance, of course: Stalin had just started another round of his dreaded purges. As with his previous liquidations, nobody knew where it would lead, or when it would end. No one was safe, not even longtime friends of Stalin's from within his own government, or their innocent family members. Max and Ivy could not trust us because, well, nobody in the Soviet Union could trust anyone.

Several days later, Joe came home from meetings at the Kremlin with a grim face, pale as parchment. I retreated into our bathroom to run the water, and Joe followed me in. "More trials today," he whispered. "Puppet trials, of course. Dr. Pletnev was among the accused."

"*Pletnev*?" I whispered, my heart faltering. "My goodness." The kindly doctor who had spent hours tending to my husband at his bedside. He had been gentle and soft-spoken, brilliant, but entirely devoid of even an ounce of political cunning.

"Oh, Marjorie." Joe dropped his head, and I noticed the new streaks of silver that laced his dark head of hair. "The sorrow I felt at seeing those men . . . the way they trembled in the prisoner's box."

I nodded, imagining the scene, even though I was grateful not to have witnessed it in person. Had I sat there, looking at these men as they were damned to death, would I have been able to keep quiet? Hide my beliefs that these trials were cruel and the sentences unjust? Suddenly I longed to go home with an urgency I had not yet felt. As I stared past my husband and toward the window, out over a bleak, windswept winter night, I felt scared. I felt homesick. I reached for my husband, and as we held each other, we wept.

⁂

AS DEVASTATED AS we were about the trials, things grew bleaker still when we awoke several mornings later to news from the West. That morning at breakfast, a flustered aide ran in to deliver the news that Hitler had marched into Austria. The next great war, the demon that had been lurking for so long, had stepped from the shadows into the reality of daylight.

My birthday a few days later was a subdued affair. We had champagne and supper in the dining room at Spazzo House. I was turning fifty-one, and we invited just the embassy staff to partake in a cake and a toast. I did not feel up for much more. For a birthday present, Joe gave me more priceless Russian art that he had acquired through Polina Molotova: a Fabergé clock of gold and rose porcelain and a silver coffee service once owned by the Romanovs. But the most surprising birthday present came not long after that, in the form of a message from President Roosevelt. He had reassigned us. "Where?" I asked, as Joe studied the telegram. "London? Paris?"

Even something less glamorous like Oslo or Copenhagen would have been welcome news. Anything to move closer to the West, closer to my girls and our homeland, as the vise of war tightened.

"Two countries," Joe answered.

I didn't like the sour-lemon look of his face. "Oh?" I managed.

"Belgium and Luxembourg," he said.

Belgium and Luxembourg. My mind called up the map. Two small countries, right in the middle of Europe. In an instant, the initial joy at the news of a pending relocation gave way to a somber realization, thick and heavy as lead: Belgium and Luxembourg were mere miles from Adolf Hitler's border.

Chapter 40

Washington, D.C.
Summer 1938

WAR WAS CLOSING AROUND EUROPE LIKE A CHOKING NOOSE, and there we were, making our way right into the center of it. But before our departure, there was lunch at the White House with the president on a blue-sky summer day. I was disappointed to see that Eleanor was not there, as she was traveling in New York, but the president welcomed us to a small table just outside his Oval Office, where we sat down to a relaxed spread of sandwiches and iced tea. The small-talk pleasantries concerning Hyde Park and Topridge, children, and the plans for Sara Delano Roosevelt's upcoming birthday party were quickly completed, and then it was on to the more pressing business at hand.

"Now, Joe, Marjorie." Franklin Roosevelt eyed each of us in turn, speaking in that jaunty, crisp cadence that was famous the world over thanks to his regular radio messages. "I'm sending the pair of you off on one of the most significant missions in Europe. You'll be looking and listening for all of us. And we're eager to hear what you find."

With that parting pep talk—or perhaps warning—we set sail, crossing the Atlantic on a mild summer wind and dropping the anchor of the *Sea Cloud* in Ostend, a northern port city of Belgium.

If I considered the size of the territory alone, our new mission seemed like a demotion; I owned land tracts in Texas that covered nearly as many miles as these small states. But given the recent developments across Europe and what the president had told us in our final days in the States, I knew this was a highly strategic post. These were two small but ancient

European kingdoms, wedged in between bitter enemies Germany and France, their people glancing nervously in each direction and wondering when and from where the war might storm in.

Our first few weeks brought with them a whirlwind of introductions and official state receptions. In Luxembourg we were presented to Grand Duchess Charlotte of Nassau, an imposing woman who held a banquet for us attended by her fleet of footmen in crimson tunics and navy-blue breeches. In Belgium we were welcomed by King Leopold, who marked our arrival with a ball and a festive parade through Brussels, his gold-liveried attendants doting on us in their powdered wigs. We ate as we had not throughout our entire time in Moscow, feasting at tables made colorful by fresh-cut flowers and golden plates heaped with rich cheeses, goose confit, and warm, fresh-baked bread, each course accompanied by a new pour of wine directly from the nearby Rhine and Loire Valleys.

But underneath the festive atmosphere of these banquets and convivial parties, the air crackled with the menace of the nearby Nazis. Even the most earnest and optimistic pacifists across the continent had finally succumbed to the grim inevitability that Hitler would not be appeased.

It was the height of summer, and the northern days stretched long over the pastures and picturesque farms of the surrounding region. From our ambassadorial residence, it was only a short, pleasant car ride past fresh-tilled fields and stone farmhouses to the banks of the Moselle River. But the idyllic summer views offered a false sense of peace; just on the other side loomed Hitler's land. With our naked eyes, we watched as the Nazi soldiers practiced their rigorous drills and marching. We saw their tanks tattooed with the large, spiderlike swastikas, their treaded wheels churning up the fertile dirt and grass. Hitler's forces were mobilizing, and we could see that they would soon be ready to march forward across a bracing continent.

And we heard from Hitler as well. Being just miles from Germany, we heard the man's nightly rants across our local radio waves. I would feel queasy as I listened to his biting tirades. Though I did not speak his language, I knew well enough what his vitriol contained: Pronouncements that the Reich had been cheated out of its land, betrayed by unfair treaties orchestrated by the Jews. Cries that the Master Race needed land for its people. Brazen promises to take back rightful German territory from Czechoslovakia and France and Poland and anywhere else.

I grew more anxious with each passing day, even as Joe and I went about our ambassadorial duties, awaiting word from Washington and our president that we should do otherwise. It seemed as if we were all living in a state of illusory tarrying, a daze, biding our time as the northern European summer passed with parties hosted by Grand Duchess Charlotte and golf outings with King Leopold. We sipped Belgian beer while staring over the dark waves of the North Sea. But when would the storm clouds appear on that idyllic horizon? When would the inevitable reckoning come?

It came in the autumn. A front of crisp air had settled over our northern region, bringing with it an abrupt shortening of days, and we were seated in our drawing room under wool blankets when the telegram arrived. "News from London, sir," Joe's secretary said, barging into the room, breathless. "Hitler has seized the Sudetenland from Czechoslovakia . . . we're awaiting the response from England."

I huddled with Joe as we clicked the radio on, feeling that the report was devastating and shocking, but also the most inevitable news that one could expect to hear. Over the next few breathless days, England's Neville Chamberlain, in a desperate attempt to pacify the Nazis, flew to Munich and met with Hitler, where the leader of England gave the German madman free rein to steal from another sovereign nation. "It's over now," I said, turning from the radio to stare forlornly at my husband. The summer idyll, the dazed denial, the foolish hopes that somehow war might be averted—it was all shattered.

Joe nodded. After a pause, still frowning, he said, "Hitler sees that he won't be stopped."

"Where will he go next?" I asked.

"I don't know," Joe said, running his fingers absently along the fringe of the wool blanket. "To the east? To the west? Both at once?"

"Well, I know something," I said, peeling the blanket off my legs and standing. "We are getting out of here." Joe nodded once more, then he followed me from the drawing room toward our bedroom.

We packed our bags that night, taking less than an hour to do so, and we hurried by car to the coast. There, we met the *Sea Cloud* and boarded the next morning, as soon as the captain could be ready for us, ordering him to set our course for London.

It was there, surrounded by relieved Londoners and journals reporting on Chamberlain's declaration that we would have "PEACE FOR OUR TIME," that Joe told me he would not be accompanying me back to America. Roosevelt had not recalled him, and there was still work to be done, now more than ever, but we both agreed that it was for the best that I return home to the girls.

The crossing could have been calm, what with the clear fall weather and the docile conditions of the sea, but the hours were a series of nightmares strung together. As the ship pulled farther from England's green craggy coasts, I began to wonder whether we had made a mistake; I missed Joe terribly—should I have stayed with him? Should I have insisted that he sail with me? Was it absolute madness that he intended to return to his post in the center of Europe, where the Nazis were poised to goose-step right up to his doorstep?

But the menace of warfare lurked not just on European land—we, too, were in the middle of very grave danger as the ship plied the cold gray swells of the northern Atlantic. The crew warned me, their expressions grim and unblinking, that we were passing through waters thick with the dreaded Nazi U-boats and torpedoes. Sensing the unsettled nerves of everybody aboard the ship, dreading the piercing sound of the alert bulletins that crossed the radios in the high-pitched music of beeps and dashes, I preferred to stay in my stateroom most of the time, taking my meals in private. I did force myself to walk the decks at least twice a day, once in the morning and once in the afternoon before supper, if only to get some fresh air and show solidarity with my crew. But I trembled whenever I looked out over the water, thinking about the thicket of destruction that lurked beneath the deceptively calm surface. *Please,* I prayed, choosing to fix my eyes to the sky instead, *please let me make it home to my girls.*

As if to scream ever louder the fact that I was crossing a war front, British RAF bombers thundered over our heads at regular intervals, patrolling from the skies for Nazi movement below. A week into our crossing, we passed a tanker with a scorched English flag, the ship's scarred carcass roiling in flames, having been fired on by some menace either below the surface or above it. I stared in horror, studying the ghost of a ship, its crew already gone—hopefully in lifeboats, but there was no way to know. As I passed near the captain's quarters to return to my stateroom, I heard the radio clicking away, SOS alerts and warnings of German activity all around us.

When at last New York Harbor came into view, I nearly wept in relief. I felt weak, having had little appetite during the trip and even less sleep. I wanted nothing more than to open the front door of my home, pull my girls into my arms, and collapse with them into my big plush bed.

But my relief was only a partial one because of my worried longing for Joe. And because I knew—even as I stared gratefully at our gleaming Manhattan skyscrapers and the blithe, bright faces of the people who walked the busy streets, oblivious of the swastika that was crawling like a poisonous spider across an entire continent—that I had crossed the Atlantic in just a matter of days. Surely it would not take long for the war to make that same crossing.

Chapter 41

New York
1939

"WHAT ARE THEY *DOING*?" JOE RAILED, HIS VOICE CRACKLING across a long-distance line from Belgium. "Has Molotov completely lost his head?"

Hitler, rather than stopping with the Sudetenland as promised, had kept marching right across Czechoslovakia, wiping the entire nation off the map. And Stalin, rather than being alarmed by this Nazi encroachment farther east, appeared suddenly to welcome German aggression, having even gone so far as to sign a pact of friendship with Berlin. The main Russian architect behind this Nazi-Soviet accord? None other than our onetime friend and dinner guest, Vyacheslav Molotov.

Joe sounded mad enough over the phone, but the truth was that both he and I were devastated. All that we had worked for in Moscow, all of our efforts to cultivate friendship and trust with the Russians had been torn asunder and replaced by their alliance with Hitler. I didn't see how the picture in Europe could appear less hopeful.

But then, that fall, the Nazis barreled into Poland, catching us all, it felt, in our sleep. It was being called a blitzkrieg—a lightning war—and to read about it in the papers, you'd see Poland had in fact been devastated by a pounding storm. France and England scrambled, hastily declaring war after years of hoping for peace. Italy, Spain, and Russia joined the side of the Nazis. All of Europe was seething, and the war promised to be worse than anything anyone had ever seen.

* * *

With the declaration of war, everything changed for us. Belgium and Luxembourg would soon be casualties of Nazi aggression, gobbled up as satellite states to feed Hitler's goose-stepping war machine. The Russians were lost to us as well, having chosen the Nazis' side in exchange for the promise of land in Eastern Europe.

As disappointing as all of this was to my husband, who had made it his life's purpose in recent years to prevent this exact scenario, there was one silver lining to the way things had fallen apart: Roosevelt knew that Joe could no longer best serve him over in Europe. Now that the Soviets were at war with the West, our president needed an adviser in the State Department who could counsel him on how to deal with the Russian menace, an expert who knew Moscow and its political machinery. My husband, FDR decided, was the perfect man for that job.

"He's coming home!" I danced around the house waving the telegram, running into the staff kitchen and announcing the glorious news to anyone I found at home on that rainy afternoon in late autumn. Joe had wired to tell me he'd accepted Roosevelt's job offer of Special Adviser to the Department of State, where he would counsel on Soviet policy and draw on the other European relationships he had spent years so skillfully cultivating.

I couldn't have been more excited. Ever since my own safe return home, I had been sick with worry whenever I thought about Joe right there in the middle of the Nazi web. On top of that, I knew that his stomach pains continued to plague him. Now all I needed was his safe crossing, and having made the passage for myself, I knew that that was far from guaranteed.

The weeks passed and autumn darkened to winter as I remained in New York, awaiting Joe's return. Deenie wrote dutifully from Mount Vernon, telling me about her fall semester drama performance. Adelaide and Eleanor visited a few times a week, wrangling me out of the house to go shopping or to dine at The "21" Club. Colby kept me abreast of General Foods business and the latest news from the meetings. I did my best to stay busy, attending shows and visiting museums, walking the park whenever the weather allowed it. But in spite of my efforts at distraction, I felt like clawing the air, I was so impatient to hold my husband safely in my arms.

And then finally, shortly after a subdued Christmas and a quiet New Year at home in New York with my girls, when I thought I could not make it another day, my Joey arrived home. Paler and thinner than I would have liked, and a bit agitated by the stress of the recent months and his journey across the Atlantic, but in one piece. At last we were both in America, and we were both safe. Or, at least, that was what we thought.

Chapter 42

Washington, D.C.
January 1940

HAVING LIVED THROUGH TWO RUSSIAN WINTERS AND AN OCEAN full of Nazi torpedoes, I was no longer daunted by a few sour society dames in Washington. So with Joe's new position at the State Department, we decided we would make our primary residence in the capital, and I found us a lovely redbrick rental in the north of the city while I scoured the area for a more permanent home.

Besides, it now appeared that with the war on and everything else going wrong in the world, most people had other things to gossip about. And I was being discussed in other, more favorable ways; that January, the Women's National Press Club told me that they wished to thank me for my service as Ambassadress to Russia, Luxembourg, and Belgium by putting on a lovely tea in my honor. Alice Roosevelt, my old friend and the longtime leader of D.C. society, toasted me there over finger sandwiches and orange scones. Eleanor Roosevelt, the *other* First Lady, also came, bearing her husband's warmest regards, and it was hard for me not to laugh as I noticed how those two cousins avoided meeting in the packed room.

All the biggest Washington newspapers sent reporters, each one jockeying for my time and an interview. Even Betty Beale, the grande dame of Washington gossip, was in attendance. She stepped tentatively toward me when we made eye contact, perhaps even feeling a bit sheepish about the many harsh words she'd written in my honor, but her smile as she shook my hand seemed earnest enough. "Mrs. Davies, it is so wonderful to see you safely back home here in Washington."

I nodded, accepting her handshake as if we were old friends. "It's good to see you, too, Ms. Beale."

"Oh, please call me Betty." She tipped her chin and said, her voice lower: "I hear you collected quite a few Russian treasures while you were over there."

"Indeed I did."

Betty angled her body toward mine and said, "I know we are all salivating to learn more about your time abroad."

"I'll give a lunch," I said. "You can all come and see for yourselves."

I sent out invitations for a reception in my home, and in a marked change from just a few years prior, all who were invited now accepted with pleasure. Thrilled to be back in America and entertaining in a land of peace and abundance, I threw myself into the preparations, filling the rooms of our home with fresh-cut flowers. I heaped the table with platters of fresh fruits and cheeses, shrimp cocktail and small bites of filet mignon. In our living room and our library, I displayed our priceless Russian art and jewelry, glimmering like a second buffet of precious stones atop my tables and shelves. Beside that I laid out dozens of photos of our time abroad, as well as European newspaper clippings that I'd meticulously collected and kept. But the best detail of the day was that I had a special guest of honor, and I introduced her to my guests before it was time for lunch. "Ladies, thank you so much for coming. Now, it is my special honor to introduce you to Her Royal Highness the Grand Duchess Charlotte of Luxembourg."

Joe and I had used our contacts in the State Department to help the beleaguered royal flee Luxembourg ahead of Hitler's invasion, and I was hosting her as my guest while we found her a more permanent residence, eager to return the hospitality that she had so graciously shown us. Charlotte was a great success throughout the afternoon, what with her statuesque presence and her booming voice. My guests seemed to thoroughly enjoy themselves throughout the meal, and then while perusing my colorful displays of priceless Russian treasure. The afternoon, I decided, was an unabashed triumph.

Betty Beale lingered as the rest of my well-dressed guests offered their thanks and farewells. Charlotte had gone upstairs to rest, and so eventually it was just the two of us who stood in my bright front hall, the smell of the fresh flowers perfuming the air around us. Betty smiled, arching an eyebrow. "What a lovely luncheon, Mrs. Davies."

I waved my hands. "You can call me Marjorie," I offered. *I have a feeling we'll be seeing plenty of each other, whether I wish for it or not.*

"Too kind," Betty said, her eyes eager and attentive as she glanced around the interior of my home, scouring the space for any detail she might have missed. "Thank you again for an exquisite afternoon. Quite impressive that you now number not only American presidents but also European royals among some of your close friends."

"Charlotte . . . the grand duchess . . . is wonderful," I said. And then, leaning forward, I added, "We've been through so much together. The stories I could tell you."

Betty took my bait, her features going positively alight. But then a moment later she remembered herself, primly folding her hands before her waist as she straightened, saying only: "One can imagine." A momentary pause, Betty's eyes roving once more over my front hallway. And then she turned back to me and added, "The grand duchess told me today that the leaders in Luxembourg have honored you with the Order of the House of Savoy."

I nodded. Indeed they had. And then, leaning toward the columnist again, I smiled demurely as I said: "It's funny: She's the royal, but Charlotte has remarked how my lifestyle intimidates her. How my land and property and wealth make her feel modest in comparison."

For once, Betty Beale looked as though she had nothing to say.

❖

I WAS DELIGHTED to be back in America, especially in the summer when I had my girls with me. Deenie, now sixteen, was home from Mount Vernon for the break, and my older girls, Adelaide and Eleanor, had cleared their calendars to spend several weeks with me. And so, for the first time in years, we enjoyed a delightful summer as a family at Topridge.

After years in Europe, watching as the thickening clouds of war took shape on the horizon, I was determined to relish a season of peace with the people I loved most, and the Adirondacks were just the place to do it. We filled those long days with canoe excursions up and down the St. Regis or waterskiing off our dock. We hiked the pine-hemmed trails, enjoying picnic lunches before sprawling views of the lake and the wooded peaks. Evenings were relaxed, with games of charades or cards, dinners of sliced ham or roast beef on the deck, dessert of roasted marshmallows or our favorite treat, Adirondack pie—flapjacks cooked on the grill and doused in maple syrup. After dinner we would gather in folding chairs around the campfire, and Joe and I would tell the girls our stories of Russia and Belgium and the London coronation.

Fall found me back in the capital with Joe and busier than I'd ever been. Now that I was back in easy contact, I resumed my responsibilities on the board of directors for General Foods, and that meant monthly meetings in New York City. In between my trips back and forth, I took up my volunteer work for the Red Cross once more, encouraging my friends to support them as well, knowing what a prolonged war in Europe would mean for so many.

But the biggest job came when Roosevelt won reelection to an unprecedented third term that autumn and the president asked Joe to oversee his inauguration. It was an honor to be asked, and I was proud of my husband, so I vowed to help however I could.

I loved to host, and I was good at it, but this job would present a new challenge, even for me. Roosevelt was making history, and as Joe's wife, I would be expected to kick things off with the largest gala in Washington history, one to which all of our nation's governors and their wives would be invited, along with congressmen, senators, political donors, cabinet members, diplomats, and other dignitaries. My home was a hive of activity for months as I finalized the guest list and readied our rooms to host more than a thousand of the world's most distinguished guests.

"You nervous, Mumsie?" Joe asked, standing beside me in our doorway as the first of our invitees began to file in. It was Secretary of State Cordell Hull, I noted, suppressing my grimace—the man had been outspoken in his criticism of Joe's appointments as ambassador. Now he was coming into our home, accompanied by the popular senator from Missouri, Harry

Truman. And there, behind him, walked Eleanor and Franklin, laughing about something as they made their way slowly up our front walk, the president leaning heavily on his wife's arm for support. I straightened to my full height, assuming a bright smile beside my husband as I offered Cordell Hull my hand and a warm nod of welcome.

Nervous? Perhaps I felt a little nervous, yes. The leader of our country was about to enter my home along with a thousand other luminaries in order to attend a party over which I would preside. But who could do this better than I?

NO SOONER DID I put my house back in order and catch my breath from Roosevelt's inaugural festivities than I was invited to speak in New York to a crowd of thousands on the topic of American-Soviet relations and America's place in the war-torn world. Though I was well versed in hosting and could now boast that I'd entertained presidents, royals, and movie stars, speaking onstage in such a massive forum would be out of my depth, and so I brought Adelaide and Eleanor with me to help calm my nerves.

Sitting in a private dressing room before my speech, halfheartedly sipping from my glass of ice water, I trembled. Adelaide noticed, and she put a hand on top of mine, speaking in a low, steady voice: "Mother, you've been practicing for days. You know the entire speech by heart."

I looked at my daughter a moment as I took in a slow, fortifying breath. Then I managed a smile, saying, "You're right, dear."

A staffer entered the room just then. "Mrs. Davies? It's time for your speech."

I rose from the chair and left my dressing room, butterflies dancing in my belly as Eleanor and Adelaide remained at my side all the way down the long hallway. Bright bulbs poured white-hot light on the stage. I heard my name, but I barely heard the words of introduction or the rumble of polite applause as I climbed to the podium and looked out over a field of attentive faces. The crackle of flash powder, cameras clicking as journalists scratched away with their pencils. I could no longer see Adelaide or

Eleanor. *Mother, you've been practicing for days. You know the entire speech by heart*. She was right. I did. And the words came to me then. I opened my mouth, reminding myself to speak into the microphone, to speak clearly and slowly, even though my stomach felt like it might flip itself. I began: "To none in this world is the outcome of this war more vital than to women."

I saw my daughters just then, seated in the front row, their pale, beautiful eyes fixed squarely on me, their mother. Their faces proud and encouraging.

I went on: "If the Nazi totalitarian system should dominate our world, the status of women would be horrible to contemplate."

Ladies seated throughout the audience nodded, agreeing. I was speaking for them. And for Deenie, Adelaide, and Eleanor. For myself. For all the women who would be affected by what I had seen on the border of Germany and through the waters of the Nazi-patrolled Atlantic. "Those of us who believe in freedom, who believe in opportunity, who believe in the innate goodness of the human race, we will not allow the conditions that would crush our rights, that would bring an end to self-respect and liberty for all, and especially for women."

At the end of my remarks, the audience leapt to its feet, roaring in approval. I could see my daughters where they stood in the front, beaming. The flash of more cameras, and I thanked the audience. I had dreaded making that speech, but now that it was over, I was certain that it had been the right thing to do, if for no other reason than to show my daughters that it was right to speak for what they believed in. That was what I had done: Marjorie Merriweather Post was a mother who wanted to make the world better for her children. A wife who championed the cause of women. I hoped my words would matter.

Just months later, Hitler did the unthinkable and turned on his Russian allies. Though stunned, Joe and I could not help but feel immense relief, even though we knew it spelled terrible things for the Russian people in the short term. In the long term, it would ultimately be good for the entire world. "Hitler, in his egotistical mania, has pushed the Russian bear right into the Allied camp," Joe noted as we stared, breathless, at the news reports. And that meant that my husband was suddenly the undisputed expert on our new military ally. His work at the State Department was both exciting and endless.

And yet, as busy as we already were, our lives turned upside down yet again at the end of that year. It happened just before Christmas, the world growing even more frightening and unknowable with the Japanese attack on Pearl Harbor. Joe and I huddled beside the radio as our president shared the grim news: thousands of innocent and unsuspecting Americans dead, our Pacific base turned into a wasteland of flames, so much blood and treasure lost in mere hours. And no matter how hard Joe and I had worked for friendship and peace, America was going to war.

Chapter 43

Washington, D.C.
January 1942

THE ENTRY OF AMERICA INTO THE WAR BROUGHT WITH IT JUST one piece of good news: Maxim and Ivy Litvinov were coming to Washington. Coming to stay, in fact, as Maxim had been named by Stalin to replace the outgoing Soviet ambassador, Konstantin Umansky. I planned to welcome our Moscow friends with a splendid party, and I used my newfound status as celebrated District hostess to ensure that the entire capital was in attendance.

The Russians were suddenly not only Hitler's enemies but also America's friends, and our president had made it clear that we were to treat the Litvinovs as such. My guest list for this gathering thus included senators, congressmen, ambassadors, reporters, members of Roosevelt's cabinet, Harry and Bess Truman, and of course, my new friend Betty Beale, who told me, her eyes wide, "I had to be here, Marjorie, darling. It's the biggest to-do in town."

The night was a cold one by Washington standards—though of course Ivy and Max would not find it so—but a thin dusting of snow gave the grounds of our home a lovely pearled appearance. Inside, the house sparkled, with our Russian paintings covering the walls, our tables set with our priceless dishes and crystal from the Romanovs. Dressed in a sheath gown of silver silk and a choker of diamonds, I put on my warmest smile as I saw my guests of honor approach. "Ivy, my dear friend, it is such a pleasure to have you here with us." I could tell by her expression that Ivy was a bit stunned, taken aback by the steady procession of my gowned and tuxedoed guests, by the small army of liveried servants who milled about offering flutes of chilled champagne and hors d'oeuvres of pâté and caviar. A spread of oysters and lobster filled one banquet table; boards of charcuterie filled another. The air was fragrant with the aromas of hothouse flowers and perfume and jockeying self-importance.

"Marjorie, my dear, thank you." Ivy took my hands in her own and leaned in for a kiss. "But goodness, you call this winter? It is so warm here."

"We hope you'll find it so. Ah, here, for you, with our heartfelt welcome." I gave her the package I had wrapped for her before the party. She opened it, smiling when she tore aside the tissue paper to see what was inside: a loaf of bread and a small pinch of salt, held in a fine porcelain bowl from the American Sandwich Glass Company.

"And this, Ambassador, is for you," I said, turning toward her husband.

Litvinov accepted and then unwrapped his package. "*Mission to Moscow,*" Maxim said, reading the title aloud. "By Ambassador Joseph Davies." Maxim and Ivy both turned toward my husband, their faces questioning.

"You wrote this?" Ivy asked.

Joe nodded. "All about my time in the Soviet Union. President Roosevelt himself asked for this book. It's all of my official memos and letters to the president and the State Department. Journal entries. Reports. All previously classified information. Our president wants the American people to see things as they really are in Moscow. Show them that the Russians are not our enemies—the Germans and the Japanese are."

"Published by Simon and Schuster, and a bestseller already," I added. As the proud wife, I could not help but chime in. I, after all, had been the one to compile many of the documents to send to his publisher, as Joe had spent large portions of the past months too ill to rise from bed for more than a few hours. And now I wanted my husband to feel proud, too. "People cannot get enough of it. We want to show the public that the Russians are people just like us, and my Joe—"

"Marjorie, that'll do," Joe interrupted, with a quick pat of my hand as he flashed me a strained smile. "Now you're my literary agent?"

"No," I said, my voice sounding like that of a chastened child. "Just your proud wife."

"I think they get the idea." Joe turned to Maxim, beckoning him to walk toward the tables of food. "Ambassador, shall we?" I remained in my place, a bit off balance, but forcing myself to keep a gracious smile on my features, hoping in silence that it was just his stomach troubles again.

⁂

JUST AS WITH the Great War, this global conflict meant that things had to change in my own home as well. "Our boys are going off to war," I said to my social secretary, Margaret, that winter during one of our morning meetings. "Which means we are going to be making some changes to my calendar."

"Yes, Mrs. Davies. Changes . . . what sort of changes?"

"This isn't the time for me to escape to Florida or Long Island for swimming and parties. It is the time for me to get to work." With that declaration, I closed up Hillwood, Topridge, and Mar-a-Lago; all my hosting would be in Washington and would have a purpose. That spring and summer I gave parties to raise money for the Red Cross, I funded performances of the National Symphony Orchestra to raise money for the army and navy, I opened a public kitchen in New York City where any member of the armed services could eat for free, and I raised money for the growing number of refugees who were scattered across Europe, particularly those from the Soviet Union.

And my days of pleasure cruises across the seas were over, that much I knew—at least for as long as Hitler had his U-boats haunting the waters. And so I offered my beloved *Sea Cloud* to the navy. "She's a patriot, just like I am," I said to Admiral King, Chief of the U.S. Navy, when I made my offer. At the rate of a dollar a year, my massive ship was theirs on lease until we had won the war. Admiral King told me they would use her as a convoy carrier, to transport American sailors across the waters, patrol for German subs, and provide safe passage through the dangerous waters that I knew firsthand.

And my contributions to the cause were not going to stop there, I learned. Deenie, who was done with high school and studying acting at the American Academy of Dramatic Arts, volunteered for a USO tour to perform for our forces on the Mariana Islands. I hated the thought of her going to the South Pacific; I felt as if I might as well have been sending a child off to war. But I knew there would be no stopping her, just as there had never been any stopping me.

The most unexpected moment of the war happened early the next spring, when Margaret came to my sitting room to announce a surprising visitor. "Mrs. Davies?"

I looked up from my armchair, where I sat reviewing the minutes of the most recent General Foods board meeting. "Yes?"

The young woman clasped her hands before her waist, jutting her chin forward as she declared, "The . . . er, the president is here to see you."

I rose from my chair, putting my papers aside. "He . . . he is?"

"Yes, ma'am."

"Where is Mr. Davies?" I asked.

"Mr. Davies is already in the drawing room. We've shown the president in to him. They await you."

I flew down the stairs and found the two men seated before the fireplace. President Roosevelt looked relaxed in a pinstriped suit, a straw boater resting in his lap. Several dark-suited men, the president's security guards, stood sentry-like near the doorway and throughout the hallway. "Ah, Mrs. Davies!" The president smiled affably when he saw me, but he didn't rise. Lingering leg paralysis from an earlier bout of polio gave our commander in chief more and more trouble these days, Joe had told me, even though the broad public did not know this fact.

"Mr. President, it's an honor," I said. *And a surprise.* "Can . . . can I offer you something, sir? Something to drink perhaps?"

"As a matter of fact, there is something I'll be asking for, but not to drink. Please, Marjorie, come sit. This affects you, after all."

My stomach clenched. Joe's face was unreadable. I lowered myself into the empty armchair across from Roosevelt. The president looked from me toward Joe, and then he said, "I realize this visit is unexpected, so how about I cut right to it?"

Joe and I both nodded. "Outwardly, the war effort is going well," the president said, his highbrow manner of speaking so familiar to me after the many fireside chats and addresses I'd listened to throughout his more than ten years in office.

"Yes," Joe answered. I could tell by my husband's creased expression that he had been caught just as unaware as I had by this drop-in.

"But Stalin is a tricky fellow," Roosevelt went on, cocking his head to the side. "It's no secret to you, Joe, that Churchill and Stalin loathe each other. Churchill doesn't trust Stalin, and Stalin suspects Churchill of imperialist intentions. Stalin feels that he has spent more blood than all the rest of us combined, and he's not entirely wrong—those Reds have been mowed down on the Eastern Front something fierce. And Stalin has grown impatient with it. He is enraged with us for not opening up additional fronts. He thinks we're deliberately trying to bleed him white. Churchill has a plan, but Stalin won't hear it. We can't let the whole damned thing fall apart. Not this late in the game, when we are so close."

A pause. Silence, but for the rhythmic ticktock of our Fabergé clock on the mantel. Out in the hallway one of the security guards coughed. Roosevelt broke the silence: "I need to get through to Stalin. To convince him that we are all on the same side. That we want to see the Nazis whipped just as much as he does." The president looked squarely at my husband, his eyes burning with an intensity that belied his genteel manner of speech. "I need you in Russia, Joe. The name Stalin means 'Man of Steel' and that is the damned truth—the man is well-near impenetrable. But he trusts *you,* and that's not something that I can say about anyone else."

I waited until the president was gone, but I did not mince words once I had my husband alone. "You can't go, Joe."

He didn't offer any reply, merely sat there in the same chair, his finger tracing the line of his chin—back and forth, back and forth—in infuriating and inscrutable silence. I, on the other hand, had no use for silence. "To be clear, Joe, he's asking us to move back to Moscow. We can't do it."

My husband looked at me, meeting my eyes for the first time since Roosevelt's departure. "Would you like me to refuse the president of the United States, Marjorie?"

I could not recall the last time Joe had called me Mumsie or Blue Eyes, I noted with a twinge. But this was no time for sentimental musings. I exhaled, trying to bridle my exasperation. "Joe, this doesn't come from me. Your doctors have told you that added stress would mean more trouble. And do you remember the food over there? And *that* was during a time of peace." I wrung my hands just thinking about it; I fed him all fresh food and purées these days—made from ingredients we would never have access to in the USSR. "And the travel," I went on, "the winter weather . . . not to mention the Nazis . . . it's the last thing you should consider."

But Roosevelt did not want anyone else for the job. When Joe declined the post, the president came back with another request. "He still wants me to go"—I made to interject with all of the reasons why that would be madness, but Joe raised a hand, quieting me so he could continue—"only to meet with Stalin. Calm and reassure him. And give him a handwritten note."

I insisted that if Joe were to undertake this abbreviated assignment, he would also take his doctor with him, along with several coolers of healthy frozen foods. So Joe prepared to make the trip, and I prepared to send plenty of General Foods nourishment. On the night before his departure, as I helped him pack the last of his luggage, I noticed a sealed envelope on top of his personal briefcase. "What is that?" I asked.

Joe glanced down at the thin envelope. "That's the letter," he said.

I knew what he meant by that. "Do you know what it says?"

"No." Joe shook his head. "Only the president does. And soon Joseph Stalin will."

Yes, I thought, *as long as you make it there alive to deliver it.*

Chapter 44

New York City
March 1946

PEACE RETURNED TO AMERICA WITH A WAVE OF GOOD CHEER and one national exhale. We'd done it. Hitler was defeated. The Nazis would not rule all of Europe. The Japanese would not be storming our Pacific shores. Joe had survived his harrowing trip to Moscow and had made it back, mission well accomplished, much to the relief of both our president and me.

As peace treaties were drafted first for Europe and then Asia, the young men began to come home, heroic, and the topics on everyone's minds seemed suddenly to be weddings and babies, and I saw that firsthand in my own home. "You really think he's the one?" I stared into the gorgeous face of my *own* baby. Well, not a baby any longer. Deenie—though now she liked to be called Dina by others—would be turning twenty-three in a few months, even if her aquamarine eyes still glowed with girlish liveliness. We were having dinner together at Sardi's in Manhattan's Theater District, Deenie having just wrapped her nightly performance in Broadway's *The Mermaids Singing*. And though she was no longer up there onstage, performing for a packed house beneath the lights and the stage makeup, my daughter was fairly aglow.

"I do, Mother. I *know* Stan is the one," my daughter answered, lowering her long-lashed gaze to her left hand, where a stunning new diamond shone on her manicured finger.

His name was Stanley Rumbough, and he was as close as any man could ever come to being worthy of my Deenie. Stan was well built, with dark hair and a broad, self-assured smile. After his time at Yale, he'd spent the war years as a marine fighting the Japanese. And I knew he didn't want my daughter for her money, because as the scion of the Colgate-Palmolive fortune, he had plenty of his own.

"Where would you like the wedding to be?" I asked my daughter. All around us the bright, noisy restaurant pulsed with nighttime chatter and energy, and the waiter appeared with our plates, pork chop for me, fillet of sole for Deenie.

"I was thinking Long Island," Dina answered. "At home. Hillwood."

I smiled at this; a wedding at our home, the place where Deenie had spent so many of her childhood summers, would be perfect. But then a sour thought quickly followed: it had been Ned's home as well. *Our* home. Across the restaurant a waiter dropped a dish, sending a clatter across the crowded space, but I barely noticed. All I could hear was the one loud, unwelcome thought that now filled my mind: Ned was going to be the father of the bride. My daughter must have seen the shifting of my features, because she leaned toward me and said, her voice low and beseeching: "Mom, please, you know Daddy will be walking me down the aisle, right?"

I STOOD WITH Dina outside of Trinity Church, just a short drive from Hillwood, where, at that very minute, a fleet of servants was putting the finishing touches on the splendid banquet that would follow the ceremony. The day was clear and beautiful, but nowhere near as beautiful as my happy girl. "You look lovely, my Deenie," I said. And she did. My daughter was the image of all that a joyful bride should be: Cheeks flushed with excitement and youthful health, slender figure sheathed in a custom gown of creamy white satin woven with crystals and pearls. Golden hair pulled back beneath a long veil of delicate lace. And, of course, my favorite diamonds brightening her ears and neck and wrists.

Looking at my girl, nervous but hopeful as she stood there outside the doors through which her groom awaited, I couldn't help but think back to three previous days of my life. Thrice I'd been a bride—and married for long enough to know that it was not always an easy state. Why, just that very morning, Joe had refused to speak to me, so furious was he at the thought of having to see Ned. Would Deenie have more luck as a wife? God, I hoped she would. I prayed that this would be her only trip up the aisle.

When Ned and Dorothy arrived at the church—late, I noted with a grinding of my teeth—I handed my baby off with a cool but cordial nod and then made my way inside the church. My small mother-of-the-bride nosegay of white roses quivered in my hands; in fact, my whole body felt shaky. I did not like being in the presence of Ned, even after these many years. There Joe sat in our front pew, frowning; he'd been in a lather for days, ever since I'd agreed to include Ned. But today wasn't about Joe. Nor was it about Ned Hutton or Dorothy. Or me and my hurts, past or present. Today was about my Deenie.

As the music signaled her appearance at the top of the aisle, I turned. I kept my eyes off of Joe at my side, off of Dorothy in the pew opposite us, off of Ned at Dina's side, fixing my gaze only on my darling girl. *Please, dear God. Let Stan be the man we all hope he is. And please let my daughter find happiness in this marriage.*

I HAD HOPED that the end of the war might mean peace in my own household as well. I was wrong. For me, things should have been swell. General Foods was soaring; American families were growing, and they were hungry. That first year of peace saw sales of almost $400 million. "Your Birds Eye bet proves more brilliant with every passing year, Marjorie," Colby told me at the conclusion of our board meeting. "It's one of our best earners." I beamed at this.

And there was more good news. Ned Hutton may have been off the mark when it came to the Birds Eye investment, but Ed Close had been equally wrong about the value of our Texas land, where, just recently, ranchers had uncovered vast swaths of rich, untapped oil, which meant that liquid profit was daily spewing from the earth as quickly as we could catch it.

To my great relief, Dina was blissfully happy in her new married life—

but I could not say the same for myself, and so I proposed, in the aftermath of Dina's wedding, that Joe and I take a vacation for ourselves. A second honeymoon on the water. It was at that time that my beloved *Sea Cloud* was returned to me, decommissioned from the navy after her proud tour of duty. I was so flush with cash that I was able to remodel her from battleship back to the luxury yacht she'd been before the war. Since we finally had our beautiful boat back, why not use it to take some time together, for rest and fun and healing? To my relief, Joe agreed.

There we sat aboard the *Sea Cloud* on a breezy, white-capped day, the Caribbean beaches of St. John rising lush and green in the near distance. Our anchor was dropped, the deck was set for breakfast, and Joe drank his herbal tea as I sipped on my Postum.

Just as a young member of the crew appeared at the table with our food—Grape-Nuts and fruit for me, a melon-and-yogurt purée for Joe—a fresh gust of wind skittered across the port railing, sending a spray of water through the air. I clutched the table. The poor servant, caught as unaware as we were, momentarily lost his footing, and he reached for the nearest chair to brace himself, accidentally sending the tray of breakfast flying. My cereal bowl fell to the floor and shattered. Joe's purée tipped over, landing with a splash on the deck at his feet. The servant, mortified, fell to his knees as he tried to salvage the mess, but Joe looked as if he would send the fellow overboard. "Goddamn it!" my husband yelled, his cheeks flushing scarlet as he saw where some of the drink had stained his trousers. I winced, but Joe was not yet finished. "Can't you be more careful, boy?"

"Joe, please," I entreated, rising from my chair to kneel beside the scrambling servant. "Let's all calm down. It's fine, it's fine."

"I'm so sorry, Mrs. Davies, Mr. Davies," the poor young man gasped, looking as if he would cry. "The ship, I wasn't expecting—"

"Please, don't worry another minute," I interjected, pressing my hand to his shoulder. "Why don't you run and fetch a mop? And then tell Cook to send up another tray. It's no bother at all."

The boy nodded and then scurried off to dispatch these orders, without a look backward toward either Joe or me. My husband, meanwhile, sat in his chair, fuming as he stared down at the spilled purée. "Damned reckless," he said, his lips thin and white.

"Joe, please," I said, my voice measured, even though my heart raced. "It was hardly intentional. And the poor kid felt terrible."

"That's right! Take his side. Put your hands all over him as if *he* has been wronged."

It was too ridiculous to acknowledge. I drew in a quiet breath, trying to remain calm, hoping that if I did so, he might cool off as well. "We'll just have Cook send up another tray. No need to—"

"Oh, stay out of it, Marjorie. It's none of your goddamned business." He swatted at his trousers with a napkin, only making the stain worse, but I certainly was not going to say that to him. I sat back down in my seat in silence. But Joe went on: "You always go sticking your nose into things that aren't your concern."

I glanced toward the doorway to ensure that none of the staff were nearby before I leaned over the table and spoke to my husband very quietly: "It *is* my concern, when you speak like that to one of my staff."

"*Your* staff?" Joe turned his glower toward me. "Oh, so it's your name on the boat now? Last I checked, this boat was my property."

I sat back in my chair, my mouth falling open in a stunned gape. What was there to say in such a situation? "This anger looks ugly on you, Joe," was all I offered in reply.

Joe's dark eyebrows lifted as he laughed, a hoarse, mirthless sound. "Oh. So now you're going to tell me not only how I should speak, but also how I should look? Anything else you want to add to the list, Marjorie? Want to castrate me while you're at it? Serve up my balls with some Birds Eye frozen peas? Maybe it'll make you millions, dearest."

I turned from him toward the water, where the waves shifted in and out of sharp white peaks. I needed to stay calm because when he was like this, there was no matching him, no reasoning on the summit of his rage. So I shrugged, taking a sip of my drink.

He tossed his napkin onto the table, waving his hands in dismissal. "Maybe if my wife wasn't constantly rubbing my face in shit, I wouldn't think everything looked so goddamned shitty."

I resisted the urge to wince, instead pulling my eyes from the water and fixing my gaze squarely on him. "I know you're not feeling well, Joe, and that you're not yourself, so I'm going to excuse myself from the table. I hope that by the time we reach port, you'll be ready to apologize for this inexcusable behavior."

Just then the servant reappeared, a fresh tray in his hands, a contrite expression plastered to his features. "Thank you," I said, rising from the table and offering the young man a reassuring smile. "I'll take mine to my stateroom with me. I seem to have lost my appetite for the moment."

I'd told Joe I understood, and that I'd give him a pass on account of his stomach pains, but inwardly I knew that it was more than simply a case of his not feeling well. And it was not a single episode of bad behavior, either. Joe's vitriol was becoming so regular that the servants had started to stutter and flee from his presence. But even more troubling, it wasn't just our staff who had felt his temper and foul mood—it was my daughters as well.

I'd invited the girls to meet us in Cuba for the second leg of this cruise. It had been years since they'd enjoyed the *Sea Cloud,* and they had always loved any opportunity to come aboard. And yet, all three of them had declined. "Why would you pass up the chance for a cruise through the Caribbean?" I'd asked, stunned, when I telephoned Adelaide from the captain's room.

I could hear Adelaide sigh on the other end of the line. Eventually, after a pause, she said: "It's not the cruise we are passing up."

This startled me. "Oh?"

"It's . . . Mother, it's the company on board."

Things had changed for him, and for us, in recent years. Once the most in-demand expert on Soviet affairs and a regular confidant and colleague of the president's, Joe had seen his influence wane dramatically of late. Now that Roosevelt was gone and President Truman was in the White House, my husband no longer had a close friend in the Oval Office. In fact, Harry Truman, along with his inner circle of George Kennan, Averell Harriman, and Dean Acheson, seemed to have no use for my husband. "Why don't you invite Truman to Topridge?" I'd suggested early on in Truman's first term. "Or aboard the *Sea Cloud*?" We'd been close with many presidents before, and I was sure that we could make friends with this one as well.

So Joe took my advice. I overheard the phone call, listening in as he said: "I'd love for you to visit my camp up here on the Upper St. Regis. Great spot. Bring the wife and daughter—I'll set them up with canoes, hiking guides, whatever they'd like." Joe never mentioned that it was in fact *my* camp. But I didn't bring that up. There was no point, since the president politely declined the invitation.

With Hitler defeated and the Japanese wiped out, American foreign policy had careened swiftly and staunchly toward an attitude of anti-Soviet sentiment. My husband, a onetime defender of Molotov's and a friend of Litvinov's, someone who'd shared multiple cordial meetings with Joseph Stalin and had spent years advocating for partnership with Moscow, was suddenly seen as a pinko and a Commie.

We'd thought we had some good news when Warner Bros. bought the rights to adapt Joe's book, *Mission to Moscow,* into a film. But when it came out, Joe was lambasted from coast to coast. Dozens of newspapers called it propaganda for the Soviets. And though American audiences uniformly hated the film, Soviet audiences loved it. Even Joseph Stalin. That did not help.

The first few years after the war saw us firmly ensconced in Washington, since Joe was too sick to do much traveling and his physicians were in the capital. We were going less and less to New York. Manhattan had been my home with Ed Close—Joe hated that. Hillwood had been my home with Ned, the site of so many blissful summer days and nights—Joe hated that even more. The upkeep on both places was turning into more trouble than they were worth, since every time I proposed a trip to either spot, it ended in a fight with Joe, and so I sold both properties.

I hoped that Joe would see these efforts for what they were: my willingness to part with the pieces of my past that reminded him of the other men. I was firmly behind him and with him in making our life together in Washington, as he wanted. So then why did I fear for how that life might look?

Chapter 45

Washington, D.C.
Spring 1952

ALICE ROOSEVELT FIXED ME WITH HER WRY, BLUE-EYED GAZE as she said, "My dear Marjorie, you're the type of gal who has lifeboats for her lifeboats."

"I think that's a compliment, Alice. But either way, I thank you for calling me a gal, rather than the old matron I am."

"You?" Alice leaned close, and I saw the mischief of her beloved late father in that cool, twinkling smirk. "Hardly. You know, Marjorie, that everyone in town wanted an invite to this party of yours? They're calling you Duchess Davies."

"Coming from the lady who is called the Other Washington Monument, it means a lot," I replied.

"Overly tall and thickheaded as stone, that's me." Alice linked her arm through mine, and suddenly we were young girls whispering about the city that had been the adopted home to us both for so long. "We've done our time in this place, you and I, haven't we?" Alice sighed, surveying the colorful scene before us, and then she declared: "You've made it magical tonight."

I looked around. Alice was right: my brand-new home did look splendid. The grounds were in the full throes of a glorious southern spring—balmy, lush, with the last spears of gentle late-evening sunshine falling across them and the lights of the nearby monuments twinkling on like electric starlight. Dreamlike as the place appeared, it had taken weeks of hard work and meticulous planning, and I had left no detail uncovered. I'd timed this gathering with precision; after that many springs in Washington, I knew certain rhythms, one being that the flowers were at their finest exactly one month after my dogwoods blossomed.

So there we were, surrounded by a garden bursting with color, Nelson Rockefeller and Mamie Eisenhower mingling over chilled champagne, admiring my magnolias and azaleas, my rosebushes and cherry trees. Inside, my bright home was fragrant with my hothouse jasmine and orchids. In addition to the flowers and the guests, the house was resplendent with my Russian antiques on full display. Sprawling banquet tables were set with an engineer's exactitude, each setting meticulously measured and spaced, sparkling with golden plates and cutlery, crystal glasses, and cut-glass bowls filled with bite-sized cubes of fresh melon and strawberries.

One of my guests, a young woman, stood before me. She had an attractive face with large brown eyes and a short bob of stiffly coiffed dark hair, on top of which rested a straw hat with pale blue flowers. I knew her last name; she was the wife to a junior senator by the name of Lyndon Johnson. *From which state?* These senators filed in and out of the city so often. The woman looked shy as she stepped forward and said, "Mrs. Davies, I have to introduce myself and thank you. My name is Lady Bird Johnson."

"Mrs. Johnson, of course," I said, accepting her gloved handshake. "So good of you and the senator to come."

"Well, we wouldn't miss it. I knew this meant I had to buy a fancy new hat," she gushed, and with that her southern accent triggered my memory—her husband served from Texas. "It's just such a treat to be invited. To meet you, Mrs. Davies. I was telling Lyndon, my husband, everything you touch seems to turn to beauty."

"That's nice of you to say, Mrs. Johnson," I answered. Just then a flurry of activity near the door, followed by the appearance of several dark-suited men, drew my attention away. "Ah, if you'll excuse me, Mrs. Johnson. President and Mrs. Truman have just arrived. But it is lovely to meet you. Lady Bird, you said, right?" She nodded, her gaze following me as I crossed the garden.

I greeted the president as Bess Truman pulled me in for a friendly hug. Photographers snapped us from all angles as we talked. Across the garden, Alice Roosevelt had a small group of congressmen laughing beneath my crab apple tree. Of course Betty Beale was circulating with the bearing of a well-dressed German shepherd, less interested in the passed appetizers than in gobbling up morsels of delicious District gossip.

Yes, everything was as it should be as the sun set and my candles dispersed their twinkling glow. Even the weather had cooperated, with just the faintest breeze to keep my guests cool. But the one thing I could not control was Joe's mood; as the night went on, even though the air stayed lovely and my guests enjoyed their way through cocktails and then dinner and finally dancing, my husband's face went from sulky to surly.

I tried my best to ignore it, for the moment, and play the part of hostess. I knew it had been cold comfort to finally have an answer to the stomach pain that had bothered him for years, almost since the beginning of our marriage: intestinal cancer. With the diagnosis, Joe had undergone treatment. I'd nursed him through the months of recovery, and our follow-up appointments had brought with them the best news for which we could have hoped: he was clear of cancer and thus free of the stomach pain.

And yet, his mood had seen no improvement. If anything, I felt that it had gotten worse in recent months. On that night, my husband—the diplomat, the onetime gregarious center of any gathering, the friend of presidents and world leaders—sat stiff and unsmiling in a chair on the far side of the darkening garden. I saw it, but I wasn't going to let it spoil the evening, not when I'd worked so hard to pull it off.

I made the announcement at nine o'clock that we would begin the dancing. "It's called square dancing. If you've never heard of it, I just ask that you give it a try. I can't keep up with these dances the youngsters are doing. What do they call it now—rock 'n' roll? Anyhow, gentlemen, please feel free to take off your jackets. Ladies, feel free to kick aside your heels. I want this to be fun!"

My string octet had packed up for the night, and now a fresh set of musicians started up, this one playing fiddles and banjoes, drums and a harmonica. Having been plied with plenty of champagne and lighthearted chatter, my guests gamely made their way to the dance floor. Joe had told me before the party that there was no way he would dance, so I grabbed Nelson Rockefeller and pulled him to the center of the dance floor with me. My guests filled in the space beside us: Ike and Mamie Eisenhower, Betty Beale paired with General Omar Bradley. Even Harry and Bess Truman joined in, the president's dinner jacket tossed aside and his sleeves rolled up.

After the set, I excused myself, saying I was going to catch my breath with a glass of lemonade. I made my way toward my husband and took the empty seat beside him. Sipping my glass of lemonade, I leaned close. Then, sounding more chipper than in fact I felt, I proposed, "Come on, Joey. Dance one with me?"

He scowled, shaking his head. A moment later, Alice appeared at our side. I noticed with a pang of embarrassment that my husband did not turn to greet her, nor did he offer her his chair. She didn't seem to mind, instead saying, "Darling, it's a wonderful evening you've put on. And to think, you once worried you had no friends in this town but little ol' me."

THE KNOCK CAME on my bedroom door shortly after midnight. I was sitting before my mirror in a silk wrapper, removing the final pins from my hair. "That'll be all, thank you," I said, dismissing my maid, who left the room with her eyes cast downward, her frame appearing to tremble as she passed my husband in the doorway.

"Joe, I'm exhausted," I said, meeting his eyes in the reflection of the mirror. "It was a lot of work getting that party ready." It was true. I was weary. And most certainly not in the mood for a quarrel.

But apparently my husband, so dour all night, had experienced a sudden burst of energy. He entered my room uninvited, and my heart dropped when I saw him shut the door, closing us in together. And then he said, "But you had the energy to twirl like that for Nelson Rockefeller. Or, I'm sorry, was it Lyndon Johnson?"

I turned to face him. "Both," I answered, my voice toneless.

"I beg your pardon?"

"I danced with both of them, Joe. Nelson is an old friend. And Lyndon I met tonight. He and his wife couldn't have been more gracious. Did you get a chance to speak with them?"

I heard the quiver in his voice as he ignored my question and said, "And you couldn't have been more hospitable to him, that Senator Johnson."

I couldn't help but sigh, my frustration ill-masked as I answered: "Maybe if *you* put some warmth and energy into it, you'd have a few more friends in this town."

It was a blow, and I knew that as soon as I said it, as soon as I saw my words hit their mark, causing Joe's dark-eyed glower to flicker in a momentary wince. My husband was not well liked in Washington, not anymore. "I don't need friends in this town," he answered, his voice like gravel. "They're all a bunch of phonies."

"All right," I said, my entire body sagging with exhaustion as I looked desperately toward the shut bedroom door. Why couldn't he just leave? All I wanted was to climb into bed and sleep until Joe was in a better humor.

But he was not done. Staring at me, his brows stitching together, he declared: "And you're the biggest phony of 'em all."

That was it; I'd had enough—of his jealousies, his dark moods, his biting words intended to wound and defeat me. I sighed again, rising from my chair and crossing toward my bed, my exhaustion getting the better of me as I voiced exactly the thought that crossed my mind in that instant: "The only thing I've been phony in, Joe Davies, is pretending that I still loved you all these years. That you were a man worthy of me."

He charged toward me then with chandelier-shaking footsteps, and for a brief instant, I was afraid that he intended to actually hurt me. And perhaps he *did* intend to, but changed his mind at the last minute—perhaps he decided it wouldn't be worth the price. There were servants just on the other side of my bedroom walls. I was well connected. I had friends who were journalists, friends who were presidents. I had more money than he had and could afford better lawyers.

Instead he picked up the nearest valuable, a dish of rose-pink porcelain in the shape of a shell, in which I kept some of my favorite jewels. He took it and hurled it at the wall, where it smashed into a thousand pieces. "*You've* been pretending to love *me*?" he sneered, his cheeks flushing crimson. "Could have fooled me! That was some piss-poor performance you put on. I hope you don't expect any awards. You're an even worse actress than that piddling daughter of yours."

My veins went cold, the blood chilling inside of them. "Get out."

He huffed a laugh. "Like hell I will. This is *my* place. My name's on the deed."

I looked to the shattered shell on the floor, my jewels scattered like glittering birdseed across the Aubusson carpet. It could never be repaired. But I could leave before anything else could be broken. "Then I'll get out. This conversation is over, Joe. This marriage is over."

DIVORCE MADE JOE angrier, if that was even possible. Meaner, too. But we had so much together: twenty years of life, a marriage that had taken us all over the world, and so many vestiges of those years that still mattered to me, even if I could do without ever seeing the man again.

There was no hope of walking away with any sort of fondness intact, but I wanted the divorce to be as quick as possible. I wanted to be done with him, and so, as much as it hurt, I gave him the house. He could have it. Much as I'd labored over that home and those gardens, they would always remind me of my time as Mrs. Davies. I would start fresh in a new place of my own.

But all of the treasure in it! Our Russian antiques and objets d'art. The Fabergé pieces, the Romanov dishes, the imperial jewels, the priceless paintings. I'd found them and I'd bought them. Joe had never had the eye—or the funds—to amass a collection on the scale of what we now had. But he did not see it that way. "Oh, that's rich, Marjorie. You only got the stuff because *I* was the ambassador," Joe said smugly, staring at me across the table at one of our dreaded and interminable legal face-offs. I knew the holes in all of what he said. He did as well; he remembered all those afternoons I'd spent plodding through warehouses, scouring the tarp-covered piles to pluck out those treasures. He'd never seen what I'd seen. But now, to spite me, he'd claim it all as his own.

"I just want to be done," I said to my team of lawyers that afternoon, after four hours of rancorous haggling had proven fruitless in reaching any sort of settlement. Further days spent like that would make me sick; I could no longer bear to be in a room with him.

"If you want it over and done with, Mrs. Post," my attorney, a man named Charles Littlefield, said, staring at me with an expression equal parts sympathy and cool pragmatism, "then the solution is to just split it all."

I crossed my arms and frowned as I considered this, eventually asking Mr. Littlefield: "How would we do it?"

"Right down the middle." He dropped his hand as if it were a blade slicing the air. "We don't haggle over every piece. Who knows how long that would take? We just draw a line through it, and you each get a side."

I sighed, staring toward the door. On the other side, Joe sat with his team. After a long pause, my heartbeat clamoring in my ears, I squared my shoulders and looked at Mr. Littlefield, saying: "Fine. We'll split it. Only let's get it over with."

It did go quicker, but it was far from the perfect arrangement. As a result of this legalistic compromise, Joe got some of my most cherished pieces; the sourest pill to swallow was when he marched smugly off with my massive oil painting of Russia's most beloved tsarina, Catherine the Great, a priceless piece that I'd delighted in since the moment I'd found it.

But I got my peace. And so, in the end, it was a price I was willing to pay.

I RETREATED TO Sun Valley for several months while the news broke across the capital. And goodness, was that the right decision—I saw just how right a decision it was as I stared at my morning's copy of *The New York Times* and read the words:

EXTREME MENTAL CRUELTY

Those relentless reporters had, somehow, gotten hold of our divorce papers, and they were sharing with the entire world the cause I'd submitted to the court in my suit. *Extreme mental cruelty.* It was true. But I'd been trying to keep that one away from the scavengers and the gossips. Not even entirely for Joe and our families, but for myself as well.

Well, I'd failed.

What followed was more headlines—weeks of salacious gossip and breathless speculation. Nothing in our lives was sacred. Had he cheated? Had I cheated? They wrote of Joe's temper. Of his feuds with my daughters. Had I lost interest because Joe had lost his glamorous political influence? They wrote of my lavish lifestyle and how a man couldn't help but feel like my pet, albeit one kept in the finest of golden muzzles. Some writers jabbed that Joe had been given his just deserts for abandoning Emlen all those years ago. Other vicious people called me a "Serial Cereal Bride," naming me as "Mrs. Close-Hutton-Davies," just in case anyone had forgotten that this was my third marriage to end in divorce.

I looked at all of these articles through eyes needled by tears, sensing the gloating that was so evident behind much of the ink, and I knew that people were speaking about me back at home. *Home.* Joe had our house, which meant that I no longer had a home to return to.

When I felt that I could not possibly feel any lower, I got a phone call. I heard the brassy voice, and immediately my entire body perked up, drawing strength from the steel in my old friend's words: "My dear, it's Alice. How the hell are you?"

"Hi, Alice, it's good to hear from you." I sighed. "I've been better."

"But you've been worse, too. So let's remember that."

"I suppose that's true." I stared out the window, at the stunning jut of mountains under the western bluebird sky. Just then a hawk was drawing a slow loop in and out of my view.

"Quite frankly," Alice went on, "I wondered what took you so long."

I couldn't help but laugh at this, a rueful exhalation.

"Now, Marjorie, I'm being entirely serious here. I know a thing about scandals, and I know a thing or two about unhappy marriages." It was true; Alice had been married to Nicholas Longworth for decades before his death, and I wondered if even a single one of those years had been happy or harmonious. Perhaps the only truly joyful years of her adult life had been after she'd given birth to another man's baby; but Alice Roosevelt had never let anyone see her mope. And neither would I.

I hung up the phone decided: I was not Mrs. Close-Hutton-Davies. I was not a homeless divorcée with her confidence shattered and her treasure plundered. I was not a Serial Cereal Bride whose misfortune made for juicy chitchat and flashy newspaper headlines.

Would I love again? Perhaps I would. Would I marry again? It was not impossible. Though sixty-eight years old and drained by the years of unhappiness with Joe, I still felt the deep warm embers of energy and hope. And I was enough of a romantic to know that it would be foolish to say absolutely no. But of one fact I was certain: I would never again make myself small in order to allow a man to feel big. I would never again root my home in another's name, or put my own name aside to take up a man's. I had been a leader, mother, businesswoman, and philanthropist all along. There was going to be no more denying that.

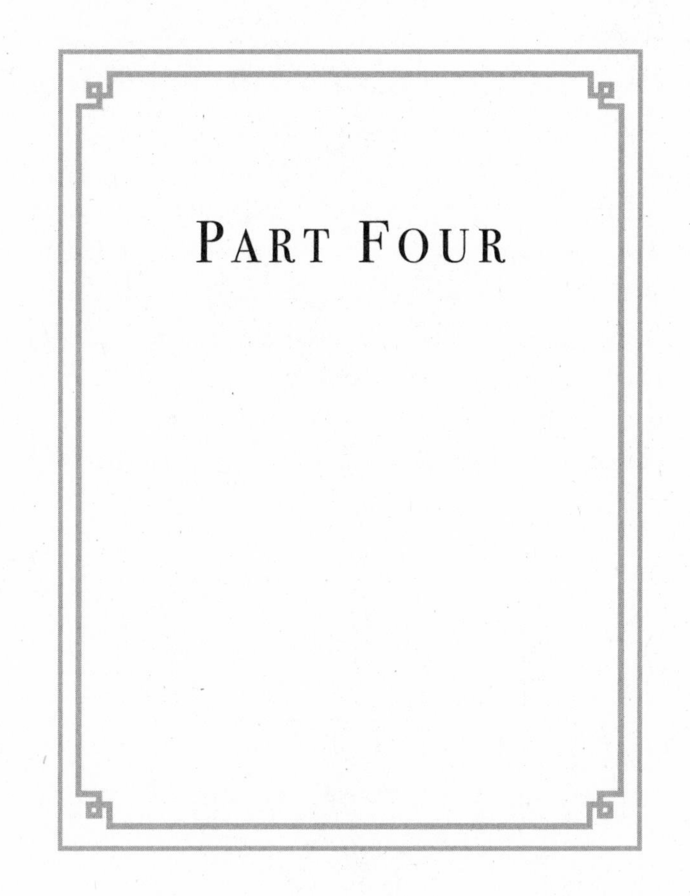

Part Four

Chapter 46

Hillwood Estate, Washington, D.C.
July 4, 1957

"MOTHER, YOU LIVE LIKE AN EMPRESS." ADELAIDE STOOD AT my side, hooking her arm through mine.

"That may be," I answered, with a shrug of my bare shoulders. "But I don't have an emperor picking up my bill."

As I looked out over the grounds of my new estate, open that night for the first time to guests, a glittering and well-dressed crowd of hundreds, it was true that the scene could have been plucked directly from an oil painting of a bygone imperial court; but I knew better than anyone the amount of hard work it had taken to produce that tableau of merriment and beauty.

I'd always thrived when put to work on a meaningful mission, and for the past couple of years, my mission had been building my best and final home. This would be the ground on which I would finally lay down my roots, separate from any man, and I'd known that this property was for me when I had first toured it and the agent had told me the name: *Arbremont—Wooded Mountain* in French—that sounded an awful lot like *Hillwood,* the name of my beloved home on the Gold Coast. So I'd bought the estate and translated the name, and then I had set about making it into a home that would suit me in every inch.

I rebuilt walls and fireplaces, ripping out dark, old paneling to bring in custom pale wood and glistening ivory marble from France. I redesigned the front stairway so it could curve like one belonging in a Parisian palace. I tore down ceilings so that they could be rebuilt even higher. I covered the walls with my stunning art from the tsars and other European nobles, and draped my ceilings with chandeliers from empresses. I constructed a new high-ceilinged pavilion, where I could hold dances or give viewing parties for the latest American movies with my massive new projector.

Because my gardens here were even more extensive than the ones I had cherished at my previous estate, I made sure that mine would be a house perpetually adorned with flowers, both inside and out. My bright breakfast room was wrought entirely of glass, packed with orchids and overlooking my roses and azaleas. All along the ground floor, French doors gave easy access onto terraces and lawns that burst with greenery and color.

The finished product was such that even *I* could say that it was blameless on that summer night. The air hung warm, and my gardens and tree-covered hills were leafy and green, with the nearby Rock Creek Park offering its lush backdrop. My guests milled about, moving easily throughout the high-ceilinged ground floor and the rolling gardens, admiring my walls lined with Fabergé eggs forged in every shade and precious stone, holy icons and chalices, diamonds belonging to the tsarinas and plates belonging to the tsars. Knowing that my Russian collection surpassed the splendor of any museum exhibit here in the States, I'd displayed my treasures as if we were in fact in a museum, and little golden knobs beneath my pieces could be pulled out to reveal written descriptions of each priceless artifact. In the library, oil paintings of my family members hung alongside a photograph of my old friend Winston Churchill and a model of my beloved *Sea Cloud*.

And it was in the library that I stood as Betty Beale approached me just a few minutes into my party. I turned to her with a warm smile.

"Mrs. Post! Just when I thought it couldn't get any better."

"Thank you for coming, Betty." I accepted her hearty hug. "It's lovely to see you."

"Oh, but my eyes are about ready to spring out of their sockets," she gushed. And then, leaning close, she added, "I hear those French doors gave you a bit of trouble." Her lips curled upward in a questioning grin.

"Yes," I said, nodding toward the glass doors that gave way from my library out over my back gardens and, beyond that, acres of woods pierced by the rising spire of the Washington Monument. "But I wasn't going to pass on a chance to have that view." Both my architects and my contractors had grimaced when I'd told them of my plan to carve out new doors that would show the Monument from inside my home, but they'd seen, after several arguments, that I was not going to give in.

"My dear Mrs. Post, had you not been able to move the glass doors to get the view you wanted, you would have just relocated the Monument itself, isn't that right?" Betty Beale said, admiring the scene as she stood at my side.

We both laughed at this; I owed this woman my warmth. Just that week, ahead of my grand party, she'd published a lengthy article calling me "Marjorie the Magnificent." Lauding not only my expertise as "America's Most Fabulous Hostess," but also, more important, my work in both business and philanthropy. "My dear, I must thank you for the lovely write-up," I said, my voice low and meaningful.

Betty put her hand on mine. "It was easy to do."

As I looked at this woman, once so opposed to my entry into Washington society, so critical of my decisions, I realized that I now considered her a genuine friend—like so many others in this place. Perhaps I did not need to feel like a failure, even if all of my marriages had been labeled thusly.

As a white-gloved footman approached and Betty accepted a flute of chilled champagne from him, she turned to me, raising her glass and saying, "I won't ever hear there's no such thing as magic. You've waved your wand, Mrs. Post, and I've stepped into a world of it."

I thanked my footman but declined the champagne, answering my friend: "Not so much magic as time. And money. But I'm home at last. This is finally *my* home. And I can tell you this much: I ain't moving again."

Just then, a stirring toward the bright front entryway, and both Betty and I turned. "Now what?" she asked, her eyes narrowing with her reporter's intensity. "They are quite dazzling, aren't they?" A young pair had entered, both tall and slim, the good-looking young man with a thicket of honey-brown hair and a self-assured smile. Even more striking was the statuesque, big-eyed brunette on his arm.

I knew their names immediately. "Ah yes, that's Rose Kennedy's boy. Jack is his name. And his wife is Jacqueline. They call her Jackie."

"Ah, that's right." Had Betty been holding a pencil, her hand would have been scratching away; I could see from her keen expression that she was instead filing it all into that incomparable mind of hers. "She's a Bouvier, isn't she?"

"Yes," I said. "And I know his parents from Palm Beach. I've known Jack since he was a youngster. Excuse me, Betty, but I think I'll go say hello."

I sailed toward them, arms extended, and reached for Jack to give him an embrace in greeting. And then I welcomed his shy, dark-haired wife, who looked regal in a sheath gown of lilac silk, cream-colored gloves wrapped around her thin forearms, tasteful pearls at her neck and wrists. "Jackie, thanks so much for coming to Hillwood," I said. "Glad this young man finally has someone to keep an eye on him."

"Mrs. Post, it's such an honor to meet you," Jackie Kennedy replied, her lips forming a coy smile, her words breathy, as if she were confiding some secret. "Everybody likens Jack and me to some fairy-tale romance, but my, this is a place for fairy tales if I've ever seen one."

As the servants announced the start of dinner, we all made our way to the tables, set alfresco on the patio, the music of Copland and Sousa mingling with laughter and the tinkling of china and crystal. Once the sun went down, we enjoyed the fireworks bursting across our capital, the backdrop of the nearby monuments illuminated beneath our velvety summer sky.

"Happy Fourth!" my guests hollered, clapping. "Happy Independence Day." I joined in the cheers. It was the night to celebrate America's independence, and my own as well.

NOW THAT I had established for the press and the gossip circles that I was back, settled in my splendid new home and ready to host again, the columns began churning with fresh gossip and speculation. *"She's America's Hostess, known for throwing the best dinners and the liveliest dances. Now she just needs to find her dancing partner."*

"Is it true what I'm hearing, Mom?" Deenie—no, *Dina,* now that she wanted to be called by her movie star name, Dina Merrill, heralded as she was as our country's next Grace Kelly—was at Hillwood for a visit that autumn, and she stared at me with a teasing smile on that mild, sunny Wednesday morning.

"Well, that depends."

"On?"

"On what you are hearing."

Dina sighed. "They say you're being courted by some Texan oilman. And that you're madly in love."

"That so?" I couldn't help but chuckle at that. It was a new man each day, according to those pesky reporters, but I had not yet heard of this latest one. "Well, he sounds great. I'd like to meet him."

Dina laughed a moment, but then her features turned serious. "Do you really think you would marry again, Mother?"

I weighed my words carefully, answering after a long pause: "Not anytime soon, my dear. And certainly not with anyone I've already met."

I could see my daughter's chest deflate with a relieved exhale.

"My goal now is to do good for this world that has given me so much. Wealth is a great responsibility, more than it is a privilege."

"All right," Dina said, her tone tentative. "But, you have not ruled it out entirely?"

"Ruled what out?"

"Mother!"

I chortled. "Deenie, when you've been around as long as I have, you learn to never rule anything out."

And so, because I was happiest when I was at work, I set to work. As much as I loved studying art and collecting antiques, music had also always played a meaningful part in my life, going back to my youth as a dance student in Battle Creek and right up to the present, when I'd rebuilt my home specifically to include a ballroom. I did not want classical music or traditional dancing to fall into distant memory in the era of rock 'n' roll, so I had decided to endow a program through the National Symphony Orchestra called Music for Young America, in which the orchestra would put on concerts for students and teach our jukebox-crazed youngsters about the importance of the classics.

I gave generously to schools—to my beloved Mount Vernon Seminary but also dozens of other high schools and universities throughout the country. I donated to the Boy Scouts, to the Red Cross, to churches and food pantries and hospitals. I tried to help anyone who asked, whether an organization that sent a formal letter or petition or simply an individual who worked in my kitchen who had the look of someone struggling. I never wanted thanks. And yet, the thanks came rolling in, in the form of medals and buildings bearing my name, awards and parties given in my honor.

But the best thanks of all came at the end of that year, just before Thanksgiving. My daughters appeared in my bedroom one cool, clear morning and insisted that I put on a blindfold. For weeks I'd been told not to walk out toward the woods past my rose gardens. I knew they were working on something out there, with the groundskeepers and the gardeners and I did not know whom else. It had been difficult not to take a peek, but I'd stuck to my word.

"You promise you haven't cheated?" Dina asked, as she settled the blindfold in place over the bridge of my nose and took my hand.

"I haven't cheated and I haven't the foggiest idea what you're about to do to me," I answered, taking my first tenuous steps as she led me out of my bedroom.

My daughters did not remove the blindfold as they guided me down the front stairs and out onto the back terrace, from where I was led by the hand toward the garden. There, on the flagstone path, I was permitted to blink my eyes open as we walked past bushes, past the magnolia and cherry trees, until eventually we came to something I had never seen before: a round patio giving out over a view of the grounds. And there, etched into dappled marble, were the words:

FRIENDSHIP WALK, HILLWOOD
DEDICATED BY HER FRIENDS
AS A TRIBUTE TO
MARJORIE MERRIWEATHER POST
FOR HER GENEROUS NATURE
LOVE OF BEAUTY
AND DEVOTION TO HUMAN NEEDS

"My goodness!" I looked around, seeing the flagstone circle with benches, hemmed by trees and shrubs as well as small busts of bronze eagles and four larger statues, each one a charming cherub.

"Each of the four seasons," Adelaide explained as she showed me the carved marble figures. "And look, their pedestals are inscribed with the names of your many friends."

"And what's this?" I looked at a marker embedded in the middle of the patio and read aloud the inscription: FRIENDSHIP OUTSTAYS THE HURRYING FLIGHT OF YEARS AND AYE ABIDES THROUGH LAUGHTER AND THROUGH TEARS.

"Words spoken by Tsarina Alexandra, the last empress of Russia," Eleanor explained. The woman who had perished along with her husband the tsar and their five young children; the woman whose family treasure filled my home.

Dina came close and handed me a rolled paper. "From your friends, Mother."

"So many," I said, uncurling the list—an endless catalog of names.

"Almost two hundred gave to help make your Friendship Walk," Adelaide answered. THROUGH LAUGHTER AND THROUGH TEARS, my inscription said. At that moment, surrounded by my girls, presented with the love of so many at a place they'd seen fit to label Friendship Walk, I felt myself filling with both.

Chapter 47

Washington, D.C.
Fall 1957

THE FACT OF THE MATTER, PLAIN AND SIMPLE, WAS THAT I ENjoyed being in love.

My heart was not yet too tired or unwilling to try it again, even after the aches it had suffered. So when I met a charming, attractive man by the name of Herbert May at a luncheon at Adelaide's home, it happened that my heart began to swell with new excitement.

I arrived that afternoon feeling relaxed and happy, dressed in a one-shoulder gown of navy, stunning blue diamonds formerly owned by Napoleon and his empress at my neck and ears. The luncheon, which was to raise money for my alma mater, the Mount Vernon Seminary, was for about fifty people, and Adelaide had set up tables and chairs in her drawing room. As the meal was announced, my daughter whisked me toward my seat and introduced me to a tall, well-dressed man who was assigned to the same table. "Mother, please meet Mr. Herbert May. He's been very generous to the school."

I smiled at the gentleman, momentarily taken aback by his trim appearance, his well-tailored suit of dark charcoal and neatly combed gray hair. As Adelaide walked away, he reached forward and took my hand. "Mrs. Post, how are you?"

"Mr. May, thank you for supporting our efforts today. It's lovely to meet you."

He cocked his head, a kind, affable smile creasing the skin around his dark green eyes. "Actually, Mrs. Post, we've met once before."

I stood back on my heels. "We have?"

He nodded. "Years ago. You were hosting a party for the hospital in Palm Beach."

"Ah," I said with a nod. "I'm sorry I didn't remember."

"I don't blame you," he said, waving his hands. And then he leaned toward me, and I caught a whiff of his clean, soapy scent as he said, "But of course I didn't forget you."

"Please, everyone, take your seats," my daughter said to the room, and Mr. May hastened to pull my chair out for me. As I accepted this cordial gesture, I noted with delight that he was in fact seated beside me.

"What do you do, Mr. May?" I asked, stealing a sideways look at him as I spread my linen napkin across my lap.

"A little bit of everything, and yet nothing nearly as important as the things you do," he answered.

"He's being modest," Adelaide said as she flitted around our table, greeting guests, ensuring that the settings were all in order—she truly was my daughter.

I arched an eyebrow toward Mr. May. "I'm vice president at Westinghouse," he said.

I sat up a bit straighter in my chair, staring at Mr. May with increasing admiration—and interest. Not only charming, this man, but also intelligent and successful, from the sound of it. Was this attractive charmer married? I stole a quick glance toward his hand as he sipped his water; I didn't see anything on his finger to indicate that he was.

"*There* you are." Just then, a young woman with a shapely physique and a bob of glossy, dark auburn hair slid into the vacant seat on Mr. May's other side. "I've been looking for you."

"Ah." Mr. May turned and greeted the young woman with a familiar smile before placing a kiss on her round, rouged cheek. I tried not to let my features sag, even as my heart did.

Mr. May turned back to me and said, "Mrs. Post, please meet my lovely Margot."

This Margot was young, early twenties I guessed. Well, that settled it. Of course a man as attractive and finely mannered as Mr. May was not unattached. And what interest could he possibly have in someone like me when he could have this woman, decades my junior? I did my best to summon a smile as I said, "Margot, it's so nice to meet you. My name is Marjorie."

"That is Mrs. Post to you," Mr. May said, leaning toward the young woman as he gave a playful pinch to her soft cheek. And then, turning to me with a wink, he added: "My daughter."

My stomach flipped—his daughter! And yet, for him to have the daughter, there had to be a wife. "Where is Mrs. May today?" I asked, attempting a casual tone.

"Ah, my Sara. She . . ." Mr. May looked down toward the white tablecloth, clearing his throat a moment before answering: "She is no longer with us."

Not married, then. A widower. And most likely still pining. "Twenty years ago," he said. At the front of the room, Adelaide announced the start of lunch, and a fleet of servants appeared from the kitchen bearing trays heaped with salad and bread rolls.

"I am so sorry," I said, my voice low in the loud, cheerful room. A white-coated waiter placed our salad plates before us.

"Pneumonia," Mr. May said, nodding. "But I have her," he said, gesturing with a smile toward Margot, who was now engaged in conversation with the fellow at her other side. "And our three others."

"Then you are a blessed man in that," I said.

"And you? Of course I know Adelaide is your daughter. And a lovely young lady she is. Do you have other children?"

"I have three girls," I said, not attempting to hide my beam.

"Well, I hope for their sake they take after their mother."

I picked up my salad fork. After a brief moment, Mr. May turned to me and said, "Mrs. Post, do you—"

"Oh, please call me Marjorie."

"Only if you'll call me Herb."

"All right, then, Herb, you have a deal."

"*Marjorie,*" he said, grinning as he made a dramatic display of saying my name. "It's a very musical name. Mar-jo-rie."

"And to think, my daddy turned it into Budgie."

He laughed; so did I. "Not as musical, that," he said.

"Not quite."

"Well, Marjorie, may I ask you a philosophical question?"

"Goodness. You can try, Herb, but I can't make any promises about my answer. I usually don't get philosophical until after the bread course."

He smiled. And then, after a pause, he went on, "Tell me this: Do you believe that it's possible to have love more than once in a lifetime?"

That was unexpected. But then, so was pretty much everything about how this luncheon was unfolding. I considered the question for a long moment, finishing my bite of salad before venturing to offer an answer. Eventually, sitting up in my chair and tipping my head toward my dining companion, I said, "Herb, I not only believe it to be possible. I *know* it to be possible."

Herb nodded at this, his green eyes flickering as he raised his water glass and took a sip. "I agree."

By the end of the lunch, as it came time for Adelaide to take to the dais and make her pitch for the fundraiser, Herb and I were consumed in a conversation entirely of our own, and I think it was safe to say that we both very much hoped it would be possible to find love again.

⁂

"MARJORIE, MY DEAREST, are we completely dotty?"

It was a clear spring night, the mild air heavy with the perfume of a thousand new blossoms, the sky pierced by a bright scattering of stars over a horizon lit by the nearby monuments. Herb and I lay alone, entangled, on the soft lawn of my back garden at Hillwood, engaged in something that neither one of us had expected to be doing that evening: discussing the possibility of marriage.

Well, perhaps we had both known it *might* happen that evening, the discussion of marriage, but now that we were actually taking up the topic, it struck me that marriage might in fact be a reality into which we were ready to plunge. Herb had been on his own for twenty years, a widower with four now-grown kids and a successful career. I'd been married three times, was seventy-one years old, had almost $300 million to my name, and homes more grand than any palace—and yet, what did any of that matter if I didn't have love?

I did love Herb. Even more so because I had not thought it possible that, after the disappointments of Joe and everything before that, I'd ever meet anyone like Herb, so kind and affable and determined to enjoy his life in a way so well suited to my own. I could see him fitting in perfectly with me at Hillwood; he loved my art, he took genuine interest in learning about my gardens, and he admired my priceless jewels with the curiosity and interest of a museum curator. I had my charity work firmly established, and Herb relished the idea of joining my efforts. Like me, he enjoyed supporting schools and youngsters and loved the symphony, and he also urged me to take a greater role in supporting the National Ballet, a cause close to his heart.

Now, with his arms around me, the fresh scent of his Guerlain cologne mingling with the nighttime perfume of my peonies, I saw only one way to answer his question: "Herb, I think we just might be."

"The plain truth of it, my dear," Herb said, his hand tracing a slow line up my back and across my shoulders, then softly up my neck and to my cheek, where he angled my face toward his, "is that you're the only woman I've known since my wife who makes me feel this way." At that I leaned forward and gave Herb a long, soft kiss, eventually pulling back to burrow my face into the curve of his neck; I loved how I fit there, just right. I thought I'd be happy to stay there all night. Herb breathed out, a quiet, contented sound. After a long pause, he said, "Heck, I think now is as good a time as ever." He rose from the grass, breaking the close stillness of our embrace.

"Herb?" I asked, the confusion evident in my voice.

"Just wait here one minute, would you? I'll be right back." With that he dashed off, back into the house. Was there a ring inside? Was he really going to propose, right then and there? I fidgeted in my place on the lawn, my body suddenly astir with excitement. I'd say yes, if he asked right then. Why wouldn't I? What more could I hope for in a man, in a companion? But when Herb returned just a short while later, the box he held in his arms was much larger than anything that would hold a ring.

"What's this all about?" I asked, looking at the velvet parcel.

Herb placed it on the grass before me. "Open it up," was all he offered in reply.

"All right . . ." I slowly undid the large bow from the top. As I did, the box seemed to jump. I startled, looking to Herb with an eyebrow lifted.

"Go on, open it," he said once more.

I slowly tipped the top off, peering inside. In the darkness, I could just barely make out a soft, round shape. And then I heard a high-pitched yip and nearly leapt from my spot on the grass. "What?" I gasped. I looked back down into the box. "A puppy?" I reached my hand inside and felt a mound of the most soft, velvety fur. "Oh, Herb. A puppy?"

"A miniature schnauzer," he replied.

"Well, hello," I cooed, lifting the light little body out of the box, nuzzling the plush fur with my cheek. "For me?"

"If you'd like him," Herb replied.

"I adore him," I said. And I did. I'd always loved dogs of all sorts, and this little fellow was irresistible.

Herb chuckled. "He's a cute little fellow, isn't he?"

"Oh, my darling, he's precious. But what should we call him? What is your name, you little one?" I held the pup's tiny face just inches from mine and stared into two blue eyes. As I did so, the pup moved quickly, sticking out his scratchy little tongue to land one quick, wet kiss on my face.

"What a scamp!" Herb laughed. "Stealing a kiss already. Easy there, little fellow, or I may just get jealous."

"That's perfect," I replied.

"What is?"

"We'll call him Scampi. What do you think of that?" I brought the puppy to my neck for another snuggle. "Oh yes, that'll do quite nicely, won't it?"

"I think he's about the luckiest scamp in the world, is what I think," Herb said. "To have found his place with you. Just like I have."

I HAD TO let Betty break the news. She'd proven herself to be such a good and loyal friend. And so a few weeks later, after I'd told my family and Herb had told his, Betty wrote in her evening column that Herb and I were to be married. I received a copy of the article on the early May night that it came out, and since Herb was up in Pittsburgh on business, I settled into my bedroom to read it on what was a rare quiet evening at home.

The phone rang just a few moments later, interrupting my rosy twilight reverie. "Mother." My middle daughter's voice was stern on the line. "Have you completely lost your head?"

"Now, Eleanor, calm down. I told you and Adelaide that we were planning on this, and it shouldn't come as any particular surprise that Betty—"

"No, not about Herb," my daughter said dismissively. "You know we all love him. He's everything Joe wasn't—kind, upbeat, generous. And I do believe the two of you will be very happy."

I gripped the telephone receiver, confused. "Then . . . why are you worried about my head?"

"Because, Mother." Eleanor exhaled, and I heard her frustration transmitted through the line. "Why did Betty Beale have to break the news *tonight?*"

"Well . . . why not?" I asked.

"Have you not heard? Joe just died."

Joe, dead. And the ink on my happy announcement not yet dry. The gossips and journalists feasted on that for weeks. As I was not invited to partake in any of the gatherings or the memorial in Joe's honor, I left Hillwood, sick from the attention. Sick from the ghoulish way in which the press fed on my marriages and divorces, making even my moments of happiness into tawdry or macabre morsels.

Herb and I would keep a low profile, and we most certainly would not have a big or celebratory wedding. We wouldn't invite the Washington social set or provide any further fodder for the newspapers. I remembered how the press had buzzed around at every single one of my previous weddings, so we decamped to Adelaide's house and had a small service with just the family in her drawing room. We did not need the grandest party—the flowers, the cake, the gown, the glamorous guest list. I'd had that before, and look how it had turned out. This time, I would get it right. This time we would start our union with just those we loved and each other. "Older and wiser," I joked, as my groom gave me a kiss on the morning of our wedding. Older and wiser, and yet made new by this surprising new love.

Chapter 48

HERB DIDN'T NEED MY MONEY, ANY MORE THAN I NEEDED HIS last name, so both of those matters were easily decided. What took us more time was the matter of where to live. I loved Hillwood and I'd spent years, and millions, making it the home perfectly suited for me. But Herb was a Pittsburgh man—his work was in Pittsburgh at Westinghouse and, more important to him, the home in which he had raised his children was in Pittsburgh. So we agreed to split our time. But there was someplace else I also needed to go. *Home*. We'd used that word so often in our recent discussions. And now *home* meant a place that I needed to see, and needed to show to my new husband if he really wanted to know me.

I had not visited Battle Creek for more than just a brief in-and-out business trip in more than four decades. Battle Creek had been my formative home, yes, the place of my girlhood and the soil from which everything in my life had sprung. But then it had become Leila's town. Leila had won it when she'd won my papa, and I'd yielded it to her.

But now Leila was dead. A visit to Battle Creek no longer meant a run-in with that woman, that imposter who'd fancied herself as Mrs. Post and Battle Creek's unofficial first lady. So I was ready to return to the place that had made me. The place that had made Papa's fortune when he'd turned an old barn into a place filled with new ideas and new foods that would go on to change the world. And I was ready to make my peace with the people there—both the living and the dead.

Just a few months prior, I had stepped down from my position on the General Foods board. I had served both directly and through my family for fifty years—or closer to seventy, if you counted the years I spent gluing labels and raking hot bran in the barn as a youngster—and I had felt ready to enter a new phase of life. I would continue to focus on my philanthropy and other charitable causes while relishing the time with my family—my new husband, my children, and my grandchildren. Along those same lines, I'd decided to put my *Sea Cloud* up for sale a few years earlier. Not only did it remind me of times spent with two husbands whom I no longer wished to remember, but with its massive size and crew, and its even more massive price of upkeep, it had become more of a burden than a joy. And besides, my new husband, being a businessman, liked to fly.

"Let's buy a jet," I suggested one mild afternoon. We'd just returned to Hillwood from a weeklong trip to Pittsburgh, traveling quickly back to the capital aboard one of my husband's company planes. It was so much faster than traveling by train or car, and I knew we'd use a jet of our own for trips up to Topridge and down to Mar-a-Lago.

Herb, however, looked at me askance. "My dear," he said, "do you have any idea how much it would cost to buy a jet of our own?"

"No," I answered honestly. "But I can look into it."

"It would cost millions."

Luckily for Herb, I had millions.

We decided on a Vickers turboprop jet, which would be roomy enough for us to bring a crew and attendants as well as plenty of guests and family on our trips. I gutted the plane's cabin and filled it with plush couches and throw pillows in an apricot and silver floral pattern. Low lounge tables would be well suited for games of cards, work, or meals. A galley kitchen would allow an on-plane chef to prepare our dishes—with General Foods ingredients, of course—and white-coated attendants would be on hand to serve. And because I had always been the hostess to have lifeboats for my lifeboats, I quite liked the idea of having backup pilots for my backup pilots, so we made sure never to fly with fewer than three ready pilots on board.

Herb smiled when he told me his idea for the name. "I was thinking the *Merriweather*."

I nodded, grinning in agreement. "I think that sounds perfect."

So, on a clear, crisp day that autumn, we boarded the *Merriweather*—Herb, Adelaide, and I—and took off for Michigan. The purpose of the trip was more than simply to take my husband and daughter for a stroll down a long-unseen memory lane. I had recently given $150,000 to Battle Creek

Central High School, and I'd urged my General Foods board to make an additional gift of $100,000, all to help build a new sports complex and stadium, for which the school had thanked me by naming it C. W. Post Field. As a further thanks, they'd invited me out for the opening football game.

If I was eager to see my hometown once more, the people there seemed to share my feelings of warmth, because the crowd welcomed me like a queen returning home after a long absence. The moment my *Merriweather* touched down, we were cheered at the airport by a huge gathering of local photographers, journalists, town leaders, and residents. As I made my way with Herb and Adelaide down the steep steps of the plane, locals clapped and members of the high school marching band serenaded us. People queued up for a chance to shake my hand and take a picture; others showed me press clippings or old photographs they had saved having to do with Papa and even with me as a young girl.

A sleek Packard limousine awaited, and we made the short ride to the new complex through a town I barely recognized. Several familiar names were already stamped on many of the local facilities—the hospitals, the hotels, the theaters and parks—Kellogg and, even worse, Leila. I glowered, saying aloud to my daughter and husband: "It's right that Papa will now have his name marked in this town."

A few minutes later we arrived at the stunning new sports grounds, where a massive archway bore my daddy's name: C. W. POST FIELD. "Now, that's more like it," I said, exiting the car to yet another crowd of cheering and jostling onlookers.

Though the day had dawned clear, as we entered the stadium and settled into our seats, a chilly autumn rain began to fall. Knowing that we were there to watch a nighttime football game, I had dressed for cold weather in one of my heaviest Russian furs, but I hadn't prepared for the rain. As the team kicked off on the field below, I pulled my collar closer around my shoulders.

"Excuse me, Mrs. Post?"

"Yes?" I glanced upward to stare into the face of a high-school-aged boy who was at that moment opening an umbrella beside me. "We are here to keep you dry, ma'am."

"That's awfully kind, young man," I said in reply. "But I can hold my own umbrella."

"No, ma'am." The young man shook his head.

"It would be our honor," said the student beside him, as all around us, half a dozen students unfurled their own umbrellas to create an impenetrable canopy over our small huddle.

"Well, this is some service you get at the C. W. Post Field," I said, smiling appreciatively from my seat on the cold bleacher.

"What can we get you to drink, Mrs. Post?" asked another youngster.

"I'll take something warm if you have it."

"How about a mug of Postum, ma'am? We hear that's your favorite."

I smiled, nodding at the student. "That'd be perfect."

"And you, Mr. May? Miss Close?"

Adelaide accepted another Postum. Herb said, "I'll take something a bit stronger if you have it." So they brought two warm Postums for Adelaide and me and a brandy for Herb, and together we watched and cheered as my hometown Bearcats took the lead against the team from Muskegon.

The rain continued to fall. By halftime, the bleachers and the ground were soaked, even as our steadfast pack of students continued to hold their umbrellas over our heads in their best efforts to keep us dry. My fingers ached from the cold, but I tried not to show my discomfort. Herb fidgeted in his seat. "Say, could you hold that a bit closer, young man?" Herb asked, coaxing the student nearest him to step closer. A few minutes later Herb asked the fellow: "How about a blanket? Could that be arranged?"

"Of course, sir." The youngster dashed off to fulfill Herb's request, soon reappearing with a blanket bearing the Bearcat logo. "There you go, Mr. May."

Herb nodded approvingly, giving the young man a pat on the shoulder. "Just put it in my lap, would you? And how about another brandy? I'm doing my best to stay warm." The young man skipped off once more, quickly returning with a fresh brandy for my husband.

"Aren't you a helpful young man?" Herb smiled, taking the drink in his hand. "What's your name?"

"It's Jerry, sir." The poor kid was soaked through but smiling politely.

Herb, looking dry and merry beneath his umbrella and blanket, fresh drink in hand, reached forward and gave the young lad another pat, this one on his lower back. "Jerry. You're just what we needed tonight. Here, sit down right beside me. This blanket is plenty big. No reason you should be shivering here while I'm toasty."

Herb continued to talk to the young man throughout the game. Jerry answered Herb's questions respectfully, telling my husband that he was a senior at the school. He was hoping to go to Madison the next year for college. Finally, as we neared the last few minutes of the fourth quarter, I leaned forward, inserting myself into the conversation: "Jerry, you and your friends have saved us tonight. As a thank you, how about we fly you all out to Washington, D.C., for a school trip? You won't have to worry about the travel or the hotel. I'll have my staff arrange it all. How would you like that?"

"Aww, Mrs. Post!" Jerry smiled, his flushed, sheepish face turning from Herb toward me. "Really?"

"Yes," I answered, nodding.

"That'd be wonderful. Thank you!"

"That's a great idea, Marje." Herb leaned forward, angling toward the boy as he added, "Be sure to let us know when you're in town, Jerry. We'll have you over to the house. My wife here has lots of nice things we can show you."

Just then the Bearcats scored, taking back the lead in the final minutes of the game, and the crowd erupted in soggy cheers. I looked around. Battle Creek residents had welcomed me back with warmth and openness. The facility was top-notch in every way, a worthy monument to my father's legacy in the town he had called home. It even looked as if we would win the football game. And yet, as the night went on, as Herb sent that poor boy back for yet another brandy, and urged him to bring his body and the umbrella even closer, the warmth in my stomach turned chilly and hard as a stone.

Chapter 49

Hillwood Estate, Washington, D.C.
Fall 1962

"NOW, WHAT'S ALL THIS ABOUT?" I'D RETURNED FROM PITTSburgh to Hillwood on a crisp October morning to find dozens of my favorite staffers from Topridge and Mar-a-Lago assembled in my front hall, along with the people who ordinarily worked in the home. With them stood Adelaide, Eleanor, and Dina, each of them with an expectant, animated smile fixed in my direction.

"Oh boy, am I in trouble for something?" I asked, looking around the bright, packed space.

Margaret Voigt, my secretary, stepped forward. "Mrs. Post, we have something for you."

As a group we made our way outside, and there on the back lawn I saw a gracious new flagpole extending up toward the blue autumn sky. I gasped, marching toward it for a better look. One hundred names were inscribed at the base, names of so many people who had lived and worked in my homes, people who had come to feel like family as they'd spent their days alongside me and my own.

I turned, glancing into the face of Charlie Cronk, a man who had served as one of my security guards for five decades. "What did you do this for?" I asked, my throat tight with the promise of tears.

Charlie smiled, folding his thick hands in front of his waist as he answered: "Well, Mrs. Post, you've turned seventy-five, and we figured that was an important birthday. And so we wanted to do something as a thanks for your many kindnesses. Your deeds speak for themselves, and we, your crew, wish to honor you."

I was overcome. Raising my hands, I declared: "All right, that's it! You all get the afternoon off!" We spent the rest of the day playing lawn games outdoors, enjoying the grounds in the fall sunshine, sipping on apple cider and champagne. Herb had flown to New York that morning—a trip he'd organized as part of his patronage of the ballet—but the rest of us remained at home, and we had a great big picnic supper, the staffers' kids running around with Scampi and laughing along with the adults.

As the sun set before us over the Mall and the monuments, and I sat nibbling happily on a dinner of cold chicken and apple crumb cake, I turned to my daughter beside me on the checkered picnic blanket. "What a special day." I took Dina's hand in my own. "Only thing missing is Herb, and then it would have been perfect."

I didn't miss the expression that flickered across my daughter's lovely features. But what did it mean, that look? And then suddenly Dina remembered herself, assuming an expression of placid agreement as she nodded. "What?" I asked, shifting on the blanket as I stared at her beside me.

"Nothing." She glanced away, her fingers smoothing the picnic blanket. Then, after a moment, she added, "I just wish he were here with you as well."

THE NEXT MORNING dawned clear and bright, and I smiled with delight when I looked out my window and saw my new flagpole gracing the lawn—what a wonderful gift that had been. I hadn't heard from Herb in New York the night before, but I greeted the arrival of my secretary, Margaret, shortly after breakfast. She came into the room with the morning mail in her hands.

"There's a package here for you," Margaret said, her glasses perched primly on the bridge of her nose. "It struck me as odd because there's no return address. Would you like me to open it for you?"

"No, bring it here." I put my drink down and brandished the letter opener that Margaret handed me, slicing the tape.

"Photos," I said. I looked at them, still a bit groggy with sleep, but it took only a moment before the blood began to thrash in my veins. And then I gasped aloud, as if the photos had burned me to the touch.

Herb.

Herb at Mar-a-Lago, lounging by the pool, sleek and suntanned and entirely nude.

Herb, his silver head resting in the lap of some young fellow, also sleek and suntanned and entirely nude.

Herb, kissing a golden young man on the lips.

Herb, nude, his hands roving freely over the muscular thighs of another naked man.

There were others; there was a pile. I shook my head, blinking away the images. And yet, they were scorched into my mind, however badly I wished it weren't so. My vision swam. "Mrs. Post?" Margaret, confused, stood alert beside the bed. I groaned.

"Don't come any closer," I ordered, my voice a shudder. Nobody could see this. Nobody could know this. Nobody but me.

Powerless to resist, I looked down and flipped through the remaining photos in that wretched pile. They did not get any better. Herb, laughing with these men. Herb, entwined with these men. Herb, his hands all over these naked men. Their bodies entangled, their skin glistening from pool water and sweat and salty ocean air and God knew what else.

"Mrs. Post, you've gone white as a sheet. What is it?" Margaret stepped forward and glanced at the pile. Now I was too dazed to protest, too dizzy with shock and rage, and my secretary gasped aloud as she scanned the photos strewn across my lap. "Mr. May?" Margaret's face mirrored my own shock.

I nodded. I was aware, vaguely, of a bird trilling outside my window, settled somewhere in my beautiful gardens, but all I could really hear was the frantic pumping of my heart in my ears. "What are you going to do?" Margaret asked.

But I did not know how to answer that question. Not right then. Right then, I was wondering something else. I was wondering: How could I be a woman of such good fortune, and yet have the worst luck of all when it came to the men I loved?

Chapter 50

Winter 1963

DINA LAY BESIDE ME IN MY MASSIVE BED, NEITHER OF US dressed in anything more than our silk wrappers, nibbling halfheartedly from breakfast trays. Heartache made me lazy, and it sapped my appetite. It sapped my will to get up. To get dressed, to face the day with its many prying eyes.

"It's a blow, to be sure," Dina said, taking a slow sip from her coffee. "But you can't tell me that . . . well, that you didn't know?"

"Didn't *know*?" I angled toward my daughter. "What do you mean?"

"About Herb. The . . . way he was." Dina replaced her coffee cup in its saucer, shaking her head. Then her eyes narrowed as she held me in her appraising, blue-eyed stare. "Mother. You really mean to tell me . . . this is a surprise to you?"

"Of course this is a surprise to me," I huffed in reply, certain that my confusion was apparent on my face. "You mean . . . you mean to tell me that you're *not* surprised?"

Dina cleared her throat, fiddling with the bedcovers that pooled around her lap. Her voice was low as she answered: "Well, he was a lovely man. So kind to you. And he loved to do all the same things as you. I thought he was a wonderful companion for you."

I leaned backward, falling into the heap of plush pink pillows, my mind as restless as a feather in a hurricane. Not only had my daughter seen it—the truth—but she'd seen it plain enough that she'd assumed there was no way I had missed it. And yet, somehow, I had.

Was I really so very blind? Or perhaps—and this was a possibility even harder to reckon with—had it been willful on my part? A refusal to acknowledge what I *did* in fact see? Like that unseemly attention to that young man at the football game on our trip to Battle Creek. The times when Herb had smiled a bit too comfortably at male waitstaff. His love of the ballet that sometimes seemed to go beyond merely appreciating the art of it—trips with the male dancers; weekends away, ostensibly for fund-raising; all of those late, scotch-soaked evenings with the troupe in which I did not take part. How could I have been such a fool? How could I, Marjorie the Magnificent, America's most exacting hostess, shrewd business-woman with millions in the bank, overseer of everything—a staff of thousands, homes as fine as palaces, parties for presidents and queens that went off without a single false note—have missed the plain truth of the man sleeping right beside me?

"Well, it took me a while," I said, heaving a sigh as Dina continued to hold me in her concerned, blue-eyed gaze. "But now I see."

"What will you do?" my daughter asked.

"Divorce," I said, my voice resolute, even if a bit weary. "It's the only way."

Funny how it didn't get easier, ending a marriage. Even when I knew it must be done. Even though this would be my fourth time. It still hurt in the deepest places of my heart to watch this life we'd built together crumble—and with it, my hopes for a long and harmonious happiness.

The best way to proceed, then, was to do it fast and clean. Herb had little say in the matter, given the nature of the parcel I'd received in the mail. I told him my decision and he accepted it with a grim nod, a silent exhale that seemed to take the fight out of his entire frame.

"The staff can help pack up whatever personal effects you will be taking from Hillwood," I said, clutching Scampi in my arms, clinging to the pup as if he might be able to offer me just a single drop of comfort.

"All right, Marjorie," Herb said, his eyes fixed on the carpet. I stood there, mute, unsure of how to proceed. Was that all? But then Herb raised his eyes, sweeping them upward to meet my own hollow stare, and he looked in that instant as if his face were the final, weakened defense holding back a rush of despair. If his mouth were to open, the dam would break. And break it did, with one long shudder of his chest, a sudden torrent of tears, as he spoke at last, only to say, "Oh, Marjorie. My dear, dear girl. I'm sorry." He repeated it over and over. "I'm sorry. I'm so very sorry."

What was I to say to that? Eventually, I managed only: "So am I, Herb. So am I."

Unlike with some of my past divorces, I didn't feel white-hot rage or disgusted dislike for Herb at this parting. I knew him, even in spite of the truth of those photographs, to be a kind man. A good man. He had not been jealous or cruel to me, ever. In fact he had always supported me in my efforts and had eagerly celebrated my joys at my side. Now that it was over, he was not trying to take my home from me or steal any of the treasures that mattered to me. Even though this divorce was arguably the most sordid and shocking of them all, Herb's behavior toward me, at the end, remained decent and dignified. And so I saw no reason why we could not part ways as friends. In that, at least, we seemed to be aligned.

⁂

"MOM, YOU COULD have run General Foods. Goodness, you could have run the State Department. You can do absolutely anything in the world once you set your mind to it. Why do you have such trouble with husbands?"

"I honestly don't know, Eleanor. But I can assure you, I'm asking myself that same damn thing."

My daughter and I sat on the dock at Camp Topridge, overlooking a lake brushed dark blue by dusk, Scampi snoring peacefully in my lap. I'd come to this camp in the woods to heal and rest, just as I'd done so many times before. D.C. was roiling with summer heat and the scandal of my fourth, inglorious divorce. Young men, whether telling the truth or not, had been all too willing to come forward and name themselves as Herb's lovers, speaking openly to the papers about their tawdry times with him. God help me if there had really been that many.

But here, in the pristine and wooded quiet of the Adirondacks, I did not need to hear about it. I could enjoy this respite with my family. My daughters, my grandchildren. I was working very hard to focus on what I did have: my health, my family, the homes I loved, and the opportunities that existed because of my family's history. I had many lovely things in my life—even if I never had any luck in choosing a husband.

We passed a quiet summer. I swam, I rested, I walked the woods. I watched the kids play tennis, and I joined them in their rowdy croquet tournaments. At night we built campfires and we played cards, and I fell asleep to the low and mournful calls of the loons that skimmed the lake's glassy surface. In the morning I awoke to pine-dappled sunlight, breathing deep of the clean mountain air. As the days shortened and autumn rolled in, I found myself feeling strong and rested. Ready to return to Hillwood, lest the press corps or the gossip circles dare claim that Marjorie Merriweather Post had ceded her spot as the District's most fabulous hostess.

"I've always loved the ballet. Why, I've seen performances everywhere from Moscow to Paris to New York. And I'll continue to support this place, just as I always have." I spoke to a scrum of reporters outside Washington's National Ballet, where they swarmed on the night of the season's opening performance, their flashbulbs popping and pencils scribbling.

It was my grand reentry into society, and it had been a strategic choice. Herb, now living in Florida, had long loved the ballet—and its dancers; that we all knew. But I had supported it as well, and I appreciated the beauty of the performances, the art of the sets and the dances. And knowing that Herb was gone, that there'd be no chance of any awkward run-in, I had figured it was a good time to show up with my head high. I wore my hair swept back, laced with sapphires, and Napoleon's blue diamond around my neck to match my gown of shimmering satin. I chose creamy white gloves that reached to my elbows and Cartier earrings with diamonds the size of grapes. And a calm, self-assured smile to complete the look.

I heard the murmurs as I swept into the theater and made my way to my personal box, but I greeted those around me with warmth and ease. "How was your summer, Mrs. Post?"

I turned toward the voice and looked into the pretty face of a woman I knew, a wife to a congressman. Betty Ford was her name. "It was lovely, Betty, thank you. And yours?"

"Fine. Gerald and I were in Virginia with the children." She smiled, and then said, "It's good to have you back, Mrs. Post."

I looked around the spacious hall, at the brightly dressed ladies and their tuxedoed gentlemen. The lush curtains poised to lift at any moment over a stage for which I had helped to pay. The string and wind musicians tuning up in the pit below. "Betty, it's good to be back," I declared, giving her my most convivial smile. And it was.

Chapter 51

Mar-a-Lago, Palm Beach, Florida
1968

"MRS. POST, THE PRESIDENT AND FIRST LADY ARE HERE TO SEE you."

"Thank you, Frank. You can show them in." I smoothed the ripples of my slate-blue skirt and rose, my spine going straight, my heart speeding to a gallop.

"Mrs. Post, it's wonderful to see you again." The president reached forward for a handshake.

His manner was friendly, his words colored by his famous Texas twang, but Lady Bird positively gushed as she looked around the space—her eyes absorbing the soaring vaulted ceilings ribbed with Venetian arches. The chandelier in burnished gold leaf. The friezes and Italian frescoes coloring the walls, vases overspilling with my garden's fresh-cut petals. The mahogany and silk armchairs arranged around marble-topped end-tables. To breathe in was to smell balmy air, flowers, and seawater. To listen was to hear the faint lapping of nearby waves, the chipper warbles of the tropical birds that flitted throughout my lush gardens and cloistered walkways. "Oh, Mrs. Post, how wonderful to be here. Every time I step into one of your homes, it's like I've stepped into some beautiful Neverland."

"Well, thank you, Mr. President, Mrs. Johnson, for coming all this way. I realize that you've got one or two other things on your plate."

The president heaved an audible sigh, a rueful smile creasing his face, and I saw the care of his office etched in his features, even as he tried to sit in my paradise and appear relaxed. Lady Bird, too, showed the faintest of cracks in the veneer of her usual poise and polish—the way she folded and then unfolded her gloved hands, the way her eyes darted about the room but failed to fix on any one spot for too long. I felt for the pair of them, even if I did not agree with them on everything.

"I'll cut right to it," I said. "I'm a planner. I always have been. And I realize that I'm getting older and I won't be here forever. And so I'd like to offer this place." I raised my hands, sweeping the grand room with my gesture. "I'd like to offer it to our government. Free of charge. To see it used as a Winter White House."

Both the president and first lady stared at me, unmoving in their shared and stunned silence. I went on: "We started with nothing, the Posts. And we've come to inhabit homes as nice as this one through hard work, yes, but also the opportunity that America offered to us. My daddy believed that and so do I. I'm dating myself here, but I was born not too long after the Civil War, when our nation was almost ripped in half. I've lived through the First World War—of course, to us it was simply the Great War, because we never imagined anyone would be foolish enough to start another one like it. But then I lived through the Great Depression and, sure enough, another World War. And so, to see what's happening these days . . . to see our country once more trying to rip itself apart. People burning our flag on the streets outside the White House. Spitting on soldiers returning from Vietnam. Shooting our leaders like King and Kennedy—well, you know all about that. You know better than anyone." Johnson nodded, his face grim. He'd risen to the presidency only after Kennedy had been assassinated.

"I just can't stomach any of it," I said. "As a nation we've got our problems, sure. And we aren't perfect. But I believe we could accomplish a lot more good by pulling together rather than tearing one another apart. Anyways, I'd like to do my part. And if this place can provide any use . . . Well, what do you think?"

"Well, Mrs. Post." The president heaved a sigh as he looked to his wife, then back to me. "It's certainly incredibly generous. I don't think anyone has ever doubted your patriotism. Or your commitment to making our nation a better place. For all who live here."

"Thank you, sir."

"It's an exciting proposition, to be sure," he went on. "One I wish I could accept right here on the spot. But the reality is complicated."

I sat back in my chair, folding my hands in my lap. "Isn't it always?"

The president nodded as he said, "We'd have to get the blessing of the branches of the federal government, as well as the National Park Service and the Department of the Interior. Congress would have to sign off on it, if we were going to make it an official government property. The Park Service would be tasked with the ongoing management."

"Goodness," I said with a sigh. "Never realized it'd take an entire government to manage what I myself have been doing all these years."

"You said it," the president answered, a wry grin turning up his lips. "How many rooms is it, Mrs. Post?"

"One hundred and twenty-six."

A whistle. "All right," he said, nodding. "Let me speak to my team. Of course I'd love it. It's just a question of whether or not the United States government can manage it. I don't think we are any match for you, Mrs. Post."

I planned everything—I had done so all my life. So how could I do anything differently when I knew the end was coming? Knowing what a unique and fortunate life I led, and knowing how hard I'd worked to make each home a place of not only beauty but also significance, I made similar arrangements for all of my properties. Camp Topridge and its hundreds of acres of Adirondack woods and waterfront would go to New York State, thanks to plans worked out with my good friend Governor Nelson Rockefeller, whose family I'd known since my first days as a young bride.

And my beloved Hillwood would become a part of the Smithsonian Institution. My husbands had complained of living in a museum, after all, and so it was only natural that Hillwood's next phase of life would be just that. This place that had been my bulwark against the torrents of marriage and divorce, scandal and joy, the place I'd designed with such loving precision, the home in which I'd watched my children and grandchildren celebrate birthdays and holidays. Where I'd sat down to lunch with presidents and royalty. I'd put painstaking care into every inch of that home, designing it to my exact specifications, and I could not imagine some other buyer coming in and undoing all of that. What if some greedy developer decided to tear it down and build a strip of soulless apartment buildings on the estate? It made me ill just to think of it.

And the treasures inside! Treasures that had taken a lifetime and several fortunes to amass. I had to protect it, and I wished to share it with the world. Everything would be preserved there for the public to enjoy. My 275-carat diamond choker, a gift from Emperor Napoleon to his Habsburg bride. Empress Eugénie's blue diamonds. The diamond crown Tsarina Alexandra wore on her wedding day. Marie Antoinette's earrings. Furniture and tapestries and dishes that had filled Versailles and the Winter Palace and the Tuileries Palace. Handwritten letters from Franklin D. Roosevelt and Winston Churchill and John F. Kennedy. Portraits commissioned by Habsburgs and Bourbons and Romanovs—and then, too, by Posts.

Chapter 52

THE TRUTH WAS, I WAS FINALLY BEGINNING TO FEEL THE AGE in my body. I, who had been taught to rise each morning and face the day without a drop of caffeine, was beginning to feel tired. I was ready to slow my pace and simply enjoy the gifts of my years—my family, my homes, my friends. All of the beauty that I had amassed around me.

Life took on a certain rhythm, albeit one that moved to a slower beat. Each morning I would take breakfast—still Post cereal, still my Postum coffee substitute—in bed, Scampi nestled beside me under the covers, and then I'd rise to get a massage. After that I'd sit in my dressing room, looking out over the grounds as my silver, waist-length hair was combed and styled. And then I would dress. I still enjoyed dressing in beautiful gowns, and so for the night of my eightieth birthday, I did just that, preparing for a performance by the National Symphony Orchestra. I slid into a floor-length gown of icy light blue, pairing it with Marie Antoinette's diamond earrings. When I was dressed and ready, I turned from the mirror toward my waiting daughter. "What is the plan for this evening?" I asked Eleanor. For once, I had relinquished the role of organizer and hostess, instead allowing my girls to take the reins for the night's activity. And I had little idea of what they had hatched.

Eleanor rose from her chair and strode toward me, weaving her arm through mine. "Just a night of music," she said, but a coy smile lit her features, and I guessed that there was something she was not telling me.

As I entered the massive, bright interior of our city's new concert hall, the Kennedy Center, I was stunned by the throngs who rose to applaud and greet me. Rows of beloved and familiar faces looked on from around a crowded theater decorated with fresh, fragrant flowers. Everyone was dressed in finery of silk and satin, tuxedoes and bow ties. As I gasped and took it all in, the players of the National Symphony Orchestra struck up a rousing rendition of "Happy Birthday," and my children and grandchildren, friends and neighbors, sang to me.

When the lights finally dimmed, I was treated to an evening filled with Brahms and Tchaikovsky, Mozart and Beethoven. As I sat in my box with Dina, Adelaide, and Eleanor beside me, their husbands joining us along with my grandchildren, I breathed in the pleasing aroma of fresh flowers mixed with perfume. I listened to some of the best musicians in the world playing their lovely classical pieces. And I felt a flush of warmth that slowly filled my entire body. This, I believed, was peace.

I kissed my grandchildren and sons-in-law goodbye at the end of the concert and left the hall with my daughters. As we made our way through the early-spring night toward my waiting Cadillac limousine, Adelaide, at my side, asked, "Did you enjoy it, Mother?"

"Enjoy it?" I considered the question, choosing my words with care. "Why, there's never been a birthday like it."

My eldest daughter gave my arm a squeeze. "Mom, there's never been a lady like you."

We packed into the plush interior of my car. My daughters remained close, and I spread my arms wide, pulling all three girls into my embrace. The chauffeur, Frank, smiled back at us from behind the wheel. "Where to, Mrs. Post?"

"Home, Frank."

Frank touched his cap and shifted gears, and the car began to glide forward through the pleasant Washington night, down the wide avenues, past the glowing monuments, and back through the park toward home. Back toward a place stocked with treasure—the treasure of all those beautiful memories and moments, each one a jewel to color a long life that was lived with purpose and intention, with warmth and passion. A life made ever richer by curiosity and generosity. A life in which I spent gladly of the riches of my heart. A life that has been a truly beautiful thing.

Epilogue

Palm Beach, Florida
Winter 1973

FIVE DECADES AFTER HOSTING A FABULOUS *ZIEGFELD FOLLIES* gala to raise the funds for a new hospital near Palm Beach, Marjorie Merriweather Post found herself hospitalized in that very place, receiving treatment for pneumonia.

Following her stay at the Good Samaritan Hospital in West Palm Beach, Marjorie flew aboard the *Merriweather* one final time, bound for home. At Hillwood, Marjorie spent the final months of her life surrounded by family and friends.

Marjorie Merriweather Post passed away at Hillwood on September 12, 1973, at the age of eighty-six. Her ashes remain there today, surrounded by her beloved roses.

Author's Note

"I can't count all the things that she has done for this city. . . . I'd take the odds she can't even remember them." Thus spoke reporter Roy Meacham about Marjorie Merriweather Post during a 1966 radio broadcast honoring the singular woman who serves as the subject of this novel. While Meacham was referring primarily to Post's philanthropic work as it related to her then hometown of Washington, D.C., I was so struck when I encountered this quotation because the statement hit on the very sentiment that I myself had felt many times over while researching and then writing about Marjorie Merriweather Post and her extraordinary life. She did *that*? She lived through *that*? She met *him*? She befriended *her*? She was *there*? She built *that*? Marjorie Merriweather Post lived her long life to the fullest; hers was a grand and epic story from start to finish, and it is my great fortune to write fiction inspired by her.

Speaking of living life to the fullest, there is enough information on Marjorie Merriweather Post's long, lavish, and layered life that one could write fifty novels about her, each with a different story arc and each stretching hundreds of pages. Marjorie lived and loved in such a way that her comings and goings (of which there were many) were noted to the day, sometimes to the hour. And unlike some of the long-deceased female figures about whom I've had the privilege of writing, Marjorie's is a relatively recent life—her third daughter, Dina Merrill, passed away while I was researching this book—and because of that temporal proximity, much of Marjorie's life is well documented and accessible.

So first, I offer my humble thanks and most profound respect to the historians, curators, biographers, and archivists who make the information pertaining to Marjorie Merriweather Post so readily accessible and abundant. These individuals honor and offer up the facts of Marjorie's life as a result of their countless hours of interviews, archival review, scholarly study, investigative research, and meticulous stewardship. I am a very thankful and humble beneficiary.

Nancy Harris, former oral historian and curator for Hillwood Estate, Museum and Gardens, is the reason I first stepped into Marjorie Merriweather Post's rarefied and inspiring world. A friend of my husband's family, Nancy gave me the first tip years ago. "Do you know about Marjorie Merriweather Post?" she asked me one Sunday at my mother-in-law's table. I'm ashamed to admit that, when asked that question, I knew nothing about Marjorie Merriweather Post other than the fact that her name sounded vaguely familiar. Nancy then offered just a few fast facts: about the Post Company, about Marjorie's four very different and dramatic marriages, about how Marjorie lived like an empress with her world-class art collection and her capacious households. Years ago, as an undergraduate at Yale, I had taken a course on the history of American nutrition, and we had learned about the fierce rivalry between the Posts and the Kelloggs and their founding of America's new breakfast industry—a rivalry and a set of characters that would change life for all of us. So I was immediately intrigued. Nancy encouraged me to visit Hillwood, and that was the best tip of all. Since then, I have been obsessed, and I have thanked Nancy by sending her endless follow-up questions, everything from "When did Scampi the dog die?" to "Why do you *really* think Marjorie and Ed Close split up?" Thank you so much, Nancy, for your generosity and kindness and willingness to offer insight and support as I have worked on this book for years. I hope you do not regret giving that first tip.

Nancy Rubin Stuart has written the definitive biography that tells the story of Marjorie Merriweather Post's life in its entirety. Nancy spoke to countless family members and friends of Marjorie's, studied innumerable newspaper and journal articles, combed the archival family scrapbooks and letters and more—and the result is the brilliant and comprehensive work *American Empress: The Life and Times of Marjorie Merriweather Post*. Stuart provides direct quotes from fascinating interviews with Marjorie's daughters, grandchildren, friends, and colleagues that offer invaluable insights and perspectives. Stuart's work shines a light not only on the minutiae and daily details that made up the comprehensive whole of Marjorie Merriweather Post's life, but also fleshes out a portrait of her as a complex and compelling human. I cannot recommend the biography highly enough for all who feel moved by Marjorie Merriweather Post's life and are inspired to learn more.

The Hillwood Estate, Museum and Gardens is quite literally a sprawling treasure trove. When you walk into Marjorie's final and beloved home, you step into her world. You see the clothes hanging, crisp and tidy, in her closet. You see that her private powder room was an explosion of pink, because that was her favorite color until the end. You see the couch where she took naps, the Friendship Walk she cherished, and the pavilion where she hosted world leaders and society legends for dances and movie screenings. As her daughter Dina said of Hillwood when she visited it as a museum: "It's as if Mother could walk in and sit down to dinner." If you have read this book and have come to understand the exacting standards of Marjorie Merriweather Post as a hostess and homeowner, then you know that that statement speaks volumes. At Hillwood, you see what mattered to Marjorie. Portraits of empresses may cover her walls, and letters from presidents sit atop her furniture along with rows of Sèvres porcelain, but the faces of her smiling daughters hang by her bed, and mementoes of her family and her many adventures occupy pride of place. Marjorie Merriweather Post came alive for me at that beloved home of hers. I would recommend not only a visit, but also checking them out on social media: @hillwoodmuseum on Twitter and Instagram.

My thanks go to Estella M. Chung, director of collections at Hillwood Estate, Museum and Gardens. Estella has given us a biography organized by themes in Marjorie's life, *Marjorie Merriweather Post: The Life Behind the Luxury*. Estella's other work, *Living Artfully: At Home with Marjorie Merriweather Post,* is a stunning compilation of photographs, handwritten notes, quotations, menus, and other original source material that once belonged to Marjorie and her daily world, each of which provides fascinating and precious insight into her life and legacy.

My gratitude and appreciation go to Mike Curtin, attorney for Marjorie Merriweather Post and her estate. Thank you for speaking with me about your memories of Mrs. Post, particularly her incredible attention to detail and meticulous care that were so evident in your working relationship with her.

My thanks go to the Historical Society of Battle Creek and Battle Creek's Church of Christ Scientist for their generous time and willingness to answer questions and share source material that proved invaluable as I worked to imagine and understand Marjorie's life as a girl. Many thanks also to my friend Amy Salas, who helped me to understand the feel of growing up in Cereal City U.S.A. and the legacy of the food empires that were built there more than a century ago. Also incredibly illuminating and informative as I worked to understand those early years of Marjorie's life was her father's biography, *C. W. Post, the Hour and the Man* by Nettie Leitch Major.

I am grateful to the Greenwich Historical Society, and in particular curator and archivist Christopher Shields, who shared old maps of Marjorie's neighborhood as well as copious newspaper articles, and who answered questions about the Posts' and Closes' neighbors, the train lines, the boating culture, and more. Those materials and conversations allowed me to better understand Greenwich as a community during the early 1900s, when Marjorie lived there.

I am endlessly grateful to the Crow family for allowing me to visit Camp Topridge, a singular place that held a uniquely meaningful spot in Marjorie's heart until the end of her life. The Crow family has not only preserved Marjorie's legacy there at Camp Topridge with beauty and care—everything from her monogrammed towels to her swimsuit, her family photos and so much more—but were so generous to allow me to visit and stay overnight in Marjorie's cottage, much of which is preserved as she left it. I felt like I was in a museum. That visit with the Crows was a trip and an opportunity I will forever cherish. Sitting by the lake, looking out over the same view that meant so much to Marjorie, I said a prayer of gratitude for this woman's life and a prayer that I would be able to do her story justice.

My thanks go to Misha Belikov and Igor Korchilov for helping me to understand Russian culture and history, for explaining the nuances and legends of the Russian diplomatic world during the Cold War, and for helping me to gain critical insight into Marjorie's years in the Soviet Union serving as the first U.S. ambassadress and mingling with the top officials of the Kremlin. Thanks to Igor for helping me to answer all sorts of questions, ranging from what Madam Molotova might have served during a wintertime luncheon in her dacha to how Marjorie Merriweather Post would have first introduced herself when meeting formidable Soviet commissars. Thanks to Misha for your patient and willing explanations of some of the finer points of spoken Russian. And especially helpful and informative in understanding the years in the Soviet Union was Joseph Davies's memoir, *Mission to Moscow,* which includes the ambassador's personal letters, journal entries, dispatches to the State Department, photographs, press clippings, and more. Much from the sections of this novel set before, during, and after Marjorie's time in Moscow were informed directly by that invaluable source material.

Thanks to Rose Guerrero, research director, and the staff at the Historical Society of Palm Beach County for photographs, newspaper clippings, and archival materials on Marjorie's time in Palm Beach. And my thanks go to Jim Simpson for all that he shared with me about Mar-a-Lago and to Earle and Carol Mack for their generous friendship and for speaking with me about Palm Beach society and Marjorie Merriweather Post's lingering legend and legacy on South Ocean Boulevard.

Thanks to Marya Myers Parr, to whom this book is dedicated, for always reading my first and roughest draft, and for hosting me in Washington, D.C., so that I could visit Hillwood. And to Kate Calligaro for tipping me off to the many ways that Marjorie Merriweather Post's legacy continues in Washington to this day through the programs she founded and the buildings she once called home. And to Bernadette Castro for her enthusiastic and thoughtful sharing of Nettie Leitch Major's *C. W. Post, the Hour and the Man* and for informing me of the history and legacy of the Post family in their former Gold Coast neighborhood on Long Island.

My job as the writer of historical fiction is to gather up and absorb many different details and facts and then attempt to get at the emotional truths that reside therein. The history, the dates, the individual people, and the facts of Marjorie's life—these all provide the raw material with which I may then build a story, offering up an imagined narrative to the reader. Marjorie had so many roles throughout her life: daughter, wife, mother, businesswoman, advocate, philanthropist, press target, press darling, hostess, trailblazer, collector, diplomat, style icon, friend, and more. She lived through four very different and very passionate love stories, taking on four different last names, only to return finally to the very name that had been hers all along. In my opinion, this is ultimately the story of a woman finding her own indelible strength and identity, and embracing a power and a life force that set her apart. Is this a love story? Yes, it is many different love stories and I believe the most powerful one of all is the love story that Marjorie Merriweather Post ultimately found with herself.

Nothing about the grandiosity with which Marjorie traveled, entertained, dressed, or lived had to be embellished for this novel. In fact, I had to leave details out. Some of her precious stones were in fact the size of pieces of fruit. And yes, she did own those fabulous pieces of art, jewelry, and dishware that had belonged to the likes of Empress Catherine the Great of Russia and Napoleon, emperor of France.

And the same goes for the extent of her philanthropy and generosity. Nothing that I describe in this novel, from the Great Depression to Marjorie's wartime efforts to her gifts to schools, hospitals, students, or other individuals, was embellished. In fact there were many acts of largesse both grand and quiet that I had to leave out for the sake of writing a book under a thousand pages. And because Marjorie did so much of her good anonymously and without seeking credit, I'm sure there are lists of good works about which we may never hear.

The life story of Marjorie Merriweather Post reads like the stuff of legend—and I believe it was indeed the stuff of legend. But, more than that, I don't know that I've ever written about a woman whom I've admired and, well, *liked,* as much. Marjorie loved beauty, and she was the first to admit that she had been blessed with many beautiful things over the course of a very privileged life, but it was in how she used her wealth and privilege to make this world more beautiful for others that I found her so particularly compelling. Marjorie was honored by the United States Congress as an individual who "derived particular joy out of her ability to give happiness to others." And she said, "My wealth would have been a burden on my soul if I did not find ways to share it with others." That says so much, and so I'll leave the final words on the topic to her.

I offer my heartfelt gratitude to the many partners who have worked tirelessly to make this book a reality. My profound thanks especially to Lacy Lynch, an incomparable literary agent and friend, and to Dabney Rice, Jan Miller, and the entire team at Dupree Miller.

To my editor Kara Cesare, how truly *magnificent* to work with you on another book, thank you for everything. And to the entire team at Ballantine and Random House, with special thanks to Kim Hovey, Jesse Shuman, Loren Noveck and your assiduous copyediting team, Taylor Noel, Debbie Aroff, Michelle Jasmine, Kara Welsh, Jennifer Hershey, Susan Corcoran, Virginia Norey, Paolo Pepe and the art department, and Gina Centrello, it is my privilege to work with you all.

Words do not suffice to properly thank my family and my friends. My parents, my siblings, my in-laws, nieces and nephews, girlfriends: I love you and I appreciate you more than I can ever say. Erin Levy, you are a truly beautiful individual in every way. To the book reviewers, bloggers, influencers, and the amazing community of writers and readers whom I feel so fortunate to call my friends: thank you for making this solitary job feel so communal, full, and supportive. Early readers who slogged through drafts, and you, the reader who is now holding this book in your hands: thank you for joining me on this journey. And finally, my love and thanks to my children and my husband, Dave, who are writing my favorite story each day.

Further suggested reading:

Nancy Rubin Stuart, *American Empress: The Life and Times of Marjorie Merriweather Post*

Estella M. Chung, *Marjorie Merriweather Post: The Life Behind the Luxury*

Estella M. Chung, *Living Artfully: At Home with Marjorie Merriweather Post*

Nettie Leitch Major, *C. W. Post, the Hour and the Man*

Joseph E. Davies, *Mission to Moscow*

Mark Kurlansky, *Birdseye: The Adventures of a Curious Man*

Harvey Kaiser, *Great Camps of the Adirondacks*

About the Author

Allison Pataki is the *New York Times* bestselling author of *The Traitor's Wife, The Accidental Empress, Sisi, Where the Light Falls,* and *The Queen's Fortune,* as well as the memoir *Beauty in the Broken Places* and two children's books, *Nelly Takes New York* and *Poppy Takes Paris*. Her novels have been translated into more than twenty languages. A former news writer and producer, Pataki has written for *The New York Times,* ABC News, HuffPost, *USA Today,* Fox News, and other outlets. She has appeared on *Today, Good Morning America, Fox & Friends, Good Day New York, Good Day Chicago,* and MSNBC's *Morning Joe*. Pataki graduated cum laude from Yale University with a major in English and spent several years in journalism before switching to fiction writing. A member of the Historical Novel Society and a certified yoga instructor, she lives in New York with her husband and family.

allisonpataki.com
Facebook.com/AllisonPatakiPage
Twitter: @AllisonPataki
Instagram: @allisonpataki

About the Type

This book was set in Dante, a typeface designed by Giovanni Mardersteig (1892–1977). Conceived as a private type for the Officina Bodoni in Verona, Italy, Dante was originally cut only for hand composition by Charles Malin, the famous Parisian punch cutter, between 1946 and 1952. Its first use was in an edition of Boccaccio's *Trattatello in laude di Dante* that appeared in 1954. The Monotype Corporation's version of Dante followed in 1957. Though modeled on the Aldine type used for Pietro Cardinal Bembo's treatise *De Aetna* in 1495, Dante is a thoroughly modern interpretation of that venerable face.